Praise for the novels of Brenda Joyce

The Masquerade "dances on slippered feet,
belying its heft with spellbinding dips,
spins and twists. Jane Austen aficionados will delve
happily into heroine Elizabeth "Lizzie" Fitzgerald's
family.... Joyce's tale of the dangers and delights of
passion fulfilled will enchant those
who like their reads long and rich."
—*Publishers Weekly*

"Joyce brilliantly delivers an intensely emotional and
engrossing romance where love overcomes deceit,
scandal and pride....An intelligent love story with
smart, appealing and strong characters. Readers will
savor this latest from a grand mistress of the genre."
—*Romantic Times BOOKclub* on *The Masquerade*

"A powerhouse of emotion and sensuality, *The Prize*
weaves a tapestry vibrantly colored with detail and
balanced with strands of consuming passion and
hatred. Joyce writes lush stories with larger-than-life
characters and a depth of sensuality and emotion
that touches chords within the reader and keeps
them coming back for more."
—*Romantic Times BOOKclub*

"Joyce's latest...romance is truly a pleasure to
read, given its involving plot, intriguing characters,
and the magic that occurs as the reader becomes
immersed in another time and place."
—*Booklist* on *Deadly Kisses*

"Another entertaining blend of danger and desire."
—*Booklist* on *Deadly Illusions*

ALSO BY BRENDA JOYCE

The de Warenne Dynasty
The Masquerade
The Prize

The Deadly Series
Deadly Kisses
Deadly Illusions

**Watch for the next book
in Brenda Joyce's de Warenne Dynasty**
A Lady at Last
Coming August 2007

**Brenda Joyce and HQN Books
are also excited to introduce**
Dark Seduction
**The first book in the exciting new
Masters of Time series
Coming May 2007**

The Stolen
BRIDE

BRENDA
JOYCE

HQN™

ISBN-13: 978-0-373-77184-4
ISBN-10:   0-373-77184-3

THE STOLEN BRIDE

This edition published by arrangement with Harlequin Books S.A.

® and TM are trademarks of the publisher. Trademarks indicated with ® are registered in the United States Patent and Trademark Office, the Canadian Trade Marks Office and in other countries.

www.HQNBooks.com

Printed in U.S.A.

ACKNOWLEDGMENTS

I want to thank Lucy Childs once again for reading everything I write and always being so enthusiastic and supportive while offering really helpful criticism. I want to thank my editor, Miranda Stecyk, for being as enthusiastic, as supportive and a great editor (keep on cutting!) as well as being willing to work with me on an insane and manic schedule. I also want to thank Cissy Hartley at Writerspace for her support, patience and utter diplomacy, time and again, and the great job she has done taking care of my Web sites. I want to thank Theresa Myers for her enthusiasm and brilliance and always taking on copywriting at the last moment! And I want to welcome two new members to my team, designers of dewarennedynasty.com and mastersoftimebooks.com! Thank you, Laurel Letherby and Dorie Hensley, for such wonderful support, unflagging enthusiasm and unfailing creativity!

This one is for the new team!
Cissy Hartley, Laurel Letherby, Dorie Hensley,
Theresa Myers and Miranda Stecyk.

I couldn't do it all without you guys.
Thank you so much!

PROLOGUE

Askeaton, Ireland, June, 1814

THE CALL OF THE UNKNOWN. It was there, around him, inside him, an urgent restlessness, the call to adventure. It had never been stronger, and it was impossible to ignore for a single moment longer.

Sean O'Neill paused in the courtyard of the manor home that had been in his family for almost four hundred years. With his own hands, he had rebuilt the stone walls he faced. With his own hands, he had helped the town craftsmen replace the empty husks where the windows had once been gorgeously colored stained glass. He had knelt on the ancient floors inside, carefully replacing the broken stones alongside the Limerick masons. With an army of housemaids, he had carefully salvaged every burned sword in the front hall, all family heirlooms. The huge tapestry there had been burned beyond repair, however.

And he had plowed the charred and blackened fields alongside the O'Neill tenants, day after day and week after week, until the earth was brown and fertile again. He had overseen the selection, purchase and transport of the cattle and sheep that had replaced the herds and flocks destroyed by the British troops in that fateful summer of 1798. Now, as he stood by his mount, the saddlebags full, a small satchel attached to the saddle horn, lambs frolicked with their dams in the hills behind the house, beneath the blush of first light.

He had rebuilt the estate with his sweat, his blood and even at times, his tears. He had rebuilt Askeaton for his older brother in the years Devlin had been at sea, a captain in the royal navy, engaged in war with the French. Devlin had returned home a few days earlier with his American bride and their daughter. He had resigned his commission and was, Sean knew, at Askeaton to stay. And that was how it should be.

The restlessness overcame him then. He wasn't sure what it was that he wanted, but he knew that his task here was done. Something was out there waiting for him, something huge, calling to him the ways the sirens did the sailors lost at sea. He was only twenty-four years old and he smiled at the rising sun, exhilarated and ready for whatever adventure Fate thought to hand him.

"Sean! Wait!"

He was briefly incredulous at the sound of Eleanor de Warenne's voice. But then, he should have known she would be up at this hour and that she would catch him as he prepared to leave. She had been his shadow since the day his mother had married her father, when she was a demanding and irrepressible toddler of two and he was a somber boy of eight. As a child, she followed him around like a puppy its new master, at times amusing him and at other times annoying him. And when he had begun the restoration of his family lands, she had been at his side on her knees, chipping out broken stones with him. When she had turned sixteen, she had been sent to England. Since then, she didn't really seem like little Elle anymore. Uncomfortable, he turned to face her.

She hurried toward him. She had always had a long aggressive stride, never the graceful gait of a proper lady. That hadn't changed, but everything else had. He stiffened, because she rushed toward him barefoot and clad only in a white cotton nightgown.

And in that heartbeat, he simply did not know the woman who was calling out to him. The nightgown caressed her body like a silk glove, indicating curves he could not recognize, flattened against her by the dawn breeze.

"Where are you going? Why didn't you wake me? I'll ride with you! We can race to the chapel and back." She halted abruptly, her eyes going wide, staring at the saddlebags and the satchel. Her smile had vanished.

He saw her shock, followed by comprehension, but he was still struggling with his own surprise. He would always think of Elle as an awkward child, tall and skinny no matter her age, her face thin and angular, with her hair in waist-length braids. What had happened to her in the past two years? He wasn't sure when her body had developed such immodest and feminine curves or when her face had filled out, making it a perfect oval.

He looked away from the neckline of her gown, which he decided was indecent. Then he looked away from the swell of her hips, hips that simply could not belong to her. His cheeks were warm. "You can't walk around in nightclothes. Someone might see you!" he exclaimed. He had sat across from her at supper last night. But he had been uncomfortable then, too, especially because every time he glanced at her, she had smiled at him, trying to hold his gaze. He had done his best to avoid eye contact.

"You've seen me in my nightclothes a hundred times," she said slowly. "Where are you going?"

He dragged his gaze directly to hers. Her eyes hadn't changed, and for that, he was relieved. Amber in hue, almond in shape, he had always been able to look at her eyes and read her every mood, her every thought, her every expression and emotion. He saw that she was afraid. His reaction was immediate, and he smiled reassuringly at her. Somehow his duty had always been to ease her fears, whenever she had them. "I need to go," he said quietly. "But I'll be back."

"What do you mean?" she gasped in disbelief.

The Elle of his childhood had always been able to read his every thought and mood, too. She had grown up, but she still understood him, even without his having to elaborate. Carefully, he said, "Elle, something is out there and I need to find it."

"What?" Her eyes were filled with growing horror. "No! Nothing is out there—I am *here!*"

He became still, their gazes locked. He knew, as did everyone in their two families, that she had harbored a wild and foolish infatuation for him for as long as anyone could remember. No one knew precisely when, but as a child she had decided she loved him and that she would marry him one day. Sean had been amused by her claims. He had always known that she would outgrow such nonsense. They didn't share a drop of blood, but he considered her a sister.

She was the daughter of an earl—she would marry a title or wealth, or both. "Elle." He spoke calmly now. He chose to ignore that remark. Surely she no longer clung to such beliefs. "Askeaton belongs to Devlin. He's home now. I have this feeling that there is something more out there for me. I need to go. I want to go."

She was pale. "No! You can't leave! There is nothing out there—what are you speaking of? Your life is here! We are here—your family, me! And Askeaton is yours as much as Devlin's!"

He decided not to refute that, as Devlin had actually purchased Askeaton from the earl eight years ago. He hesitated, trying to find the right words, words she might understand. "I have to go. Besides, you don't need me now. You've grown-up." His smile failed him. "You'll be sent back to England soon and you won't be thinking of me then. Not with all your suitors." He found that notion odd and unpleasant. "Go back to bed."

A look of pure determination crossed her face and he tensed. When Elle had an objective, nothing could stop her from attaining it. "I am coming with you," she declared.

"Absolutely not!"

"Don't you dare leave without me! I am going to

get dressed. Have a horse saddled for me!" she cried, whirling to race back inside.

He seized her arm, pulling her back around. The moment he felt her soft full body against his, his brain failed him. He instantly jerked away from her. "I know you have always gotten your way with everyone, including me. But not this time."

"You have been acting like an idiot ever since I came over last night! You've been avoiding me! And don't you dare try and deny it. You won't even look at me," she exclaimed. "Now you say you're leaving me?" She was so distressed and angry that she was breathing hard.

He folded his arms across his chest, his gaze dropping to the bodice of her nightgown, where he could clearly see the shape of her full breasts. He was shocked with himself. He lifted his eyes instantly to her face. "I'm leaving—not *you,* I'm just leaving."

"I don't understand," she said, tears coming to her eyes. "Just take me with you!"

"You're going back to England."

"I hate it there!"

Of course she did. She was a wildflower, not a hothouse rose. Elle had been raised amongst five boys, and she had been born to ride the Irish hills on her horse, not to dance the quadrille in a London ballroom. She stood there, looking devastated, and in that moment time fell away and she appeared all of eight years old, not eighteen, crushed with disappointment and hugely vulnerable. Tears tracked down her cheeks.

And instantly he took her in his arms, as he'd done a thousand times before. "It's all right," he began. But the moment he felt her breasts between them, instead of her bony chest, he pushed away. He felt his cheeks flame.

"Are you ever coming back?" she demanded, clinging to his arms.

"Of course I am," he said tersely, trying to back up.

"When?"

"I'm not sure. A year or two."

"A year or two?" She began to cry. "How can you do this? How can you leave me for so long? I already miss you! You're my best friend! I'm your best friend! Won't you miss me?"

He gave in and reached for her hand. "Of course I'll miss you," he said quietly. It was the truth.

Their gazes locked. "Promise me. Promise me that you are coming back for me."

"I promise," he said.

And he realized as they stared at each other, as the tears rolled down her face, their hands remained tightly clasped. Gently he pried himself loose. It was time to go. He faced his mount, reaching for the stirrup.

"Wait!"

He half turned and before he could react, she threw her arms around him and pressed her mouth to his.

He realized what was happening. Elle, little Elle, tall and skinny, fearless enough to leap off the old ruined stone tower behind the manor and laugh while doing it, was kissing him on the mouth. But that was impossible, because there was a woman in his arms, her body soft and warm, and her lips open and hot.

He jumped away, aghast. "What was that?"

"That was a kiss, you fool!" she shouted at him.

He wiped his mouth with the back of his hand, still stunned.

"You didn't like it?" she said in disbelief.

"No, I didn't like it," he almost shouted. Furious now, with her and with himself, he leaped astride his horse. Then he looked down at her. She was sobbing, but soundlessly, covering her mouth with her hands.

He could not stand it when she cried. "Don't cry," he said. "Please."

She nodded, ashen, fighting the tears until they stopped. "Promise me again."

He inhaled. "I promise."

She smiled tearfully at him.

He smiled back, and it felt oddly tearful, as well. Then he lifted the reins and spurred his horse into a gallop. He hadn't meant to leave at a madcap pace, but her distress, which he had caused, was far too much to bear. When it felt safe to do so, he finally glanced back.

She hadn't moved. She stood by the iron courtyard gates in the white nightgown, watching him leave. She raised her hand, and even from a distance, he felt her sadness and fear.

He raised his hand in return. Maybe this was for the best, he thought, shaken to the core of his being. Then he turned away, cantering down the roadway, not toward Limerick, but to the east.

When he topped the first hill he paused a final time. His heart beat hard and fast, disturbingly. He turned his mount to look down on his home. The manor was as small as a toy house. A small figure in white posed by the front gates. Elle hadn't moved.

And he wondered if what he was looking for was already within his grasp.

CHAPTER ONE

October 7, 1818, Adare, Ireland

IN THREE DAYS, she was getting married. *How had this happened?*

In three days, she was going to marry the gentleman everyone thought perfect for her. In three very short days, she was going to be Peter Sinclair's wife. Eleanor de Warenne was afraid.

She leaned so low over her galloping horse's neck that she saw nothing but his dark coat and mane. She spurred him, urging him to an even faster, more dangerous pace. She intended to outrun her nervousness—and her dread.

And briefly, she did. The sensation of speed became consuming; there could be no other feeling, no thought. The ground was a blur beneath the pounding hooves of her mount. Finally, the present had vanished. Exhilaration claimed her.

Dawn was breaking in the pale sky overhead. Eventually, Eleanor became tired, as did the stud she rode. She straightened and he slowed, and instantly, she thought about her impending marriage again.

Eleanor brought the bay stallion to a walk. She had reached a high point on the ridge and she looked down at her home. Adare was the seat of her father's earldom, an estate that reached into three counties, encompassing a hundred villages, thousands of farms and one very lucrative coal mine, as well as several quarries. Below, the ridge turned to thick forest and then into the achingly lush green lawns and riotous gardens surrounding the huge stone mansion that was her home, a river running through them. Although first built in Elizabethan times, very little of the original structure remained. Renovated a hundred years earlier, the front of the house was a long three-story rectangle, with a dozen columns supporting the roof and the triangular pediment above it. Two shorter wings were behind the facade, one reserved for the family, the other for their guests.

Her home was filled with family and guests now. Three hundred people had been invited to the wedding and fifty guests, mostly Peter's family, had been crammed into the east wing. The rest were staying at village inns and the Grand Hotel in Limerick.

Eleanor stared down at the estate, breathless and perspiring, her long honey-blond hair having come loose from its braid, wearing a pair of breeches she had stolen ages ago from one of her brothers. After her come-out two years earlier, she had been required to ride astride in a lady's proper riding attire. Having been raised with her three brothers and two stepbrothers, she had decided that was absurd. She had been riding at dawn since then, so she could ride astride and leap fences, an act that was impossible in skirts. Society would find her behavior shocking—and so would her fiancé, if he ever discovered she was inclined to ride and dress like a man.

Of course, she had no intention of letting that happen. She wanted to marry Peter Sinclair. Didn't she?

Eleanor could not stand it then. She had thought her grief and sorrow long since gone, but now, her heart broke open. She had wanted to marry Peter, but with her wedding just days away, she had to face the terrible and frightening truth. She was no longer certain. More importantly, she had to know if Sean were alive or dead.

Eleanor walked her mount down the hillside. Her heart beat swiftly and painfully, stirring up feelings she had never wanted to again entertain. He had left her four years ago. Last year, she had come to terms with his disappearance. After waiting for his return for three interminable years, after refusing to believe the conclusion her family had drawn, she had woken up one morning with a horrific comprehension. He was gone. He wasn't coming back. They were right—as there had been no word, he must be dead.

She had locked herself in her room for several days, weeping for the loss of her best friend, the boy she had spent a lifetime with—the man she loved. On the fourth morning, she had left her rooms, going directly to her father.

"I am ready to marry, Father. I should like you to arrange a proper match."

The earl, alone in the breakfast room, had gaped at her in shock.

"Someone titled and well-off, someone as fond of the hunt as I am, and someone passably attractive," she had said. She had no emotions left. But she added grimly, "Actually, he must be a superb horseman or we will never get on."

"Eleanor—" the earl had leaped to his feet "—you are making the right decision."

She had warded him off. "Yes, I know." And she had left before he might inquire as to her sudden change of heart. She had no wish to discuss her personal feelings with anyone.

An introduction had been made a month later. Peter Sinclair was the heir to an earldom, the estate seated in Chatton, and his family was well-off. He was her own age, and he was handsome and charming. He was a superb horseman and bred Thoroughbred racehorses. She had been wary of his English background, having been chased improperly by some English rakes during her two Seasons, but upon meeting him, she had liked him instantly. His behavior had been sincere from the first. That very night, she had decided he would suit. The match had been arranged shortly thereafter, due to her enhanced age.

Suddenly Eleanor felt as if she were on a bolting horse, one she could not bring to a halt. A horse-woman her entire life, she knew the best recourse would be to leap off.

But she had never bailed from a runaway, not once in her twenty-two years. Instead, she had exerted her will and skill over the animal, bringing it under her control. She tried to remind herself that all brides were nervous and it was not uncommon. After all, her life was about to forever change. Not only would she marry Peter Sinclair, she would move to Chatton, live in England, run his home and soon, bear his children. God, could she really do this?

If only she knew what had happened to Sean.

But she did not know his fate, and she was probably never going to learn of it. Her father and Devlin had spent years searching for him, using Bow Street Runners. But his name was not an unusual one, and every lead had turned out to be false. Her Sean O'Neill had vanished into thin air.

Once more, she blamed herself for ever allowing him to go. She had tried to stop him; she should have made an even greater attempt.

Abruptly Eleanor halted her mount and she closed her eyes tightly. Peter would be a perfect husband, and she was very fond of him. Sean was gone. Not only that, he'd never once looked at her the way Peter regarded her. It was a great match. Her fiancé was kind, amusing, charming, blond and handsome. He was horse-mad, as was she. As the English debutantes she had once been forced to attend would say, he was a premier catch.

Eleanor quickly moved the stallion forward. At this late hour, she was lying to herself. Peter was a dear man, but how could she marry him when there was even the slimmest chance that Sean was alive? On the other hand, she couldn't break the contracts now!

Suddenly real panic began. She had been a failure in London. She had hated every ball, where she had been snubbed because she was Irish and tall and because she preferred horses to parties. The English had been terribly condescending. She was going to be a failure in Chatton, too—she was certain of it. Even if Peter had never questioned her background, once he got to know her he would be condescending, too.

Because she wasn't proper enough to be his English wife. Proper ladies would not dream of riding astride in breeches, let alone doing so alone. And while a few were brave enough to foxhunt, ladies did not shoot carbines and fence with masters; ladies loved shopping and gossip, which she abhorred. Peter didn't really know her—he didn't know her at all.

Ladies don't lie.

It was as if Sean stood there beside her, his silver eyes oddly accusing. If only he hadn't left her. How could it still hurt, on the eve of her wedding, when she had invested the entire past year of her life in her relationship with Peter?

And Eleanor knew she was on that runaway horse yet again. Her wedding was in three days and until recently, she had been pleased. In fact, she had been very caught up in the wedding preparations and she had been as excited as her mother. It would be the scandal of the decade should she now call it off. She was having bridal jitters, nothing more. Peter was *perfect* for her.

Very purposefully, Eleanor halted and closed her eyes, trying to find an image that would chase away, once and for all, every fear and doubt she had. She saw herself in her wedding dress, the bodice covered with lace and pearls, the huge satin skirts boasting pearl and lace insets, the train an endless pool of satin trimmed in beaded lace. Peter was standing beside her, blond and handsome in his formal attire. They were exchanging vows and Peter was raising her veil so he might kiss her.

The veil was removed from her eyes. Peter was gone. Standing before her was a tall, dark man with shockingly silver eyes.

Ladies don't lie, Elle.

Eleanor could not bear the renewed surge of grief. She did not need this now. She did not want this now.

"Go away!" She almost wept. "Leave me alone, please!"

But the damage was done, she thought miserably. She had dared to let him back into her mind, and now, just days before her wedding, he wasn't going to go away. She had known Sean O'Neill since she was a child. His mother had been widowed by the British in a terrible massacre, and her own father, a widower at that time, had married Mary O'Neill, taking Sean and his brother in. Although he had never legally adopted the O'Neill boys, he had raised them with his own three sons and Eleanor, treating both boys as if they were his own.

There were so many memories now. Even as a tot, she recalled thinking Sean a prince, never mind that his family had been impoverished Irish Catholic gentry. Toddling after him, screaming his name, she had tried to follow him everywhere. At first he had been kind, allowing her to piggyback on his strong but scrawny shoulders or leading her back by the hand to her nurse. But his kindness had become irritation as Eleanor grew into a small child. She would hide in the classroom to watch him at his lessons and then advise him on how to do better. Sean would summon the tutor, ordering her put out, telling her to mind her own affairs. Unfortunately, even at six, Eleanor's math was better than his own numbers. If he thought to escape the day's lessons, she knew, and she would follow him out to the pond, also intent on fishing. Sean had tried to scare her with worms but Eleanor had helped him bait his hooks instead. She was better at that, too.

"Fine, Weed, you can stay," he had grumbled, giving up.

He would ride across the Adare lands with his brothers, an almost daily event. Eleanor had a fat, old Welsh pony, and she would follow, refusing to be sent home. More times than not, with vast annoyance, Sean had caved in to her, allowing her to send the pony home and letting her ride double behind him.

Her favorite ploys, though, had been to spy or steal. Sometimes she hid in a closet to eavesdrop on Sean, overhearing the most fascinating young male conversations—most of which she had not understood. At other times she would take a beloved possession—his favorite book, his penknife, a shoe—just to make certain he hadn't forgotten her. When he realized, he would chase her furiously through the house or across the grounds, demanding the item back. Eleanor had laughed at him, loving the chase and knowing he could not catch her unless she allowed it, as she was too fast for him.

An ancient ache was assailing her, yet she realized she had been smiling, too. She found herself standing some distance from the stables, her stallion now contentedly grazing, and tears pricked at her eyes. Sean was gone. In her heart she might yearn for his return, and she might still miss him terribly, but what good was that? Irrefutable logic demanded that if he could come back—or if he wanted to—he would have returned by now. Common sense also proved a very painful fact: he had never once in their entire lifetime indicated that he felt anything but brotherly affection for her.

Eleanor realized that a man was approaching, having come out of one of the many entrances of the house. Instantly she recognized her oldest brother, Tyrell. He was so terribly preoccupied with affairs of state, the earldom and the family that they did not spend much time together, but there was no one more dependable or more kind. One day, he would be the family patriarch, and every problem and crisis, both personal and otherwise, would be brought to him for resolution. She admired him tremendously; he was her favorite brother.

Tyrell paused before her and she was very pleased to see him. Tall, muscular and dark, he smiled at her. "I am relieved that you are all right. I saw you from a window and when you dismounted, I feared something was amiss."

Somehow Eleanor forced a smile. It felt sad and fragile. "I am fine. I decided to let Apollo graze, that's all."

Tyrell's dark blue gaze was searching. "You were never one to dally in bed, but I thought we had an understanding that you would not ride about this way while we have so many guests."

Eleanor tried to keep smiling, but she avoided his eyes now. "I had to take a gallop this morning."

He was blunt. "What is wrong?"

She stiffened, Sean's image filling her mind. Oddly, she thought she could feel him with her now, somehow. Shaken, she glanced around, but only a gardener and his boy were passing on the lawns behind her.

Tyrell caught her free hand. "Most brides would love some extra beauty sleep, sweetheart," he said kindly.

"Extra sleep will hardly make me shorter," she managed tartly. "True beauties are not as tall as most men—and taller than their own husbands."

His smile was brief. "Have you decided that you wish a taller husband? It is a bit late to change grooms."

Damn it, her first thought was that her head barely reached Sean's chin—even in her boots. Dismayed Eleanor bit her lip. "I am very fond of Peter," she somehow said. "I don't care that we stand eye to eye when I am in my bare feet."

"I am glad, because he is very smitten with you," Tyrell said seriously. "Last night during the dancing, he could not take his eyes from you. He also partnered you three times. A fourth time would have been scandalous." He laughed.

Eleanor did not. "That is because I am a ghastly dancer, missing every other step." She met his gaze. "Do you really think he is smitten? I am bringing a fortune to the marriage."

"It is rather obvious that he is besotted, Eleanor. Why are you crying?"

Eleanor tensed. She was ready to tell Tyrell everything, she realized. She so needed a confidante. "Tyrell, I am confused," she heard herself whisper.

He gestured at a stone bench, his expression kind. Eleanor handed him the stud's reins and walked over, sitting down, that odd desperation coming over her. "I do care about Peter. He is so witty and so considerate, and I have enjoyed the time we have spent together. You know I detest balls, but these past few months, with Peter attending me, I really haven't minded."

"He has been good for you, Eleanor," Tyrell said seriously. "The entire family is agreed on that. He is turning you into a rather proper and conventional lady."

"I have truly tried to be ladylike," she said.

Ladies don't lie, they don't steal and they don't spy, Elle.

Panic overcame her and she stood. "Tyrell! Sean is haunting me now. I can't do this! I really can't! We should call off the wedding— I don't care if I remain an old maid on the shelf!"

His eyes were wide. "Eleanor, what has brought this on?" He spoke with a wary tone.

"I don't know!" she cried. "If only we knew where Sean was—if only we knew what had happened to him."

Tyrell was silent.

She filled that silence. "I am aware that you think he's dead. I know what the Runners said. I still miss him," she whispered, and to her shock, she realized she missed him so much that it was like a knife stabbing through her heart.

Tyrell put his arm around her. "You have loved him your entire life and he has been gone for four years. I am certain a part of you will always miss him. Peter is a great match for you, Eleanor, in every possible way, and I cannot tell you how pleased I am that he is genuinely in love with you, too."

She barely heard. "But how can I really go through with this when I am feeling this way? I am so unsettled! I almost feel as if Sean is here to stop me from going forward! I am going to be Peter Sinclair's *wife*. I am going to bear his *children*. I am going to live in *Chatton*." And she gazed pleadingly at her brother.

"Even if Sean were here, which he is not, would it really make a difference?"

"Of course it would!" Then she flushed. "I comprehend your point. He never cared for me the way that Peter does. I know that, Ty. Why do I have to be thinking of him now, of all times?"

"All brides become exceedingly nervous before their weddings, or so I have been told." Ty smiled reassuringly at her. "Maybe you are looking for excuses to delay the event, or to even walk away?"

She studied him. "Maybe you're right. What should I do?"

Tyrell touched her. "Eleanor. You waited for almost four years for him. What do you think to do? Wait four more years for his return?"

Her heart wished to do just that. She finally said, "He's not dead, Ty. I know it. I feel it. He is very much alive. He has hurt me terribly, but one day, he will come back and tell us what happened and why."

"I hope you are right," Tyrell said grimly. He put his arm around her again. "A very wise person once said that we do not choose love. It chooses us. True love never dies, Eleanor."

"What am I to do?" she begged.

It was a thoughtful moment before Tyrell spoke. "Frankly, I am not surprised that now, on the eve of your wedding, you would be tormented by thoughts of him. Given the past, it would be odd if you did not think of him now. But that doesn't necessarily mean that you should forsake your marriage to Sinclair."

Eleanor started. "What do you wish to say?"

Tyrell hesitated.

Eleanor seized his sleeve. "Ty, you may be frank."

His jaw was tight. "I wish for you to have a life of your own. A home and family of your own, a future with the joy of children. Sean has never returned your feelings, and we do not know where he is or if he will ever return. Sinclair is offering you a genuine future. I think it would be mistake for you to jilt him now. You will not find this opportunity again. Not because of your age, a hindrance enough, but because Sinclair is such a good match for you."

Eleanor realized she did not care for his meaning. She slumped onto the stone bench, consumed with despair and doubt.

Tyrell spoke again, with great care. "Sinclair is an honorable man. He is, by birth, nature, breeding and character, a true gentleman. I do think, should you go through with the wedding, he might have some trouble ruling his roost. But I don't think he will care! He has fallen in love with you, Eleanor, and I very much approve of that. Are you genuinely considering breaking the contract on the off chance that Sean will soon return and, even more improbably, realize that he loves you?"

She was so overwhelmed she could barely think. Tyrell was right. She was being absurd. And she had given her word to Peter Sinclair.

"Of course, if you do not care for Sinclair at all, I would not want you to marry him," Tyrell said softly. "But from what I have seen, you seem genuinely fond of him. I have been pleased to see you laughing again, Eleanor. And I never thought to see you smile during a quadrille."

Eleanor inhaled and made her decision. "I am so fortunate." She did not feel fortunate at all. "What woman is allowed to make such an important choice? What choice is there to make? Peter is titled, wealthy and handsome, he is kind, and he loves me. I must be the biggest fool in the land to be thinking, even for a moment, of breaking my marriage for a man who doesn't want me—a man who isn't even here, a man the whole world thinks is dead."

"You have never been foolish," Tyrell said with a smile. "But I am relieved that you will go through with the wedding. I can barely begin to describe the pleasure a family of your own will bring you."

She just looked at him, reminding herself once

again how fortunate she was while trying to push Sean's dark image out of her mind. She must never entertain it, or her doubts, again. "You scandalized all of society by choosing Lizzie over your duty, Ty. You married for love—for true love—so I am not sure I am going to enjoy all that you have."

"You won't know, not if you don't try," he said. "I would never encourage this union if I did not have great hopes for it. I want you to be loved and I want you to be happy, Eleanor. We all do."

She threw her arms around him. "You are my favorite brother! Have I ever told you that?"

He laughed. "I believe you have," he said with an affectionate smile. "And, Eleanor? Please, do not become too proper!"

She finally smiled. "As it is an entire ruse, you need not fear a shocking transformation of character! Is not my current attire proof?" She gestured at her breeches.

He did not look down. "On that subject, I must object. Eleanor, please promise me you will return to your riding habit if you must gallop at dawn? At least until after the wedding—and the honeymoon. I would then advise you to humbly ask Peter for his permission to ride astride. I have no doubt you can convince him of anything you truly desire."

She sighed. "I will try to be humble, Ty. And you are right. I do not need a scandal of my own making now. I will steal into the house so no one sees me. Are the gentlemen up and about?"

"A large group is intent on fishing today, so yes, they are in the breakfast room. I suggest you go in through the ballroom. The ladies remain asleep, of course, except for my wife." His soft smile was instantaneous.

She quickly envisioned her escape into the house, and her planning calmed her. "Thank you, Ty. Thank you for your pearls of wisdom." She stood. "You have soothed me. I have come to my right mind. I feel much better."

Tyrell kissed her cheek. "I happen to believe you are making the right decision. I think, in time, your love for Peter will grow. I think there is every chance that, once you bear his children, there will be no regrets. You deserve all life has to offer. Sinclair can give you that."

"Yes, you are right. You are always right, in fact." She grinned at him. It never hurt to flatter the heir to the estate.

He laughed. "My wife would disagree. You need not be obsequious, my dear."

"But you are the wisest of all my brothers! Can you take Apollo back to the stables for me?" she asked in the same breath.

"Of course."

Eleanor hugged him and strode toward the house, looping past the west wing so she could take the terrace to the ballroom.

Tyrell remained still, watching her. His smile faded. He had been terribly fortunate in his own life to avoid a prearranged match and to marry for true love. Eleanor remained as deeply in love with Sean O'Neill as she had ever been—it had never been more obvious. These past few months she had been acting a charade. He could not help himself now, for his wife had made him a romantic. He wished that circumstances were different—he wished she were marrying where her heart lay. But it was not to be, and Sinclair was offering her a future. Even if Sean did return, he could offer her nothing now.

He tensed. He had just kept the truth from his sister and he dearly hoped that in doing so, he had done what was right.

For last night, well past the conclusion of the supper party, Captain Brawley, currently in command of a regiment stationed south of Limerick, had requested a private audience with the earl. Tyrell had attended, as was his right. And the young Captain had informed them that Sean O'Neill's whereabouts had been discovered.

Shocked, they had learned that Sean had been incarcerated in a military prison in Dublin for the past two years. Their disbelief and horror growing, they were told that Sean had been charged with and tried for treason. There was no explanation for his lengthy incarceration or the failure of the authorities to hang him, much less to bring the facts forward to the family. Then Brawley had announced the most shocking news of all. Three days ago, Sean had taken the prison warden hostage and he had escaped.

Sean O'Neill was a fugitive now, wanted by the authorities, a bounty on his head.

And at any moment, Tyrell expected him to appear at Adare.

CHAPTER TWO

EVERYONE KNEW that hell was blazing fire. Everyone was wrong.

Hell was darkness. It was darkness, silence, isolation. He knew—he had just spent two years in it. Three days ago, he had escaped.

And because the light of day hurt his eyes, because everyday sounds startled and frightened him, because he was being pursued by the British and he did not intend to hang, he had been hiding in the woods by day and making his way south by night. He had been told that there were men in Cork who would help him flee the country. Radical men, men who were traitors, too, men who had nothing to lose except for their lives.

It was almost dawn. He was covered with sweat, having traveled from the prison in Dublin to the outskirts of Cork in just three nights by foot. Once he had realized he might never be let out of the black hole that was his cell, he had started to use his body to keep it strong, beginning to plan his escape. Exercising his body had been simple—he had found a ledge on the wall and he had used it to hang from or to pull up on. He had used the floor in a similar manner, pushing up until his shoulders and arms ached. He had tried to keep his legs strong by practicing fencing exercises, concentrating on lunges and squats, but his body was not used to walking or running or covering any distance at all. The muscles he had not used for two years now screamed at him in protest and pain. His feet hurt most of all.

Exercising his mind had been excruciatingly difficult. He had focused on mathematical problems, geography, philosophy and poems. He had quickly realized he must keep his mind occupied at all times—otherwise, there was thought. Thought led to memory and memory led to despair and worse, to fear. Thought was to be avoided at all cost.

In his hand, he carried a burning torch. The torch was his greatest treasure. Having been immersed in almost total darkness for two years, a source of light was as important to him as the air he breathed, or as his freedom. The torch felt as weighty in his hand as a king's ransom. Sean O'Neill looked up at the sky as it turned a dark, dismal gray. He no longer needed the light if he dared to go on. The sole other survivor from the village of Kilvore had instructed him to proceed to a specific farm as swiftly as possible, and he knew he must go on, somehow transcending his fear. He carefully extinguished the torch.

The Blarney Road he was on was made of rough and rutted dirt, and led into the town's center. Somewhere up ahead was the Connelly farm. He had been assured that there he would find comfort and aid.

His heart beat hard and heavily as he walked through the woods, not daring to use the roadway but keeping parallel to it. From the width of it and the wheel ruts, he saw that it was well used. In the three long nights he had been traveling, he'd avoided all roads and even dirt paths, keeping to the hills and the forest. He'd heard troops once, but that had been a hundred miles north of where he now was. Only hours from Dublin, he'd heard the cavalcade of horses and had peered out from some high rocks on a hilltop. Below, he'd seen the blue uniforms of a horse regiment. The last time he'd seen cavalry, two dozen men had died—as had innocent women and children. In real fear, he had melted back into the woods.

The sky began to turn a pale pink. Today, clearly, it would not rain. His tension began, creeping over him, a companion both familiar and despised. But he was too close to run to the ground now. He would suffer the daylight, no matter what it cost him. Already the sounds of an awakening forest were making him start and jump, the birds beginning to sing merrily from their perches in the branches overhead. As had been the case each morning since his escape, their song brought tears to his eyes. It was as precious, as priceless, as the unlit torch he carried.

The road rounded and a cottage became visible, the roof thatched, the walls stuccoed, two sows rooting in the mud in the front yard by the well. A single cleared cornfield was behind the house, a smaller lodge there.

Sean paused behind a tree, breathing hard, but not from exertion. As alert as he was, it was hard to see across the road and to the house and the hut beyond. His eyes had become so weak. He finally glimpsed a movement between the house and the field—it was a man, or so he thought. He hoped it was Connelly.

Sean looked up and down the road but saw nothing and no one. Not trusting his poor eyesight, he strained to hear. The only sound he heard was that of myriad birds, and after a moment, he also decided that he could detect a soft rustling of leaves, the whisper of a fall breeze.

He thought he was very much alone.

More sweat pooled.

His heart pumped with painful force now. He stepped from the woods and onto the road, almost expecting a column of troops to mow him mercilessly down. But not a single soldier appeared, much less an entire column. He tried to breathe more easily, but he simply could not. He was too afraid.

He blinked against the brightening sky and pushed across the road.

The man saw him and halted.

Sean cursed his vision and strode on. He tried to summon up his voice, the effort huge. Just before his solitary confinement, there had been a murder within the prison, and much mayhem had followed. He had been badly beaten, and in the riot, his throat had been cut. No physician had been sent to attend him and for a while, he had been at death's door. He had healed, but not fully. He could no longer speak with any ease; in fact, forming each word took tiring and painstaking effort. Of course, there had been no one to speak to for two years, and once he realized that he could barely talk, he had not even tried.

Now, he forced the word from his throat and mouth. "Conn...elly?" And he heard how hoarse and unpleasant he sounded.

The man hurried forward. "Ye be O'Neill," he said, taking his arm.

Sean was shocked by his touch, and alarmed to realize he had been expected. He flinched and jerked away from the other man. "How?" He stopped and fought for the words a child could so easily utter. "How…do…you know?"

"We got our own secret post, if ye get my meaning," Connelly said. He was a big, burly man with a long red nose and bright blue eyes. "I been sent word. Ye better get inside."

A flurry of messages must have been relayed, sending the news of his escape and his need ahead of him. Sean followed the big man into the house, allowing himself to feel a small amount of relief when the front door was solidly closed, barring the outside world.

"The missus is already with the hens," Connelly said. "Ye be John Collins now." He spoke swiftly, but as he did, his gaze took in Sean's appearance with growing concern. "Ye look like a skeleton, me boy. I'll feed ye and give ye a blade fer your face. Damn those bloody Brits!"

Sean simply nodded, but he reached for the thick beard on his face. There'd been no shaving for two years.

Connelly hesitated, then spoke, "I'm sorry about what happened in Kilvore. I'm sorry about it all, an' I'm sorry about yer wife and child."

Sean stiffened. An image formed, blurred, a sweet face with kind and hopeful eyes. Peg had faded into an indistinct and painful memory that was colorless, even though he knew her hair had been shockingly red. His gut twisted, aching.

He had grieved at first, for many months; now, there was only guilt. *They were dead because of him.*

"Ye got no choice but to leave the country. Ye know that, don't you?"

Sean nodded, glad to have his thoughts interrupted. He had learned how to avoid all memory of his brief marriage, except in the wee hours of the night. "Yes."

"Good. Ye go straight down Blarney Road to Blarney Street. Ye can cross the river at the first bridge. Follow the river, it'll take you to Anderson Quay. Cobbler O'Dell will put you up."

Sean nodded again. He had questions, especially as to when he would be able to find a passage and how it would be paid for, but he was suddenly exhausted and he was also starving. He'd had a single loaf of stale bread in the past three days. Worse, speaking was a terrible chore. He tried to find and form the words. "When? When…will…I…leave the country?"

"Sit down, boyo," Connelly said, his expression grim. "I don't know. Every day at noon, ye go to Oliver Street. The pub there, it's right around the corner from O'Dell. Ye look fer a gentleman with a white flower pinned to his jacket. He will be able to tell you what ye need to know. I'm only a farmer, Sean."

Sean struggled. "Noon." He tried to clear his throat. Even his jaw felt odd, rusty, weak. "Today? Should I...go today?"

"I don't know if the gent will be there today or tomorrow or the next day. But he's good. He's real good at helpin' patriots. His name is McBane. Ye don't want to miss him."

McBane, Sean thought. He nodded again.

Connelly turned and went to the larder. He returned with a plate of boiled potatoes and a large chunk of bread and cheese. Sean felt saliva gathering in his mouth.

The supper table was set in white linens, with Waterford crystal wineglasses, imported china and gilded flatware. Huge chandeliers were overhead, towering candles flickered on the table and liveried footmen carried sterling platters of venison, lamb and salmon. The women wore silks and jewels, the men black dinner coats and white shirts and ties. Perfume wafted in the air....

He jerked, shocked by a memory he had no right to have. He refused to identify it or the man it belonged to.

Instead, he tore off pieces of bread and cheese, devouring them almost in the same instant. The only past he wished to remember was the recent one—his life at the Boyle farm. Otherwise, he would never be able to pay for what he had done to them.

THE NOISE WAS DEAFENING.

Sean paused once inside the barroom's door, overwhelmed by the cacophony of sound. The instinct to clap his hands over his ears to dim the sound was almost impossible to resist. The raucous conversation and laughter, the scraping of wood chairs, the clink of tin, was a barrage of sound that threatened to immobilize him. As it was, he was rigid with the tension it had engendered in him. And the bright lights were blinding.

He had left the farm within an hour of first arriving there and had followed Connelly's instructions. It had been easy to find the cobbler, who had put him up in a small room over his shop. It had been hugely difficult to make his way through the awakening and bustling city. He had been shocked by the sight of so many people, both on foot and on horseback, or driving wagons and carts. There had been so much pedestrian and vehicular traffic. He had seen one-horse gigs and two-horse curricles and even large coaches. And then there had been all those barges on the river. There had simply been so much movement, so many people, so much chatter, conversation and noise. And there had been so much dirt, soot, smoke and refuse. He felt strange and alien, like a farmer from the far Northwest who had never been in a city before.

In the few short hours he had been in town, his senses had not become accustomed to the sensory overload. Now, in the pub, he had to hold a hand over his eyes. Briefly, he felt a surge of panic and it was not for the first time. There were too many loud people in this single room, he thought, and his first instinct was to flee.

Yet he remained capable of reason. His mind knew that the overcrowded public room was far preferable to the small box that had been his cell. And he told himself that he would eventually become accustomed to the noise and the crowd.

Someone entered the barroom, brushing past him as he did so.

Sean did not think. The dagger appeared in his hand, a reflex meant to ensure his survival, so swiftly that no observer would have seen any movement. But the moment he grasped the carved handle above the lethal blade, the moment he held the dagger chest high, poised to slice the intruder's throat, some sanity and even humanity returned. Sean stopped himself. He braced hard against the wall, panting, subduing the urge to defend himself, the urge to kill in that defense, reminding himself that he was not a beast, never mind the past two years of being caged and fed like one. He was a man, even if he was the only one who might think so.

He leaned his head against the wall. In truth, he no longer knew who or what he was. Maybe he had genuinely become this creature of the night, a man who would kill without provocation, John Collins.

Despair suddenly clawed at him, but he had enough talons in his flesh and he shoved it savagely aside.

"Hey, boyo, beg yer pardon," the very drunken man said, glancing at him.

He had stolen the dagger from the warden when he had taken him hostage. Sean now hid the weapon, having flipped it deftly so that the blade faced up his arm, against his shirtsleeve, the worn handle hidden in his hand. He knew he needed to smile—it was the polite thing to do, the way a gentleman would behave—but he could not perform the task. Suddenly, he desperately wanted to manage the act. He ordered his facial muscles to do so, but they were so ill-used that a brief attempt produced no change in his expression. Sean gave up, staring at the unwanted interloper.

The man's eyes widened with fear. He hurried away.

Sean stood very still, his breathing hard, the ugly sounds of the drunken crowd still surging over him and through him, waves of disturbing sound pounding inside his head. Maybe it would be better once he was on a ship, once he was put to sea.

He pushed through the crowd, carefully avoiding all physical contact. He had glimpsed a small corner table far in the back, in the shadows, against a wall, and he made his way to it. When he reached it, he felt safer, relieved. Two crooked chairs were there, but neither satisfied him. With his foot, he shoved one chair against the wall and only then did he sit. His back was protected, and he could see the entire public room and everyone inside it.

He gazed out at the thirty or forty men present, all drinking, laughing, speaking, some playing at die or cards, and he once again felt like an outcast. These men were Irishmen, just as he was. Once, he had been prepared to give his life defending them against tyranny and injustice, and he almost had. Now he felt no kinship with them. Except for confusion and surprise, he felt nothing at all.

It was then that he saw the man in the fine blue wool jacket approaching, a wildflower in his lapel, a small satchel in hand. Because he feared a trap, Sean carefully let the dagger reverse itself in his hand, and he laid it on his thigh, beneath the table.

The gentleman saw him and paused before the table. "Collins?"

Sean nodded, responding to his alias. Then he gestured at a chair.

The man sat. "I was given your description," he said. "Unfortunately, you look exactly as a dangerous escaped felon might." He was grim.

Sean ignored the remark. The man was tall, with tawny hair. His jacket was well made, his trousers tan, a fine wool. He noticed his waxed shoes. This man was clearly from a privileged background. The odds were that this was the gentleman Connelly had described, someone named Rory McBane.

It took him a moment to speak. It seemed easier than it had been that morning. "Are you…alone?"

"I haven't been followed," McBane said, studying him as warily. "I was very careful. And you?" He leaned closer, as if he hadn't been able to clearly hear Sean when he had spoken.

Sean shook his head. The man continued to stare, far too closely, as if trying to decide whom he was aiding and abetting now. Perhaps McBane knew he was wanted for murder—perhaps he knew he *was* a murderer—perhaps he was afraid.

"Everything you need is in the satchel." McBane broke the tense silence. With his boot, he moved the satchel toward Sean. "There's some coin and a change of clothes. Passage has been booked to Hampton, Virginia, on an American merchantman, the *U.S. Hero*. She sails the day after tomorrow on the first tide."

He would soon be free. In a matter of days, he would be sailing across the ocean, away from the British, away from Ireland, the land where he had been born, the land where he had spent most of his life. He knew he must thank McBane, but instead, his heart stirred unpleasantly, as if trying to tell him something.

Whatever it was, he didn't want to hear. In a few days, he would no longer be hunted. Soon, he would be able to look at the sun, hopefully without using his hand as a shield, and he would never have to hide in the dark again. He would never be surrounded by cold stone walls and a barred iron door. He would never sleep on ragged stone floors with only the rags on his body for warmth, for comfort. He would never have to eat water laced with potato skins and bread crawling with maggots. He was going to America and he would be free. They would not find him there.

He should be elated or relieved, but he was neither of those things.

Crystal tinkled. Perfume wafted. Soft conversation sounded. And amber eyes, bright with laughter, held his.

Sean stiffened, shocked that his mind would suddenly do this to him. He felt ill, almost seasick. Maybe he was losing his mind, once and for all. He simply could not go to where his mind wanted to take him. There was no returning to that other lifetime! Panic claimed him.

"You need a good razor," McBane said, cutting into his thoughts, the interruption a welcome one. "I saw a Wanted poster. You look too much like it. You need to get rid of that beard."

Sean just stared. He had used Connelly's blade but it hadn't been of a good quality. McBane was right. He needed a real razor, a brush, well-milled soap.

And his mind had become intent on mayhem.

Silver eyes, bright and pleasant, stared back at him from a looking glass. A handsome, dark-haired man was reflected there, shaving in the morning. In that reflection, velvet draperies were parted. Outside, the sky was brilliantly blue and the overgrown lawns were fantastically green. The ruins of a tower were just visible from the window. So was the sea.

Sean! Are you going to dally or are we riding to the Rock?

"Are you all right?" McBane asked.

Sean tensed. He could not understand the question. What was happening to him? He could not think about the ancient past. When he married Peg Boyle, hoping to one day love her and determined to be a father to her child, as well as to the child she carried, he had made his decision. The only woman he had to remember was Peg. Now, he deliberately recalled her lying in his arms, battered and beaten and bleeding to death.

"Look, Collins, I understand you have been through hell. We are on the same side. I'm an Irishman, just like you. I heard it whispered that you're noble by birth, which gives us a common bond. You don't look well. Can I be of some help somehow?" McBane seemed perplexed but he was also concerned.

Sean could not find any relief in the present now. He found his voice but made no attempt to raise it. "Why…are you doing this?" He had to know why a gentleman would risk his life for him.

McBane started. "I told you. We are countrymen, and I am a patriot. You fought for freedom one way. I fight for it another way—usually with my pen—but sometimes I aid men like you."

Sean forced his teeth to bare, trying to smile, but McBane flinched. "Thank you," he heard himself say roughly.

"Is there anything else that you need?" McBane asked.

Sean shook his head. All he needed was to sail far away to a different land, a different life. Once he did that, maybe his mind would stop trying to torture him with glimpses of a life he was afraid to recall.

McBane leaned across the table. "Lie low then, until the *Hero* departs. I am leaving Cork tonight, but I can be reached at Adare. It's only a half day's ride from here and our mutual friends can get word to me there."

Sean knew his body remained perfectly still, but his heart leaped with a painful and consuming force. He felt as if McBane had just stabbed him. Was this a trick, after all? Or was his mind cruelly teasing him again? Had McBane just referred to *Adare?*

McBane stood. "Godspeed," he said.

Sean, stunned, did not reply.

McBane made a sound, and something like pity flitted through his eyes. Then he started through the crowd. Sean remained seated, paralyzed. He should let McBane go, otherwise he knew he was going to lose the last of his iron will. But what if McBane was a part of an elaborate trap?

He was not going back to prison and he was not going to hang.

Sean followed McBane with his eyes. He waited until he was almost at the front door. He had been correct to assume that McBane would not look back. Sean leaped up, grabbing the satchel, and reached the door an instant after McBane passed through. Then he followed him into the night.

McBane walked down the narrow and dirty street, his strides long, even jaunty. Making certain that he was soundless and invisible, Sean followed, his longer strides taking him closer and closer to his unsuspecting prey. And then he reached out, seizing him from behind, turning him face-first into the nearest wall. McBane stilled, clearly understanding that a struggle would be futile. "You…do not…go to Adare," Sean rasped, fury now uncoiling within him. "This…is a jest…or a trap."

"Collins!" McBane gasped. "Are you mad? What the hell are you doing?"

Sean jerked on the man's arm, close to breaking

it. "What…do you intend? What kind…of clever ruse…is this?"

"What do I intend?" McBane gasped against the wall. "I am trying to help you flee the country, you fool. We should not be seen together! My radical anti-British views are well-known. Damn it! There are soldiers everywhere in town!"

Sean pushed him harder into the wall. "You cannot be going to Adare. This is a trick!" he cried. Speaking a whole sentence without interruption caused his entire body to break out in sweat.

"A trick? You are mad! I heard they had you in solitary for two years. You have lost your mind! I am going to Adare as a friend of the bride and her family."

And Sean lost all control.

Adare was his home.

The green lawns and abundant gardens of Adare were so spectacular that summer parties from Britain would request permission to stop by to visit them. Huge and grand, the visitors would often request a tour of the house, as well, and it was usually allowed, if the countess or earl were in residence.

He was shaking. No, Sean O'Neill had been raised there. He was John Collins now.

"You are as white as a sheet," McBane said. "Would you mind releasing me?"

But Sean didn't hear him.

During the morning, there had been lessons in the sciences and the humanities with the tutor, Mr. Godfrey. The afternoons had been spent fencing with an Italian master, rehearsing steps and figures with the dance master and learning advanced equestrian skills. There had been five of them, all young, handsome, strong, clever, privileged and more than a bit arrogant. And then there had been Elle.

"Collins."

He came back to the present, to the street in Cork where he continued to hold McBane against the brick wall of a house. The damage was done. He had dared to allow himself the luxury of recalling a piece of the past to which he no longer had any rights. He loosened his hold on McBane, wetting his lips. He had to turn around and go back to his flat over the cobbler's shop. He did not. "There…is a wedding?"

"Yes, there is. A very consequential wedding, in fact."

Sean closed his eyes. He did not want to remember a warm and verdant time of belonging, of family, of security and peace, but it was simply too late.

He had a brother and sister-in-law and a niece; he had a mother, a stepfather and stepbrothers, and there was also Elle. He could not breathe, fighting the floodgate, struggling to keep it closed. If he let one memory out, a thousand would follow, and he would never elude the British, he would never flee the country, he would never survive.

He was overcome with longing.

Faces formed in his mind, hazy and blurred. His proud, dangerous brother, a fighting captain of the seas, his charismatic and rakish stepbrothers, the powerful earl, his elegant mother. And a child, in her two braids, all coltish legs...

He stepped away from McBane, sweat running down his body in streams. McBane appeared vastly annoyed as he straightened his jacket and stock, then concern overtook his features. "Are you all right?"

McBane had mentioned a *bride*. He looked at the man. "Who is getting...married?"

McBane started in surprise. Then, slowly, he said, "Eleanor de Warenne. Do you know the family?"

He was so stunned he simply stood there, his shock removing every barrier he had put up to prevent himself from ever traveling back into the past. And Elle stood there in the doorway of his room at Askeaton, her hair pulled back in one long braid, dressed for riding in one of his shirts and a pair of Cliff's breeches. *This was impossible.*

"What is taking you so long?" she demanded.

"We are taking the day off! No more scraping burns off wood! You said we could ride to Dolan's Rock. Cook has packed a picnic and the dogs are outside, having a fit."

He tried to recall how old she had been. It had been well before her first Season. Perhaps she had been thirteen or fourteen, because she had been tall and skinny. He was helpless to stop the replay in his mind.

He was smiling. "Ladies do not barge into a gentleman's rooms, Elle." He was bare-chested. He turned away from the mirror and reached for a soft white shirt.

"But you are not a gentleman, are you?" She grinned.

He calmly buttoned the shirt. "No, you are no lady."

"Thank the Lord!"

He tried not to laugh. "Do not take the Lord's name in vain!" he exclaimed.

"Why not? You do far worse— I hear you curse when you are angry. Boys are allowed to curse but ladies must wriggle their hips when they walk—while wearing foul corsets!"

He eyed her skinny frame. "You will never have to wear a corset."

"And that is fortunate!" Her face finally fell. She walked past him and sat down on his unmade bed. "I

know I am so improper!" She sighed. "I am on a regime to fatten up. I have been eating two desserts every day. Nothing has happened. I am doomed."

Now he had to laugh.

She was furious. She threw a pillow at him.

"Elle, there are worse things than being thin. You will probably fill out one day." He could not imagine her being anything but bony and too tall.

She slid off the bed. "You're saying that to humor me. You told me I'd stop growing two years ago, too."

"I am trying to make you feel better. Come. If you beat me to the Rock, you can stay here an extra day."

Her eyes brightened. "Really?"

"Really." He grinned back. "Last one to the Rock goes home today," he said, and he started to the door.

She cried out and ran past him, flying down the stairs.

He was laughing, and when he got in the saddle, she was an entire field ahead.

He turned away from McBane, trembling. He couldn't do this. He couldn't stand there in the cool autumn afternoon, letting his mind wander. He needed to get on that ship and sail far away, to America.

How old was she now?

The last time he had seen her she had been eighteen. He desperately wanted to shut his mind down now, but it was too late. The unforgettable image had formed. Elle stood in the white lace nightgown, next to Askeaton's front gates, a small, forlorn figure as he stared down at her from the rise in the hill. She did not move. He didn't have to be near her to know she was crying.

Promise me you will come back for me.

He was very ill now, and he could barely breathe. "Who…is she marrying?" Had she fallen in love?

"What is this about?" McBane demanded. "Do you know her?"

Sean looked at McBane, finally seeing him. He had to know. "Who is she marrying?"

McBane seemed taken aback. "The groom is an earl's son, Peter Sinclair."

The moment he realized that she was marrying an Englishman, he was disbelieving. "A bloody Brit!"

McBane said carefully, "He has title, a fortune, he is rumored to be handsome, and I have heard it said that they are a very good match. In fact, my wife told me Sinclair is besotted and that she is very happy, too. Look, Collins, I see you are distressed. But you will be even more distressed if a patrol finds us standing about gossiping on the street. You need to go back to wherever it is that you are hiding until you leave for America."

He was right. Sean fought to come to his senses. He was leaving in another day for America. It was a matter of life and death. What Eleanor did, and whom she was marrying, was none of his affair. Once, he would have protected her with his life. But he had been a different man and that had been a different lifetime. Sean O'Neill was dead, killed shortly after that terrible night in Kilvore. He was a murderer now, with a price on his head.

Even if he wanted to, there was no going back, because Sean O'Neill did not exist.

There was only a pathetic excuse for a man, more beast than human, and his name was John Collins.

He looked at McBane. "You're right."

"Godspeed, Collins. Godspeed."

CHAPTER THREE

"BEFORE THE GENTLEMEN retire to our brandies, I should like to make a toast," the earl of Adare said.

Everyone became silent. The long, linen-clad table was filled with all fifty houseguests, the entire de Warenne family—except for Cliff, who had yet to arrive—and Devlin and Virginia O'Neill. It was set with Adare's best crystal and china and gilded flatware from Holland. Two low, lavish floral arrangements were in the center, from the countess's hothouse gardens. The earl sat at its head, the countess at its foot. Eleanor saw that her father was smiling.

He was a handsome, silver-haired man in his early fifties with the demeanor of a man born to privilege and power. But then, his entire life had been dedicated to serving the earldom, his country and his family. His blue eyes were warm and benign as he looked down the long table, first at his family and then at their guests. Finally his gaze returned to her.

She could not quite look him in the eye. He was so pleased that she was marrying Peter, and she did not want him to guess that she had remained nervous all day—just like the witless debutante brides she scorned. Her earlier conversation with Ty had not had a lasting effect. Peter sat beside her. He had been attentive all evening, and he was very handsome, too, in his dinner clothes. At first, it had been so hard to smile and laugh and pretend that nothing was wrong when she was still so uneasy. Eleanor didn't care for the taste of wine and more importantly, its effect on her mind, but tonight she'd had not one but two entire glasses of red wine. Miraculously, it had calmed her down.

She had instantly enjoyed Peter's every single word and had been laughing for most of the night. She hadn't realized how amusing he was. And she wondered why she had never realized how *extremely* handsome he was, too.

Those ridiculous, marriage-mad debutantes with whom she'd had to spend so much time during her two Seasons would think that Peter was more than a premier catch—he was *the* catch of all time. Why hadn't she invited Lady Margaret Howard and Lady Jane Nettles to her wedding? They would be green with envy. Pea-green with envy, in fact. She had heard their husbands were *fat*.

If it wouldn't be remarked upon, she would have another glass of wine, never mind that supper was over. Then she would simply float through the rest of the evening.

Peter murmured, so no one else might hear, "Are you all right?"

She smiled at him. "It has been a *lovely* evening."

His brows arched in mild surprise. "Every evening is lovely if I share it with you."

She felt herself melt, oh so pleasantly. Had she really been in doubt of their union? "You are a romantic, Peter." She laughed, playfully poking his arm.

He started. "I have always been a romantic when around you."

She fluttered her lashes at him. How fortunate could one get? *Why* had she been so upset earlier? She could not quite recall.

The countess was seated at the foot of the table. Lord Henredon, Peter's father on her right. Mary said softly, "Darling? We are all waiting."

The earl cleared his throat, his gaze going from his daughter back to the table of expectant faces. "I cannot begin to say how pleased I am that my dear, beautiful daughter has finally decided to marry. I am even more pleased that she is marrying young Sinclair. Obviously her change of heart required the right man. I do not think I have ever seen her happier. To the bride and groom. May your future be filled with love, peace, joy and laughter." He raised his glass.

Eleanor smiled at her father, not able to decipher what he was talking about, and she looked at Peter, who was looking at her as if she were a goddess from Mount Olympus. His eyes were shining. Or was her vision dancing? Maybe Tyrell was right. Maybe this man was in love with her and she would one day find herself in love with him. Eleanor smiled at Peter. Maybe she was falling in love, then and there. Maybe she was already in love. Hadn't she agreed to marry him because he was the right man for her?

Her father had said something about a change of heart. She frowned. How could her heart change? She had found the right man, obviously—although he did not have gray eyes.

She felt confused. Peter's eyes were blue, not gray. Maybe she needed more wine. If she were not already in love, another glass would certainly do the trick.

"I would also like to thank Lord and Lady Henredon for their aid in planning this monumental wedding, and I want to thank all of our guests for being here. I especially want to thank Mr. and Mrs. McBane, Lord and Lady Houghton, Lord and Lady Barton, for being here with us tonight, on this first of hopefully many more joyous family occasions. And finally, I want to thank young Sinclair. Peter, thank you for making my daughter so happy." He sat down, glancing at Eleanor again with a fond smile.

"I should like to second that toast and add one of my own," Tyrell said, smiling as he stood. "To the man who dares to marry my sister. Keep her happy or you will have to account to all five of her brothers," he said.

Sinclair smiled. "I will live to keep Eleanor happy," he said gallantly. Then he seemed perplexed. "I beg your pardon—Eleanor has four brothers, does she not?"

Eleanor felt her smile fade. She had three brothers and two stepbrothers. Everyone knew that. Didn't Peter know it, too? But Sean was gone, missing—and he was the one who had gray eyes.

"Did I say something wrong?" Sinclair asked in bewilderment. "Cliff has not arrived yet, but he would make four."

Eleanor stared at the linen table cloth, suddenly sad in spite of the wine. Where was Sean? Why wasn't he here? Didn't he want to come home?

The wine had made her a lackwit. Sean wasn't there, so how could she get married? There couldn't be a wedding without Sean, because he was the one she was supposed to be marrying. Suddenly Eleanor felt a surge of panic.

"I am sorry, Eleanor," Tyrell murmured.

She looked at him, the effects of the wine gone just like that, like being thrown in a tub of frigid water. She was marrying *Peter,* not Sean. She loved *Peter*—or she almost did—and she had to have a third glass of wine before the evening was *ruined*.

Devlin O'Neill spoke. Once an infamous captain in the British Royal navy, he remained bronzed, his hair sun-streaked. "I am sure you have heard the rumors, Peter. I have a younger brother but he disappeared four years ago. No one has seen or heard from Sean since."

Sinclair started. "No, I hadn't heard. Good God, I am terribly sorry, Sir Captain!"

There was no wine left in her glass. Eleanor stared at the crystal, almost wishing that she had never met Sean, because he was ruining what was supposed to be the happiest day in her life. And she *was* happy, wasn't she? She liked the way Peter looked at her and the way he smiled. She had been happy a moment ago! She was going to miss Sean forever—she missed him now—but she was marrying a wonderful man, the most perfect man, even if he was English.

And she was overcome with confusion. She liked

Peter very much; sometimes she thought she loved him. Missing Sean—who had gray eyes—had nothing—*nothing*—to do with her wedding.

"Peter?" She smiled at him. "I should like another glass of wine. Very much," she added, but he was not given the chance to respond.

"To Sinclair," Rex de Warenne said. He had lost his right leg in the war and now he reached for his crutch and pushed to his left foot. "The perfect husband for our sister, as he will dedicate his life to her. Eleanor, no bride could be as fortunate."

Eleanor just stared at Rex, wondering if he was mocking her. He had changed so much since he had come home from the war. "I am the most fortunate woman in Ireland," she said with the heat of utter conviction.

Everyone looked at her.

Eleanor wondered, aghast, if she had just *slurred*.

Rex's dark brows lifted in skepticism. "Really?"

Eleanor met his dark, penetrating gaze and thought he might know exactly how she was feeling. But then, he was very fond of wine—and brandy—especially since he had lost his leg. Maybe he would get her another glass of wine—*discreetly*, just in case she had committed the terrible faux pas of becoming foxed in polite company.

Ladies don't get foxed, Elle.

Eleanor jumped in her seat, whirling to find Sean. But no one was standing behind her.

"Eleanor? What is it?" Peter asked quickly, concerned.

"Is he here?" she managed, clinging to the back of her chair.

The earl stood decisively. "I think we should adjourn to our brandies. Eleanor?"

Eleanor realized she had been about to sit backward in her chair. Sean wasn't there. She was so disappointed it was hard to face the right way as the men all stood. She felt far too many curious regards coming her way.

Peter remained seated beside her. As the men left, Rex limped over to them, using his single crutch. He was very dark and muscular, and almost the spitting image of Tyrell, except that his eyes were brown, not blue. "I am sorry, Eleanor. I should not burden you with my foul mood on this, your joyous occasion."

She had stopped understanding him years ago, when he had first returned from the war, embittered as well as wounded, but she did not have a clue as to what he meant now. She smiled. "Oh, Rex." She waved at him. "You are my favorite brother and you can do no wrong. You do know that, don't you?"

He glanced at Peter. "I beg your pardon." He took

her arm, tugging her away from the table, which he somehow did in spite of the fact that he had to rely so heavily upon his crutch. "You are in your cups!" he exclaimed, keeping his tone low.

"I am, aren't I?" She beamed. "Now I begin to understand why you so enjoy drink. Would you sneak me another glass of wine? Red, if you please?"

"I will not," he said, appearing torn between amusement and horror. "Do you think to purposefully sabotage your wedding?"

Eleanor decided to analyze the word *sabotage*. "Hmm. Sabotage, that means ruin, does it not? But in a political manner? Is sabotage a political act? Why are we discussing sabotage?"

"You should go to your rooms," Rex said firmly, but his mouth was quirking as if he were trying very hard not to smile.

"Not until I have been kissed—and soundly, too, I might add." She walked away from him, smiling at her betrothed.

The ladies had adjourned to a separate salon. Peter was waiting by himself at the table. "Is everything all right?" he asked.

She was surprised by the question. "Of course it is." She took his arm, looping hers with his. "I am with you," she added.

He blushed. "Eleanor, you never imbibe. Maybe I should summon one of your sisters-in-law and bid you good-night for the evening."

"That is a stunningly bad idea!" She pressed closer. "We haven't had a moment to ourselves all day," she said softly. "Won't you join me for a look at the stars?" She wondered if she should tell him that she would love a kiss.

He blushed. "I was going to suggest just that. You have beaten me to it," he said.

"I am good at beating boys—and men," she told him frankly. "I ride and shoot better than everyone."

He started, his eyes widening with surprise.

"Oops," she murmured. *Ladies don't ride and shoot,* she thought. *Ladies don't swear and they don't lie.* "Ladies don't lie," she added.

"I beg your pardon?"

Maybe conversing wasn't the best idea. She smiled and pulled him toward the terrace doors. He relaxed, allowing her to lead.

SEAN LEAPED UP the terrace steps. The terrace was deserted and unlit, and even before he crossed it, he could see into the house, where a gathering of some sort was in progress. He rushed to one of the huge windows and stared into the dining room.

Standing at the head of the table was the man who had taken him in after the murder of his own father, who had raised him as his son, who had fed him and clothed him, who had taught him nobility and honor, who had loved him as if he were his natural-born son. Sean clung to the stone wall of the house, his knees useless.

And then he saw his brother.

Devlin stood, a tall, powerfully built leonine man, his wife at his side. Sean had rebuilt Askeaton for Devlin, and he would do it all over again in an instant, if he had to—just as he would give his life for his older brother, too.

He swallowed hard. Devlin's beautiful wife, Virginia, seemed very happy, and he was fiercely glad for her and for them. She had saved his brother's soul years ago and for that, he would always love her.

His stepbrothers were also rising to their feet and he could vaguely hear them speaking. The mood was festive, warm, light.

And it was almost impossible not to recall every moment spent in that room with his father, his brothers, his mother and Elle. Like the surging tides of the Irish Sea, moments and feelings swept through him, over him, demanding attention, inspection, remembrance. He fought his recollection of an early

Christmas morning, of a dark, wintry afternoon, of pleasant evenings in front of the fire, of family, male camaraderie and brandy. He had to shake himself hard to free himself from the past.

Why was he doing this? Reminding himself of the life he had left behind was not going to help him elude the British and flee the country. In a few minutes, he would steal a fresh mount from the stables and return to Cork. He would be there before dawn, and when his ship set sail from Cobh he would be on it.

But he wouldn't leave just yet.

He was doing this because Elle was getting married, he reminded himself.

Sean pressed his face to the cold glass, watching Tyrell clasp Devlin's shoulder. The two men were laughing about something as they followed the other men from the room, and it became impossible to deny the yearning to go inside and become a part of that family one more time. He desired it so badly he could taste it, but he made no move to do so. He was wanted for treason and he had no intention of bringing the earl and his brother and stepbrothers down with him.

The women were rising now and preparing to leave. He recognized Virginia, and Tyrell had his arm around a lady with titian hair. The rest of the departing crowd was meaningless to him, except for his mother. She was smiling as she led the ladies from the room. The countess remained as graceful and elegant as ever, but he saw that she seemed older. He didn't fool himself—his disappearance must have distressed her to no end.

Then Sean realized that one woman had walked away with Rex. His gaze slammed back to her—and his heart stopped.

For one instant, he was paralyzed. She had changed—but he would know her anywhere. And there was so much relief, huge and consuming, that he almost collapsed against the window. *Elle.*

Nothing was left of the gawky, intrepid child—but then, if he dared to recall his last night at home, the young blossoming woman he had left four years ago had been anything but childlike. He hadn't forgotten how tall she was, but the planes and angles of her face, like the planes and angles of her body, had finally vanished. She had become lush and voluptuous. The gawky child was now a beautiful woman, capable of stunning a man senseless.

Watching her charm his brother, he felt his world turn upside down.

Sean panicked. What was he doing, anyway? He had expected to return to a slender young woman who had never been kissed, a young woman whom he saw only as a friend and sister. Now she laughed at Rex, her smile dazzling, and he could almost hear her then.

Have I ever told you that you are my favorite brother?

Words Elle had said to every one of his stepbrothers and to Devlin, to everyone but him.

Realization struck him with the force of lightning, causing him to stagger. He was staring at Elle with need and hunger.

It was impossible, he thought, incredulous and aghast. He could not desire the woman he had considered a sister for most of his life. His body was responding as it would to any beautiful female, due to two years of celibacy, his only relief inflicted by his own hand.

She was walking away from Rex and smiling at a blond gentleman, looping her arm in his. He briefly looked at her escort, realizing that he was her intended, Sinclair. The man was handsome and privileged, with the bearing of a born aristocrat. Sean despised him on sight.

Sean realized he was shaking and desperate. He was furious with her, with Sinclair, with himself. Of course Elle had grown up. He had every right to be surprised by the beauty she had become, but he had no right to any other feelings. And where the hell was she going with Sinclair, anyway? He returned to the window and realized that the dining room was empty.

The moment he heard the terrace door open, he also heard her laughter, and while the sound was familiar, it was also strange and new. Her laughter had changed. It had become sultry; it was *seductive*.

He pressed his back to the wall, waiting for them to come into view, and as he waited, he realized that his loins were stiff and full. But he barely had time to absorb that terrible fact when they appeared, strolling to the balustrade. They were so engrossed in one another that he did not think they would notice him in the shadows against the house. She moved differently now, too. Her stride was long but there was a sensuous quality to the sway of her hips—a quality he instantly hated. She moved like a woman who knew she was being appreciated and admired, pursued and watched.

"Have I told you how lovely you are tonight?" Sinclair asked, taking both of her hands in his.

Sean felt like choking him into silence.

"I don't think so," Eleanor said, a smile in her voice. "But if you did, you can always tell me again."

She was flirting! Since when had Elle learned to flirt?

"You are so beautiful," Sinclair said thickly, and Sean hated the rough tone of his voice. They should not be out on the terrace alone, at night. Where the hell was everyone, anyway? She had four brothers to chaperone her. Why wasn't someone doing precisely that?

"And you, sir, are far too gallant and far too charming," Elle returned softly. "I am so fortunate to be marrying such a man!"

"A man cannot possibly be too charming or too gallant, not where you are concerned," Sinclair whispered.

Did he know that his lady love was a hellion? Or had Elle given up her wild gallops, her fist fighting, her swear words? Did she still hunt and fish? Or was she now a debutante and a flirt?

"I am pleased that you are so charming," Elle whispered back. "I find you very charming indeed, even if your eyes are blue."

Sean had not a clue as to what that meant, and apparently, neither did Sinclair.

There was a strained silence then.

Sean felt like smashing the wall, because he knew that Sinclair was preparing to kiss her.

"May I? May I kiss you, Eleanor?" he asked.

"I thought you would wait *forever* to ask." She laughed.

In disbelief, Sean watched Sinclair take her into his arms, slowly lowering his face to Elle's. The moon chose that moment to come out from behind a single cloud, vividly illuminating the lovers. Sinclair had fused his mouth to hers—and she was kissing him back wildly, clinging to his shoulders.

He leaned against the stone wall, furious and paralyzed, panting hard, but he refused to look away. He could not comprehend the sensual woman in the other man's arms— Elle, who was kissing him and making small, breathy sounds of pleasure and delight. He pulled at his breeches. She might be a woman now, a very desirable woman, but they had grown up together and he had no right to the lust in his loins.

"I've been kissed, Sean!"

He jerked, words she had spoken many years ago suddenly coming to mind. And it was as if she was eleven years old again to his seventeen, and they were standing there in the stables at Adare, amidst the straw and the horses, and she was grinning mischievously at him.

HE HAD SPENT WEEKS pursuing a tenant's daughter— a buxom blonde with a pretty smile and two dimples. Suddenly he was in the straw with her, his hands beneath her skirts, and she was weeping in pleasure and he was so close to unbuttoning his breeches and moving inside her. He began to do so, taking her hand and guiding it to where he was stiff and hard. And he heard a giggle.

Instantly, he knew Elle was spying—again. All lust vanished. Furious, he leaped to his feet, pulling his pants together as he did so—only to find her perched on the top edge of the stall, grinning at him. Realizing that she had seen everything, he felt his cheeks burst into flames, and his anger erupted. She knew, because she leaped down from the top of the stall, alarmed.

He threw open the bolt and ran through the stables after her. But instead of fleeing, she stood in the stable yard, warily waiting for him. He halted abruptly, as wary. "You are in jeopardy now," he warned, meaning it.

She stuck her tongue out at him.

"I am going to box your ears—hard—and tell Father what you have done."

She pranced, just a little. "But you can't catch me."

She was right—she was as fleet and as lithe as a deer. "I don't enjoy being spied on."

"Do you love her?" she suddenly asked.

"No!" The moment he spoke, he regretted it, as it

was none of her affair. "Come here, Elle." He took a step toward her.

She shook her head, backing away. Then she grinned. "I've been kissed."

He felt his world become oddly still. "I hope you are lying, Elle."

She grinned hugely at him. "No. Jack O'Connor kissed me last week behind the chapel."

Sean was shocked. And then he whirled into action, striding back to the stables, calling for a groom and a horse.

Eleanor ran after him. "Where are you going?"

"I am going to kill young Jack O'Connor." He meant it. He had never been more furious—Elle was just a child!

Eleanor grabbed his arm. "Wait! Don't! It was my fault!"

Sean faced her grimly. "Did he kiss you, or not?"

She bit her lip. "I kissed him. Like this." And she threw her arms around Sean, actually leaping up to kiss his lips.

He hauled her off. "You threw yourself at that boy?"

"Why not? You kiss all the girls! And all the ladies! You are a rake! Father says so."

Recently, he and his brothers had been tearing up the countryside, testosterone raging. He flushed. "You can't spy on me anymore! I'm not a boy now, Elle! You'll see things you shouldn't!" He was truly aghast.

"Like you putting your hands down her bodice— and touching her between her legs?" She smiled mischievously at him, then mimed, "Oh, oh, OOHH!"

He'd had enough—a boxing of the ears would not do. Sean reached for her, but she darted quickly away. He set chase, determined to somehow corner her so he could thrash her at least once. She started to laugh, putting a tree between them and dancing just out of his reach every time he tried to seize her. She might be as quick as a hare, but he had fortitude, and sure enough, in a few more moments, she started to scowl, clearly becoming bored.

"All right, I give up," he said quietly, turning away.

She sighed and left the safety of the tree, and he whirled and grabbed her by her ear.

"Ow! Ow!"

He shook her well, not once, but twice. "The next time I catch you spying on me, I am turning you over my knee, as if you were five or six."

"All right! I'm sorry! I swear!" she begged, wild-eyed.

"Ladies don't swear—but then, you're a hellion not a lady. Let's go." Not releasing her ear, he started to walk away from the stable, Elle in tow.

"I am sorry—and I won't swear!"

"You're not sorry—and you'll probably swear at your wedding!"

"Don't take me to Father!" she begged, a tear falling.

He halted. In spite of what she had done—and what she had seen—he did feel sorry for her. He transferred his grip to her arm. "Did you really kiss Jack?"

She hesitated. "Yes, I did, but on the cheek—not the mouth."

"I thought so." He sighed. "Ladies don't lie, Elle, they don't kiss boys, and they don't swear."

"I hate being a lady," she pouted.

He had to smile—and she smiled back.

"Eleanor—I love you."

Sinclair's breathless declaration jerked Sean back into the present. He didn't want to remember the past, but he didn't want to watch Elle making love to another man, either. Sinclair held her face in his hands. The man was visibly shaking and Elle, damn it, was smiling at him—as if she were in love.

"I am trying very hard to be a gentleman," Sinclair whispered, "but you make it almost impossible."

"It's only the two of us," Elle murmured. "No one

will ever know if you are being a gentleman tonight or not."

Sean started to step forward to intervene but caught himself in the nick of time. Was she suggesting that Sinclair take even more liberties? She had been such a wild and headstrong child, he knew she was a wild and passionate woman. Had she already taken her fiancé to bed? Elle never denied herself anything that she wanted and he knew her well enough to know that she wouldn't care at all about her virginity, but that she would most certainly like bed sport.

And they were kissing again.

Sean slammed his fist into the wall then. Where the hell were her brothers, damn it? Was he going to have to witness her lovemaking all night? Because he didn't think he could stand it.

Elle leaped out of Sinclair's arms. "What was that?" she cried, glancing quickly around.

He forgot about his dilemma, willing himself into invisibility as he sank as tightly as he could against the wall.

"What was what?" Sinclair asked, his tone disgustingly thick again.

"Didn't you hear that?" Elle asked, appearing bewildered. "Are we being spied on?"

"Darling, who would spy on us?"

"Rex, is that you?" Eleanor demanded, scowling now.

"Oh, God," Sinclair said. "Your brothers are very protective of you—which is laudable, of course, but each and every one has privately made it very clear to me that I had better be a perfect gentleman until we are wed." Sinclair cleared his throat. "Perhaps we should go back inside."

Elle shook her head. "Oh, don't mind them! They are all swagger and high commands. I can manage Ty, Rex and Cliff. Have no fear! I am enjoying being kissed, Peter," she added boldly.

Sean felt like grabbing her by the ear as if she were eleven years old and shaking her until time went backward and she was an innocent, if vexing, child once more.

Suddenly the terrace door opened and an odd footfall sounded. Sean recognized Rex—and then he realized that he had lost half of his right leg and he was using a crutch. He stared, shocked.

He hadn't known.

But then, he had been gone for so long, how would he have known that his stepbrother had suffered such a wound?

Rex limped over to the lovebirds. "I thought it might be wise to interrupt this enchanting tryst. The two of you are not married yet." He smiled, but without mirth.

And in that single instant, Sean recognized a kindred spirit—Rex had changed from the inside out. Although he had never mourned the loss of his own soul, he ached for Rex's loss now.

"I am twenty-two," Elle exclaimed. No other woman would ever refer to her advanced age. "I hardly need a chaperone."

"Oh, I think I can easily disagree with you," Rex said. "Shall we?" And it was not a question, but an order.

Elle was annoyed. "Oh, I forgot, you outrank me, *Sir* Rex," she said with heat.

So Rex had been knighted, Sean thought. He had undoubtedly won that title on the field of battle and Sean was pleased for him.

"Only until you are wed," he said calmly, gesturing the lovers inside.

Sean watched Elle display her infamous temper, huffing as she swept by him, with Sinclair, chagrined, following. Sinclair would never be able to keep up with Elle, he thought, but he felt no satisfaction. He was thinking now about the fact that in two nights, if he had understood correctly, Elle was going to be in that man's bed, with every right to be there.

Suddenly Rex stiffened.

Sean stopped breathing, aware that Rex had just sensed his presence on the terrace.

Rex, posed to enter the house, shifted on his crutch and turned, his glance taking in the entire terrace— including the wall where Sean stood hiding.

And for one moment, Sean could have sworn that Rex had seen him, that their eyes had met.

But he was wrong, because Rex turned and limped into the house, leaving Sean alone outside, swallowing the bitter aftertaste of all he had just seen and heard.

CHAPTER FOUR

IT WAS A NEW DAWN. Eleanor had not been able to sleep more than an hour or two, fighting the effects of the wine, and when she had, she had dreamed not of Peter, but of Sean. In her dreams, Sean had come home, but he had changed, and there had been something dark and disturbing about him. She had woken stunned, for one moment believing that her dreams were real. And when she had realized they were only dreams, utter disappointment had claimed her.

Today she raced her stud as hard as he could go. Bending low over the bay stallion's neck like a New-market jockey, she urged him around a particularly sharp turn.

A man stepped directly into her path.

Eleanor hauled hard on her reins. The man just stood there, unflinching, as if he were made of stone. The animal lunged back to stand and Eleanor reacted.

She had never been more furious. "Fool!" she shouted, raising her crop, her instinct to strike him down. "Do you wish to die? Did it not cross your mind to get out of my way, or are you a madman seeking suicide?"

She urged the bay forward, intent on going around him, but he seized her reins.

Her fury escalated dangerously, but with it came fear. No one had ever accosted her on her father's estate before. She spurred the bay—and their gazes clashed, then held.

Her heart ceased beating, and then thundered wildly, in disbelief and elation.

Sean was standing there on the trail before her. Sean had come home.

And she knew, immediately, that something terrible had befallen him. In that space of a single heartbeat, she saw that he was thin and scarred. *But it was Sean.* With a glad cry, she leaped from her horse. She rushed him so swiftly that she almost knocked him off his feet. Throwing her arms around him, she clung.

She began to cry.

She had missed him so much. Only then did she fully realize that it had been like having her heart ripped from her chest while it continued beating.

He did not move, but he made a noise, raw and harsh.

That sound cut through her exhilaration, her relief. She realized she was clinging as tightly to his lean, muscular frame as she could. She was afraid to let go, afraid that if she did, he might vanish into thin air. His chin cupped her head and her face was tucked into his chest. Sean had always been lean but now he was only muscle and bone, with no flesh to spare. And that rough sound had been filled with pain and anguish. *What was wrong?*

But he had come home—he had come back to her, *for* her. A huge pressure swelled inside of her, a powerful combination of all her feelings both past and present, of having missed him so much and of needing him now. She still loved him; she had never stopped. Eleanor smiled up at him.

He did not smile back. His face was wary and he moved stiffly away from her.

Eleanor started—he could not be wary of her? She reached for him to embrace him again. "I knew you would come back."

But he deftly dodged her. "Don't."

She somehow breathed. "Sean, don't *what?* You're home!" she cried.

He didn't answer, but his intense regard never

wavered. When she looked into his eyes, trying to make some sense of his behavior, they became flat and blank before he looked away.

She was shocked. They had never kept secrets from one another; his expressive eyes had always been open and unguarded with her. His beautiful gray eyes could shine with laughter, with affection, with kindness, or they could darken with intent, with determination, with anger. How often had they shared a private look and each had known exactly what the other one was thinking?

And his face had changed, too, she realized. It was gaunt and hollowed. She saw the scars on his cheek and throat and she shuddered—someone had slashed him with a knife! "Oh, Sean," she began, reaching up to touch a white crescent on his face, but he flinched.

She went still. His expression was guarded. Her first instinct was right—something was very wrong. Whatever he had suffered, she was there now, to help him though it. "Are you all right?"

"You're engaged," he said. He spoke in a whisper that was barely audible and his voice was hoarse, as if had recently lost it. He was looking at her with such shattering intensity that she hesitated.

"What?" she began, confused.

But he was not looking into her eyes now. His gaze had slipped to her mouth and then it veered abruptly to her chest. She was, in fact, wearing one of his old, cast-off shirts. His gaze slammed to the knotted leather belt at her waist—or to her hips. Suddenly Eleanor was aware of how she must look in a man's breeches. She had been wearing men's attire for years—Sean had seen her dressed in such a bold fashion a thousand times—but in that instant, she felt immodest, indecent, naked.

Her body hollowed.

For the first time in her life, Eleanor understood desire. For the space inside her was so empty that she ached, and in that instant, she understood the necessity of taking him inside so he could fill it.

She had thought she had felt desire before. She had enjoyed Peter's kisses, certainly, and before Sean had left Askeaton, she had looked at him and wished to be the recipient of his flattery, to be taken into his arms, to be kissed by him. In that moment, she realized she had been playacting, pretending or even hoping to feel the way a woman was supposed to feel when she loved a man. But she had been too young and too innocent and she hadn't felt this way at all. The pressure in her was combustible and consuming.

It was so hard to speak. "You came home," she

said slowly, trembling. Now, she was cautious. She wanted to take his hand—as she used to do, lightly and innocently—but she was afraid to reach out. Somehow, in the previous moment, everything between them had changed. "What happened? Where have you been?" she asked.

His eyes locked with hers, just for an instant before he looked aside. "I heard you're getting married," he said again, slowly, spacing out his low, rough words. And he lifted his silver gaze.

She bit her lip, taken aback. Hadn't she secretly fantasized about his return in the nick of time to save her from wedlock to another man? "Sean. I am affianced," she began. But she did not want to discuss Peter or her marriage now.

"The wedding—" he paused, as if it was hard to speak "—is in two days."

She didn't even think about what she would say. She smiled tremulously at him. "It is a mistake. I'm not marrying Peter."

His eyes flickered.

And she had to touch him one more time, even though she was afraid to perform such a simple gesture. She reached out to him, brushing his hand. She wanted to seize it and *never* let go. "It's been so long! Everyone thinks you're dead, Sean. I almost believed it, too. But you promised. You promised me you would come back and you did!"

He didn't look at her now. "I'm sorry. I didn't want…to hurt anyone."

He was acting so oddly and speaking so strangely. It had become awkward, as if they were strangers now, but that was impossible—they were best friends. "What's happened to you? What happened to your voice? Why are you so thin? Why didn't you send word? Sean…you've changed so much!"

"I couldn't send word." He looked briefly, unemotionally, at her. His eyes had become even flatter and darker than before. "I've been…in prison."

"Prison?" She gasped in absolute disbelief. "Is that where you got those scars? Oh, God! Is that why you're so thin? But why would you be in prison? You're the most honest man I know!" But this began to explain his prolonged absence and his utter lack of communication with her and the family.

He stared at the ground. "I shouldn't be here." He glanced up, at her, through her. "I escaped."

The implications of what he said hit her then, hard. "Are they looking for you?"

"Yes."

Her mind scrambled, fear rising. He was not going back to prison. Nothing would stand in her way of helping him now! "You must hide! Were you followed here?"

"No."

She was relieved. "The stables? You could hide in a spare stall there."

He did not reply.

She was unnerved. What did that intense look mean? "We're best friends, but I am so nervous!" She laughed and the sound was high and anxious. "You need to hide."

"I am not...staying."

She had misheard. He had just returned; he could not leave her now. It was a moment before she could find her voice. "What do you mean?" she asked carefully.

He looked away, at the branches overhead, or at the skies beyond. "I am leaving...the country."

"You just came home!" she cried, desperate and frightened, and she seized his hand. It was hard and calloused and that, at least, was familiar.

He pulled his hand free, his eyes wide and incredulous. He shook his head, not speaking.

It was dawning on her now that he would not let her touch him. But they had grown up together and in the past, she had done more than reach for his hand— she'd leaped on his back as a small child and crept into his bed after a nightmare. She'd ridden astride behind him. Even when she'd been older, she held his hand when she felt like it, and he must have clasped her shoulder or her elbow a million times.

His rough whisper brought her eyes to his. "You've changed."

Of course she had changed. And although his words were entirely dispassionate and without any innuendo, that shattering intensity had returned. In response, she went still and she instantly recognized the fist of desire as it slammed into her.

Somehow she nodded. She spoke with great care. "I've grown up. You've changed, too."

Tension seemed to fill the clearing. It crackled like fire, dancing between them, heated and bright. Was she mistaken, or was Sean feeling the same need, the same desire, that she was? He had never before looked at her so intently as he had just done. There had never been so much awkwardness and tension. In the past, the pull between them had been easy and light—a natural affinity, a bond of affection. What else could this strain mean?

She shuddered. "How long were you in prison? What did you do?"

He stared at her, his eyes turning blank. "Two years."

She gasped.

"There was a village. It's gone now."

She had been steeped in the history of her people, her land. That history was one of plunder and outright theft, of birthrights lost or stolen, of rape, murder. One of the worst massacres in Irish history had taken Sean's father. She didn't have to know the details to understand him now. There had been a protest or an uprising and the British troops had been called in. Whether rightly or wrongly, defense of the landed gentry had resulted in the destruction of an entire village. And Sean had been involved.

He had spent his entire adult life taking care of Askeaton, and that had included guarding and even defending the rights of every Irish tenant on estate lands. She did not have to ask which side he had been on. She was almost paralyzed with foreboding. "Did British soldiers die? Did you bear arms?" Bearing arms in Limerick County was an act of treason, as was disputing British authority; the county had been placed under the Insurrection Act before Sean had left.

He nodded. "Yes, soldiers died. Arms?" He was angry now. "We had knives and pitchforks."

Had a chair been available, Eleanor would have sat down. She knew she had blanched. She didn't know where the uprising he spoke of had occurred, but it didn't matter. If soldiers had died in a violent confrontation, Sean was in dire jeopardy. He might even be a traitor. She was terrified for him now. "The winter before last, they hanged over a dozen men, Sean, and deported dozens others! The charges were insurrection! Father is no longer the magistrate here—he chose to step down. Accusations of bias were made against him. He dared to defend some of our people! Captain Brawley is the commander of the garrison in the county and he has been acting as chief magistrate." She realized she was in tears. She wiped her face; she had no time for weeping now.

"I am sorry," he said, appearing grim and disgusted.

She shook her head. "He and Devlin both perjured themselves in the hopes of saving some of the accused. He stepped down because he could not keep the county under control—because he could no longer protect our people." She forced herself to recover her composure. She strode to him but he stepped back from her, as if he knew she was going to reach for him. His determination to keep a physical distance between them had already dismayed her, but now, it was beginning to frighten her, too. What had happened to him, to make him so wary, so distant?

"Sean, I don't care what you did—nothing has changed for us. You're my best friend and I will do anything for you. Anything!" she stressed fervently. "Sean, why won't you let me embrace you?"

"*Everything* has changed."

She wished she could look into his eyes and comprehend his every thought the way she once had. She was sure he was angry, but she could not fathom why. And she had no clue as to what he meant. "You have been through a terrible ordeal, which is obvious. My feelings for you haven't changed. My loyalty remains. I will help you hide and then we will go to Father and somehow resolve this, so you can be free to come home."

His eyes widened. "You are not going to the earl!" he exclaimed hoarsely. "Do you want him… named…a conspirator? Do you want the earldom… forfeit? Traitors do not keep their titles…their land!" He was so agitated that he was shouting, but in that terrible whisper of his.

She was aghast. "Were you charged with treason?"

He nodded darkly, his eyes flashing now.

"But they hang traitors!" she cried. Executions were summary and swift.

He waved at her, hard, a dismissal. "Cease." His chest was rising and falling rapidly, an indication of his stress. "I am going to America."

She reeled. America was so far away! Yet he was

right in that her father must not be a conspirator to his crimes. The pages of Irish history were filled with stories of forfeited titles and lands. But Sean must not go to America. "You do not need to run away to America," she heard herself say with desperation. Panic had overcome her now. "Devlin can help us."

He jerked, and for one instant, she thought he was reaching for her. But his hand fell to his side. "Not *us*. And he is not helping me."

She flinched. "Devlin will want to help you. He is one of the wealthiest men in Ireland and he is still well connected with the government. In fact, he has many cronies in the Admiralty—"

"No!" He suddenly towered over her. His lean body was shaking wildly, uncontrollably. "Why won't…you understand? The man who left… four years ago…he isn't coming back!" He seemed furiously angry, his eyes bright, his face flushed.

Eleanor was almost cowed, but she was relieved to see him passionate about something, anything at all. "He did come back. He's standing right here!"

"He died," he shouted in that dismal whisper. "Sean O'Neill is dead."

Eleanor recoiled, horrified by his words, and worse, by the fact that he wanted her to believe them.

"I am John Collins! I am not dragging

Devlin…into hell." His dark stare glittered wildly, almost madly.

She was terrified, but not of him—she was terrified of what had happened to him. "If Sean were dead, I would know it!" She swatted hard at his chest. He jumped, eyes widening in shock. She hit him again, this time with her fist, the blow a solid one. "If Sean were dead, he would not be trying to protect his brother! I don't know who John Collins is and I don't care to know!" Then she swatted at her tears.

And she saw that he was fighting for composure now. Realizing the enormity of the struggle, she became still. She slid her hand over his cheek just as the tremors ceased. He started, his gaze flying to hers. He was roughly shaven, but she didn't care. *She loved him more than she ever had, and that was impossible. Touching him, even in such a simple caress, instantly sent a vast churning into motion inside her. There was so much love, so much fear and so much need. If only he would take her into his arms, she might settle for that, never mind the urgency in her body.*

"Don't cry."

She hadn't realized that tears continued to well in her eyes. The dam broke then, and the tears raced hard and fast down her face. "How can you ask me not to cry when you are a fugitive from the British? When you plan to leave your home again? When I need to hold you and touch you and you won't let me? Will you ever come back? And you are so thin!" She wept.

"Don't," he said, his tone thick. "Elle."

The tears ceased. It had been so long since he had called her his own private nickname and her heart yearned for what suddenly felt impossible—to have him smile at her the way he always had when he was no longer furious with her. She did not move, because she still cupped his rough cheek and his oddly flat eyes had a light in them now, or was it the glimmer of tears?

He shifted so that her hand dropped to her side. "The earl can't help...Devlin can't help," he said very quietly. "You need to understand."

"No! I do understand. But Devlin *can* help. He would never run away from this, from you, like a coward! He has missed you, Sean, almost as much as I have."

"I killed a soldier." He cut her off. "There was a trial. I am a traitor. No one...can help. I am going to America...tomorrow."

Had he hit her with his fist she could not have been more stricken. He would leave *tomorrow?* She reeled, staggering backward. And he instinctively reached out to steady her.

His large hand, strong and hard and capable, painfully familiar, closed on hers as it had countless times before. But his touch had changed. His touch now went through her entire body, because it was that of a man and she had become, just moments ago, a woman. She met his gaze. There was no choice to make. She was going with him.

"Sit down…before you swoon."

He knew very well that she had never fainted once in her entire life. She ignored him. "When does your ship sail?"

His thick black lashes lowered, hiding his eyes, and he let go of her, turning his back to her.

"When does your ship sail?" she demanded, moving to step in front of him and forcing him to look directly at her.

"Tomorrow night," he said slowly. And when he finally met her eyes, she saw a shimmer of guilt there.

He was lying to her. Eleanor was disbelieving— Sean had never lied to her. So much had happened to him, and so much was happening now. Two facts were glaring, though. He needed to hide until he left—and she was going with him. "I'm coming with you."

He flinched and stared, wide-eyed. "You're getting married."

"I am coming with you and don't even think to

stop me," she said fiercely. He had left her once and she would never allow him to leave her behind another time.

This time their gazes clashed. "No...you're not," he said very firmly. "You have a *wedding* to attend. *Your* wedding."

And for the first time since Sean had so suddenly appeared on the trail, she really faced that fact. What was she going to do about Peter? She could not marry him now.

"What's wrong?"

"Can you still discern my every mood and feeling?" Her question was sincere.

He hesitated. Clearly reluctant, he said, low and harsh, "Perhaps."

She searched his gaze, but it was impossible to fathom any of his thoughts or feelings. "Then you must know I can't marry Peter now."

He was still. "You were fond of him...last night."

Because he spoke so strangely, in a low whisper, and because his voice had changed, his tones rough and raspy, it took her a moment to comprehend his words. "What are you speaking about?" she began, and then she felt her cheeks flame. "You were there? No, it is impossible! You were not there, last night? Were you?" Eleanor suddenly recalled the evening in some very humiliating detail. She had been *foxed*. She had *slurred* at the table in front of Peter's family and fifty other guests.

His face didn't move, except for his lips. His tone was incredulous. "Why were you not chaperoned?" His stance had changed. His legs were braced defensively, as if he rode one of his brother's ships.

Eleanor was stunned—and horrified. For she thought of being outside on the terrace with her fiancé being kissed and wanting even more kisses. Her cheeks burned. "How much did you see?" she managed. She had been worse than improper. She had been *brazen*. She had been *bold*.

"Everything," he said, turning away from her. His strides were restless now. Eleanor suddenly noticed that he was moving differently, as if he was stiff and sore.

She found a rock and sat down. Should she attempt an explanation? What could she say? "I am fond of Peter—"

"I don't care," he said, uttering the words rapidly, and surprising her because of it. He had now turned red, too.

"He is my fiancé," she tried.

"So you will become English?" His tone was mocking.

She shook her head. "We will live in Yorkshire—I mean, we were going to live there, in Chatton, but—"

"You've changed!" he exclaimed, and for the first time that day, his voice rose above a whisper. "You hated those two Seasons.... Elle would never leave Ireland!" He paused, but whether it was because of the exertion of speaking so rapidly and angrily or because he had said all he intended to, she did not know.

"I don't want to leave Adare!" she cried.

"Then don't!" he cried back, his voice rougher than before. He coughed and seemed angry that his voice had begun to fail him. "Does he know... that you can shoot...antlers off...a buck...moving in the woods?"

She was dismayed. "Sean, stop. I see that it hurts you to speak so much." She was on her feet, reaching for him. His voice was getting lower and more inaudible with every word he spoke.

But he shook his head furiously. "Has he...seen you...dressed...like a man?" he cried, tripping over his words now, his voice dripping sarcasm as well as wrath. "Has he seen you...in breeches! Boots! The knotted belt!"

"Sean, stop!"

"He doesn't want Elle!"

"Why are you doing this?" she begged.

"He wants that woman…the coquette!"

She shook her head in denial. "I have changed. I am a woman now and you had no right watching me kiss Peter! And you're right—he doesn't know me. But how could you disappear for four years? *How?* And then you come back and spy on me? And now you think to leave again—without me!"

"Yes!"

She struck at him with her open hand.

He caught her wrist before she could hit him.

She hadn't meant to strike at him, for he was hurt and she loved him. But he had been badgering her so cruelly about Peter—and Peter was irrelevant to them now. She wanted to tell him all of that, but her own voice failed.

For she looked into his eyes and they were blazing. And she realized the light she saw there was not just anger but jealousy. He hadn't let her wrist go; in fact, in seizing her wrist he had pulled her forward and her thighs were pressed against his legs. Her heart was already speeding uncontrollably but now it skipped, wildly, as she realized how hard his muscular thighs were. Hard…and male. Instinctively she shifted her weight and her breasts brushed his chest. Her nipples stiffened, hurting her, and she began to swell. She thought she might explode if he pulled her forward another fraction of an inch.

He became utterly still, except for his harsh breathing. And in that moment she realized that she would give anything to be in Sean's arms and his bed, making love to him wildly, passionately, with no inhibition, touching his hard, scarred body everywhere, with her hands and her mouth, and letting him touch and kiss her that way in return. And he knew, because his gaze veered sharply to her mouth.

"You're right," she breathed. "Peter doesn't want Elle. But you do."

His grip tightened and he pulled her even closer. Her nipples scraped her chemise and shirt and through the linen, his chest. His eyes widened and then he let her go.

"No. Elle was a child. Elle is gone."

Eleanor stared at him, trying to recover her composure, while he paced, tense and shaken. "Sean. I am here. I have grown up, that's all."

He made a harsh sound, an attempt at mirthless laughter.

She walked slowly toward him. His expression twisted and he stared for so long that she thought he wasn't going to speak. Then she realized he was summoning up his words. "You…belong…to Sinclair."

"No! I belong to *you!*"

He jerked in shock, turned and began hurrying away.

She ran after him, drawing abreast of him. "You need to hide. I can help."

"I'll hide in the woods…for tonight."

"And then you will leave? At dawn?" she demanded.

He hesitated. "Yes."

Her resolve strengthened. She would be packed and ready to leave at dawn, as well. In fact, she had the beginnings of a bloody brilliant idea. "No, not in the woods, it's too dangerous."

He glanced at her, his face filled with wariness.

"You can hide in my rooms."

CHAPTER FIVE

EVERYTHING WAS AT STAKE now and Eleanor knew it—Sean's life and his freedom, and her future with him. She refused to think about the fact that he had not agreed to let her journey to America with him. She refused to think about the years they had shared, when he had never once suggested that he might love her back. Instead, she would think about the way he had looked at her and the desire she had felt pulsing between them. She could not have misinterpreted that.

They had agreed that he would remain in the woods for the day, as there was no way he could steal into the house without, in all likelihood, being detected. Now that she knew he was back and being searched for by the authorities, she feared the imminent arrival of British troops. He seemed remarkably calm and unafraid, insisting he would hear their approach long before they could ever find him.

Their plan was that he would go up to the house during the supper hour, when the family, their guests and the staff were occupied.

She'd finally had a moment to actually assimilate all that had transpired. She would never stop loving Sean, but he was a convicted traitor now. She knew that each and every member of her family would fight for his freedom and his good name, if they were given a chance. She also knew that no one, not her father, her mother or her brothers, would ever condone a match with him now.

If he had returned home with the same status as when he had left, it would not have been hard to convince her father to allow her to marry for love. Sean's family was an ancient one, and once, his ancestors had been great earls, ruling half of Ireland, but he had been born the younger son of an impoverished Irish Catholic nobleman. His father had actually leased Askeaton from Adare, even though those lands had once belonged to the O'Neills. Yet the earl would have given her hand in marriage to his own stepson, and he would have gifted them with a small estate. Their life would have been a simple one; Eleanor would not have cared.

The earl would never approve of such a marriage now, not that Sean had offered for her. And no one would allow her to run away with him, if they ever suspected her plans. It saddened and distressed her that, so suddenly, her great family was being torn apart.

But they would spend the night together, and she could barely wait to be with him again. She had to know everything that he had been through. He had become so distant, like some dangerous stranger. Surely his wariness toward her would ease. And his insistence that Sean O'Neill was dead was absurd. Sean O'Neill was very much alive, even if he was thin and scarred, his voice strained and hoarse. He had been wounded somehow, but he wasn't dead. The wounded healed, and Sean would heal, too. Eleanor intended to make certain of it.

Although he remained a short distance away in the woods, she missed him terribly. She wanted to sit close to him, his arm around her, the way they once had. She wanted to see him smile and hear him laugh. It had been so long! Did he even know that Tyrell was married and that he had two children? Did he even know that Devlin now had a son as well as a daughter? There was so much to share. And if she were very daring, she would encourage him to kiss her.

The tension inside her spiraled wildly. In spite of the dire circumstances, in spite of the changes in

Sean, she was *happy*. He had come home and she would never let him go without her again.

Eleanor had reached the flagstone terrace and she slowed, glancing cautiously around. Her morning rides were usually over well before seven, before the sun had a chance to shake the chill of the prior evening. Well, it was past seven now, and the sun was high and warm. If it were close to eight, her father and her brothers and any number of their male guests were having breakfast in the morning room. Ladies rarely came down before ten or half past that hour.

Rex appeared before her, having been seated alone on the terrace. Eleanor jumped nervously. He smiled, limping toward her. "Did I give you a fright?" he asked curiously.

"Yes, you did," she said even more nervously. His expression was oddly calm and flat.

His gaze traveled over her. "You seem to be riding a bit later than usual."

He was suspicious, she thought in alarm. Rex was as solid and dependable as a rock, never mind his recently acquired sardonic humor. He had always been close to Sean—they were the exact same age. If she were not determined to be with Sean, she would go to him for help and advice. But she contained the impulse. Sean had been very clear that he did not want anyone in the family involved in his escape, and Rex would no more wish to see her running off with him than the earl or his brothers would.

He smiled very slightly. "You are very flushed. It's not that warm out," he said.

She swallowed hard, thinking of Sean, who so needed help.

"Is there something you wish to tell me?"

She was almost certain that he was suspicious of her. She managed a smile. "I am running late, and I rushed here from the stables. The last thing I wish is for one of the Sinclairs to see me dressed like this."

"Do you want me to see if the path is clear?" he asked.

She nodded and seized his left hand, as he always kept his crutch under his right shoulder. "That would be wonderful."

His eyes softened with kindness. "Come on," he said. "I'll go first."

A few moments later, Rex signaled that the salon was clear, and she darted through it, into the hall and safely upstairs. A maid was passing. Instantly Eleanor changed the plans she had made with Sean. "Beth!"

The plump girl paused, curtsying. "My lady." She never blinked at the sight of Eleanor in men's clothes standing in the hall at such an hour. Beth, while very pleasant and helpful, was rather dull and somewhat dim-witted, a fact that worked in Eleanor's favor. So many of the staff indulged in the gossip that ran rampant below stairs.

"I should like for you to go to the kitchens and fill a sack with a loaf of bread, a very large hunk of cheese—any kind will do—some meat if it is available and a bottle of wine. It need not be chilled," Eleanor said. Sean had told her he could wait until the evening to eat, but she was not going to heed him now.

Beth nodded. "Wine, bread and cheese," she repeated.

"In a sack. If Cook asks, you may tell him it is for me. You are to leave it outside the back kitchen door," she instructed, hoping all of this would not be too much for Beth to manage. "And do not forget some meat, if we have it."

Beth left to obey her orders.

Eleanor took a deep, calming breath. She was so overwhelmed with the stunning development of Sean's return that it was hard to think clearly. He also needed clothes. She hurried up the hall, knocking on the door to the room that was Cliff's. As a privateer who spent most of his time at sea, pursuing one fortune after another, he was rarely home. She had learned from a blushing maid that he had appeared late last night, well past the midnight hour but in time to join some of their guests for a few games of whist.

There was no answer and she shoved open the door.

The room was a large, lavishly furnished one with blue walls, a marble fireplace and a large canopied bed in its center. As there were so many bed coverings, it was hard to tell, but her brother most definitely seemed to be in its midst. "Cliff!" she demanded, striding over.

He jerked upright, his chest bare, looking positively stunned to see her, and Eleanor realized he was not alone. She felt herself turn red as the woman next him hid under the covers.

"Do you ever knock?" he exclaimed. Like all the de Warenne men, he was tall, well built and handsome to a fault. Like Eleanor, he had dark blond hair, but his was riotously streaked from the sun and years at sea. He was as bronzed as the pirates he hunted.

"You just returned home. Can you not keep your hands to yourself for even a single evening?" she cried. Of all of her brothers, he was the one infamous for being a rake.

"Can you not see that I am preoccupied?" he growled. "Might you leave?" He was now blushing.

She began to enjoy the moment. Cliff was never

discomfited and she wondered who the woman was. Her gaze strayed in the nameless lady's direction. He had stopped enjoying housemaids at the age of fourteen—which was when he had run away from home on his first adventure—therefore the lady in his bed was one of her wedding guests. And that would undoubtedly make her a member of Peter's family or the wife of one of his close friends.

"That's enough," he said. Pulling a sheet around his waist so effectively he must have performed the feat a hundred times, he leaped from the bed.

Eleanor quickly backed out of his reach. "I need some clothes." She turned her back to him and ran into the hall.

"I can see that!" He barked at her.

She kept the bedroom door slightly ajar. She heard him pulling on his trousers. "No, Cliff, I need a pair of your breeches and a shirt—and a jacket," she added. The moment she spoke, she realized the mistake she had made, in her eagerness to see Sean properly clothed, and she turned around.

He walked into the hall and stared at her. Carefully, he closed the door behind them.

She bit her lip, turned to flee. "Another time."

He caught her arm. "You are half-naked," she said

pointedly. She herself didn't care, but a passing maid would surely faint.

"What are you up to now?" he asked, ignoring her remark. "You're getting married tomorrow afternoon. If that isn't enough to make you into a proper lady, I don't know what is. Has your fiancé seen you dressed like this?" He was judgmental.

She stared sweetly into his vivid blue eyes. "The maid who let you in last night said she first thought you were a highwayman—and then a pirate."

He understood and folded his very solid and muscular arms over his equally solid and muscular chest. "I may choose to dress as a barbarian, but you do not get to choose how you dress. Besides, I came directly from my ship."

She sighed. "Cliff, just give me the clothes. I'll explain—but not now."

His gaze was searching. "Are you in trouble?"

She became still. Cliff had come directly from his ship. "Are you berthed in Limerick?" she asked slowly, her heart beginning to thunder in her chest.

"And if I am?"

She bit her lip. Cliff had been the master of his own ships, sailing the globe for four or five years now, and he had a record which spoke for itself. Last year alone, he had captured eleven prizes, an astounding feat. At the age of twenty-six, he was already recognized as being one of the great privateers of his time. Sean did not want Devlin involved, and he was right—Devlin had a wife and two children and their ancestral home to pass on to his son. But Cliff was an adventurer at heart. He had no wife—he would probably remain a bachelor until he died. And he had enough courage for ten men.

He could sail them away to freedom, she thought. But how could he be convinced to allow her to come along, when she had yet to even convince Sean?

"Eleanor, what trouble are you in?" he asked very sharply.

She decided to put Cliff off for a bit. "Can you give me the clothes now and meet me later? I will tell you everything then."

"When?" he demanded, at once suspicious.

"Meet me before supper in the gallery," she said. She tried to smile at him. "I will explain. But I do need the clothes now."

"You're running away, aren't you? You're running away from Sinclair, disguised as a man."

"Cliff!" She tried to protest.

"Eleanor, you don't have to run away. Good God, where would you go? How would you live? If you don't want to marry Sinclair, we will go to the earl together and tell him. I will back you."

Tears came to her eyes. "You would have been my favorite brother if you had been here just a little," she whispered.

"Let me get dressed. Then we'll speak with Edward," he said. Oddly, he never called his father anything but the earl or Edward.

She touched his arm. "I am not running away," she said, and she wasn't—at least, not the way he thought. "I want to tell you everything, I do, but I can't—not until later."

He studied her. "I am confused and I freely admit it. Do you intend to marry Sinclair?" he asked.

She shook her head. "No. Not anymore."

His gaze hardened. "So you will jilt him at the altar?"

"I wish it could be different, but it can't!" she cried.

"I am not waiting until suppertime to find out what is going on," he said with heat. "But don't tell me you are not running away. I can see it in your eyes. You've never lied to me, Eleanor."

"You were never here," she exclaimed. "I was ten when *you* ran away. Cliff, I need some time. Please. I am twenty-two, not two or three or ten! I know what I am doing. Let me borrow the clothes, and meet me

at six tonight. And don't mention what we have discussed to anyone!"

His refusal was there, in his piercing blue eyes.

"Please," she begged.

He finally nodded. "All right," he said. "But I am
not pleased."

She turned away before he could see her smile. He
had not been easy to manipulate, but in the end, as
she always did, she had gotten her way.

WHEN SHE RODE into the glade where she had left
Sean, there was no sign of him anywhere. For one
moment her heart stilled, and she was afraid he had
left her again.

He stepped out of the woods. "What are you doing
here?" he cried hoarsely. "I told you…I would come
to the house tonight!"

She slipped down from her horse, dressed now in
a dark, ladies' riding habit with a jaunty brimmed hat,
having ridden sidesaddle. "I was not going to let you
starve all day."

He was angry. He grabbed the horse's reins as she
removed the sack of food and wine from the saddle.
"Damn it! Elle…were you followed?"

"No, I was very careful." She focused on the
bundle in her arms. Being with Sean again was
simply overwhelming in every possible way.

"It's almost noon!" he exclaimed. "Someone must have…seen you."

She gave him a bright look. "I am not a fool. I pleaded a headache to avoid all female company and then went down to the stables by myself. Here. There's bread, wine, cheese and some ham." She handed him the sack.

He was staring at her, so she smiled back. "There's a nice change of clothes in the oilskin," she added.

"Thank you," he finally said, grim and grudging at once. He sat down in the dirt, opening the bag. He glanced up at her, then bit into the cheese. In that moment, she felt how hungry he was. Eleanor went still, realizing she had been right to bring him food now. In minutes, he had devoured it all.

Had they starved him in prison? she wondered. She looked away so he would not realize how upset she was.

Suddenly he said, "Elle, I didn't leave anything for you."

She inhaled and turned, smiling. "I'm not hungry."

His gaze met hers. "You're always hungry," he said softly.

The present slid away, and she knew he felt it, too. She had always had a huge appetite for a woman and no one knew it better than Sean. She thought of those long days at Askeaton when she had labored at his side to rebuild the manor house from charred ruins; they had taken their meals on the floor, seated cross-legged before the hearth. "I had a huge breakfast," she lied.

"Do you want some wine?" he asked, standing up. This time there was no mistaking that he was moving stiffly and awkwardly, as if hurt.

"No, thank you," she answered.

He uncorked the bottle with a very frightening dagger. Then he hesitated, their eyes meeting.

She understood. "I don't mind—you will not offend me by drinking from the bottle."

He nodded and tipped the bottle. A look of sheer pleasure crossed over his face and she suspected he had not had a sip of wine in years. Her heart broke for him. The gentleman remained, there inside the felon, and he was trying to reappear, whether Sean knew it or not.

She took the opportunity to really enjoy the sight of him. He might be thinner than he had once been, but he had always been the most stunning man she had ever set eyes on, and that had not changed. The planes of his face might be harder and sharper, but every angle was beautiful and perfect. When they were children, he had been so beautiful, while she had been so plain, that they had both been teased about it.

And in a way, his body was perfect, too. Because he bore no fat, every movement caused an interesting reaction in the muscles and tendons there beneath his dark skin. There was no mistaking how hard and strong his body was. Her glance strayed to his narrow hips and she recalled the times she had so brazenly spied on him making love to the local wenches. Sean had been a rake as a young man, and she had glimpsed far more of his perfect body than she should have. She lifted her eyes, aware of blushing, thinking about the fact that he was excessively virile, vaguely aware that he had become so still. What would it be like to taste him? What would it be like to have him kiss her—really kiss her?

"Don't," he suddenly warned.

She tensed, their gazes locking. "I'm…not…doing anything." She cleared her throat. "Sean, are you hurt? You are almost limping."

"I'm tired," he said slowly. "I'm sore," he admitted.

She tried to imagine spending two years in a cell with no opportunity to hike or ride. In one way, she and Sean were alike—neither one of them liked the indoors at all. "You need to rest."

"You need to go…back to the house. Your behavior this morning…has been too suspicious."

"I'd like to talk to you first," she said earnestly.

He faced her warily.

She stiffened. Why did he think to guard himself against her? "Sean, I am on your side—only on your side. You do know that?"

He was rigid and at first, unresponsive. "Elle… it's not a clever idea…for you to help me in any way."

She knew better than to argue. "Cliff returned last night."

Sean's expression relaxed. "How is he? Is he still cruising the West Indies and West Africa, fighting corsairs…taking prizes…shipping wine and silk… seducing Hapsburg princesses?"

"*Has* he seduced an Austrian princess?" Eleanor smiled. That would be just like her reckless brother. "Yes, he is never home—he is always at sea. He has made a fortune, I think. He hasn't changed very much," she added.

Sean's mouth moved, as if he wished to smile. "That's good.… Cliff may be a rogue, but he's the youngest son. He can do as he pleases.… He is fortunate."

"Just as you did as you pleased?" She heard herself ask, thinking of the night he had left her.

His jaw flexed and he turned away from her.

She seized his arm from behind. "I'm sorry!"

Tension rippled through him as he faced her, withdrawing his arm. "I'm sorry…I hurt you."

She stilled.

His gaze moved from her eyes to her mouth and then back up to her eyes. "I wouldn't…do it again."

"I am so glad you have come home!" She was an instant from reaching for him, from taking his handsome face in her hands. He must have sensed what she wanted, because he stepped farther away, watching her carefully now.

She wet her lips. "He has ships."

Sean's eyes flared.

"He has fast, fighting ships. He has a ship in Limerick. Sean, Cliff can help us leave the country!"

He seized her before she had any idea he was crossing the glade to come to her. "What did you tell him?" he demanded, releasing her as swiftly.

"I haven't told him anything yet!" she cried. "But he has guessed that I am about to run away. He thinks I do not want to marry—and he is right."

Sean stared. "I think not."

"I beg your pardon?" She was confused.

"If you did not want Sinclair, then why were you…in his arms last night?"

She felt her cheeks burn. Sean hadn't put any distance between them, safe or otherwise. His gaze was riveted on hers. Desire filled her now. "I wanted," she whispered, wetting her dry lips, "to know what it was like to be kissed."

His silver eyes flickered, brightening.

She prayed that he would kiss her.

"Don't," he said tersely. "Don't ever play me… the way you play Sinclair!" His chest rose and fell, hard.

For one moment, she had believed Sean would kiss her. She dismissed his remark, as she did not even want to attempt to decipher it. "I'm a woman now," she tried. "Sean, surely you can see that!"

He held up his hand as if warding her off. His hand trembled. "Why won't you listen? Why are you looking at me that way? I won't be played… Eleanor!"

"I have no idea what you mean. I am not playing you or anyone. Sean, I have missed you terribly."

"But you won't listen! I'm not that man…I'm not him."

She shook her head. "I will never believe that."

"Whatever it is that you want…I cannot give it to you now. Stop looking at me!" he cried desperately.

"I can't. You must know how much I missed you and how much I love you." The moment she had mistakenly confessed her feelings, she flushed.

His eyes went wide, half fury, half surprise. His

voice became a croak. "Go back to Sinclair... Eleanor.... Your future is in *England*. Your future is with *him*."

"Now it's not. It's with you, in America, or wherever it is that you decide to go!"

He was shaking, but so was she. "You're so stubborn...headstrong...a brat! I'd forgotten how impossible...you can be."

"And you are wasting your time trying to convince me that you are some kind of criminal, some kind of terrible man!" But his words had hurt her immensely. Did he really see her as a spoiled brat? Had she deluded herself into believing that he saw her as a woman—a woman he wanted?

A hard cold mask settled over his face. "But I am a criminal...I am a murderer...an outlaw."

She shook her head. "Why are you doing this? Do you want me to be afraid of you?"

"You should be afraid of me," he said, his gaze slamming to her mouth, his entire body shaking.

And then there was simply no more room for doubt. His look was male, potent and hot. It was crude and base, but clear. And now she understood his tremors—they were the tremors of desire. She didn't think, but reacted, reaching for him slowly, taking his hand, raising it to his face, his mouth. "I don't care that soldiers died because of you. I don't care that you were in prison and that you escaped and are a fugitive now. I will never be afraid of you, Sean."

"Then you're a fool," he said harshly. He pulled her hand away from his mouth but held it tightly between them and her knuckles brushed his chest. "When will you understand? Sean is gone. But I'm here. You can call yourself Elle…or Eleanor, I don't care. I've been locked up for two years. Tempting me now…is not a good idea. You *need* to be afraid of me. You need to be afraid of me *now*."

It was a moment before she actually understood his meaning. And because his eyes were blazing, and she saw the wild lust there, she shrank. "Oh my God! Are you trying to tell me that you have no feelings for me—that you simply need to use a woman, any woman, right now?"

He stared and then, his mouth firming, his eyes hardening, he nodded. "Yes."

His cruelty cut her like a knife. "I don't believe you," she gasped. He could not have changed so much. "You would never use *me*. You would *die* before using me."

His grasp on her hand tightened painfully and for one moment, she was in shock. Had he turned into a complete and frightening stranger after all? But all he did was slide his gaze over her dark brown riding habit as if stripping it away from her body. "*Sean* would die first," he said softly, his meaning clear.

"No." She didn't try to pull free from him because every instinct she had told her that she would not succeed. "You may be a traitor but you are not a monster. I don't know why you want me to think otherwise, but I refuse."

He released her and gave her a hard, angry look.

She turned and walked away from him, more shaken than he could know. She couldn't breathe—but she would never believe that Sean would hurt her. He had been her protector, her savior, her friend. But he had changed, after all. The question was, how much, and how irrevocable was it? She leaned against a tree, panting. For a moment, if she dared to be honest with herself, she hadn't been certain what he would do. She wanted Sean O'Neill to desire her, to make love to her; she always would. And she was determined to get rid of that felon who had taken Sean over.

He was suddenly standing behind her.

Eleanor tensed but did not move.

An interminable moment passed before he spoke to her back. His breath feathered her nape, her ear. "I meant it. You need to be afraid…and you need to go."

She fought for air. She fought for him, for them.

"I am not afraid of you, Sean. And if you want me that way, it is because I am both Elle and Eleanor, not because you are a felon in dire need of a woman."

He made a harsh sound. "You need…to give up."

She turned and found them face-to-face, his chest inches from hers. "I am not giving up on you."

His eyes flickered.

But it still took courage to lift her hand. She caressed the scar on his cheek to prove to him that he had not succeeded in chasing her away. "You don't bite, after all. I know you better than you know yourself."

He jerked his face away from her hand. "You're crying…again."

She hadn't realized. She let her hand fall to her side. "You're hurting—and I hurt, too, when I look at you."

"I don't want your pity!" he exclaimed.

"I don't pity you. I ache for you and all you have been through. And when you will let me, I will comfort you."

"I won't be here," he said darkly.

Very carefully, she met his gaze. How could she reach him? Not the man he was insisting that he had become, but the man he really was? "Do you remember the first time I fell off that Welsh pony, the old sorrel?"

Watching his face, she saw his eyes light up.

He remembered, she thought, thrilled. "I was so

insulted that he wouldn't take that log. I wanted to show off my horsemanship but I was only four or five years old."

Sean looked away, his gaze blank now. "I don't remember."

He *had* remembered—she knew it. "I tried to make him jump the log and instead, he was nasty and he stopped. I flew right over his head."

Sean walked away from her, his body rippling with his every step. Then he muttered, "I recall that pony. He was too old to jump a blade of grass, much less a log."

She had to laugh. "Yes, he was. I adored him."

He turned, his mouth suddenly soft. "Yes, you did." He stopped.

She just looked at him.

He said, very deliberately, "There's no point in discussing the past."

She disagreed. He had been smiling, maybe not visibly but in his heart, and she had felt it.

"You used to call me Weed, which I hated, and you used to box my ears when I was truly annoying and chase me through the entire house."

"I don't remember any of it," he said, the muscles in his jaw flexing

"Once, I hid in the attics. You couldn't find me!

Suppertime came and there was an uproar down-stairs. Father was furious because I was missing." She almost laughed. "He was furious with you, Sean, when I was the culprit. You were punished— I think he took your hunter away for a week. I was patted and stroked and hugged and kissed when I finally came out of my hiding place."

"You were six years old and you had everyone eating out of your hand."

"So you *can* remember the past, when you want to."

"But I don't want to remember…any part…of it!" He was angry now. And his words were becoming thick.

She went still. His anguish was obvious. "Let me help you."

"You have helped. You brought food…clothes."

"You have never needed me more," she said with utter determination. "I will not abandon you now, when you are in so much trouble."

He suddenly looked sharply at her and she realized her choice of words had been too literal. Because she could feel all of his needs now. Having grown up with three very virile brothers, a virile step-brother and Sean, she understood that a man's needs were very different from her own—they were far more consuming. And a terrible plan came to mind.

"Maybe I do remember calling you Weed. I also used to call you Brat." He paced the clearing.

"Now you are changing the subject." She swallowed. "We can continue to rehash the past tonight. I had better return to the house before I am truly missed."

His face closed off even more. "It's not the best of ideas…. I had better stay in the woods…. I can travel by night."

She was alarmed. "No!" She rushed to him. "Sean, there is so much to discuss! So much has happened while you were gone! Don't you want to hear about Tyrell's marriage? And Gallant is a champion. Do you remember him? He was a gawky foal when you left! Sean—you can bathe. In hot, sudsy water. I've already arranged for a meal— there's pheasant, ham and cod, salmon and roasted guinea hen. There's a Burgundy wine you will love!"

He was pale. "You think to bribe me?"

"If that is what it takes," she said grimly.

"I am tempted…but my answer is no. I am leaving…and I am not coming back."

Very carefully, she grasped his hand. He started; she ignored it. She had never been more determined. "Did you mean what you said earlier? Have you really been celibate for two years?" she asked softly.

He jerked away. "What the hell?"

She felt thick and heavy inside of her body now. "I think you were fourteen when you had your first mistress. I know—I spied."

His face was rigid. "You would know…you were spying…as always."

"And from that moment on, there were so many light skirts." She was hoarse. Her pulse had slowed. "Two years? I can't imagine you being without a lover for so long." She had stepped outside of herself. Somehow, she was a seductress with the most ancient allure of all.

He was flushing now and he was also rigid. "Why are you doing this?"

"How did you manage? Did you dream about a lover?" she whispered, her cheeks hot. "At night, could you feel a woman's touch, her soft body?"

He just stared at her, but his silver eyes burned.

"Maybe it was my body that you dreamed of, my touch," she murmured.

He flinched.

"You know how I feel about you," she whispered. "So come to the house tonight, Sean, because I will take care of you."

And she knew she had succeeded, because his hunger was there between them, huge and rising.

CHAPTER SIX

SEAN HAD THE SAME DREAM every night. He'd had the same dream so many times that he knew he was dreaming the instant it began, but that did not decrease his panic, his fear, his horror. Paralyzed, he could only watch the events of that bloody night unfold, helpless to prevent the massacre of the villagers and the murders of his wife and her son.

Peg smiled at him, but the question was always there in her faded eyes: Why don't you love me, Sean?

He wanted to go to her and beg her forgiveness and tell her that he did love her, even though it would have been a lie. Circumstance had dictated that he marry her and they had both known it.

"When will you give me my boat back?" Michael appeared, his skin oddly gray, his hair, once crimson, almost black.

Sean had punished him that night for being rude to his mother by taking the carved toy away. It had been a gift from his father, a sailor who had disappeared at sea. The small toy remained in his pocket now, even as Sean slept. He was not given a chance to reply.

The mob of angry villagers appeared and he knew he had to stop them from marching up the road to Lord Darby's estate. He knew what would happen if they appeared at those iron front gates. He knew it because he had been there, not just three years ago on that bloody night, but as a child, the day his own father had led a similar mob against the British. He tried to tell them that no good could come of this but his voice wasn't working—he couldn't get the words out. His panic escalated. He tried to seize the arm of Boyle, Peg's father, but he didn't seem to notice. He tried to seize Flynn, but he vanished before his very eyes and the estate was burning, the soldiers were there, and he was there, his dagger in the gut of a redcoat, a boy really, and then the boy looked at him, meeting his regard, the question there unspoken, why? And when Sean laid him down he was looking up into the blazing blue eyes of a British officer. Colonel Reed was staring at him with hatred.

Sean understood what Reed intended. He tried to chase him, but the officer was galloping away and he could not catch up. The days passed by him and he was still running madly to the cottage where he was hiding his family, and even as he ran, he knew what he would find and he was sick with dread and desperation. Too late, he was there, but the house was an inferno, too late, he screamed for them both, but Michael was nowhere to be found and when he found Peg, he held her as she lay dying....

Sean cried out, sitting up, sweat pouring down his body.

For one moment, he was somewhere else, in the midlands in a small, starving village just a few miles from Kilvore. For one moment, there was smoke and fire, shouts and retreating hoofbeats and he choked, sobbing over his dying wife and their lost child. He gasped for air.

Sanity returned, and with it, reason and reality. He was not back in Kilvore. He was not beside the burning inferno where his wife had died. He shoved to his feet. He was standing alone in the woods. The horse he had stolen yesterday in Cork was grazing some short distance away, hobbled so he could not wander.

Sean was trembling violently and he knew he could not stop it. He could only wait for the tremors to pass. He walked to the edge of the glade, knelt and vomited.

He sat back on his heels, closing his eyes, recalling that he was at Adare. His home—the home where he had been raised from the time he was eight years old—was on the other side of the woods. In that huge house was the earl, whom he loved as a father, his mother, his brother and stepbrothers.

He stood. Elle was there, too.

But she wasn't Elle anymore. His gut tightened, his heart lurched. The panic came, and it was so huge that he couldn't even try to deny it to himself.

She had become a beautiful woman, a woman he barely recognized. But she was still stubborn and fearless, even if the skinny child had vanished. He could insist to himself that it was natural for him, in his celibate state, to be responding to her body, her beauty. But he hadn't really noticed any of the women he'd passed on the streets in Cork. Even the cobbler's pretty daughter had evinced only a vague and passing interest.

He had meant every word when he had told her that she should be afraid of him. He wanted her to fear him, his lust and the British who were after him—he wanted to chase her away. He hated the way she looked at him. He hated that she seemed to love him still, perhaps more so than ever. But she had refused to be frightened and she did not seem to be running away. Worse, she had offered him her *bed*.

Maybe he was the one who was afraid of her.

She had offered him her body.

But he would never accept her offer, even though

the mere thought of it increased his arousal. He was not going up to the house tonight, because her offer came with strings. He could try to convince himself that Elle was gone, but she wasn't. She still worshipped him, and he saw her love every time he looked into her eyes. She might be prepared to give him her body, but she wanted his heart in return.

And that was never going to happen.

Even though he was certain Sean O'Neill was dead and buried, some part of him remained, because he couldn't use her, even if he desperately wanted to. And it was only in part because she now belonged to another man. He did not want to hurt her more than he already had.

Besides, he was leaving and she was marrying the other man. God, he hated Sinclair! Yet he had known from the moment he was old enough to understand the politics of dynasties that Elle would marry a title and, if possible, a fortune. And he felt as if he might explode out of his skin. He had the frantic urge to stop the wedding. Worse, his body raged to accept her damnable offer and take her to bed. He could not understand himself anymore.

Instead, Sean fought the inexplicable anger. It was a very good match, in spite of Sinclair being an Englishman. He was going to America anyway. And there was no possible way that she was coming with him. Because they would chase him and if he were caught and she was there, she might suffer the same fate as Peg.

He knelt and vomited again.

Where had that notion come from? He wondered, feeling dizzy now as he leaned against a tree. He wasn't taking Elle with him because he wasn't rotten enough to make her a mistress and he would never take another wife. He wasn't taking Elle with him because she deserved her titled heir and his fortune and a future filled with peace.

I am coming with you.

I want to go hunting, too!

Sean tensed. A memory he did not want to entertain threatened him.

IN BRAIDS AND DRESSED for riding, she was glaring and stomped her foot. He sighed. He had known this would happen if she ever learned that they were going hunting for two days. He had begged Tyrell not to mention their hunting expedition to her. This particular week he hadn't been able to shake her from his trail for more than a few minutes. "You're nine years old and you are a girl, even if you seem to wish you were a boy. You're not coming with us," he said firmly.

"Yes, I am," she said, stamping her foot again. "And so what if I wish I were a boy? Being a girl is stupid! I hate dolls. I like hunting! I like fishing! I like worms! I'm not too young— Father took you hunting when you were nine!"

"How would you know? You were a baby then." Annoyed, he turned and started to leave his room. She followed.

"I asked him, and he told me."

He stopped in his tracks and she crashed into his back. "Has anyone ever told you that you are too clever for your own good? You're not coming, Elle. If you're not careful, you might turn into a boy—and then you will die an old maid!"

She began to cry. "I hate being a girl! I hope I turn into a boy so I can be just like you."

There was no reply to make to that. Worse, he was feeling sorry for her and guilty for being cruel, so he rolled his eyes and left. Amazingly, a few hours later, as the hunting party set out, there was no sign of Elle. He wondered if it was possible that she had given up, but he highly doubted it. Was she sulking in her room? Was she still crying? His heart stirred. Her tears were usually a matter of theatrics, but he hated it when she cried anyway.

A few hours later, they were many miles from

Adare. They had stopped to rest, water the horses and take some refreshments. Sean had actually forgotten about Elle as Cliff was regaling them with the story of his latest conquest—the lady being half a dozen years his senior and the bride of one of Father's elderly friends. But then Elle's fat red pony wandered into the makeshift camp and he was without his rider.

Fear briefly paralyzed him.

They split up to search for her. He was afflicted with images of her lying on the trail, her neck broken—one of the most common causes of death. This was his fault, he kept thinking, and he prayed that she was all right. If anything dire had happened to her he would never forgive himself...

He found her walking up the trail, looking dirty and unhappy, but unhurt. When she saw him, her face lit like a harbor beacon and she cried out, running toward him, holding her arms out.

He leaped from his charger and ran to her, hugging her hard. "What were you thinking?" he cried, almost angry. Then, cupping her cheek, "Are you all right?"

She nodded, her eyes huge and serious. "Sean, I fell asleep!"

He could not believe she had fallen asleep on her pony. He pulled her back into his embrace, holding her tightly there. "In an hour it will be dark, and there are mountain lions and wolves out here," he said thickly. "Elle, promise me you will never be so foolish again."

She regarded him seriously. "I only wanted to come with you."

SEAN SAT DOWN at the base of a tree. He wasn't fifteen anymore and she wasn't nine. Once, she had manipulated him as easily as he could whistle and snap his fingers for his dog. Those days were over. No one could manipulate him now, much less Elle— especially because she wasn't that annoying child anymore.

You know how I feel about you. Come to the house tonight and I will take care of you.

He stood, instantly and painfully aroused, choking on the air. She had been indulged far too greatly as a child. He suddenly wished to box her ears, as if that act might set her straight. But she hadn't ever tried to be a lady while growing up and clearly, nothing had changed. Convention did not interest her and she chose to ignore propriety. No wonder Sinclair was smitten.

He covered his face with his hands. Someone had to rule her with an iron hand. Once, that someone would have been him. But she had a father and three brothers to take up the slack. One of them, or possibly even Devlin, had to speak seriously with her. No woman of her station and rank should ever proposition a man so boldly. Such speech was simply dangerous.

What had she been thinking?

You know how I feel....

Come to the house tonight....

Sean looked at his mount. He should be getting on his horse and riding as rapidly as possible from Adare.

He was not going up to the house tonight.

Even if that meant he was never seeing her again.

"REX," CLIFF SAID. He paused on the threshold of a small library. Rex had his back to him, staring at the empty fireplace. He was clearly disturbed and brooding.

But Rex turned instantly at the sound of his voice, smiling, and he limped toward Cliff. They embraced, exchanging solid slaps on the back. "How are you?" Cliff asked. He hadn't been home in over a year and when he had, Rex had not been at Adare, although he had seen him at Harmon House in London the previous winter.

"I am well. And you look well," Rex said, looking him up and down. "Even the fine clothes cannot disguise the fact that you have become a heathen, Cliff."

Cliff laughed. He knew his hair was too long but otherwise, he had not a clue as to why people thought he looked like a barbarian or a golden-skinned Moor. No one knew that he lived with a knife in his belt, a stiletto up his sleeve and a dagger in his boot—even with a suit, he never wore shoes. "I think you have become fanciful. What passes in Cornwall?"

Rex shook his head. "Absolutely nothing."

Cliff walked to a bar cart where he poured two bourbons. "Then why spend most of your life there? I should go mad from the boredom."

"I have been making improvements to the estate. It is my living," Rex said, accepting the drink.

Cliff knew that he and Rex were as different as night and day. Still, he could not understand why anyone would want to seclude themselves on a Cornish estate in the middle of nowhere. "I hope you have a beautiful mistress warming your bed."

"I have willing maids," Rex said. "I can't afford a beauty."

Cliff's smile faded. He couldn't imagine bother-ing with a housemaid. Last night, he had espied Lady Barton playing whist and had managed to include himself in the game when her card partner had decided to retire. A quick flirtation had produced exactly the result he desired. If a woman were not extremely beautiful, he was not at all interested. Maybe he should procure a beautiful courtesan for his brother. It would surely help him pass the time.

"Why are you staring? You are rich and good-looking. You do not need to pay for service. I do."

Cliff made up his mind. He would send Rex a gift, a very seductive and alluring gift. "I didn't mean to stare. If you are determined to be a gentleman farmer, I will not try to dissuade you. And some women have found you infinitely more attractive than me." That was the truth. Surely Rex did not think himself handicapped because of his amputated leg?

Rex shook his head. "I do believe that is ancient history, brother. And it was my uniform they admired."

Cliff was suspicious, although Rex was right on one point. The ladies had adored any soldier in uniform during the war, especially a cavalry officer.

"I sense a scheme," Rex said abruptly. "I hope I am not involved. You have always been too reckless for your own good. It amazes me that you remain alive, considering your current status."

He had no intention of mentioning the present he intended to bestow on his brother; it would be a surprise. "As a privateer?" It was how he preferred to label himself, should a label be necessary, and when in society, it was.

"As a pirate hunter, who is but a hair's breadth away from drowning or the gallows," Rex said.

Cliff flashed a white grin. "In Barbary, they behead their enemies. The Moors and Turks do so, as well. The Spaniards have a new trick—it is called walking the plank."

"How pleasant for you." Rex took a seat, stretching out his unscathed leg. Absently he rubbed the remainder of his right thigh, which ended above the knee. "You and Eleanor are so very alike." He seemed distracted now.

Cliff sat eagerly. "Good! The very subject I should wish to discuss."

"The similarities you share with our sister?"

"So you still have some wit? No, brother, I wish to discuss our little sister and her impending marriage."

Rex smiled, but it did not reach his eyes. "You wish to compare notes?"

"I most certainly do," Cliff said grimly.

ELEANOR HAD BEGUN TO PACK, planning on taking only a small satchel with her. But as she did so, she started thinking about Peter and the fact that their wedding was scheduled for the very next day.

Her heart lurched. If only Peter were cruel, cold and ugly. But he was none of those things; he was handsome and kind. He was going to be jilted. She wished he could somehow be spared the heartbreak.

An image suddenly crossed her mind, of Peter standing at the altar, waiting for her arrival. But the bride never appeared.

There would be confusion at first. Everyone, both family and guests, would assume her to be late. But then there would be chaos when one and all realized that she had disappeared—worse, run off.

Eleanor stiffened with dread. No one knew Sean was present, so no one would guess that she had run off with him, but she was very much in the public eye because of her impending wedding. A search party would be manned. The authorities would be summoned. As she stood there, with a few belongings scattered across her bed, she realized that if she left Peter, she would lead the British right to Sean!

Stunned, Eleanor realized that the wedding must be canceled this very minute. She must instantly shed her status as a bride. But her father would never agree to break the signed contracts at the eleventh hour— not without a very good reason.

She could not lose Sean again. There had to be a

solution—and in that moment, she knew what it must be.

She must somehow convince *Peter* to jilt *her.*

He must be the one to withdraw from the marriage contract.

Eleanor didn't think twice. She raced through the house. Peter was sitting outside on the terrace with his sister, Lady Barton, and her husband. Lady Barton was a beautiful and elegant blond woman. Her husband was a bit older and somewhat dour in countenance. Eleanor managed to greet everyone pleasantly enough even though she was trembling with determination now.

Lady Barton came to stand beside her. "You must be so terribly excited, Eleanor. I remember what my wedding day was like! I simply could not wait to walk down the aisle in my wedding gown."

"I am very pleased, my lady," Eleanor somehow said. Her lips remained stretched in a smile that felt impossibly stiff. How she hated doing this!

Lady Barton patted her arm. "Do call me Dianna, my dear. Would you care to take a stroll? I noticed your brothers entering the maze."

Eleanor realized she was perspiring. "Actually, I had hoped to take a stroll with my fiancé." She sent Peter a smile and realized her look had undoubtedly been beseeching.

Peter raced to her side. "I should love to stroll with you, my dear," he said.

Lord Barton spoke up. "Dianna, I am scheduled to tour the estate with his lordship. I am afraid I must leave you to your own devices."

"Oh, darling, never mind. I am sure I can amuse myself." Dianna pecked his cheek as he nodded at everyone and left.

"Do you wish to join us?" Peter asked his sister.

"Oh, I would not think of intruding." She beamed. "Do enjoy yourselves. I shall wander the gardens."

Eleanor suddenly glimpsed Cliff standing at one exit to the maze. She turned to look at Lady Barton and realized she was staring after him. Society was notorious for its affairs and she realized that Lady Barton had been in her brother's bed that morning. She just couldn't care.

"My dear?" Peter prompted.

Eleanor allowed him to take her arm and they left the terrace slowly. Her heart raced with her nervousness and dread. He deserved love and loyalty, and certainly not the ill treatment he was receiving.

"You are so quiet!" he exclaimed. "Is everything all right?"

She met his blue eyes and saw that he was worried. "I wish to apologize for my behavior last night."

His eyes widened, and then he blushed. "I very much enjoyed watching the stars with you, Eleanor," he said, low.

She did not want to go anywhere near the subject of his kisses and her inebriated responses to them, but that was precisely what she must do. She swallowed and said, "My behavior was terribly improper. I beg your pardon!"

He took both of her hands, halting her. "Darling! There was nothing improper about last night. Tomorrow afternoon we will be man and wife."

She knew she was red. Her mouth was also terribly dry. "I was foxed," she said.

He was clearly taken aback by her bold statement. "I do realize that."

She bit her lip. Lying was utterly distasteful to her, but there was no other choice. So she would try to convince him that she enjoyed drink far too much. "I do enjoy a glass of wine—or two."

He started. "Darling, I have never seen you drink, other than a single sip of champagne, in the entire time we have known one another."

Her cheeks were on fire. "I didn't want you to know."

He stared, stunned. "What are you trying to say?"

"I am a bit like Rex," she managed, feeling terrible.

"You mean…I don't believe it! I understand his leg hurts him, but he drinks in the morning—he drinks at noon! Do not try to tell me that you drink all day, too!"

She couldn't. "No, I just meant, I am fond of wine—and its effects. A bit too fond…for a lady. I didn't want you to be surprised—after we are married."

He appeared suspicious of her. "Eleanor, if you insist you like a glass of wine, then I am pleased. We have a wine cellar in Chatton, and while I should not admit it, the wines are French, the finest in the country. We will be able to enjoy a fine bottle every night! It is my preference, in fact, not to drink alone."

She turned away. Well, that ploy had certainly failed.

"Every lady I know enjoys a good glass of wine or sherry. Or do you like brandy and a cheroot, too?"

She worried the ribbon on her gown. "No, I don't drink brandy and…" She stopped. "I have heard that in Paris, there are women who smoke."

His eyes bulged. "Yes, there are. They are not ladies. You are not going to tell me that you smoke?"

He was horrified, she realized, with no satisfaction.

She stared. She realized that she should be telling him the truth. She should tell him that he was wonderful, but she simply couldn't marry him because she was in love with someone else. "I ride."

Relief flickered in his eyes. "Excuse me?"

"I ride a stallion, astride, in men's attire. It is more comfortable than a riding habit," she added.

A terrible moment ensued. She knew her cheeks were crimson. "Eleanor, why are you doing this?" he asked slowly.

"You must know these things, if we are to wed," she somehow said.

"I do know about your dawn rides."

She gasped. "You know?"

He smiled at her. "I watch you when I can. You are magnificent. You ride as well or better than any man I know. Watching you gallop that stud at dawn is breathtaking," he said. "I will confess that I was shocked. Not by your skill as a horsewoman, but by the manner in which you dress. But then I realized you could not ride as you do if you were not astride. It would be a physical impossibility. And I understood that you must dress in that manner. I am glad you have confided in me, dear."

Eleanor was stunned. "How can you be so complacent? Ladies do not ride astride in breeches!" she cried. "It is a terrible faux pas."

"But you do, and you *are* a lady—the lady I love. Why don't you understand? I have never met a woman like you before. You are so proud and beautiful and so original! Why do you think I am smitten? My God, Eleanor, I have never felt this way about anyone and I never will, because there is no one else like you."

She felt her legs collapse. He helped her to a lawn chair. Peter loved her for who she was, not what she had appeared to be. How could this be happening? Desperately she looked at him as he knelt before her on the grass. "Don't you want a proper lady in your home?" she begged. "The English are so frightfully proper!"

"I am not that way. And my friends are not that way, either. They already adore you! Well, the gentlemen admire you as I do. I am sure a few of the ladies are rather jealous of the attention you receive." He smiled tenderly at her. "Why are you so distressed?'

Here was an opening and she should seize it. She could tell him that she had loved Sean forever and that as fond of him as she was, she simply could not go forward with the wedding. But Sean was but a few hundred meters away. She must not tell anyone the truth; no one must ever know that he had been at Adare, not until they were safely gone.

"I am not certain I am the right wife for you," she managed.

"It doesn't matter." He pulled her close. "*I* am very certain that you are perfect for me."

ELEANOR HURRIED BACK to her rooms, torn between despair over her relationship with Peter and an acute awareness that in a few hours, she would be with Sean once more—and that their time together was running out. If she failed to appear at her wedding now, if she ran away with Sean, she could be the cause of Sean's capture and death. She was at a terrible loss. She could not be his downfall and she was beginning to realize that she was going to have to let him go to America without her. Her mind had become blank and she could not come up with a plan that would allow her to escape with Sean. Wasn't his freedom more important than anything else? Wasn't love about sacrifice? But this was too painful to bear. And suddenly, two men blocked her path.

Rex smiled at her, but without mirth. "Are you in a rush?" he asked politely. But there was nothing polite about his stance as he barred her way.

She looked from his odd smile to Cliff, who was helping him impede her progress upstairs. His expression was almost identical and she knew that she had been discovered.

She turned to flee but someone seized her—it was Cliff. Reluctantly she met his gaze. "We'd like to chat with you," he said in a strangely neutral tone.

She felt like a child again, caught in some stupendously inappropriate act, about to be severely punished. But she wasn't a child and these were her brothers. She could manage them both at once, if she had to. She inhaled for some courage and smiled. They could not know that Sean was hiding in the woods or that she intended to see him that evening and, if she dared seduce him, she would make love to him, too. If they ever suspected her intentions, they would move mountains to stop her.

Rex indicated that she should precede them into an adjoining room, a small salon used on the rare evening, when only one or two family members were present. Eleanor walked inside uneasily, followed by both men. Cliff closed the door behind them.

"How is the bride?" Rex asked, his gaze searching.

"Very nervous, but that is expected, is it not?" She looked from Rex to Cliff.

Cliff said, "I thought you had decided to jilt Sinclair at the altar."

Dismayed, she looked at Rex and saw that he was hardly surprised by Cliff's comment. "I see you have betrayed me," she said to Cliff, but she was too distressed to be angry with him. "How much did you tell him?"

Cliff smiled. "Everything I know and suspect."

She hugged herself, wondering what he meant, exactly. But did it matter? She was supposed to marry Peter tomorrow, and if she did not, they would search for her—and find Sean. If Sean was captured, he would hang, and it would be her fault.

She was going to have to go through with her wedding and let Sean go. And if that were the case, Cliff and Rex could help Sean flee to safety. Sean would be furious over her betrayal, but she had heard Cliff brag that he had never been outrun at sea, or defeated there in battle. He had spoken with such quiet confidence that she knew it was the truth.

Did she dare give Sean up? Did she have the strength?

Rex spoke. "Last night, you were in love—or so it seemed. Today you are jilting your fiancé at the altar, and gathering men's clothes! How odd this sudden turn is, especially as I know you well. You are not unkind. If you were to change your mind about Sinclair, I know you would be speaking with Father now. My little sister would never jilt her groom at the altar."

Eleanor knew she must be selfless, but she was paralyzed; she could not speak.

"Has something happened, Eleanor," Rex continued softly, "to change your mind about Sinclair?"

Sean might never forgive her if she betrayed him,

but he would be alive and he would be free. "Every bride has nerves." She was shaking. "Every woman has moments of indecision." She needed all of her courage now.

Cliff studied her suspiciously. "The sister I grew up with knew her mind and always got what she wanted. What is it, Eleanor? What has you on the verge of tears? Why do you think to jilt Sinclair? Why were you scrounging for my clothes this morning?"

An image flashed in her mind, of Sean's heated silver stare, but lust wasn't love. She certainly knew that, having seen her brothers racing after more women than she could ever count. If she gave him up now, she wouldn't see him that night. Would there even be a goodbye? She felt a tear slipping down her face.

Before Eleanor could speak, Rex said, "Who are you running off with, Eleanor?"

She could do this. She thought of the lifetime they had shared, the happy warm moments filled with so much affection, trust and laughter. She saw Sean smiling, his face unscarred, his eyes open and unguarded. Maybe, one day, in America, he would become the man he'd been before.

"Is Sean here?" Rex asked grimly.

She met his dark, penetrating eyes, and nodded.

"He…" She could barely speak. "He is in dire need. He needs you both." Then more tears fell. She felt sick.

"Where is he?" Cliff demanded, but quietly. His palm covered her shoulder. "You know we will do anything to help him, although I might kill him for hurting you this way."

She managed to look at him through her tears. "He is in mortal danger—but he thinks, as he always does, to protect everyone but himself!"

Cliff and Rex exchanged a potent look. Rex spoke. "If you have been in contact with Sean, then you know that his crimes are exceedingly serious and we must race the clock."

She was so anguished that the fact that both of her brothers seemed to know about Sean's status as an escaped felon only mildly surprised her. "When did you find out? And why was I not told?"

"Two nights ago, Captain Brawley stopped here to ask the earl and Tyrell what we knew. As we knew nothing until that moment, we had nothing relevant to impart to him," Rex said.

"Was anyone going to ever tell me the truth?" she managed to ask with bitterness.

Cliff spoke. "I think one and all decided that you did not need this distraction on the eve of your wedding. Clearly, that judgment was the right one."

"And when did you learn the truth about Sean?" she cried, finally becoming indignant and even angry. "Oh, let me guess! The moment you walked in the door! I am merely a woman, so I did not need to know that the man I have loved my entire life was still alive and in dire need of my help!"

"We understand that you still believe yourself to be in love with him, but he needs to flee the country, and I intend to help him do so. He needs my help, not yours, Eleanor." Cliff stared. His expression was one she had never before seen and she realized this must be how he appeared on his ship when about to do battle with his enemies.

Eleanor shook her head. "He begged me to keep his confidence. He is afraid that the earldom will fall, that Devlin will lose his estates—and he is right."

Cliff's dark brows slashed upward. "And you, also, planned to run off with him. I hope, Eleanor, that you have come to your senses, because jilting Sinclair on the morrow and fleeing with Sean could only hurt him, not help him."

"I have realized that!" she cried. "But you would not understand! You have never been in love! I have missed him so terribly these past years, I thought I might die from heartache. Now, you will sail him to foreign shores! I will never see him again and I will never be able to convince him that I am the woman he must love."

"Where is he?" Cliff had clearly decided to ignore the outpouring of her heart.

"In the woods." She briefly told them how to find Sean.

"He is hurt?" Cliff asked, clearly making plans.

"He is scarred and thin, and his voice is weak and strange. He is terribly wounded, not physically, but in his soul." She had to sit down and she collapsed into a chair.

"So he is physically able to ride and to walk?"

She glared at him. "Yes! But he is filled with pain, Cliff! Not that you can possibly understand."

He was rigid. "I despise seeing you so distressed, but given the circumstances, I am not sorry he has rejected you. Sean has no future now. *You* have no future with him. Your future is with Sinclair."

"You are arrogant and obtuse!" she cried, ignoring his surprise. "I hope you are struck by Cupid's arrow one day and that the lady realizes you are nothing but a boor."

"You are my only sister, and it is my duty to look after you and do what I think is best," Cliff said, his jaw flexing. He turned to Rex. "I prefer that we leave Father, Ty and Devlin in the dark. I will send a man to Limerick to order *The Fair Lady* readied to set sail. I'll meet you downstairs in five minutes." And before Rex could even nod, he had strode from the room.

Eleanor wished she had a book to throw at his departing back, or any object in hand, but she did not. She glared after him instead.

Rex pulled an ottoman forward and sat down beside her. He handed her an immaculate handkerchief, embroidered with his initials. She accepted it, wiping furiously at her eyes.

"I understand," he said quietly. "I understand the extent of your love—or at least, I think I do—and I also understand the extent of the sacrifice you are making."

She stilled, meeting his kind brown gaze. "Thank you."

"You are very brave, Eleanor, but your courage has never been in question."

"My heart is broken," she replied.

"He is a fool," Rex said with heat. "And I intend to tell him so. Any man—except Cliff, obviously—would give his right arm to be so well loved."

"Before the war, you were a romantic. You are still one, I see," she managed to say.

He touched a curl. "I will arrange a farewell for you."

She gasped in surprise, and then she seized his hands. "Thank you, Rex…thank you!"

He smiled. "What? You will not insist I am your favorite brother?"

She had no words left. She merely nodded, using the linen against more tears.

He took up his crutch and stood. "You have done the right thing for our stepbrother."

Eleanor closed her eyes against the stabbing pain. It was a moment before she could speak. "I know," she said.

CHAPTER SEVEN

SEAN SLIPPED THROUGH the window of Eleanor's room. Once inside, he had to pause. He had been in her room countless times, but not since he had left four years before.

He pushed past the heavy gold velvet draperies there and slowly looked around. Once, her bedroom had been blue and white; now, it was green and gold, lush and feminine, the bedroom of a woman, not a child. It felt and looked and even smelled terribly sensual.

He saw the table, set for one. She had made certain a meal was waiting for him. His heart stirred with gratitude. Then he thought about Rex and Cliff, looking for him in the woods. She had betrayed him and that infuriated him, but he had easily eluded his brothers. He shouldn't have come. He should be on his way to Cobh. But he had to say goodbye. He could not leave otherwise.

Her image filled his mind now, as she had been

the first moment he had seen her yesterday night, in Sinclair's arms, passionate and breathless and clinging to the other man's shoulders. He wished he could forget her damnable offer; even now, he was acutely aware of it and it was affecting him terribly. A huge tension filled him but he intended to ignore it. He understood now that he needed release. There would be whores on the ship—there always were.

He'd never used a whore in his entire life. From the time he'd lost his innocence, there had always been young women in pursuit of him. But they had wanted Sean O'Neill, the dashing younger son of an Irish nobleman, the stepson of an earl. None of those past lovers would look at him twice now, not that he cared. He wouldn't look at any of them a second time, either.

And as he stood in Eleanor's luxurious accommodations, he wondered for the hundredth time how his life had come to this. How had he become such a stranger, even to himself? He wanted to remain disconnected from that other man, that boisterous yet solidly dependable younger son who would do anything for his family and who had a penchant for the ladies. The bridge to that past remained and he saw it in his mind's eye, a trestle bridge spanning a huge gaping gulf of events, emotions and time, but it was rotting and pieces of it were missing. What would it take, he wondered, to completely sever the connection, to watch that bridge released from its cables so it might shatter on the deadly rocks of mistaken choices below?

His two years spent in prison had not been enough to destroy it, he now realized. While there, he had believed the past completely erased. He had been wrong.

A new life in America might do the trick. If not, he would have to throw stones at that bridge, day after day, until it finally came down.

Suddenly he saw the old stone bridge that was on the roadway between Askeaton and Adare. It spanned a particularly deep part of the river that was an offshoot of the Shannon. As boys, he and his brother had leaped from the bridge a hundred times, but that was only half the fun. The currents were strong at certain times of the day and once in the river, it would sweep them swiftly downstream, through a series of rapids, until it bent and slowed in a calm pool. They would leave two horses at the pool, riding two horses up to the bridge, one horse double, another ridden triple if all five of them were present. They would spend entire afternoons leaping off that bridge.

He didn't want to remember; it was too damned late.

"SEAN!"

He was soaking wet and shirtless, riding back up to the bridge with Rex and Cliff, Devlin and Tyrell behind them on a different mount. At the sound of Eleanor's voice, his gaze veered, searching for her, and he was already alarmed. Had she followed them? She was only six years old, but she was becoming far more than fearless recently. She was as reckless as any of them, even though she was half their age.

"Sean!"

He saw her standing on the bridge, grinning happily and waving at them in her white dress.

His heart stopped. He knew what she intended. "Elle! Don't you dare!" he screamed at her.

She laughed and lifted her skirts, revealing thick white stockings and black button-up shoes, and started to climb onto the balustrade of the bridge.

"Shit," Rex exclaimed. He rode in front and he spurred the hack into a canter.

"Elle, get down!" Sean yelled, sandwiched between his stepbrothers.

Elle stood on the balustrade now, no longer smiling, staring down at the river.

She was going to jump, he realized in horror. And Cliff verbalized his worst fears. "She is going to do it."

Sean pushed Cliff off the back of the horse, then

followed. Eleanor suddenly lifted her arms and leaped off the bridge.

He ran to the edge of the road and scrambled down the grassy and slick bank, never taking his eyes from her. She hit the water with a cry and as she disappeared beneath its surface, he saw exactly where she had gone in.

But that was not where she would surface. He knew the currents and he kept racing for a point farther down the river. He didn't look upstream now—he reached the bank and dived in.

The water rushed over him, pulling him downstream. He heard her choking and he fought to tread, an impossible task, so he could visually locate her. And he saw her white face and her frightened eyes, just before the river sucked her into its depths.

He reached out as he dived underwater and seized a piece of her skirt. He was absolutely determined that the river was not going to beat him. He fought to swim closer, against the raging current, and he put his arm around her. Then he charged to the surface, where he threw her above him. He heard her choking for air.

"I've got her," Tyrell said, taking her from him.

"Sean." Devlin seized him, helping him stay above the surface now so he had a chance to breathe.

A moment later the four of them were in the quiet, still pool. Sean stood up, trembling. The child was mad. She was only six years old; she had almost drowned! Devlin had also stood, grimly silent, but Tyrell sat in the shallow waters, appearing relieved. Elle sat with him, her eyes wide.

She looked up at him, her face beginning to lose its pallor. She started to smile as she stood. "Can we do that again?"

He charged her. Seizing her hand, he yanked her from the water, hard enough to hurt her and she cried out in protest. "Are you stupid?" he shouted at her when they were on the bank.

"If you can do it, so can I!" she yelled back.

He was so angry he reached for the closest branch he could find. She understood; she paled and backed up. "You wouldn't."

"Someone has to have the honor," he said furiously. His heart was still racing in pure terror, he realized. He wasn't sure it would ever stop.

"Sean." Tyrell took the branch from him. "She won't do it again."

Sean felt an odd moistness on his face and realized he was starting to cry. Horrified, he turned away from everyone.

Elle hurried to stand there. She took his hand, her mouth pursing. "I won't do it again. Why are you so sad, Sean?"

HE WAS STIFF WITH TENSION now. He did not want to recall any more of the past. Once, he and Elle had shared a special bond, and he would have done anything to protect her. They no longer had that bond, and she had Sinclair to protect her now.

Sean sat down on the edge of the canopied bed, the soft mattress giving way to his body instantly. He had lost his best friend a long time ago, and there was simply no going backward. Old memories did not help, they only deepened the confusion. When he looked at her now, he didn't know what to think or do. He saw Eleanor, but then he saw Elle. He was in the present, but the past beckoned. Nothing made sense anymore.

Especially not his being in her bedroom and her having made such a damnable offer.

He had to stay in the present, he decided. It was too dangerous otherwise. Elle was gone. She'd been gone for years. He had no friends. And what he needed to remember was that he was a traitor and a fugitive and she was a stranger named Eleanor.

But he still needed to say goodbye.

HAVING PLEADED a headache she genuinely suffered, Eleanor had left Peter with the men and the ladies by themselves. Supper had been interminable; all evening she had been acutely aware that Cliff and Rex had not been able to find Sean in the woods. He had disappeared and she knew he had left, as he had said he would.

It was incredible. He was gone. Just like that, as if he had never come home, a nightmare come true. There wouldn't even be a farewell.

"Eleanor, dear," the countess said, approaching from behind her.

Instantly Eleanor stiffened. It was a moment before she could breathe and turn to face her mother as she stood there on the stairs.

The countess, Mary de Warenne, was a very beautiful woman. Technically, of course, she was not Eleanor's mother, but the mother of Sean and Devlin. But Eleanor's mother had died giving birth to her. Until she was two years old, she had been raised by a nurse and her father. Mary was the only mother Eleanor had ever known and she loved her deeply. In fact, she had often secretly wished that she could be more like the countess, who was graceful, gracious and generous to no end.

Eleanor tried to smile at her.

Mary paused before her. "My dear, I can see that you are terribly distressed. Would you like to speak about it?"

"I can't."

Mary's blue eyes were searching. "All brides worry and fret before their weddings, but I am afraid that this is something more. I only wish to help."

Tears filled Eleanor's eyes. She knew that the countess had wept for Sean privately and that she had believed her son was dead. And even though her mother had given up hope almost two years ago, Eleanor did not want to raise a painful subject for her. She did not have to.

"Darling, is this about Sean?"

Eleanor nodded. "I miss him so terribly it is a pain in my chest."

"We all miss him." Mary seemed anguished then. "I thought that you had gone on with your life. I thought you genuinely cared for Peter and perhaps were even falling in love with him. Your father and I have been so pleased and so relieved that you and he seem to get on so brilliantly."

"I thought so, too," Eleanor said. "I was wrong. There is only one man I can love, and that is Sean."

The countess blanched and put her arm around her daughter. "We should sit. There is something I must tell you."

Eleanor shook her head, pulling away. "I need to go to my rooms. I am very tired. Tomorrow will be a long day." She no longer had the strength to fight her fated marriage. She could not care less what happened tomorrow.

"Eleanor! I know what it is to be fond of a man, to marry well—and to love someone else, my dear."

Eleanor had heard the love story of Edward and Mary many times, but not from either her mother or her father. She had heard it from the local lords and ladies; she had heard it from her old nurse and from the now-deceased family physician. "It's true? You didn't love your first husband?" she whispered.

Mary smiled. "I loved Gerald because it was my duty to do so. He was a good man, the father of my two sons. And in spite of his philandering, I knew that he loved me in his way and would do so until he died."

"But?" Eleanor cried.

"I loved Gerald because it was my duty, dear. When Edward rescued me and my sons from the British, after Gerald's murder, I found the kind of love and passion I had never even dared to dream of." She hesitated. "I met your father about five years after Gerald and I married, when we had just become his tenants. Although I refused to ever admit to myself that something was there between us, I knew the very moment that Edward walked into our hall that he was different, and not just a king among men.

I think we exchanged a dozen entire sentences in those five years. He was polite and correct. But Eleanor, when he finally took me in his arms for the very first time, I knew that I had never understood love—or passion—until then."

Their stories were so similar, and yet not similar at all. "What are you trying to tell me?"

Mary touched her face. "I want you to have what I have, darling."

She trembled. "I will never have what you have. I have always loved Sean. He doesn't love me. Excuse me. I am exhausted, I have to go upstairs."

"Eleanor! Please! I am so worried about you!"

But Eleanor was running up the stairs. At her door she paused, the pain in her temples acute. Now, finally, she would have the time and the privacy to grieve for losing Sean all over again. How many times would her heart break over the same man?

Eleanor stepped into her bedroom, closing the door. Then she saw the table where she'd had his beautiful meal laid out. She had forgotten to tell her maid to cancel it. She stared at the covered platters, and her heart stopped, then leaped wildly.

The dinner plate was used. Some leftovers were on it. Incredulous, she turned to the wine bottle—it was almost empty.

He stepped out from behind the heavy gold velvet draperies by the windows. Instantly his gaze met hers.

He had stayed.

He didn't love her the way she loved him, but she didn't care. She had missed him for four years and she missed him now. She had never been happier to see anyone. She ran to him, throwing her arms around him. She hugged him tightly, acutely aware of his hard chest beneath her soft breasts, his broad shoulders beneath her hands. That terrible feeling of being lost and alone, of being abandoned, of being cold, vanished.

He grasped her hands and removed them, his gaze instantly locking with hers. "You told them."

She understood. "They somehow guessed. I had to tell them you were here. They only want to help."

He shook his head. "I asked you…I begged you to keep silent. I explained…."

"They were forceful and adamant! Cliff thinks to sail you far from here, tonight."

He stared at her, his silver eyes hot and bright.

And when he did not reply, when he simply looked at her the way a man looks at a woman he wants to take to bed, she recalled her proposition— and the fact that this was their last night together. Desire slammed its huge fist into her.

He had returned to take her to bed.

She carefully lifted her gaze to look at him. He continued to stare, unmoving, but his breathing seemed labored, too. She wet her lips. "Sean."

His jaw flexed. "I didn't come here...for that."

Her eyes widened. She wasn't certain that she believed him. "Then why? Why are you here—in my bedroom?"

He half shrugged, turning aside so she couldn't see his eyes.

"Why did you return at all?" she asked, for she desperately needed an answer she could understand—and live with forever. "If you didn't come to take me with you and you didn't come to see the family, why did you come?"

"I don't know!" he cried. And he seemed distressed, too. "I heard about...the wedding." He gestured oddly now.

A huge and awkward silence fell. There was so much tension in the room, it was hard to breathe. "But you didn't come back to stop the wedding," she finally said.

Briefly their gazes locked. "No."

That was not the answer she wanted. "I have missed you so much. I am going to miss you when you leave. Sean, didn't you miss me?"

His face was tight. "In the beginning it was hard."

It was impossible to understand him now, when once she could almost read his mind. "What do you mean?"

"It doesn't matter! Not now!" He confronted her angrily.

She shuddered, afraid of what that might mean.

Before she could speak, he said, "Your dress is green."

Her heart leaped but her body became heavy and still. "Yes."

"Unwed ladies wear...*white*."

She had chosen her gown with care for the farewell Rex had promised and when she had learned that Sean was gone, she hadn't thought about changing it. Her dress was darker and deeper than a pastel green and it was a part of her trousseau. She had been supposed to wear it after her wedding, as it was more appropriate for a married woman than one unwed, both because of the color and the design. It was the most alluring gown she owned. Both the countess and Tyrell's wife, Lizzie, who had supervised her trousseau, had been very surprised to see her wearing it.

She had worn it to impress Sean. She had worn it to make him look at her the way he had in the woods—the way he was doing now—with bold, burning eyes. He had said he would not accept her offer, but then why was he looking at her this way? "A young unmarried lady is allowed to wear pastels."

"That is not a pastel," he said firmly.

He was leaving her behind. Why couldn't he understand that one night together was better than nothing? Why couldn't he understand that even if he didn't love her, she had enough love for them both? She was desperate to be in his arms, to make time cease, just for a while. She was desperate to feel his love, even if it was a pretense on his part.

"I don't like it," he suddenly said.

His words were hurtful. "It's a beautiful dress."

He shrugged, folding his arms over his hard chest. "I don't know anything…about fashion."

She bit her lip. She knew she shouldn't sink so low as to play him, but she did. "Peter likes this dress. He was staring and it was obvious. He asked me to stroll in the gardens after we finished dining, but I refused." That last statement was a bold lie.

His color deepened. "Don't."

"Don't what? Don't point out that another man finds me very desirable, when you say you do not?" She was breathing rapidly now. "And when your claims are so clearly lies?"

He jerked in surprise. "I said…I didn't come here tonight…for you."

"Then why did you come?" she cried.

"You belong...to someone else!" He was red.

She froze. "No." She shook her head. "No." She had given her heart and her soul to Sean years ago. She belonged to one man and that was him.

He seemed to be fighting to speak. "Did you... break off...with him?"

She tensed.

"I didn't...think so. Good!" He stalked away, stiffly pacing the confines of her bedroom.

She knew he was angry and upset, but she did not back off. "Sean, my offer stands."

He stumbled, then whirled. "No!"

She dared to approach him. "Sean, we have always been honest and open with one another."

His eyes were wide, wary. "That was Elle."

She sensed him stiffening in resistance and struggled to find the right words. "I know you don't love me, not the way I want you to. But Elle has grown up—I think we are agreed on that." She smiled but tension consumed her.

"Last night...you were with Sinclair...*moaning.*"

She gasped. "Let me finish, please!"

"Why?" His furious gaze moved over her face and then dropped to her décolletage. "Tomorrow…you'll be in bed…with Sinclair!" He stared unwaveringly at her.

"I don't love Peter. I don't want to marry him. But why do you care? Why are you angry? And don't tell me you're not! Sean, this might be the last time we ever see each other—*ever.*"

He faced her grimly, hands fisted on his hips. "I am not…angry. I want to talk about Sinclair!"

"No!" she cried, trembling. "I want to talk about tonight—I want to talk about making love with you—right now!"

He cried out. He was angry but he was also horrified and she knew it.

She whispered desperately, "I'm not asking for your love."

"You should…marry Sinclair!" His eyes flashed. "The union is good. Damn it. Titles, land, wealth… But you can't speak…this way! Do you understand?"

She hugged herself. "Why? Because you are so tempted that you might lose control? I meant it when I said I am not afraid of you! Make love to me, Sean. Just this one time, so I can remember it forever."

He stared at her as if paralyzed.

She stared back, and the grandfather clock in the far corner of the room could be heard ticking. A hundred seconds passed. She finally raised her hand in a plea. He flinched but was still. She inhaled and cupped his rough cheek.

His body trembled but he did not move away and as their eyes locked, she saw the battle he was waging. Then she saw his long thick lashes drift closed. She gasped and he moaned.

A knock sounded on her door.

His eyes flew open and she saw fear in them.

"Lady Eleanor?" her maid said.

Sean had paled. "The maid?"

"I'll send her away!" Eleanor cried, seizing his hand. He had been a moment away from surrender, and she knew it. The timing could not have been worse. Now his thoughts were on discovery or escape.

He shook his head fiercely. "Routine. Answer it." The desire and need that had been so brightly reflected in his eyes was gone. His gaze was hard, controlled. Eleanor could not be more dismayed. Then he pulled away, crossing the room and disappearing behind the curtains.

The window did not slam closed.

Her maid knocked again. "Lady Eleanor?"

She stood in the center of the room, barely hearing the maid, thinking about how Sean almost let her lead him to the bed. She was shaking with so much desire. Finally, she turned to let Lettie in.

"My lady, what took you so long to answer?"

Only her personal maid, whom she'd known her entire life, could be so bold. "I fell asleep," she lied, glancing at the draperies again. She knew Sean hadn't left; she could feel his intense presence.

"Let me get your nightclothes, my lady," Lettie said, going directly to the armoire and retrieving Eleanor's white cotton nightgown.

Eleanor was about to tell her that she would change later. It was late, though, and she had no excuse to make for not having Lettie help her get ready for bed, as that was what she did every single night. But Sean was standing a short distance away, hiding behind the curtains, and they had yet to finish the conversation that would have to last her the rest of her lifetime. How could she undress now?

She began to tremble. Her breasts felt fuller, the tips tingling. She had become thick and swollen in unmentionable places.

The maid had laid her nightclothes on the bed as she always did and she swiftly undid the buttons on the back of her gown. Eleanor tensed as Lettie pulled the gown over her head. She could no longer breathe; Lettie was untying the strings of her corset and loosening it.

The corset vanished. Eleanor bent to reach for her garters, feeling naked now, her cheeks on fire. Her heart beat hard and fast, and her skin tingled wildly. She could barely believe what she was doing and she was certain Sean was watching.

His lust, his need, his desperation had combined into a single tangible element and it filled the room.

When her stockings and shoes were gone, she hesitated, trembling uncontrollably and afraid her maid would notice. Sean's lovemaking was not going to be anything like Peter's gentle kisses. She somehow was certain of it. She could not wait. She needed him now.

And then her chemise was gone.

And she suddenly could not stand it. Lettie was untying her drawers but all Eleanor could think about was Sean touching her bare skin, his hands on her hips, his mouth on the side of her neck.

Suddenly her nightgown dropped over her head and spilled down her body. It was the finest spun cotton, the gown V-necked, the insets sheer, the body sleeveless and trimmed in lace. Eleanor could not move. Lettie unpinned her hair and then spread the masses out over her shoulders. Then she began to divide her hair into sections.

Eleanor swallowed so she could speak. "No. I don't want a braid tonight." Before her maid could evince surprise, she smiled firmly. "Good night, Lettie. I am *exhausted*," she added.

She thanked her maid, walking her to the door without even realizing it. Nor was she aware of closing the door and locking it. All she could think was, *Sean*. The air in her room had become so thick she was almost choking on the tension, the heat. No, she was choking on *his* tension, *his* heat.

She heard him coming.

She turned, pressing her spine into the wood.

Sean's strides ate up the distance between them. His gaze was wide, hard, fierce.

Eleanor felt a moment of extreme excitement, even fear. She had provoked him, and she saw he was beyond any control. He was aroused, so much so she could see the wide hard line in his breeches. And she felt the first spasm of uncontrollable pleasure, licking between her thighs.

He didn't stop.

She arched back against the door, gasping.

His hands seized her shoulders and their eyes collided.

It was Sean, but she had never seen him like this before. He was crazed with desperation and lust.

And then she knew she wanted to see affection and love there.

But she had enough love for them both. "Sean," she began, reaching for his beautiful face.

His eyes seared hers, his mouth inches from her lips. "Too late!" he cried. And he pulled her against his stiff, inflamed body, and his mouth opened, covering hers.

His mouth was filled with insatiable greed. She became still, grasping his shoulders, as he kissed her deeply, wetly, thrusting his tongue deep, licking her inside. Her heart burst. She swelled, and knowing it, he pressed his massive loins over her.

She'd had no idea, she somehow realized, that passion was like this. She cried out, kissing him back now, using her tongue to explore him, filled with an answering greed. He gasped in pleasure, his hands finding her breasts, and ripped her nightgown away from her.

She felt the first spasms begin as he teased her nipples into an impossible state of pleasure and pain, their mouths now fused completely. And then his chest flattened her breasts, and her spine was crushed against the door while his huge manhood slid between her wet thighs.

Eleanor became dizzy and faint with cresting desire, the throbbing excitement.

Shaking uncontrollably, as well, he pushed against her, his mouth now against the side of her neck. He was hot, wet and hard between her thighs.

Eleanor began to fly and break apart and she wept in pleasure against his mouth.

He gripped her buttocks, now bare, in his hands. "Please," he gasped. *"Elle, please, let me fill you."*

She understood that he needed her and wanted her as he had never needed or wanted anyone before. "Sean!" Ancient instinct made her lift her leg and wrap it around his waist.

He groaned, the most beautiful sound she had ever heard, helped her lift her other leg and then he was burying himself inside her.

There was a brief pain, and then there was only dark mindless pleasure, hot friction, wet heat and a deep, rich wild spasm began. He was huge, filling her completely, perfectly. And he pushed hard and fast and faster still, gasping and determined, mindless, intent. Eleanor held on to him, sobbing with pleasure, crying in release.

He cried out thickly, collapsing against her, his body convulsing, filling her with his wet heat.

The tension rippled away, vanishing. She held him, gasping for breath, loving him more than ever, so much so that it hurt. She slowly released her legs, and he let her, so her feet found the floor. She held him more tightly, beginning to understand what had just happened. "Oh, Sean," she whispered.

He stiffened in her arms.

In that moment, she knew he had regained his mind, too.

And he straightened, looking at her with wide eyes—and it was a look she had seen once and hoped to never see again.

He looked at her with shock.

"No," Eleanor began, reaching for him.

He leaped away.

"Sean! No! It's all right!" she cried desperately, attempting to smile. "I love you!"

He backed away, his eyes wide with disbelief. And then she saw his self-loathing begin.

"Don't go," she whispered. "I love you—come back."

He shook his head, backing away another step. And then he turned and strode to the window.

Eleanor wept his name.

But he was already gone.

CHAPTER EIGHT

ELEANOR STARED OUT of the window and saw him racing across the lawns, a pale blur in the dark shadows of the night. She managed to recall that he was wanted by the authorities and that many of their guests would still be up, playing cards or billiards downstairs. Only that comprehension prevented her from screaming his name.

She turned from the window, horrified. Sean could not go like this—not now!

Eleanor ran to the bed and shrugged on her peignoir, crossing the room as she did so. The hall was lit at intervals by sconces and she stumbled down it. The earl and the countess had their suite at the end of the hall, and her bedroom was the only occupied room on this floor. She raced upstairs. The first room she came to was Rex's and she did not pause. She simply barged inside.

Rex was awake. He was seated on the sofa before

the hearth, still dressed in his evening clothes, his jacket tossed aside, a glass of brandy in hand. He had been staring at the fire. When he heard her, he whirled, reaching for his crutch, which was on an ottoman by his hip.

Eleanor paused, panting.

He took one look at her and his face darkened. He set the brandy down and lunged to his foot, the crutch firmly beneath his arm. "Eleanor?"

She must never let him or anyone know what had actually happened that night. She realized her face was damp and that she must have been crying. "Rex, Sean just left the house. Please!" She stopped. She had actually rushed to him to beg him to bring Sean back. Now she froze.

He needed to flee the house, their guests, the authorities and the country, and she needed to go with him.

But nothing had changed—she was marrying Peter in the morning, so he could safely escape.

She was hot and cold, at once. She hadn't had a chance to think about what had just happened, but she did so now. Had she done the wrong thing? How could she marry Peter now? How could she not?

I didn't come...for that.

Then why did you come back?

I don't know.

She had wanted him to touch her, hold her and kiss her as if he loved her, so she could cherish that pretense. But what had happened? She had seduced him until he could not resist her. There had been a stunning explosion of passion and an even more stunning release of that passion, but passion wasn't necessarily love. And the truth was that she had wanted him to love her—the way she loved him.

Now, she thought about the look of shock and horror on his face after they had made love.

"You should marry…Sinclair!"

What did she want Rex to do? Find Sean and drag him back to her, so he could look at her with more horror and even revulsion? He didn't love her the way she wanted to be loved, and that had never been clearer.

"Eleanor!" Rex was towering over her. "What the hell has happened? Are you hurt? Did he hurt you?"

Eleanor jerked and realized that her brother was furious, suspecting the worst—that is, he was suspecting the very truth. She somehow smiled, in order to reassure him. "I am never going to see Sean again and my heart is broken. We had an argument and he left before I could bid him farewell. Can you find him? You and Cliff have to help him escape and I need to see him one last time." That, at least, was the truth. There had to be a final goodbye.

Rex stared, his face a mask of suspicion. "Was he in your room?"

She lifted her chin. "Where else would it be safe enough for us to meet?"

A very ugly look filled his eyes. "You need to tell me the truth," he said harshly.

She interrupted. "I am telling you the truth! Sean just pointed out the advantages to my marrying Peter. In fact, he wants me to marry him. And that is why I am so upset."

Rex studied her for a brief moment and nodded. "I'll try to find him. Get dressed. If I do find him, I am taking him to Limerick and that is where you will be able to say goodbye." Not waiting for her reply, he turned and went to Cliff's door. Eleanor waited another moment, to make certain Cliff would answer, which he did, and then she returned to her room on the second floor. If anyone could find Sean, it was her brothers.

She closed her bedroom door and leaned against it, recalling in vivid detail the sexual episode she had just shared with Sean. She trembled, suddenly sick at heart.

Had she been used?

She choked on the surge of anguish. There had been so much passion—she was never going to forget the way he had kissed her. But everything had happened in minutes, mere minutes—or was it seconds? He had kissed her as if he had wanted to kiss her for a lifetime—or had he been kissing her the way a man who was forced into two years of celibacy does? Had his passion meant something? Had it meant anything at all?

Eleanor realized she was seated on the floor, her back to the door.

She had thrown herself at Sean, refusing to listen to his insistence that he did not want to become involved with her. Maybe she should have listened. Maybe, for once, she should have heeded what someone else wanted, and not what she wanted. There had not been one soft smile, one tender look. Eleanor felt sick inside. But hadn't Sean insisted that he had changed irrevocably?

When Rex returned, it was dawn. Eleanor remained seated in almost the same position, hugging her knees to her chest. She had rehashed every word and every moment she had shared with Sean since his return—as well as every moment she had spent in his arms that night. There was only one conclusion to be drawn. She loved him and she always would, even as dark and different as he now was; but he did not love her in return. Once, he had loved her as a sister and a friend, but even that was lost to her now. Sean had changed, and nothing would ever be the same.

Eleanor stood, her joints stiff, her body now aching from the loss of her virginity. She opened the door and saw Rex. He was grim, and in that moment, she knew without having to be told that he had not found Sean.

"I'm sorry. He's become as wily as a fox, Eleanor. He's gone to ground." His gaze was searching.

She nodded, mouth pursed.

Rex seemed very upset. "Are you certain he did not hurt you?"

She shook her head, incapable of speech.

"Have you slept at all? It will be dawn in another half hour."

How could she sleep? "No."

He sighed then. "Eleanor, you are to be married in a few hours."

Eleanor turned away, choking on a cry. She was exhausted, mentally, emotionally and physically, and she had not one ounce of reserves left. A few days ago she had been pleased by the prospect of marriage to Sinclair; now, she was ill with dread. She needed to be rational and reasonable, but her mind was too tired to analyze anything. She could hardly jilt a high-ranking nobleman like Peter Sinclair now. So what was there to think about?

"Eleanor, you need to get a few hours of sleep," Rex said kindly.

She turned and met his soft and concerned gaze. "I love Sean," she heard herself say.

"I know." He hesitated. "Sweetheart, it is over. Even if he loved you in return, Cliff is right. You have no future with him. But he doesn't love you the way you wish. If he did, he would not have left you in tears this way. And he would not be promoting your marriage—he would be breaking it up."

His words hurt. Eleanor choked and Rex pulled her against his solid, broad chest. "Get some rest," he advised softly.

Eleanor nodded.

ELEANOR WENT DOWNSTAIRS. Sleep had been impossible. If she was getting married, she was going to need help—otherwise three hundred guests, her family and her groom were going to know that something was very wrong with the bride.

She found her sister-in-law in the kitchens, where she was discussing the banquet that would follow the wedding. Lizzie was very fond of cooking and, since marrying Tyrell, she had gradually been assuming some of the countess's duties and responsibilities. She had become Eleanor's best friend in the three years since her small, intimate wedding to Tyrell, and she was one of the kindest women Eleanor knew. Now, she took one look at her and hurried over. Eleanor knew that she was a sight. It was obvious she had been crying; her eyes were red and swollen and she was dreadfully pale.

"Eleanor? Oh, my dear, come here, let us speak," Lizzie cried, leading her from the kitchens. She put her arm around her.

Eleanor tried to smile brightly at her, but she knew she failed. "I know you are terribly preoccupied," she began, "and I cannot thank you enough for supervising the reception—"

Lizzie cut her off, clearly worried. "Eleanor! What is wrong? Are you ill?"

Eleanor bit her lip. It was hard to speak clearly. "Would you help me dress? I don't feel all that well, actually, and I know I am a sight."

Lizzie's gray eyes were wide. "You are hardly a sight," she lied, "but you seem nervous and you appear exhausted. Have you slept at all?"

Eleanor shook her head. "If you could help me with my rouge?"

Lizzie hesitated, her concerned gaze searching. "You are as dear to me as my birth sisters, Eleanor. This should be the happiest day of your life. But it's not, is it?"

Eleanor closed her eyes. Sean's image assailed her mind, not as she had first seen him in the woods, but as he strode across her bedroom, his eyes wild and hot before he took her.

"Dear, shall we sit and speak about this?"

Eleanor shook her head in negation. "Just... help me dress...please?"

"Of course!" But Lizzie took her hand and held it tightly. "Eleanor, if you are so unhappy, maybe you should not go through with it."

Eleanor met her gaze. "You are so brave. You and Ty scandalized the ton with your indiscretions. How did you do it, Lizzie?"

Lizzie smiled a little. "I was so in love, I simply refused to think about the world outside. Until that world refused to stay away. Eventually reality intruded." She stared. "Do you really wish to go through with it?"

"I don't care," Eleanor said. Her heart lurched with dread and dismay. "I *don't care*. If the wedding were in a few weeks, I might break it off, but it is in *hours*. I don't have the strength to care."

"What has happened?" Lizzie asked softly.

Eleanor was about to tell her. But she would go directly to Tyrell, the future heir to the earldom. Ty must not know about Sean. He must never become involved. "I am sad," she whispered, and she shrugged. "Once, I dreamed of marrying someone else. Those dreams are over now." Eleanor pulled away before Lizzie could reply and left her standing there outside the kitchens.

Eleanor traversed the corridor. She had no wish to run into any of their guests, and to avoid the main hall, she slipped outside so she could enter the family's wing of the house from a back entrance. She was just about to safely reenter the house undetected when she glimpsed a flash of red from the corner of her eye. She whirled to stare toward the driveway where it curved in front of the house. Even from a distance, Eleanor recognized Captain Brawley.

He had been invited to her wedding, as her father wished to stay on good terms with the British soldiers. Brawley was the ranking officer in the county and as such, the officer attending to local disturbances and affairs. Major Wilkes commanded the county and Cork and Kerry, as well. Now Eleanor saw that Brawley was with five other troops, immersed in a rather intense conversation as they sat their mounts in the front drive. She did not think twice; she lifted her skirts and hurried across the lawns toward them.

The men were about to disperse, Eleanor realized, her heart racing, all of her exhaustion gone. "Captain!" she called, increasing her pace. "Captain Brawley!"

He instantly turned his charger, his gaze going wide with surprise. "Lady Eleanor," he said, instantly dismounting. He bowed. He was in his early twenties, with jet-black hair, fair skin and light blue eyes. They were acquainted, due to his regular calls at Adare, but their exchanges had been infrequent and mundane. Although Brawley was a young man and handsome enough, he was neither a charmer nor a rake; in fact he was very serious and very intent. He was always polite, and he usually paused to have a word with her when he was at the house. All in all, she had found him very unremarkable.

She managed a bright smile, her heart racing. She had to know what the captain and his men were doing there at Adare. He had been invited to her wedding, but his troops had not. Surely he was not hunting Sean! "Captain, good morning."

"Lady Eleanor, I pray I am not disturbing you,

today of all days." A slight flush colored his high cheekbones. He was stiff in posture, although his carriage was correct.

She was in no humor for a stilted exchange now. "You are hardly disturbing me, as I am the one greeting you. You are early for the wedding—I am not even dressed." She somehow laughed, as if in gay spirits.

His gaze was on her face, though, and she was afraid he was remarking her recent tears and her unnatural pallor. "Lady Eleanor, I fear I am presuming on your time. Should I escort you back to the house?"

She smiled brightly. "Are you here for my wedding, already? It is not even noon!" She refused to be deterred.

He hesitated. "Actually, no, I have other duties to attend, but I will not miss the wedding." He smiled politely at her.

Eleanor scrambled to think. Was he there at Adare looking for Sean? What other reason could there be? She was so afraid and she realized she was shaking.

Instantly he caught her arm. "Lady Eleanor! Are you about to faint? You seem terribly pale."

She held on to him tightly, so he could not go. "Captain, you must tell me the truth."

"Let me find you a place to sit so I can summon help," he said.

She shook her head. "I am getting married in a few short hours, as you know. And because of this, everyone thinks to keep me blissfully ignorant. But I know you were here a few days ago—and I know the reason for your call, Captain."

He was grim. "Lady Eleanor, I think I must see you back to the house. It is your wedding day, as you have pointed out, and my men and I are a terrible intrusion."

Eleanor seized his arm. "Yesterday I received terrible news, news that my stepbrother Sean had been in prison and that he has recently escaped. Then I find you here, with your men! If you are hunting the stepbrother I am so fond of, then you must tell me!"

"Lady Eleanor," he said after a terse pause, "I am afraid I cannot discuss this subject."

"He isn't here!" she cried. "If Sean were here, he would come to wish me well, especially today!"

Brawley stared at her as if torn.

"Surely you do not think he is here?" She released his sleeve. "Sean and I were raised together under this very roof. I am so worried for him! And whatever they say he did, they are *wrong*. Sean is *innocent* of all the charges against him."

"Lady Eleanor, if your family thinks it best not to inform you of all that has transpired, surely I should not be the one to do so," he said firmly.

She felt tears well, tears engendered by her exhaustion, encouraged by her raw emotions. "How can I marry today not knowing if he is alive or dead? Not knowing if he is safe? Not knowing where he is?"

"Please, Lady Eleanor!" Brawley handed her his immaculate white handkerchief. "I am afraid I was instructed to search the grounds," he said. "But my orders to do so were not based on any evidence that he has been here. In fact, our search of the entire area has proved the very opposite—your stepbrother has not returned to Adare." He tried to smile stiffly at her. "So you may know that he is safe, wherever he is."

Eleanor stared into his eyes, beyond relief. "So the search is over?"

He looked away. "I am afraid not. By law, he is a fugitive, and I am under orders to apprehend him."

All relief vanished. She did not have to know Brawley well to know he was a man who carried out his duty, no matter the cost. "And that is what you will do?" she asked bitterly. "Even knowing, as you now do, that he is innocent?"

He was rigid, and he did not quite look at her now. "Your loyalty to your stepbrother is commendable. If you must know, I would be as loyal, if I were in your shoes. But I am a soldier, Lady Eleanor, and I must obey my orders."

She had a dreadful suspicion. "And what are your orders, precisely?" she asked, trembling. Traitors were hanged. There was no quarter given, and Sean had already been convicted of high treason. "Captain Brawley? You said your orders are to apprehend Sean—yet you refuse to look me in the eye!"

"He is a dangerous man!" he cried, meeting her gaze and flushing. "Why do you torment yourself this way, so soon before your wedding?"

She gripped his arm. "There is more! What aren't you telling me? And Sean is not dangerous!"

Brawley seemed to struggle with himself. He shrugged free of her. "He is wanted dead or alive, Lady Eleanor. I am sorry to be the one to tell you so."

Eleanor cried out.

ELEANOR SAT in her wedding dress before the vanity in her dressing room, both of her sisters-in-law with her. Devlin's wife, Virginia, was a petite woman with fair skin and black hair who had been born on a plantation in the state of Virginia. Virginia had just remarked how beautiful Eleanor was in her beaded and lace-trimmed wedding dress.

Eleanor could not care. She could not shake Brawley's words. Now, she prayed Sean was on a ship and bound for the Atlantic Ocean.

She stared at her ashen reflection, the diamond tiara she wore with its attached veil doing nothing to help her complexion. She appeared ill, or as if she was in mourning. But she *was* in mourning, she thought. She was mourning the loss of her best friend and the man she loved. She wondered if she would mourn forever.

And to make matters worse, she was about to go downstairs and marry Peter Sinclair, an honorable man who loved her. Eleanor knew she had wronged Sinclair last night and that she was wronging him now by marrying him.

Lizzie moved closer to Eleanor, laying her palm on her bare shoulder. The wedding gown had short, puffed, dropped sleeves, a wide, square and low neckline and huge tulip-shaped skirts. The entire dress was made of lace, sewn with pearls and silver thread; the train was a pool of satin, trimmed in the same manner. "Dear, you haven't said a word in an hour. Can we talk? Because you are frightening Ginny and me."

Eleanor closed her eyes, overcome with despair. *What was she doing?* How could Sean have done what he had, never mind her invitation, and then just left? And, dear God, she didn't want to marry Peter. It wasn't honorable or right. But she had lost her will.

She felt as if someone had beaten her into a bloody pulp, so badly she could barely move much less walk, think, talk, or even feel.

"Eleanor?" This from Virginia. "You are behaving as if someone has died. Not like a merry bride."

Eleanor looked at her pretty sisters-in-law in the mirror. Their gazes met. "Someone has died. And I do not love Peter. I can't do this." She added, choking on bitter laughter, "Peter doesn't deserve this."

Virginia and Lizzie exchanged dismayed glances. "Who has died?" Lizzie asked worriedly.

"I have," Eleanor said, remaining as still as a statue, except for her chest, which showed the signs of breathing with some exertion. "I have died. And this must be hell."

"I am going to get the countess," Lizzie said, pale with alarm. "She is with the housekeeper, I think, but she needs to be here now."

"Sean was here," Eleanor said.

Lizzie gasped, and Virginia's eyes went wide. "Eleanor, what are you saying?" Virginia cried, blanching.

Eleanor looked at her in the mirror. "He doesn't love me. I have been such a fool. Worse, I still love him."

Virginia bit her lip. "Where is he? Dear God, the troops were here the other day and then just this morning! Devlin has to know that his brother is near!"

"He left last night. He won't be back—he is going to America," Eleanor said, as if in a trance.

"I must tell Devlin," Virginia cried, already racing for the door.

Lizzie took Eleanor's hand, forcing her to look directly at her. "Why didn't you tell anyone?"

"He asked me not to," Eleanor said. "But I told Cliff and Rex."

Lizzie started; she was near tears. "I have to tell Tyrell. Will you be all right by yourself?" she asked.

Eleanor somehow nodded. "I am not getting married," she said, "not today and not ever. Maybe I will join a convent."

Lizzie started. "Stay right here," she said firmly. "Do not move until someone gets back." She squeezed her hand and left the room.

And Eleanor was alone. She brushed at a tear, angry to find it crawling down her cheek. At least Sean had a good twelve-hour start on Brawley and his men, or even more, if Brawley had still not picked up his trail.

Even after the way he had treated her and the way he had left, she was glad for him. She was always going to care, she realized, and she was always going to want him to be unharmed and safe.

She suddenly felt that she was being watched.

She looked up into the mirror—and found herself looking not at her reflection, but into a pair of intent gray eyes.

Sean stood behind her.

She stood, whirling. "Sean!" Hope blazed.

He shook his head, his eyes filled with anguish. "I came…" He stopped, his tone thick. "I am sorry, Elle," he said harshly. "I am so sorry for hurting you."

She wet her lips, her mind racing, but her heart spoke. "I love you."

He flinched. "Don't. It was wrong—I hate myself. I am sorry! How can I undo…*it? How?*"

"It doesn't matter," she whispered, trembling wildly. She wanted to rush into his arms but did not dare. "All that matters is that you're back." In horror, she realized what she had said. "Sean! They're looking for you!"

"I know," he said as thickly. His gaze was on her face, her eyes. His eyes seemed hungry and desperate, as if determined to memorize her every feature. "They left an hour ago. It's all right.… They won't catch me." He stopped. His gaze moved over her wedding dress and then went back to her eyes. "I never…want to hurt you.… Not you. I don't know what happened…or why. I am…ashamed."

He was stricken because he had hurt her. "You

didn't hurt me," she lied. "You can't hurt me," she added softly. "Nothing you say or do will ever change the way I feel about you."

He shook his head. "Don't." He fought to speak now.

She started toward him, reaching for him.

He seized her wrist, refusing to let her close the distance between them. *"Don't."*

"No!" Her mind raced. She was going with him— Of course she was. In the end, there was no other choice.

"Sinclair...tonight, Elle, you have to...pretend."

Suddenly she realized what he was saying. *He was referring to her wedding night.* "No!"

"Pretend...pain. He'll never know...he loves you."

"Stop it!" She wept. "I won't marry him, I won't. I can't!"

"No! He'll take care of you because...I cannot." His expression was twisted and his eyes were shining with tears.

She couldn't speak, she couldn't breathe. Despair choked her.

"Goodbye." He smiled sadly at her.

"No," she whispered.

He turned and went into the bedroom.

Eleanor came to life. "No!" She ran after him as

he strode to the window, which was wide open now. "Sean, you can't go—not without me!"

He ignored her, climbing out.

"Sean!" she cried, running to the sill.

He was already climbing down to the next balcony.

"Sean! Take me with you!"

He didn't look up, leaping from the rail to the oak tree. And he began to scramble down to the ground.

Her mind hardened with resolve. Eleanor turned, lifting her skirts, and ran across the room, flinging the bedroom door open. A maid was in the hall carrying a tray of refreshments, but Eleanor did not see. The maid leaped against the wall to avoid being run over, dropping the tray and all of its plates, cups and saucers. Eleanor ran down the stairs, tripping on her skirts, which she held high with one hand, her other on the railing. Behind her, her train flowed, an endless wave of satin and silk.

She realized that hundreds of guests were milling about the house. Eleanor didn't care, ignoring the gasps of surprise and the rising murmurs that sounded as she flew through the hall, amongst the crowd. People rushed to step out of her way.

From the corner of her eye, she saw Cliff flirting with Lady Barton. He saw her, straightened. "Eleanor!"

She was almost at the front door. And she saw

Peter's father, Lord Henredon, the earl of Chatton, staring at her with shock.

"Open the door, fools!" she shouted to the two liveried doormen there.

They obeyed instantly.

"Eleanor!" It was Devlin, somewhere behind her, and it was a command.

Eleanor barely heard him. She ran outside and instantly saw Sean, halfway to the stables, his strides long and rushed. She lifted her skirts and ran. "Sean!"

He started, turning, and saw her. Then he whirled and began to run away.

Eleanor saw a groom leading a horse from the stables toward him. Her resolve escalated wildly. "Sean!" She screamed as loudly as she could. She tripped now as she began to run across the grass.

He leaped astride, the horse rearing, and he looked her way. Two hundred meters separated them.

Eleanor was caught by a sharp stitch in her side and she halted, gasping for air and fighting the lancing pain. She was vaguely aware of a crowd forming outside of the house, the murmurs sharp and excited, and of Devlin and Cliff pausing behind her. One of her brothers cursed.

Cliff said, "Dev. They're back."

Eleanor couldn't remove her gaze from Sean but

she didn't have to. She knew Cliff meant the soldiers. If she looked toward the front of the house, she knew she would see the troops coming up the drive.

Sean spurred the black and galloped toward the woods, intent now on escape.

No. Eleanor lifted her skirts, screaming, and began to run after him. "Sean!" she cried. *"Sean!"* And she stopped, incapable of breathing now.

Suddenly the huge black reversed direction, so sharply it stumbled, and Sean was galloping at her.

Eleanor held out her hand.

Sean had the beast at a full gallop. He was just meters away, and their eyes met. His were light and bright and fiercely determined. Eleanor was overcome with elation. *He was returning for her.* He reached down, almost upon her.

Their hands touched, clasped.

And Eleanor leaped for the horse just as he hauled her up and she was astride, behind him. She clasped her arms around his waist and buried her face in his back. Sean whirled the stallion again; cries of shock and orders to halt sounded.

They galloped away, into the woods.

CHAPTER NINE

WHAT HAD HE DONE?

And how far behind were they?

Eleanor remained behind him as they galloped through the woods. Her hands were light but firm on his waist. She could ride just as well behind a man as she could alone—her balance when on a horse hadn't changed, even if everything else had. *What had he done?* Her breasts, soft and full, teased his back and he was acutely aware of her just as he was acutely aware of the house that was now far behind them, filled with hundreds of wedding guests. Devlin was there, too, as was the earl and his mother, and he knew they must be shocked. *He had just stolen the bride.*

He was stunned by his deed, but it didn't matter now. Sean still knew the woods as well as he had when he was a young man, racing through them in pursuit of a vagrant Elle when she was just a wild girl. He veered for the tenth time onto another deer trail, this one finally bringing them to a wide, shallow river that ran southeast from the Shannon. Eleanor had her cheek pressed to his shoulder, but now, as he halted the stallion, she shifted and straightened in the saddle. It was a relief.

Elle was no longer that blossoming girl but a full-blown woman now. They should not be running away together, just as they should not have shared a bed last night—except they had never made it to the bed. *He had taken her on the wall, as if she were a whore in an alley.*

"Sean," she said hoarsely. "We can lose them in the river."

Of course she knew what he intended. She remained the most intelligent woman he had ever met. He threw his right leg over the black's neck. He slid to the ground and finally looked up at her. He had been sick ever since he'd left her room last night and nothing had changed. She had said that it didn't matter. He felt ill. It did matter. It mattered to him. He had become a beast, not a man, and last night he had proved it.

Her golden eyes met his.

His heart seemed to catch.

She was stunningly beautiful in her white wedding dress, her cheeks wildly flushed, her eyes terribly bright. Although her hair remained pinned up, a few strands had escaped and were curling around her face. One strand lay low, a curl at the cleavage on her chest. The long train, once elegant and now filthy, still trailed behind the horse on the ground. It was torn and tattered. He was afraid that pieces of it had left a trail for the soldiers to follow.

He shouldn't be admiring her, not now, not ever. He had only returned to try to tell her how to deceive Sinclair on her wedding night and more importantly, to apologize and beg for the forgiveness he would never deserve. And he'd wanted a chance for a final goodbye. Instead, he had abducted her.

Panic surged in his chest. He still didn't know what had made him turn around. He had seen the soldiers riding up the drive. He should have kept on going straight for the woods. But she had cried his name, as she had so many times as a child, in need, in desperation, in terror and fear. He'd turned the stallion back for her without even thinking twice about it.

"Sean?" she whispered nervously, her gaze riveted to his. She was waiting for him to act.

The panic escalated wildly, consuming him. With it came fear and dread.

The British were after them both now. He had just put Elle in grave, mortal danger.

"Sean? What are we going to do?"

He jerked. *He could not do this to her.* "We'll lose them in the river," he said slowly.

"I'll walk, too," she said decisively, cutting into his thoughts. "We can move more swiftly. But I can't walk in the water in this dress."

That was obvious. The huge skirts and train would weigh her down. The words weren't even out of her mouth when he had his dagger in hand. "Sit still," he said grimly. She nodded, her eyes widening as he gripped the edge of the train and cut it from her dress. He gathered it up. They weren't going to leave clues behind for the troops, and he hoped very much that no one had espied any torn pieces of her gown on the trail.

"Give me the knife," she said in the same low, tense voice as she slid to her feet.

He suddenly realized what she was going to do. He had an image of her half naked, her nightgown ripped down the front, her face strained and flushed with passion. He felt his cheeks flame and his loins stir. He handed the blade to her. Their hands brushed, bringing a rigid response to his body and another more graphic recollection of being with her last night. She had been very soft in some places and very hard in others. He turned away, finding a broken branch on the ground. As he went to retrieve it, he heard the fabric of her dress ripping apart. He kept his gaze down, walking some distance away. He began sweeping away their tracks, working backward to the edge of the river where she stood with the stud. He placed all of his concentration on the task at hand, but even so, he strained to hear. The sound of her dress being cut had stopped.

His heart had an odd rhythm now, slow and heavy, painful. He finally looked up.

She stared back at him, as if daring him to say a word.

The skirt was gone. She wore a single linen underskirt that was all lace and pink ribbons; she'd left the beaded white bodice of her dress intact. She still looked like a bride—but one who had been abducted for all the wrong reasons; she looked like a bride who'd had her skirts cut off in order to be ravaged. He flushed and went to the stallion's head.

"How far ahead of them do you think we are?" she asked quietly.

He led the stallion into the water. The river was shallow, but the bed was all rock. He tried to think about the footing. Elle followed him into the water.

He avoided looking at her. "We could have lost them…completely," he said, wondering how she was going to walk a mile or so in that underskirt. "Or they could be…minutes behind."

She was moving very quietly behind him—a feat for a woman dragging sodden skirts. "They would have interfered."

He glanced back, saw she'd tied her petticoat around her waist, and jerked to look ahead. *She was wearing lace-trimmed drawers that ended above her knees. The garments matched her petticoat exactly. He'd bet his life the corset was white lace and pink ribbons, too.* He wiped some sweat from his brow.

"Devlin and Cliff were behind me when you came back for me. I know they'd do something to help us escape."

She was right. He hoped that whatever they'd done, it had been very discreet. And he began to realize that Elle wasn't the only one he'd placed in jeopardy. His entire family was at risk because of his actions now.

"What are we going to do, Sean?" she asked worriedly.

"We'll travel until dark…rest…then keep going." He kept his tone flat and calm.

"Where are we going?"

He glanced at her, then wished he hadn't. The water had molded her drawers to her long legs. *She had strong muscular legs, and last night, they'd been wrapped around him, hard. He had never known a woman could have such legs.* "Cork."

"Cliff has a ship in Limerick."

He told himself not to respond. The less she knew, the better. She was in danger now. *They could make her pay for his crimes—the way they'd made Peg and Michael pay.*

He was ill, unable to stop his thoughts.

HER FACE WAS WHITE with fear. "You have to stop them. Don't let them go," Peg begged. "They'll be killed, all of them. Sean, please!"

Her fear was real, and he would never forget it. He had gone after her father, a leader of the mob, because he had promised her he would intervene. Since his arrival in the village the previous year, the entire village had looked to him for advice and leadership. And because he had been overlord of Askeaton for all of the years his brother had been at sea, he had naturally assumed that position.

He had promised Peg he would stop a catastrophe, but now it was too late. Two dozen men, pitifully armed, had already confronted Lord Darby. They had lined up, not allowing his coach to enter through his own front gates. Darby had an escort—Lieutenant Colonel Reed and five men. Before he knew it, he was somehow negotiating with Darby for the reversal of an eviction, in the hopes of preventing a riot. Darby had refused.

The men had gone berserk, overturning the coach and dragging Darby out of it. Two soldiers were pulled from their horses and beaten to death; Reed and the remaining soldiers had fled. Darby was dragged to the nearest tree, weeping and incontinent. Sean had begged for his life; the Englishman had been promptly hanged.

The mob had descended on Darby's home to destroy it, ignoring him yet again when he begged them to retreat. In fury, they had set the house and grounds on fire. Defeated, unable to watch such destruction, he had turned to go home. Then the reinforcements had arrived and the massacre had begun.

When it was over, every man in the village of Kilraddick was dead, except for himself and Flynn, and a redcoat had been killed by Sean's own hand. His every instinct told him to find Peg and Michael, to take them and flee. On foot, limping from a bayonet wound, he had raced through the village. Peg was waiting, white with fear. There'd been no time to explain anything, no time to pack up their meager belongings. He'd taken her and Michael and they'd fled to the next village. The next day, he'd told her the truth, all of it. She'd wept for the deaths of her father and everyone else. And she had told him she was carrying their child.

He'd married her the following day, Michael bearing the ring he'd managed to borrow. Because no troops came searching for him, they began to hope that he was presumed dead in the Darby fire. Some of the shock began to wear off, then real grief began. With it came a burning need to avenge the dead, but he knew better.

And when Peg came to him and asked him where they were going to live, it struck him that, somehow, he had become a married man.

He had stared at her, absolutely at a loss, incapable of understanding how and when he had married this woman, a woman he didn't really know and certainly didn't love. Amber eyes had haunted him, and he had felt guilt.

Shyly, she had told him she wanted to make plans for the birth of their child. As shyly, she had told him that they needed their own home and hopefully, another farm.

He suddenly realized he had a wife he was responsible for, a son, an unborn child. They were too close to Kilvore and the garrison in Drogheda. He knew that he must take his family back to Askeaton. Lieutenant Colonel Reed would never look for him there—and even if he did, he would never assume the earl's stepson to be the same man who had been in the Kilvore Rising.

But then the impossibility of that decision suddenly hit him. How could he go home with Peg and Michael? What would his brother say? What would the earl and the countess say? What would they think?

What would Elle think?

He'd stayed in the village tap room, debating the subject, until cries of alarm roused him from his brooding and indecision. A fire had started. Glad of the distraction, he joined the men to help put it out. When he walked outside, he was shocked to find that it was dark already. And then he realized that the cottage, where he had let rooms, was in flames.

As comprehension came, so did dread. And then he saw the cavalry galloping away from the town and the cottage and he knew what had happened....

Sean ran.

Only one home was on fire, and it was his. The thatched roof was an inferno, the walls just beginning to burn. He screamed for Peg, for Michael. He tore his shirt from his body and used it to avoid inhaling the smoke. Inside, fire was devouring every stick of furniture, every cabinet and door. Fighting the smoke and fire, he found Peg unconscious on the floor, her clothes torn from her, bleeding from her wounds, clutching the toy boat. She had died in his arms and Michael had never been found....

AND NOW ELLE was at his side, with the British hunting him down.

In that moment he was terrified that the past was going to repeat itself. Nothing was as important as protecting Elle, as seeing her home safely, not even his escape. As long as she was with him, she was in danger. In fact, if the woods weren't so perilous, if he didn't fear a wild boar, he'd leave her then and there, and let her find her way back. But he couldn't leave her alone in the woods, so he would take her to Cork, where he would find her a safe escort to see her home. Men like Reed could not harm her if she was behind Adare's solid walls. But could the earl protect her from criminal charges? If they couldn't hurt her the way they'd hurt Peg and Michael, maybe they'd do the next worse thing. She would not be the first woman to be imprisoned in the Tower for the rest of her life, charged with conspiracy and treason.

No, he thought furiously, that wasn't going to happen, either. But there was so much panic that it was hard to think.

"Sean? Why didn't you leave last night?"

He did not want to think about last night, not ever again—and he especially did not want to discuss it with her. "I did leave."

"But you came back."

He chose not to answer now.

She seized his arm, dragging him to a halt in the water. Somehow he was facing her. He knew the water lapped her thighs and her skin was visible through the cotton drawers, so he refused to look— except from the corner of his eyes. "Thank you," she said softly.

He pulled away. "I told you...goodbye."

"But it wasn't goodbye. This is a new beginning," she said softly.

"Damn it! When did you become...foolish?" The words exploded from him. "You could be married...to an Englishman...Sinclair! Instead... freezing water...hunted by Englishmen!"

"I don't love Peter," she said, her tone stubborn.

His mind was treacherous, choosing that moment to recall all of last night. He almost told her she had proved that. "It doesn't matter." He turned away, continuing on downstream. "No one marries...for love."

"I beg to differ with you!" She slogged through the water, chasing him. "Father loves the countess and he chose to marry her for love! Tyrell married for love—but you wouldn't know that, because you weren't here! He was engaged to an heiress, and he carried on openly with Lizzie, living with her at Wicklow. He was prepared to give up the earldom for her. And what about Devlin?" she cried to his back. "You know as well as I do that he married for love!"

He whirled. "We have…an odd family…do we not? But Rex hasn't married for love…. Cliff will never marry! And I…" He stopped. He was breathing hard. He hadn't married for love. He had married because he had gotten Peg with child and she had needed him desperately, as had little Michael, who had begged him to be his father. He had married her because he had been too shocked by the massacre to even think about doing anything other than protect her and her child from more harm. And what had his efforts gotten him? In the end, he had done the very thing he had been determined not to do. His attempts to protect them had gotten them murdered.

"You what?" she asked in bewilderment, reaching for him.

He shook her hand off and led the stallion on. She made no move to follow. Although he was furious with himself for dragging her into his escape, he strained to hear her slogging through the water behind him. It was another moment before he heard her starting through the river after him.

Elle had always known when to engage and when to withdraw, when to push and when to let go. "We're making good time, I think," she said, as if their previous argument had not existed. "We haven't stopped. But we'll have to rest at some point, especially for Saphyr."

He doubted it had been even two hours since their escape from Adare. But she was right—they had been moving swiftly the entire time. They needed rest—and so did the horse. The sun was high but weakening, and in an hour or two it would start to descend in the west. "We'll leave the river in half an hour...turn inland then."

"Sean!" Eleanor suddenly grasped his arm. "Do you hear that?"

He didn't wait to discern if she had heard their pursuit or not. "Come." He ran with the stallion to the opposite bank, Eleanor at his side. He handed her the reins and she ran with the horse into the woods. He had kept a piece of her wedding train wrapped around his arm and now he tied it to a branch. He quickly swept the sandy area clean, covering his own footprints as he went back to the woods.

He found Elle and paused, breathing hard. Their eyes met.

Hers were searching. But the question in them had nothing to do with their pursuers, and everything to do with last night. He glanced away. Why did she keep insisting that he give her something he did not even have left to give?

And then he heard voices, faint but not far enough away. They were English. One voice was giving orders, very distinctly.

Elle turned to speak.

He clapped his hand over her mouth and in doing so, pulled her close. She went still.

He whispered into her ear, "Upriver. Close."

She nodded, her eyes huge.

He slowly removed his hand, willing himself not to think about her body, more undressed than dressed, pressed against his. With his other hand, he caressed the stallion's neck. The stud could easily give them away.

Four of them were in the river, riding in single file, their gazes going from bank to bank. And the fifth horseman was Devlin O'Neill.

At the sight of him, Sean felt his heart lurch. He knew what his brother was doing. Devlin had convinced the officer in charge to let him join the search. Devlin's reputation was notorious—he had been a ruthless commander during the war. Most of the naval command had been in fear of him, as well as in awe. It probably hadn't been difficult to persuade the officer to allow him to join the search party.

He was there to help Sean escape.

Devlin's gaze veered toward them, as if he had

somehow been able to pinpoint their location in the woods.

Sean put his arm around Eleanor and felt her tension. He wanted to reassure her, even though the soldiers were within shouting distance and he was afraid. He tried to calm her with his eyes. Sweat trickled, interfering with his vision.

Elle tried to smile at him. Her face was white with fear.

In response, Sean hugged her closer to his side. She looked up at him, her pupils dilated, her face starkly white. She trembled and turned her face to his chest and buried it there.

His heart constricted, but he held her even more tightly. He realized that, somehow, he'd put both arms around her.

"Sir," a soldier shouted, sounding dangerously close. "They must have gone to land farther down. There's no sign of any horse, any man, not here."

"And you, Sir Captain? What do you think?" The officer spoke tersely.

"I think it was clever to send half of your men north toward Limerick. There hasn't been a single sign that they have passed this way," Devlin said. "That wedding dress should have left a few tatters."

Sean met Elle's eyes. Devlin must have found the

pieces of her train and hidden them or directed the soldiers' attention elsewhere.

"I think you are right, Captain O'Neill. I think they have gone north to Limerick and we are on a false trail. If they had come this way, there should have been some sign. There hasn't been one broken branch, one hoofprint, one piece of your stepsister's dress. And, you remain remarkably calm, sir."

"I told you once—and I do not like repeating myself—my brother is no danger to anyone and the charges against him are erroneous." O'Neill flashed a cool smile. "I have seen my share of false testimony while serving Great Britain, Captain."

"If you are right, then the sooner we apprehend your brother, the sooner we can clear his name. Move out!"

The soldiers and Devlin rode their horses to the far bank, turning back the way they had come. As they disappeared into the woods, Devlin did not look back, not even once.

"He saw us," Elle whispered.

Sean became impossibly aware of the woman he held in his arms. Unbelievably, every inch of him that was male came to life, urgent and insistent, clamoring for attention, for relief. He released her, stepping away. To compose himself, he went to the black stallion and stroked him. "Yes. He led them away…from us." And Devlin would now know that he was heading for the port at Cobh, as it was a major harbor.

The younger brother in him almost wanted to chase after Devlin and ask for his help. But he was a man now, not a boy, and his brother had too much to lose.

The raging need had settled. Sean looked at Elle, who had sat down in the dirt. "They're gone…. They won't return today."

She nodded, clearly not able to speak. She did not look as relieved as she should be. She removed her white kidskin shoes, which were terribly dirty and torn.

"It was close…but we made it." He wished he could remember how to smile because he wanted to comfort her now. "Elle… They want me, not you." He could not think about Peg and Michael now. He did not dare.

She shed her stockings, as well. "That's just it! That was Brawley, Sean. I spoke with him—he's the captain—earlier today. His orders are to apprehend you, and he has full discretion as to how to proceed."

Sean quickly lowered his gaze. He understood. Brawley had permission to bring him back dead or alive.

Elle looked at her bare feet. "Devlin was trying to convince him that you are innocent—so was I. But I know the man just a bit. He is every inch a soldier. Devlin can attempt to persuade him until he can no longer speak, and it will not matter. We may have bought an extra day. But Brawley is going to do everything he has to in order to apprehend you."

He was disbelieving. "You tried to plead... bargain...with a British officer?"

She nodded. "I had no choice."

He knelt and took her by the shoulders. "I don't want you *ever...near* a redcoat...do you hear?" He almost shook her, fear and fury blinding him.

"I was trying to find out what he knew. I was trying to help!" she cried. "You're so afraid—I can see it in your eyes. It's the only thing I can see," she added in distress. "I've never seen you afraid this way."

"I'm afraid...for you!" he cried before he could stop himself.

She started, turning pale. "What?"

He closed his eyes, trembling. "We need to move.... We'll go east. There's more forest...that will be to our advantage." He met her wide gaze. "It will take longer...to get to Cork."

Elle hugged herself. "I don't want you to worry about me," she said slowly. "Sean, it's your life that is in jeopardy, not mine."

Her words pained him sharply. Later, when they

were in a safer place, in the flat in Cork, he would tell her that he planned to send her home. He did not want to engender an argument now. "We had better go," he said.

She hesitated, then slowly, painfully, stood.

He saw immediately. "What happened to your feet?" But he knew. His own feet, unused to walking, hurt terribly, but he had willed himself to ignore it days ago. He was a man, however; she was not.

"You try walking in brand-new shoes—through a river, I might add," she said, biting her lower lip.

He took her arm. "Sit down."

She obeyed, her gaze moving to his face.

He felt his cheeks warm but he ignored the way she was regarding him—with absolute faith and trust. He wished he had never known her as a young child, that he had never been the recipient of that look so many times before. He knelt and looked at one foot, becoming grim when he saw the blisters. *She was hurt, and it was up to him to manage it.* He looked up.

"I can walk," she said stubbornly.

He became aware of cradling her foot in his hand and he placed it on the ground. "You are riding... until we stop for the night," he said. "I'll use the train for bandages."

IT WAS ALMOST TWILIGHT when Devlin strode into the front hall of Adare. Captain Brawley accompanied him, his men outside. Instantly Cliff and Tyrell appeared, followed by Rex, the earl, the countess and Peter Sinclair. The latter was ashen and wide-eyed.

Devlin met Cliff's eyes. Cliff smiled slightly at him.

He knew that Cliff had ridden like hell through the woods for Limerick, and not to prepare his ship to sail at dawn, as apparently he'd taken care of that last night. He had left a false trail for the soldiers, and from the satisfied look in his eyes, the bait had been taken.

"Have you found them?" the earl asked Brawley, carefully avoiding looking at Devlin.

"I'm afraid not. It looks as if they have ridden for Limerick. I will await word from the men I sent north earlier," Brawley said.

The earl nodded. "I appreciate your efforts on my behalf, Thomas," he said. "I am desperate to find my son."

Brawley hesitated. "I know you are, my lord. Let us all hope that there is a satisfactory conclusion to this crisis." He bowed and walked out.

The earl turned to young Sinclair. "Peter, would you care to join me and your father for another drink? There is nothing more to be gleaned from this night."

Sinclair turned a bewildered gaze on Devlin. "The rogue is your brother, Sir Captain! Is this truly what you think, that he has gone to Limerick? And what of Eleanor? Everyone swears she is in no danger from him, but I am not convinced!"

"My brother is innocent of the charges against him," Devlin said, clasping the younger man's shoulder.

"He is charged with murder, sir, murder and treason!" Sinclair cried.

"Sean is a gentleman, not a cutthroat. And he is a patriot."

"An Irish Patriot, perhaps?"

"We are a part of the Union," Devlin said in his most commanding manner. "He is as much a patriot as you. Eleanor is his stepsister—he would never hurt her. To the contrary, he would give his life for her."

Sinclair finally nodded, remaining distraught. "I will never understand why she went with him."

The earl went over to Sinclair. "Eleanor has always been impetuous and rash, I'm afraid. Let us try not to worry. Sean will keep her safe and by the morrow, I am certain they will both be found. Your worries shall be laid to rest when you are able to speak with her, and we, of course, will begin to proceed to clear Sean's name and record of these terrible charges."

Sinclair stared, then shook his head and muttered, "Excuse me. I think I am going outside. I need to think."

When he was gone, Rex said tersely, "One of us needs to be with him. He could and should be a useful ally, if Sean is apprehended."

"You are right," the earl said. "Tyrell, go appease young Sinclair. Convince him Sean has been falsely tried, falsely convicted and falsely imprisoned. And when you have done that, try to convince him that Eleanor acted out of folly and love for a dear *brother.*" He was grim.

Tyrell nodded tersely and strode after Sinclair.

"What happened?" the earl asked Devlin.

"They've gone south, to Cork. They were but four miles from here, on the other side of the river. However, I made sure they left no trail and Brawley believes they have gone north to Limerick."

The earl nodded and turned to Cliff. "Can you sail at dawn?"

"I can have *The Fair Lady* in Cobh in two days at the worst," Cliff said, his eyes hard. "But what about Eleanor?"

A brief silence fell and glances were exchanged. The countess stepped into their midst, but she looked only at the earl. "She is a grown woman now, and she has never stopped loving Sean."

"And what if we cannot overturn his convictions? What if there is no amnesty? He is an outlaw, Mary, and he will have to leave the country. What if he is caught and she is with him? What if she is charged with conspiracy to commit treason?"

Mary was pale. "If he wants her with him, we will never convince her to abandon him," she said. "Darling, I know you are angry with Sean. But I know my son. He has fallen in love with her, Edward. There is no other explanation for his behavior."

"Right now, I am not sure I care how he feels about Eleanor," the earl said abruptly. "Sinclair is a suitable match—he is titled and wealthy and he is not an outlaw, placing her very life in danger."

Mary had stiffened. "So even knowing how Eleanor has loved my son her entire life, you would be set against them?"

He was as rigid. "Before Sean bore arms against the British, I would have allowed the match! I have raised him as a son—he is my son! But surely you do not expect me to allow Eleanor to marry an outlaw?"

"If that is what she wants and what he wants, then I do expect exactly that."

A terrible tension settled there in the room.

Devlin stepped between them. He gave his mother a reassuring smile, one that softened the hard angles and planes of his face. Then he faced the earl. "Edward, the point is currently moot. Marriage between my brother and your daughter is not on the table. We do not know what they intend. I do know this. Sean would never deliberately place Eleanor in danger, for, if only as a sister, he loves her too much."

"He has done just that," Edward cried. "And I am afraid for them both."

"I know you are. However, he will not be caught." Devlin spoke firmly and with confidence. "And I prefer to be the one to sail him to foreign shores."

Cliff seized his arm. "You have a wife and two children now—I have no one. I will take care of Sean. And if Eleanor is with him, I will take care of her, as well. I hate to say this, my dear brother, but I can outsail, outrun and outfight anyone—and that includes any British ship that might be sent in pursuit of us."

Devlin faced him. "If you sincerely believe you are invincible, then you are in for a letdown, my boy. There is a naval base in Cobh—or have you forgotten?"

Cliff smiled coolly. "I have never lost a battle at sea and I do not intend to start now. As for the navy there, half the sailors are impressed felons who will jump ship at the first sign of danger."

Rex limped between them. "The two of you are

going to start measuring up against each other now? I think not! Anyone who sails Sean away from Ireland with or without Eleanor, may never be able to return. Therefore I have a plan."

Mary had taken a seat, her face strained and her arms folded tightly across her chest. "Please, Rex," she said.

"Cliff can sail to Cobh, but he will be our decoy. Devlin, you must privately and secretly purchase a fast, armed ship. That ship must also be sent to Cobh, if the purchase is not made there. When we locate Sean, Cliff can set sail and lead the British astray. Devlin can then sail him to safety, without pursuit. Meanwhile I am going overland to Cork," Rex said. "If I leave now, I should arrive within mere hours of them, so their trail there will remain fresh."

A cough sounded, and heads turned. Rory McBane stood on the threshold. "I have decided to come forward," he said, "because you are going to need my help."

THE SUN HAD FINALLY SET. Eleanor had never been as pleased to welcome the night as she was just then. While Sean hobbled the horse, exhaustion suddenly overcame her. She limped over to a grassy area in the clearing and laid out the train of her dress, folding it several times over. Her arms were bare, for she had no wrap, and it was already cold. She sat down, shivering, aware of her body being sore, aware of being ravenously hungry—but she had never been happier.

Sean had come back for her. It was a dream come true, a miracle. Last night had changed *everything*. Obviously he returned her feelings, or was beginning to do so. And since they had eluded the soldiers, the worst was undoubtedly over. Soon they would arrive in Cork, and shortly they would be sailing together to America.

For nothing else could make any sense. If Sean had returned for her, if he cared about her as a woman, he must want her to go with him.

She hugged her knees to her chest, watching him. Her feet hurt, but she felt as if she were walking in the clouds above their heads. From the short distance separating them in the small glade, Sean must have felt her stare, because he glanced her way. Then his gaze skittered aside. "How are you?"

Her smile faded. On the other hand, he had been acting oddly all day. She thought she knew why—he was embarrassed about his behavior last night. Did she dare tell him that it didn't matter? What mattered was every moment from this day on.

"I am exhausted and cold and I am starving! But

I am fine, Sean." And she heard how silken her tone had become.

He stiffened. Then, very deliberately, he finished with the stallion, which began to graze. He retrieved the oilskin which had been tied to the saddle and moved closer to her. "I don't want to light a fire," he said slowly.

She understood. The British troops led by Brawley might have turned back, but anyone could stumble across them, and of course, there were other troops stationed throughout Ireland. "I think I can survive the night without a fire," she said with a soft smile.

His eyes slid up, briefly meeting hers. "You're cold. It's going to get colder.... We have nothing except that train...it won't be warm."

Instantly she thought of the most obvious way to stay warm and she smiled. In his arms, she would never be cold. And this time, there would be love between them, not just explosive passion. Her chest grew tight. "I'm not worried about the cold," she murmured.

He jerked. "What does that...mean?" he demanded.

She stood and seized his hand. "You're so afraid to even look at me!" she exclaimed. "Sean, if anyone should be embarrassed about last night, it is me."

He pulled free of her grasp. "There's bread and

cheese," he said fiercely, kneeling and ripping open the oilskin.

She hesitated, biting her lip. She recalled how it had felt to have him deeply inside of her. "Sean, my behavior was reprehensible, truly, but—"

He looked up, eyes wide. "I do not want...to discuss...last night!"

She flinched. "I know the topic is not seemly, but at least your reluctance proves you are still a gentleman."

He stood, incredulous. "My behavior was a gentleman's? Are you mad?"

She flushed, terribly uneasy now. "I encouraged you—"

"I said...do not discuss last night. As far as I am concerned...it never happened!" he cried.

She recoiled, disbelieving.

He knelt, violently slicing the hunk of cheese in four pieces and one loaf in half.

She dropped to her knees besides him. "I don't understand. Why are you angry? Are you angry with me?"

He paused, knife in hand, staring at their meal. "I am angry," he said curtly, clearly fighting to choose his words, "with myself." He looked up, his gaze hard. "I am angry...that you are involved. I am angry for using you last night." He turned crimson. "I am angry...I cannot stand myself!" He stabbed the ground.

She watched him as he stood and paced, refusing to believe that he had used her. "But you came back for me."

He whirled. "I came back…damn it…to say goodbye. You should eat!" he ordered. Then, dangerously, he added, "I mean it, Elle."

"But you didn't leave. You returned—for *me*." She stared up at him. "Didn't you?"

He stared down at her. "I wish…" A long pause ensued. "I…had not!"

She gasped, shocked, covering her racing heart with both hands. "You wish you hadn't come back for me?"

He fought for composure, or perhaps for words. "I have spent my life…my entire life…protecting you. Rescuing you…saving you. You should not be with me."

"I disagree!" she cried. "And I cannot believe we are arguing over this, when I am here with you now, and when last night, you took my innocence."

His eyes blazed. "What does that mean?"

"I thought that was why you returned for me. Because of what happened, in my rooms."

"What are you thinking?" he asked, low and harsh.

She wet her lips, frightened now. "I'm not a virgin anymore. You have a duty to marry me—and take me with you."

He just looked at her.

"Oh, my God," she whispered, hugging herself. "You are not thinking about marriage, are you?"

He shook his head. "I am thinking," he said stiffly, "about sending you home…to Adare…where you belong…where the earl can protect you."

She cried out, cutting off the sound with her own hand.

"And I am sorry," he said fiercely. "Very sorry! I never meant to take you…at all! I already told you…how sorry I am! I told you…to marry Sinclair! But I am not a gentleman—don't cry now—Sean O'Neill is gone.… I have told you…you won't listen. You can't run off with a fugitive.… Why won't you be reasonable?" he cried, gasping for breath.

She turned away, beyond shock. Last night she had offered him her bed without any strings, but when he had come back for her, she had assumed his intention was marriage. She had been wrong. Maybe it was time to listen to what he was trying to tell her. He kept insisting that Sean O'Neill was dead. She had refused to believe it. But the man she had loved her entire life would have walked away from her last night, instead of taking her innocence, if he didn't love her in return. The man she had loved her entire life would not be standing in front of her now, like this, after last night, telling her to marry Sinclair.

She faced him furiously. "Then why in hell did you take me with you? Why? If not to make an honest woman of me, why? Because I don't understand!"

"I don't know!" he cried. "I simply do not know! Damn it! You were calling my name…screaming, like Elle always did. I went back to you…like a hundred times before!"

She slapped him across the face with all of her might. The sound of her palm on his skin was as loud as the crack of a whip. "I am not that little girl you were always coddling and rescuing! I am the woman whose virginity you took. But now I am what? Your leftovers, to be tossed aside, like so much trash?"

He shook his head, his gaze oddly moist. "Sinclair loves you."

"I am not going back to him—not that he would have me! How dare you try to foist me off on him, after you slept with me!" She intended to strike him again—she wanted to strike him until he was sense-less—but he seized her wrist.

"Elle!" He spoke urgently now while she struggled to free her arm so she could punch him even harder than before. "I must protect you…please understand.

Sinclair is *English*. If you marry him…no one will chase you…hurt you. He can keep you safe!"

She jerked furiously away. "Now *you're* mad. He would never take me back after what we just did, leaving him at the altar. No one is hurting me except for you!"

A terrible moment ensued. Then, slowly and calmly, he said, "You say that you love me…like a brother…as a sister, you had to help me escape. Sinclair will believe you. There are ways…to make him believe."

She was shaking uncontrollably. "I have been a fool. I gave my body to you, and I would have given my life for you, but for what? To be treated this way? Did you ever love me at all, even when we were children?" She felt as if her heart was bleeding profusely and she started to walk into the woods.

"Damn it!" He ran after her, seizing her from behind and dragging her back into the clearing. "Where are you going? There are wolves!"

"Just now, I do not care! I want to be as far from you as possible!" she cried, twisting wildly until she had shaken him off. She swatted at the tears on her face. She was not going to shed a single tear because of him, not in front of him; but the tears fell, anyway. "I have learned my lesson. You don't love me, you never have, and I am going to stop loving you. You don't deserve my love!"

He was still, staring at her. She stared back. "Good," he said.

That was not the response she had hoped for. "Last night you used me—I believe those are your exact words. Last night, I was your *whore*."

He inhaled, eyes widening. "No! That's not... true."

She hugged herself. "I wanted you to make love to me, Sean—how foolish was that? But that isn't what happened, now, is it?"

He did not speak for a long moment. "No," he said slowly and carefully. "That's not what happened."

She hit him again and he let her.

CHAPTER TEN

HE WATCHED HER.

Elle lay with her back to him. She had wrapped herself in the train of her wedding dress, but whether to ward off a chill or for comfort, he did not know. The night had settled around them, heavy and dark but starlit. He was grateful it hadn't become as cold as he had thought it might. He knew she had finally fallen asleep because her breathing had deepened and slowed.

He sat with his back to a tree, taking the first turn to watch for troops or anyone or thing that might pose a threat. But the night was soft and quiet. An owl was hooting, the sound deep and peaceful, crickets sang their night song, and occasionally, he heard the black stallion shifting as he grazed. Had the day been different, had their situation been different, the night would have been an occasion to relish and enjoy.

But there was nothing to relish or enjoy now.

Sean had his knees pulled up to his chest, his arms looped lightly around them. Elle had fought her tears, but she hadn't truly cried, not even once. He had hurt her yet again, even more terribly than he had the night before, and he could not seem to get past the fact. How had this happened to them, when he had spent a lifetime taking care of her and protecting her from everything and everyone? Now, it seemed, she needed protection from him.

And it didn't matter that she wasn't a child anymore. It would always be his duty to watch over her. Only he had realized that too late.

His gaze shifted from her long, slim back to the woods. The troops were far north by now, he had no doubt. He had Devlin to thank for their successful escape.

But what about Elle?

I am going to stop loving you.

He did not want to remember her words. It would be for the best; he had never asked for or wanted such love, such loyalty, such trust. But her declaration did not relieve him. Instead, his body felt racked, as if it were being pulled apart. His mind remained tortured. And oddly, those words frightened him.

Taking one brief, cautious glance at the perimeter of the clearing, he laid his face on his hands. *She had changed so much; she hadn't changed at all.* He did not know what to do. Of course she had to stop loving him; she had to marry and love Sinclair. But could they ever return to being friends? He had never felt more confused. Memories washed over him. Elle as a child, tagging along with him and his brothers; Elle growing up, spying on him, even when he was in a tryst; Elle at his side, her hands blistered, her face sunburned, helping him rebuild Askeaton.

He closed his eyes tightly. Returning her to Adare and having her marry Sinclair was his priority. If he could still escape somehow, he would; if not, he would die knowing she was well-protected and well-loved. But even he was not mad enough to think she would ever forgive him for using her as he had, or for failing to return her love. They were not going to be friends again, even if he was capable of such a friendship, which he wasn't. Besides, it was highly unlikely that he would remain alive to be her friend.

What he really wanted to know was if she hated him.

He would understand if she did. She had every reason to despise him now. But he could not come to terms with the concept. Sean couldn't fathom how their relationship, developed over an entire lifetime, had come to such a conclusion, with his hurting her at every turn and her hating him for it.

It remained cool out but sweat trickled from his temple. If hating him would keep her at a distance, than he should embrace her anger and hatred. He *needed* to keep Elle angry, he realized, in order to push her away—in order to push her into the arms of another man.

The owl hooted; the sound should have been soothing, but it wasn't. His temples throbbed. Or maybe it was his chest that was aching. Elle's image remained in his mind, tearful, furious and stricken.

The night softened impossibly, a silken caress on his flesh, becoming the cocoon of sleep. Elle's expression also softened, and she was smiling at him. No, it was Peg smiling at him, so oddly faded. As he realized he was dreaming, panic began.

He did not want to go back to those nights of horror and death!

Why don't you love me, Sean?

He tensed, confused. In the dream, Peg never asked the question she hadn't been able to verbalize when alive, but her confusion had always been there in her colorless eyes.

Why won't you love me, Sean?

His heart went wild and he was shocked when she spoke again. Except this time, it wasn't Peg speaking. He stared at the woman in his arms and it was Elle, beautiful and whole and very much alive. Elle, with shining amber eyes, her love reflected there, her love and her trust. He became terribly confused and afraid. Elle should not be there, not in his dream and not on that bloody night when Peg had been raped and murdered!

He wanted to tell her to hurry and leave before the troops came; he wanted to hold her and beg her forgiveness, and then he wanted to soothe her and tell her that he did love her.

He didn't like the way the dream was going, but it was too late—the mob of angry villagers appeared and he knew he had to stop them from marching up the road to Lord Darby's estate. He knew what would happen if they appeared at those iron front gates. He tried to tell them that no good could come of this but his voice wasn't working—he could not get the words out! His panic escalated—he tried to seize the arm of Boyle, Peg's father, but the man didn't seem to notice. He tried to seize Flynn, but he vanished before his very eyes and the estate was burning, the soldiers were there, and he was there, his dagger in the gut of a redcoat, a boy really, and then the boy looked at him, meeting his eyes, the question there unspoken. And when Sean laid him down, he was looking up into the blazing blue eyes of a British officer, and

Lieutenant Colonel Reed was staring at him with sheer hatred.

Sean understood what Reed intended. Because Elle stood there now, having no idea that she was about to suffer, unspeakably and brutally, at Reed's hands. He could not let Reed murder her, the way he'd allowed his men to murder Peg and Michael. And just as he knew that, the officer vanished.

Elle was in his arms, smiling at him, her eyes filled with love.

He held her, his heart pumping madly, barely able to believe that she had escaped rape and death. He held her tightly, filled with relief, but the relief instantly changed. She was so warm in his arms, so soft, so real, and he stiffened, blinded with desire. He found her mouth and they kissed, a gentle caress of lips, and then his hunger raged beyond any control. He had never needed anyone the way he needed her. And she knew. She smiled at him, understanding, then she beckoned him. He cried out, somehow restraining himself, moving deep and slow, so ready to explode....

Sean awoke in the throes of lust, barely able to comprehend that he had been dreaming. He shot to his feet, trying to control an insatiable need. Wildly, he glanced at Elle, but she remained deeply asleep, in a state of exhaustion. The dream had been painfully real.

Even now, he was aroused. He stroked sweat from his brow, having unwittingly walked to stand over her. He was supposed to be on guard duty but he had fallen asleep. He was supposed to be protecting her from their enemies, but instead, he'd been making love to her in his dreams. He was furious with himself. He quickly turned and walked the perimeter of the glade, but all seemed as it should be. The stallion remained widely awake, the only sentry they needed.

Sean paused, inhaling harshly, trying to shake the physical urgency afflicting his hard, hot body. Was Elle now going to haunt his nightmare? He'd had the exact same dream for two years, but suddenly it had changed and she had taken Peg's place. He shuddered with fear. What did that mean? Why was his mind playing such tricks on him? She had never been in the small village of Kilvore and she never would be. She would never come face-to-face with his nemesis, Reed. And he was never going to take her in his arms that way, because it was best that she stopped loving him and returned to Sinclair. He could offer her nothing, nothing except a life on the run and the empty shell of a soul.

There was a small trickling stream just beyond the edge of the glade, and he needed to douse himself with cold water. Abruptly, he changed his mind. He could not leave her alone in the glade, not even for a moment. So instead, he crossed back to where he had been originally seated, but he did not sit. Instead he stared at Elle as she slept.

If he wasn't mistaken, in that damnable dream, he had told Elle he loved her, and it hadn't been a lie.

It had been a nasty trick of his mind, because it could not possibly be true. He had no heart left and therefore was incapable of loving anyone, which was as it should be.

ELEANOR STOOD RIGIDLY behind Sean as he unlocked a warped pine door, in a dismal, dark and very cramped hallway at the top of impossibly narrow stairs. The single room where Sean and she were about to hide was above a cobbler's shop on a street overlooking one of the many canals that ran through Cork. It was hard to believe that this was where they would stay, even if only temporarily. A rat had scurried under the stairs when they had first gone inside and there was no lighting in the cubicle entryway downstairs or on the landing where Eleanor now stood. The building smelled suspiciously like vinegar—or was it urine? The door Sean was shoving open had a gaping hole between two of the four planks. Once, it had probably been painted green.

Now, it was an ugly shade of gray in most places and a natural hue everywhere else.

Sean stepped aside and looked at her, trying to meet her eyes. "It's not much…but it's a good place to hide," he said slowly.

Eleanor refused to look at him. She walked past him, careful not to let her petticoat brush him, and paused in the center of the sparsely furnished room. Sean followed her in and shut the door, bolting it twice.

They had been traveling since the very early morning. Although Eleanor had not believed she would ever rest, she had fallen asleep almost from the very moment she had lain down and wrapped what was left of her wedding dress around her. She had slept deeply and dreamlessly, in exhaustion. The arrangement had been for Sean to stand guard for two hours and then to take his turn sleeping while she stayed awake, taking the next watch, but he had not awakened her until it was time to leave.

If he wanted gratitude, he was not going to get it. He wasn't a gentleman and he had proven it by not even considering marriage to her. He had used her body; he had made that very clear. She was never going to understand why he had come back to take her with him, and maybe it was better that she didn't. She finally understood. The man she had loved her entire life was gone. Some dark and even dangerous stranger was in his place, someone with no respect for ladies and no respect for her.

Eleanor was numb. She glanced around at the interior of the room. A tin sink was on one planked wall. There was a cast-iron stove and a basket of kindling beside it, a small cabinet above. A small rickety table and two equally spindly chairs were in the room's center, carved from cheap, pale pine. On the opposite wall was a single bed, with a red blanket and some sheets that had once been white and were now beige. Facing the door was a dirty window with faded muslin curtains, and there was one rack of pegs, from which hung a gentleman's suit, complete with waistcoat and ruffled shirt. Socks and shoes sat on the floor beneath it. The well-tailored ensemble was incongruous with the rest of the room.

"I know...you've never been...in a hovel," Sean said tersely, "but it won't be for long."

Eleanor limped over to the window and saw one of the channels of the River Lee. There were a few small barges in the river and one sloop with passengers, about to disembark from a dock. A few street vendors were on the quay, and one horse and cart was passing by. She turned away from the rather charming scene, taking a chair at the table and sitting down. As she removed her very dirty shoes, she debated ignoring him for the rest of their time together, especially as he seemed to want her attention now. But such behavior was very childish, especially when she wanted to answer him, so she finally looked at him.

He was staring at her with such intensity that she was taken aback. But the moment she met his gaze, he glanced away, his long, dark lashes fluttering over his eyes. Why had he been staring at her in such a way?

And her foolish heart turned over, hard. She inhaled. This man was a stranger, someone she did not know—someone she did not wish to know. "Yes, I cannot forget. You are sending me home, at once. And when will that be?" How bitter she sounded!

He folded his arms across his chest, which, in spite of his lean frame, remained broad and hard. Eleanor wished she hadn't noticed. "As soon as possible... I can't send you home...with anyone, Elle." He flushed. "Eleanor," he corrected himself. "I have to arrange for an escort I can trust... someone to guard you with his life."

So it was Eleanor now, she thought grimly. "And before I go, are you going to give me precise instructions as to how to delude Peter into thinking I am a virgin?" How cool and unshaken she sounded.

He flinched, his color crimson now. "Yes." He turned his back to her, hands shoved deep in the pockets of his cloth breeches.

"Maybe you had better instruct me now," she snapped. "Are you an expert in the subject of taking innocence and then educating the object of your previous affections in the art of pretense and theater?"

He faced her. "I understand...you are angry with me. You have cause!"

"I'm not angry." She smiled coldly and stood. "I have realized you are right. You have changed. Sean O'Neill is dead. As soon as possible, I should like to go home to my fiancé. I was in love before you came back, and I do not know what possessed me to look at a man like you even twice."

He paled.

She had wanted to wound Sean, and she still knew him well enough to know that she had done just that. She saw the hurt in his eyes. She should not care. It was time to go home and marry Sinclair. But, dear God, she could not help feeling that Sean had suffered enough.

His face had become a mask with no expression. He strode to the stove and began placing kindling in it.

It was cool in the room; she did not object. She saw that he was tense and angry. Eleanor wished she hadn't spoken so cruelly. She stood. "Can I help?"

"No." He used flint to light the fire and once it was burning, firmly closed the door to the stove. He did not look at her now, as he walked to a chair, pulled it away from the table, and sat down. The instant he did so, he shoved out his long legs and his head fell back. In that moment, Eleanor realized he was exhausted.

He had escaped prison just a few days ago and ever since, he had been running from his pursuers. The night before last, he had slept in the woods and last night, he had stayed up all night, watching for troops. She didn't want to feel sorry for him but it was obvious that he had no physical resources left. Eleanor hesitated, her gaze taking in every feature of his face; finally, his expression was relaxed. Her glance slid down the hard line of his throat and then to the even harder planes of his chest, rib cage and torso. The soft white shirt he wore clung.

His eyes opened, meeting hers.

She knew she flushed. "You must be tired. Why don't you take your boots off? I will keep watch." She didn't smile at him. But she was a compassionate woman and she couldn't treat Sean any differently than she would someone else in his position.

He hadn't moved from the slumped position he had assumed but his eyes remained on her now. And then he straightened, lifting one leg and reaching for his boot. He grunted.

Eleanor turned away, wanting to help him but reminding herself that he was a cad and a rogue with no conscience. *I am afraid...for you!* She didn't know why he was afraid for her, when he was the one in trouble, and she did not want to remember him saying so.

Eleanor suddenly realized that Sean was struggling to pull off his boot. He had turned as white as a sheet, sweat was dripping from his brow and he looked as if he were in pain. She could not help herself. She strode to him. "I'll do it," she said.

Their gazes collided; he glanced instantly away. "Thank you."

Facing him, she took hold of his boot and pulled as hard as she could. The boot came off but Sean gasped, blanching impossibly.

She instantly saw why. His socks were tattered rags and his feet were bloody and swollen. What had she been thinking? He had been in a prison cell for two years. He wasn't used to walking and he wasn't used to wearing boots. And she had been complaining about her three paltry blisters. "Sean," she managed to whisper, instantly aching for him.

His color was returning. He peeled off the bloody

sock, tossing it aside, and set his foot down. He reached for the other boot—she stopped his hand. "I'll do it," she said, her stomach churning.

He lifted his gaze; their eyes met and this time, they held. "Be quick."

She nodded, pulling off the other boot. This time he didn't make a sound. Eleanor knelt at his feet, removing the other bloody sock. "I need to get some water. Do we have soap?" She looked up.

He had his head thrown back and he was breathing hard. It was a moment before he spoke and he didn't glance at her. "I am fine." His shirt was wet with sweat now, too. Unfortunately she could see every clearly defined plane and line in his muscular chest and torso.

She looked away, fighting to control her fear. "You are hardly fine. And unless you want a serious infection, your feet need to be tended to, Sean." She was silent for a moment. "Why didn't you say something?"

He finally looked down at her. "I had other things on my mind." He started to stand.

She shoved him back into the chair. "I'll get the water and soap. Just sit still."

He made no comment, so she stood, seized a pail by the sink, where a bar of brown lye soap lay, and left the flat. There was a small yard behind the shop with a pump. Eleanor filled the bucket quickly, worried about being seen; but no one was in the yard. If his feet had suffered so terribly in the past few days, what other ailments did he have? She had noticed that his stride had changed, that he didn't move with the same agility that he once had. She realized that every muscle he had was undoubtedly stiff and strained.

When she entered the flat, he was in the chair, his head thrown back, soundly asleep.

In that moment, she forgot about being hurt, rejected, cast aside. She forgot about being angry. She was terribly worried about him and there was no way to fight it or her feelings. He was exhausted, hurt, and wounded somewhere deep and dark in his soul. How could she remain angry at him? If she didn't help him, who would?

As she knelt before him, she wondered where that left them. But there was no *them,* she thought as she began to carefully wash his feet. He had made that clear—and he was right. He had changed enough that there would never be a *them.* They were never going to leap off bridges and cliffs together again. They were never going to toil in a field side by side, or whitewash a wall together and then furiously paint fight. Suddenly she paused, unbearably saddened.

Her best friend was gone—and so was the man she loved. She could never forgive him for using her as he had, even if she had encouraged it. But she was going to prevent an infection, and she was also going to help him escape the country with his life.

Eleanor finished washing his feet and looked up. He remained deeply asleep, despite the stiff wood-framed chair and the uncomfortable position that he was in. And in sleep, she had the opportunity to study him. His face might be leaner now, and he had the scar on his right cheek, but his features remained very much the same, hard and handsome, at once painfully and wonderfully familiar. Staying true to her new course and new beliefs was not going to be easy, she realized grimly.

She tossed the rag she had been using in the now soiled water and stood. "Sean?" She took his hand. "Sean, go to bed." He did not stir. "Sean?"

His eyes drifted open and he gazed at her without focus.

"Come to bed," she said firmly, tugging on him.

His mouth shifted, the corners lifting. *"Elle."*

He was barely awake and she knew it. But the murmur had been a seductive invitation she recognized instantly. *And he had smiled.* Her heart exulted. She hadn't seen him smile even once since he had come home, but now, unguarded in his exhaustion, he had tried to do just that.

She would give anything to make him smile again. If she could, would the old Sean return to her?

He was standing, his hand still in hers. Eleanor tensed as his sleepy gaze drifted down to her mouth and slid slowly over her chest. Had he reached out and caressed her, her response could not have been greater. Her blood raced, her skin hummed. And his lips turned up again, his hooded gaze lingering on her hips. Before Eleanor could react, his arm slipped around her waist. He pulled her to his side, against his hard body. Eleanor had stiffened, some alarm rising—and with it, inescapable urgency.

"Come with me," he whispered, moving to the bed and as he lay down, he pulled her down with him.

Somehow she was in bed with him, in his arms. She could not do this, she thought in alarm. Yet her body had stirred, the pulse between her thighs surging. Eleanor knew he was dreaming, or caught between waking and sleep, and if she did succumb to temptation, she was going to regret it. She could not be used again, even if she wanted him desperately.

"Elle." He sighed her name, his hands closing over the back of her head, in her hair. His leg covered hers and he pressed his mouth to her lips. Eleanor's body burst into flames while she waited for his assault. It did not come. His hands slid down her back and he pulled her close while his lips brushed hers, soft, gentle and questing. Eleanor felt her body hollow, the desire so overpowering it was enough to make the room tilt and spin. And then his mouth stilled.

She stared and saw that he was deeply asleep. She hesitated, remaining in his arms, because she didn't want to move away. She shifted and tugged one arm free and lifted her hand, cupping his rough cheek. Too late, love swelled. It was never going to be over, she thought, and she was caught between elation and despair. But did she love a man who existed, or the ruined remains of one? In that frightening moment, she wasn't sure she could distinguish between the old Sean and the man lying in bed with her.

But because she remained deeply in love with the old Sean, she lay in his arms, cherishing the interlude and knowing it was only that.

A few hours later, she slipped from the bed. Sean hadn't moved once since he had passed out. Eleanor went to the window. It was late afternoon now. She hadn't slept. Being with Sean was an emotional tug-of-war, and she did not know how much longer she could bear it. She was hungry, and their bread and cheese had run out that morning. However, she wasn't leaving Sean alone, and she wasn't going to wake him, either. She had the terrible comprehension that he wasn't going to find another moment to sleep for days. How much longer could he go on like this?

Suddenly she had the sensation of being observed. She shifted toward the bed. Sean lay on his side now, facing her, regarding her with watchful gray eyes.

"You're awake," she said. She smiled a little at him, her heart leaping in excitement she was not prepared for and did not want or need.

"How long did I sleep?" he asked, unmoving.

"Four or five hours. It's late— I heard the church bells toll five o'clock."

He suddenly sat up, throwing his legs over the side of the bed. He eyed her as he stood. If his feet hurt, he gave no sign. "Did you go out?"

She shook her head.

Sean crossed the room to retrieve his boots, taking the socks from the shoes beneath the rack of pegs.

Eleanor stared as he pulled on the clean socks. "Where are you going?" she asked with care. She did not like the idea of him going out.

He didn't look up at her. "We need food... linens...more clothes." He grimaced as he pulled on each boot.

Eleanor bit her lip. He needed to heal, not walk

around town in search of necessities while trying to elude any troops he might encounter from the city garrison. "I'll go."

He straightened. "No. You wait here."

She tried to smile at him. "I think you should rest." He had given the livery man one of her diamond earrings for Saphyr's feed and board. She reached for the other earring. "There's a chandler on the corner. It's not far. I'm sure I can buy bread and cheese there, maybe some bacon. Do we have a fry pan? I'll use my other earring—we'll have credit for months."

His silver gaze had locked on hers. "What is this?" he asked warily.

She knew exactly what he meant but pretended not to. A few hours ago, she had been furious with him, after all. "I feel fine and you do not. We have always looked out for one another. I'll go out. I need some air, anyway."

His eyes were wide. "You hated me…a few hours ago."

She had to face him now. "I don't think I ever hated you, Sean, and no matter how you have changed, there's no point in being at odds. The one thing we have always been is friends."

His eyes were wide. "You think to be…friends?"

She inhaled. If she made such an offer, would he

accept it? She knew she could not withstand another rejection now.

But he did not give her a chance to speak. "You forgive me?" He was disbelieving.

She hesitated. "If you are asking if I am forgiving you for treating me as you would a casual and inconsequential lover, for treating me as you did all those farmer's wives and daughters when we were growing up, then no, I am not forgiving you for that." She wet her lips. She had no anger left. In fact, she felt very much as if she had already forgiven him. "I'll get us some supper, Sean. And more socks."

"No." His tone was hard and final.

"Why not?" she cried in real despair.

"Why not?" he cried back. "There are troops... there is a garrison...west of town!"

He was upset and she could not understand him. "Why are you trying to protect me? You need protection, not I!"

"Do not let *anyone* in," he said. "Bolt the door." He threw both bolts and strode onto the cramped landing.

She didn't hesitate. She ran after him before he could shut the door. "What are you afraid of, Sean? I don't understand!"

His jaw flexed. "I told you! No matter what I

say...you say...they will charge you as my accomplice."

He frightened her with his determination. *I must protect you!* he had exclaimed yesterday. "No one," she said slowly, "is going to accuse me of anything other than being rash and foolish, and certainly not of being your accomplice. Yesterday you said you wanted to protect me. I am not in danger, Sean. You are the one in danger."

"You are foolish now! You have conspired with me...that is treason! You will not go to prison...for *my* sins." His eyes blazed.

She became still, alarmed. Why would he speak about sins? And her intuition told her that she had found the terrible root of his wounds. "You mean crimes. You mean you do not want me to pay for your *crimes*. No one will try to make me pay for what you have done, Sean."

He turned away, trembling, and hefted the bucket. "I'll be back with water." He paused before leaving. "Bolt the door, Eleanor." He went out.

She barely heard him. Even having changed into such a dark man, his words were odd. Sean was not fervently or fanatically religious. She knew he believed in God—most men and women did. She did not think he would ever refer to the deaths of soldiers, committed in the cause of patriotism, as sins. But she reminded herself that she was thinking about Sean, the man he had once been—not the man he was now.

Her mind was drawing conclusions now, rapidly. Sean had become hard and withdrawn, he had become cold and angry. There was no more doubt in her mind that he was different. But he was not unrecognizable. Some parts of the man she once loved remained. It was dangerous to understand that, but she did—yet she would not fall victim to that comprehension, not now and not ever again.

The logic was inescapable. If Sean had referred to his crimes as sins, he was blaming himself for something terrible. Was this the cause of the changes in him?

He suddenly strode into the room with the water, and he was angry. "You didn't bolt the door!"

She hesitated, steeling her heart against him. She needed to know what had happened; she needed to know everything. "You were only gone for a moment."

"I told you...bolt the door!"

She wasn't going to argue about disobeying him. The question was there, on the tip of her tongue, and she could not help herself. "Why did you say sins instead of crimes?"

And he looked away, instantly. "It was a mistake." He shrugged, eyeing her now through lowered lashes.

"I don't think it was a slip of the tongue."

Now, when he looked at her, it was with that blank stare he had perfected.

Eleanor wet her lips. "Something happened. Something terrible—to someone. But it wasn't a soldier. You would not blame yourself for a battlefield death."

He was still, but briefly, his eyes widened with surprise. "I don't know what you mean."

Eleanor knew she had stumbled onto the truth.

He strode to the door as if to leave, but she did not move out of his way.

"Excuse me," he said harshly. His eyes were hot with anger and they flashed at her now.

She wasn't really afraid of him, and not enough to move out of his way or to back down. "It might help to talk about it," she said, very cautiously.

"No. I am going to get food and clothes."

"Is this why you've changed? Because you've kept some deep, dark secret—some sin that you've committed?" she cried.

"Don't," he said, seizing her arm.

His grip hurt and she paled. He instantly realized it and released her. Eleanor rubbed her arm, but her eyes remained on him. "Let me help you," she whispered. And she lifted her hand to touch his cheek.

He threw her hand aside. It was a moment before he could speak. "You can't…. No one can." And he slammed out of the room.

This time, she bolted the door behind him.

CHAPTER ELEVEN

ELEANOR'S ANXIETY increased. Sean had been gone for well over an hour. It could not take that long to go to the chandler on the corner for food and some other supplies. She stood barefoot at the room's single window, having changed into the breeches and ruffled shirt, so that she could watch for him. From where she stood, she could see down the wide cobbled street that ended at the Custom House, where both channels of the river met. There, numerous vessels were at berth. Most seemed to be fishing boats and barges. However, staring south where the river widened, heading toward Great Island, she saw the three larger masts of a frigate. Eleanor knew enough about ships to know that this was a fighting vessel with guns. As there was a naval base in Cobh, she assumed the battleship belonged to His Majesty's Royal Navy. The sight of the forbidding ship was more cause for concern.

Eleanor turned to glance down at the street where the cobbler had his shop. Sean was nowhere in sight. Like most Irish cities, Cork dated back to medieval times, if not beyond, but the quay was wide and lined with stucco buildings, some yellow, some green, all two stories high. Clotheslines had been passed back and forth from window to window, as if the street were decorated with flags and pennants, not shirts and stockings. Shops lined the street, and a few pedestrians were passing by, in no apparent hurry. Eleanor saw a miller's, an apothecary shop, a tailor's, another cobbler shop and a chairmaker's. From where she stood, she could not see the farthest corner, where the chandler was.

What was taking him so long?

Just as she became convinced that he was in trouble, she saw him coming up the street. Her heart leaped wildly, a response she refused to consider. But she was terribly relieved.

He was carrying several parcels. He was bringing food and more importantly, he was neither hurt nor captured. She almost smiled, but the expression never formed. He was not alone.

A small woman with a cap on her long, curly dark hair was walking alongside him, and they were clearly conversing.

And in that moment, every tryst he'd had while they were growing up came rushing to mind. Sean had been a rake as a young man, and only Cliff would have been able to compete for the honor of unabashed cad, had he not left home at fourteen. She also recalled his uncontrollable and explosive passion of the other night. He had been caged up in prison for two years—and now, some lightskirt was pursuing him.

She didn't have to hear what the woman was saying or even see her face to know that. Every instinct she had told her so.

They had paused on the street below, outside of the cobbler's shop and the entrance to the flat where Eleanor watched. The woman was plump and pretty and as she conversed, she kept touching Sean's arm. Eleanor could recognize a flirtation when she saw one. She knew exactly what was transpiring below her. If Sean hadn't taken this woman into his bed already, he would do so soon.

Eleanor gripped the sill, finding it hard to breathe. She could not possibly be jealous. She was returning home to marry Sinclair—she *wanted* to go home and marry him, because the man she really loved had changed so much that she simply could not be sure who was standing on the street below. But her reasoning did not ease her frantic emotions.

Feeling ill, she turned away from the scene, but only after Sean and the woman had parted company; the door below stairs thudding as it slammed closed.

"Elle."

Eleanor strode to the door. She paused there to take a deep breath, form a smile and calmly throw both bolts. She didn't care if he'd taken that woman to bed or intended to. The only thing that remained between them was an awkward friendship and an inescapable past. There was no future. She would ignore how saddened that comprehension made her, because it was a belief she must cling to at all costs.

He looked at her and started. "Are you all right?"

She smiled again. It felt brittle. "You were gone so long. I couldn't help but worry."

He gave her a guarded look and entered the flat. Eleanor closed the door, bolting it. He placed the paper sacks on the table while she watched. He cautiously said, "Come sit down. I'll bandage your feet."

"My feet are fine. You are the one who needs bandages. Who is your lady friend?" The words popped out and she was aghast. She felt her cheeks heat.

He straightened and their gazes clashed. "I beg your pardon?"

She bit her lip, wishing she could take the words back.

"Do you mean Kate?"

Eleanor hesitated and then shrugged as indifferently as possible.

"She's the cobbler's daughter," he said, turning and placing some items on the table. "I told her you are my sister." He seemed to avoid her gaze now.

"How convenient," she sniped unhappily.

He turned again, his gaze very hard to read. "I do not understand. She saw us come in. She is a bit…of a snoop. I had to tell her…something. I said your name was Jane." He added, "She thinks I am John Collins. Could you please sit down?"

Eleanor wanted to know if they had shared a bed. If they had been in *that* bed, she wasn't sleeping there ever again. It was not her affair, but she was hurt.

She turned away, restlessly pacing the room. How could she continue to have these feelings for Sean when he was such an enigma? It was one thing to want to help him heal his wounds and escape the authorities, but it was another to remain half in love with him—or the man he had become.

Sean's cheeks were flushed. "I didn't take her to bed…if that is what you are thinking."

He could still read her mind! "I'm not!" She smiled widely and sat down. "I didn't give it a thought." She shrugged as flippantly as possible.

Eleanor felt her color increasing. Finally, she dared to look up, and her breath became suspended. In that moment, she had not a doubt as to what *he* was thinking.

She forgot about Kate. Her stomach vanished into thin air, leaving a huge space inside that would so eagerly accept him. Sean's gaze slipped down her ruffled shirt just once before he turned away. He lifted a wrapped roll of linen. "Why don't..." He stopped. His voice was raw, but not from two years of disuse or any accident.

Eleanor was dismayed. She had no right to such a terrible hunger herself, and she understood. "I'll do it."

He nodded, handing her the linen without looking at her.

Eleanor took in the rigid lines of his body, and she unrolled the linen as he began to unpack their few groceries. The irony of the situation struck her, hard. She had been waiting for him to notice her as a woman for years, and now that he had, she was determined to fight his attraction and hers. It was beyond ironic, she realized. It was tragic.

Eleanor bandaged her other foot, feeling very self-conscious. The air in the room had become humid and thick. Now she began to think about the long night ahead of them and the fact that the flat had one bed.

"I bought a roast turkey dinner from the inn-keeper…around the block."

Finished, Eleanor straightened in her chair. No wonder he had been so long. He was careful not to look at her as he opened the small cupboard over the sink. Sean removed two plates, two tin mugs and some utensils. Eleanor saw a bottle of red wine on the table. The aromas wafting from the paper parcel, tied with string, were very enticing, but the tension in her body remained. She was in despair. She did not want to feel this way, not now and not ever.

He brought everything to the table. Eleanor stood and untied the parcel while Sean uncorked the wine. "Did you see any soldiers?" she asked, hoping to break the tension.

"No. There's a frigate in the island harbor…the HMS *Gallatine*."

They were almost on safer ground, Eleanor thought. "Do you know the ship?" She served herself, not daring to look up at him.

The cork popped loudly in the too—small, too—silent flat. "Devlin engaged it years ago… captured her from the French. I asked…she's got thirty-two cannon. Tomorrow I may go look at her."

She was startled and not pleasantly so. "How does that affect you? What difference does it make if she has nine cannon or thirty?"

His gaze met hers, then danced away. "It only affects me...if she is chasing me when I set sail."

A new, different tension afflicted her. "Did you book a passage for yourself?"

"How can I do that?" He stared at her in some surprise. "You will return home first." Abruptly he reached for the wine and poured two glasses, then stopped. "I forgot. You don't drink."

"That's all right." She had never needed the effects of a glass of wine as badly as she did then.

He handed it to her; their hands brushed.

Eleanor felt as if he had pulled her into his arms, as if he had covered her mouth with his, and it was a moment before she could breathe. Her skin was on fire, and her flesh throbbed.

He turned his back to her, drinking from his own mug. She thought she saw a tremor pass through him, but she couldn't be sure. His back and shoulders were stiff with tension. She put her mug down, untouched. "I have been thinking about it."

Very warily, he faced her. "You've been thinking... about what?" His tone was as cautious.

"I think you should leave the country before I

return home. I want to know that you have escaped safely, with your life."

"Absolutely not!" he responded firmly without pause. She searched his silver eyes and saw sheer determination there.

He turned away, tossing the rest of his wine down with visible anger.

"Our friendship may have changed," Eleanor said quietly, "but once, we were close. Once, you were my hero. I owe you, Sean. How many times did you rescue me from myself when we were growing up? In good conscience, I cannot leave you here alone."

He stared at her, his gaze hard and wide. It was a moment before he spoke. "You don't owe me anything, Elle…Eleanor. I could never live with myself…if I let something happen to you…because of what I have done."

"You can't live with yourself now," she dared. And her heart broke. "Oh, Sean! What is it?"

He started, his entire body stiffening.

She realized what she had said, and also that she was right. "What could have happened to make you blame yourself, and perhaps hate yourself, so much? Why have you changed so much? Where is the man I loved and trusted?"

"We need to eat!" He jerked a chair from the table

and sat. Then he dug his fork into his food, shoveling bite after bite into his mouth.

She had hit a nerve. She was uncovering his feelings, but not the reason for them. She sat down. Sean was halfway through the huge plate. The compassion she was so afraid of now filled her. She had never seen anyone eat as quickly, except wild, starving dogs. "Sean, I won't pry anymore. Enjoy your meal," she whispered.

He paused, the fork halfway to his mouth. Then he laid it down and finished chewing. He looked up at her, his gaze disquieting and direct.

"Please." She attempted a smile and before she knew it, she had lightly grasped his forearm. Her heart lurched wildly at the feel of so much power and strength, and she quickly slid her hand away.

His face was hard. He stared at the table, his plate or her hand, she could not tell. He lifted his fork and as she wasn't expecting him to speak, his words surprised her. "You always snooped. Spied." He continued to stare at the table—or into their past. His mouth softened. "You were impossible...I had no secrets."

She shivered. "I didn't mean to be so annoying. I loved you so! I had to be with you all the time—I couldn't stop myself."

His cheeks were pink. He never raised his eyes. "So impossible," he said softly.

She studied him as a silence fell. Was he reliving parts of their past? She trembled, desperately hoping so. In spite of the dire crisis they were in, she would give up everything to have the old Sean back.

She wet her lips. "But you rescued me anyway, all the time, even when my life wasn't in danger."

He made a sound, and it almost resembled a grudging laugh. "Yes. I did."

"Remember when you told me not to go in the lake, as it had rained for an entire week? Of course, I did not listen."

He slowly lifted his gaze. "You *never* listened."

"I got caught in some branches and I would have drowned, but you dived in to save me." She smiled. "I was eight or nine."

"Ten," he corrected. "You were ten, because I was sixteen."

She instantly understood. "How could I forget? The new governess was blond and beautiful and you were in her bed the moment she came to Adare!"

He just stared at her.

Eleanor was aware of the tension instantly changing, becoming hot and sexual. Her heart had picked up a slow, heavy beat. "She was slender and for a woman, tall."

His lashes drifted down.

She stared at him now. Sean had been besotted with Lady Celia that summer and, at ten years of age, his infatuation with the slightly older woman had been entertaining in every possible way. As Eleanor was now, Celia had been dark blond, slender and tall. Eleanor tried to tell herself not to read too much into that slight coincidence.

"You should eat," he said.

She had watched him dancing with her outside on the terrace while a midsummer ball was in progress, inside. They had been so engrossed, they had never noticed her spying from the shadows. "Were you in love?"

He shrugged. "I was always in love…it never lasted."

She met his unwavering, too bright gaze. "Then it wasn't love. True love never dies."

He made a slight and harsh sound again. "I was sixteen."

She smiled. "And when I was sixteen, Mother and Father forced me to come out. Do you remember that?"

His mouth twitched. "I felt so sorry for you."

"No one was sorrier than I!" she cried, then sobered. She had hated her Season in London and she had hated being sent to Bath, too. It had been a blur of misery and constraints; for her, coming out had been a prison, too.

But Sean had rescued her even then. She suddenly looked up and found him watching her closely and steadily. Her insides shifted. "Sean, you came down to London for my coming-out ball. God, I haven't thought about that in years. It was so awful!"

He glanced away. "I am sorry," he said slowly, "that I made fun of you in your gown."

She had forgotten. Her first ball gown had been very beautiful, but she had felt like a tall, skinny fool in it—she *had* been tall and skinny, then. Sean had laughed at her and she had punched him in the stomach, hard enough to cause him to gasp in pain and double over. She had hated him for that one moment, because he was right—a ball gown hadn't changed who she was. But when he had asked her for her very first dance, when he had escorted her onto the floor, her arm linked firmly in his, she had been both grateful and proud. She had missed some steps, but he had guided her through the figure so adroitly that no one had known. She had been terrified to begin the dance, but in the end, she had enjoyed herself.

"You danced with me," she said slowly. Her heart turning over too many times to count, she added, "And now I know exactly why I have always loved you so much."

He stood. "Eat."

She shook her head, shoving the plate aside. She also stood. "Sean, I need you. You have to come back to me the way you used to be."

He moved away, shaking his head fiercely.

"Please!" she cried. "We need to speak about the past like this. We need to go to Askeaton together and wander upstairs. Devlin never finished the third floor."

He was incredulous—or afraid.

"We can finish those last few rooms together. And whatever is bothering you will go away, I just know it!"

"It will never…go away!" He exploded in bursts of words. "Stop begging me…for what I don't have…to give!"

"I am not asking for your love," she exclaimed fiercely. "I can forsake your love. I can! But I want you back, damn it!"

He held his hand up, warding her off.

"No!" She strode to face him, pausing so close that his hand almost touched her nose. "No, you can't raise your hand and send me away as if I am a ghost haunting you. I am not haunting you, but God knows, something or someone else is. I *know* I can help."

He was breathless now. "Some secrets…are meant to be…secrets. I have changed. Prison does that to a man!"

"How bad was it?" She had to know. "Is that what happened to your voice? Is that why you are so thin?"

"It was bad…very bad…like being buried alive in a black hole."

She didn't understand. Surely he wasn't speaking literally?

"You have changed…. And you belong to someone else…. I have changed—I am a criminal… fleeing to America."

"There's one thing that will never change."

He looked at her as if he did not want to hear what was coming next.

"We can't change the past. We can't change *our* past. You are different now. It took a very painful lesson for me to learn that. But the past remains—and we share it. I don't want to forget it. I will never forget it. And if I can help you heal your wounds, if I can help you return to me, then I am going to do just that."

"No." He whirled and started for the door

She ran after him, because she had to know. "Sean, you didn't mean that you were really imprisoned in a hole, did you?" She was ill with dread.

He turned and stared at her.

"Oh, my God," she gasped, shocked, because the answer was not just in his refusal to speak, it was in his eyes. "You were in a pit—for two years?"

"It doesn't matter," he rasped.

"It matters to me!" He was even more deeply scarred than she had thought. But the physical horrors he had suffered had to pale in comparison to the guilt he was afflicted with. "I am sorry, so sorry," she tried.

"Don't." He reached for the door.

She seized his arm. "I know you are not a coward, yet you are running away from me, and from something and someone else. That's it, isn't it? You are running away, not from the British, but from whatever it is that you blame yourself for!"

He faced her, shaking her off. "You should hate me for what I did the other night."

"Oh, so now you try to change the subject? The subject isn't your taking my innocence—which I freely offered and gave. The subject is your running away now, from me, yourself and whatever you think you did."

He stabbed at the air and turned to unbolt the door.

Her anger vanished. "Sean, stop. Where are you going?"

He leaned his forehead against the door, breathing hard.

"I'll cease and desist. But my feelings won't change."

He made a harsh, disparaging sound.

"It's not safe to keep going out and you know it," she added firmly. "We are in *hiding*."

He turned away from the door. "You eat and sleep.... I'll keep watch."

She smiled a little at him. "Very well." But as she sat down at the table, aware of Sean crossing to stand by the window, her mind was not on her supper. He was running, not from her but from himself, and she was going to somehow stop that flight. She was going to find the man she loved, and bring him back to life.

A SMALL FIRE BURNED in the iron stove, but otherwise, the flat was entirely dark. They had taken turns sleeping this time; Eleanor had insisted on it. It was the darkest and earliest point of the morning, perhaps an hour or so before dawn's first light. Sean was soundly asleep in the room's single bed. Eleanor sat by the window, but as the street below was entirely dark, there was simply nothing to see. She didn't mind. She had rested well and she was very pleased that she had managed to convince Sean to take a turn in the bed. She knew he remained exhausted, because the minute he had lain down, he had become utterly still, clearly falling asleep in that single moment.

She was glad to have some solitude; now, she could think carefully and she could plan.

Sean had been cruelly imprisoned in solitary confinement in a pit. Whenever she thought about it, she ached, and she had never hated the British forces more. One day, someone was going to pay for what they had done to Sean. Her mind was made up.

But that was the past. If she was really going to make every effort to resurrect the old Sean, she certainly wasn't going home anytime soon. She sensed she was making progress. Every moment they spent together was raising old and important memories. He was beginning to welcome them and he was beginning to smile.

Their past was going to pave the way for their future; it had to. And even if he never loved her the way she had always wanted him to, she would settle for far less now. She was committed and determined. One way or another, she was going to help Sean heal his wounds and find himself again.

She stole another glance at him as he slept. It was hard not to watch him, and when she did, her heart stirred with so much longing and so much love. His chest was rising and falling in a slow, even manner and he hadn't moved a muscle since first falling into the bed.

But watching him while he slept had other effects on her, too. He was dying inside from guilt, self-loathing and God only knew what else, but he remained the most virile, attractive man she had ever seen. Now she was intimately familiar with his long lean body, and when she thought about the brief interlude of passion that they had shared, her mouth became dry and her body quickened. She was always going to desire him and that desire would always feel explosive, she thought. But because she was making a bargain with herself and God, if He was listening, she would have to control that longing.

Suddenly he stirred on the bed. Eleanor thought he might be waking up.

He thrashed restlessly and muttered something in his sleep.

He was dreaming. She decided not to disturb him and turned back to the window, finally noticing a gray finger of light in the dark sky.

Sean cried out.

Alarmed, Eleanor turned, only to see that he was apparently still dreaming. Sweat was shining on his brow and his shirt was wet, molding to his hard frame. In concern, she stood, trying to decide whether to wake him or not.

He began sobbing. "No."

Eleanor froze at the sound of broken male weeping. And then she hurried over to him, aghast. "Sean." She laid her hand on his shoulder.

But he was still now, his breathing deep and even once again. His cheeks were damp with tears, however. What had he been dreaming about? What had he been crying over? It had only been a dream, but there was no doubt in her mind of his torment. Whatever haunted him in his waking hours was haunting him in his sleep, too.

She hesitated, then gave in to every urge she had. She sat down by his hip and took his hands in hers. Comforting him was a double-edged sword and she wet her lips before saying his name, the need to slip into his bed with him stunning her. If she dared, she would put her arms around him and hold him close, but only to comfort him. She was afraid her treacherous mind and body would attempt far more.

His hand covered hers, grasping her tightly. "Elle!"

Eleanor started, because his cry was one of alarm and fear and even panic. "Sean, wake up," she began.

"No! Elle, damn it, not you, it's Peg!" Suddenly he threw her hand away, shooting to a sitting position, his face blanching. His gaze was horrified but unfocused.

And she clasped his shoulder to comfort him, but her mind raced. *Who was Peg?* Had she even heard him correctly? Was he dreaming about another woman?

Suddenly his gaze met hers. He was turning an odd, sickly shade of green. He leaped from the bed and ran to the opposite side of the room, where he retched into a chamber pot.

Eleanor became very still, hugging herself.

He continued to retch, the heaves now dry.

She slid from the bed, too concerned to be afraid of his rejection. Eleanor went to him and laid her hand gently on his back as he knelt over the chamber pot. "Sean, it's all right. It's me, Elle. You were having a terrible dream, but it's over now."

He remained kneeling, breathing hard. Tension had turned his back into an unyielding knot of muscles.

"Sean?"

He breathed again. "I hear you." Another ragged breath. "I'm fine."

He wasn't fine but she did not say so.

"Elle, give me a moment. Please," he said harshly.

She nodded and moved away, so he could recover his composure and clean up.

He stood, staggering a little, as if on a storm-tossed ship and not quite balanced. Then he went to the sink. She carefully avoided watching him now while her mind raced with possibilities. He washed his mouth out with wine. She saw him use his sleeve to wipe the leftover tears from his face.

What did a woman named Peg have to do with her, with them and with his recent past?

He slowly turned to face her, staring. "It was just a dream.... I must have eaten rotten food.... Did you get sick?" Only then did he look away, indicating that the conversation was a ruse.

He was clever, but not as astute as she. "No. I suppose I am fortunate. Can I go downstairs and get some fresh water for you? We need more water anyway." She smiled as if nothing had happened.

"I'll go."

"Sean." She approached. "What were you dreaming about?"

He froze. "I don't recall."

"You called my name."

He turned red but didn't look her way. "I don't remember."

Eleanor inhaled and touched his sleeve. "Sean, who is Peg?"

He seemed stunned.

She swallowed. "I heard you call out to a woman named Peg."

"It was a dream," he cried.

"I know. But it upset you, and we dream about our lives sometimes—"

He cut her off rudely. "I don't know anyone named Peg." He removed both bolts from the locks and left.

Eleanor realized that he remained highly distressed. He had forgotten to close the door, but she made no move to do so. Sean was lying. She had seen the lie in his eyes. He knew who Peg was—he just didn't want to tell her.

She felt real dread. What had happened to him, to make him dream so graphically and with so much anguish? And who was this other woman? Was he weeping because of her? Did he love this woman?

Eleanor was stricken by the possibility. She didn't bother to try to tell herself that he could love someone else and it wouldn't matter. Nothing would be as hurtful. Nothing he had done could hurt as much. All she had been feeling would be pitiful in comparison to what she would feel then. Sean belonged to *her,* even if he never loved her back. There *couldn't* be another woman—it was beyond impossibility.

But she had to recover her own composure. She couldn't help him if she remained so shaken. A part of her wanted to forget she had ever heard him cry out another woman's name; another part of her was determined to find out the truth about Peg.

She was so afraid.

Sean returned with two buckets of water. He kicked the door closed, then placed both pails by the sink. "It's almost light out. Do you want some fresh scones?" he asked quietly, as if she had never caught him dreaming, weeping and vomiting afterward.

Succulent aromas were drifting up from the bakery down the street. "I'm not hungry."

He glanced at her, then quickly looked away. Walking over to the window, his hands deep in the pockets of his breeches, he stared outside.

Eleanor's heart began to thunder inside of her chest. Very carefully, she said, "Do you often have nightmares?"

He turned, leaning against the wall. "No."

"That's a relief." She wet her lips, aware of his second lie in as many minutes. "Sean, do you really think the British are looking for you so far south? You said the prison you escaped from was in Drogheda."

He folded his arms across his chest. "The prison was south of Drogheda," he said. "What are you trying to ask me?"

So much for discretion, she thought. "I was just wondering," she began, "if you were in prison for two years, where were you the other two years?"

His eyes widened. "I was in a village...you wouldn't know it."

He was reluctant to discuss those two years with her. More dread came. "Maybe I would..."

"You wouldn't. What is it that you want to know?" He stared coldly now.

She hugged herself. Their gazes held. "I think… you know."

He turned away rigidly. "I have no idea," he finally said.

"You were gone for four years!" she cried. "Being in prison these past two years explains half of your absence. What were you doing the other two years?"

He faced her. "You should give up."

"Why?"

He shook his head.

"Why?" she cried.

"You won't like…the answer!" he shouted, agonized.

She had known it. She had simply known it, from the moment she had heard him cry out another woman's name. "You were with Peg."

"Stop," he demanded. "Just stop!"

"Were you? Was there another woman? *Is* there another woman?" she demanded, shocked.

"I was helping them—that's all!" he cried back. "Why do you still…snoop…and pry? Why, damn it?"

He had spent two years helping some other woman? Helping her do what? She was stricken and Sean knew, because he went to her, clearly fighting his own temper. When he had regained some composure, he said harshly, "It doesn't matter, Elle.... You are going home to Sinclair.... I am going to America."

"It matters," she managed. "It matters very much." She seized his arm. "Did you love her?"

He flinched.

And Eleanor saw that her fears had been right.

"No," he said, stunning her. He spoke slowly now. "No, I did not."

CHAPTER TWELVE

"THIS IS IMPOSSIBLE," Tyrell said, pacing. "I am sitting here in my home doing nothing, while Eleanor and Sean are out there, somewhere, Sean fleeing for his very life."

He paused in front of the hearth, where his wife was seated on the sofa with the countess. Lizzie stood and went to him. "Rex is in Cork—he sent word. Cliff should be there by the morning. Your father is halfway to London to petition for a pardon. Ty, someone has to be here."

"I realize the earldom supercedes everything— believe me, I do." He was bitter. "Duty traps me once again, it seems."

Lizzie exchanged a look with the countess. "I know you would prefer to gallop to Cork and search every shop and house there by yourself, but the earldom does take precedence. Sean would not want you to involve yourself and, in doing so, jeopardize all this family has and stands for."

"Devlin has gone to Cobh to make his purchase," the countess remarked. Her face was pale with strain and fatigue.

"And if his part in this is ever discovered, Dev has everything to lose, as well," Tyrell said fervently. "As for my dear friend McBane, I could strangle his scrawny neck for waiting an entire afternoon before telling us what he knew!"

"He is a traitor, too." Lizzie defended her brother-in-law. "You should be thanking him for helping Sean in the first place, when he did not even know who he was."

"Thank God for Rory," the countess whispered. "Lizzie, how is your sister managing?"

Lizzie's sister, Georgina, was married to McBane. "She is remarkably calm. I feel certain that Georgie has had prior knowledge of Rory's clandestine affairs." Lizzie went to her mother-in-law and took her hand. "They are all strong, determined, brave men. Oh, Mary, I know what you must be feeling, I do, because I love Eleanor dearly and having heard so much about Sean, I love him, too! Our men will save the day. You must believe it, for I do."

Mary embraced her. "The day you became my

daughter was the biggest blessing our family has ever had," she said.

"Finally, something I can agree with," Tyrell stated.

A knock sounded on the door. Tyrell turned. "Enter," he said tersely.

A servant bowed. "My lord, a Colonel Reed is here to speak with you. He claims the matter is an urgent one."

Tyrell glanced at his wife and mother. "Send him in."

"That won't be necessary." A handsome blond officer in the blue uniform of the Light Dragoons strode briskly in, his blue gaze hard and cold. "Lord de Warenne, we meet at long last." He bowed. Some sarcasm clung to his words.

"Colonel," Tyrell said cautiously. He turned to face the ladies. "We should like a private moment."

"Of course." Lizzie smiled at him and taking the countess's arm, they hurried out.

"Would you like any refreshments?" Tyrell asked politely, very wary now. He had never heard of this officer and did not know him. He was afraid that any news he might be bringing would be unfortunate. "Wine, scotch, a whiskey?"

"No, thank you." Reed smiled, a mere curving of

his thin lips. "I am here in regards to the escaped convict, Sean O'Neill."

Tyrell was instantly furious at his brother being referred to in such a condemning and frankly disrespectful manner, but he merely inclined his head. Losing his temper would not help Sean, and he would do everything in his power to help him now. "Obviously." His tone was calm, quiet. "Is there news?"

"No. The hunt continues. I should like you to tell me what you know."

"What I know?" It became much harder to control his temper, as anger turned to rage. "My stepbrother was imprisoned for two years and this family was never apprised of it. What I know?" he repeated coldly. "My stepbrother was convicted of treason—yet this family never knew of any trial. I know nothing, sir."

"I am sure the army has already apologized to your family for the breach of etiquette."

Tyrell tried to breathe. "Losing my stepbrother in a prison—leaving him in solitary confinement for two years—is hardly a breach of etiquette."

Reed sighed. "Yes, it was terribly bungled, was it not? I am not here to defend the prison system in Ireland. Did O'Neill contact you after escaping?" Reed stared.

"No."

"But he was here yesterday. Three hundred guests saw him."

"I saw him, as well. That was, frankly, the first time I saw Sean in four years." Tyrell realized that he needed a drink and he poured himself a stiff Irish whiskey.

"So you did not know he was living in Kilvore, prior to the rebellion there?"

"I was informed of that only recently, after Sean's escape. I do not know the village."

"It is a small farming village in the midlands, south of Drogheda. And when O'Neill married, he did not write a letter to you or anyone in your family to share the happy news?'

Tyrell was genuinely stunned. "He is married?" And all he could think of in that moment was Eleanor. She would be devastated when she learned of this.

"I see you are surprised."

"None of us have heard from him, not since he left home, and that was four years ago. Colonel Reed, you seem like a reasonable and astute man. There may have been a rising in Kilvore, but I can assure you that my stepbrother was not involved. He has been part of the aristocracy here in Ireland since the day my father married his mother, when he was a small child. Someone else led those peasants, sir." But the problem was that Sean had always been on the side of the farmer and the peasant. Tyrell feared the worst.

Reed's pale brows lifted. "But he is not a nobleman, now is he? His father leased land from Adare, did he not? The family is Catholic, are they not? There are no titles, and other than what Sir Captain O'Neill has amassed for himself in his naval career, there is no wealth."

"Is there a point that you wish to make? My stepbrother was raised in a bedroom just down the hall from my own, sir, and he has enjoyed every privilege that I have. My brother is innocent of treason, sir. Someone else led the villagers."

Reed smiled coldly. "I can assure you that he led the villagers. I was there, Lord de Warenne."

Tyrell stiffened in dread. "You must be mistaken." *But this was what he had secretly feared.*

"You are very loyal. But then, the Irish are a loyal lot, Catholic or Protestant, are they not?"

Tyrell was precariously close to losing his temper now. "Do not slander us, Colonel. Not here, when I am gracious enough to allow you into my home."

Reed was not taken aback. However, he apologized. "I do beg your pardon. That was not my intent." He was brusque. "Your sister, Lady Eleanor. I wish to speak with her."

"So do I. Unfortunately, as I am certain you know, she is not here." The change of topic relieved him.

"So she has not returned, after running away with your stepbrother?"

"She has not returned," he said flatly. How he rued the day he had not told Eleanor that Sean was an escaped felon. If he had told her, he might have realized beforehand what she would do when Sean came home, and half of this crisis would not exist. "And she has not *run away* with Sean. She has always been impulsive, sir. She has always been headstrong and rash. I feel certain that she was overjoyed to see Sean again, after four long years of separation, and that joy caused her to behave as she did. Her eagerness to speak with him would cause her to call out to him as she did. I am certain she did not think about her actions. She merely wished to see him and speak with him."

"Really? On her wedding day?" Reed almost laughed.

He kept his face still when he would have loved to smash the other man's nose. "Really. My sister happens to be in love with her fiancé. This is hardly a laughing matter, Colonel."

Reed remained amused. "I apologize. Do you

think she was in contact with O'Neill since his escape—before they *left* Adare together yesterday?"

"Are you calling my sister a traitor, sir?" Tyrell asked, becoming cold inside. And now he was afraid for Eleanor. This man was a threat, not just to Sean, but to Eleanor, as well.

Reed's smile vanished. "Of course not. But I should like to get all of my facts straight. Why would Lady Eleanor leave the wedding with her *stepbrother?*"

"I believe I have already explained that to you. And to answer your previous question, Colonel, my sister had not heard a single word from Sean in four years—not since the night he left his home."

"Then answer this—why did O'Neill take her with him?"

"I do not know," Tyrell said, and finally, he was speaking the truth. Sean's actions made no sense. "When they were growing up, Sean and Eleanor were inseparable, in spite of the seven-year difference in their ages."

"So they are very close," Reed remarked shrewdly.

"They *were* very close," Tyrell corrected.

A pause ensued. Then Reed said, "The gossip goes two ways. I have heard it said he has abducted her and will use her to get out of the country." Reed's stare became intent.

"My stepbrother is a gentleman, Colonel. He would never abduct his own sister."

"O'Neill is responsible for the deaths of seven soldiers, and a prison inmate. That, my lord, does not make a gentleman."

"Circumstances are extenuating. Sean is innocent of all the charges leveled against him. I know it." Tyrell stared at the officer in his most intimidating and condescending manner, when he knew nothing at all.

But Reed stared coolly back. "Others say Lady Eleanor is no genuine sister."

He tensed. "I beg your pardon?"

"I have heard it whispered, even in your stables, that Lady Eleanor is more than O'Neill's stepsister, and that she is in love with him."

"My sister is in love with your countryman, Lord Sinclair," Tyrell insisted, his eyes flashing. He must not allow Reed to ever learn the truth of Eleanor's great love for Sean.

Reed smiled, but his gaze was unflinching. "I suppose we shall see. If you learn of O'Neill's whereabouts, it is your duty as a British citizen to apprise me of it. I am certain you know that failure to do so would make you a conspirator to his crimes."

"I shall be the first to tell you where he is," Tyrell said, an outrageous lie.

Reed finally laughed, the sound flat and mirthless, and walked out.

Tyrell waited until he had heard the front door close. Then he kicked the door to the salon closed with all of his might and the wood cracked.

He was very grim. Sean was in dire jeopardy, but so was Eleanor.

Worse, Reed was a very dangerous adversary; Tyrell's every instinct told him that.

IT WAS ALMOST NOON. The sky outside was graying, threatening rain. Eleanor sat on the bed, hugging her knees to her chest. Sean had been gone for a few hours and she could not relax until he had safely returned. He had left the city to take a look at the frigate that remained hovering just past the city limits, and he had said he had other affairs to conduct.

She had been afraid to ask what those affairs were. But she knew, didn't she? He had to buy his passage to America and he also had to find an escort to take her home, never mind that she was not going to Adare now. She was not leaving Sean like this. *And what about Peg?*

She hugged her knees more tightly to her chest, aching with hurt. Who was this other woman who was so important to him that he dreamed of her? Had he spent the entire two years before his incarceration with her? Eleanor was so afraid. He had said he didn't love her, but that wasn't a relief.

She dreaded the truth but she had to know everything. She was determined to withstand whatever it might be. If she did not, how could she help him find his way back to the man he had once been? However, she was prepared for a battle. Sean did not want to discuss the past four years with her. He had made that terribly clear.

Outside, the skies broke open and it began to pour.

Eleanor ran to the window to close it. As she slammed it down, she saw Sean racing up the street and she sagged against the sill in real relief. A moment later he was banging on the door. She hurried to let him in.

He came inside, soaking wet. Eleanor closed and bolted the door behind him. She turned. "Are you all right?" she began, about to ask him where he had been. But she stopped.

He had shrugged his wet shirt off, revealing his beautiful, lean torso. But as he turned to drape the shirt over a chair, she was confronted with a dozen long, snakelike white scars on his back. She gasped, realizing that he had been brutally whipped.

He whirled in surprise.

She began to shake, she was so sick. "Sean! What happened?!"

He stood still, his surprise vanishing, his eyes becoming guarded. "You already know. I was in prison."

"They flogged you?" she cried.

He stared at her. "It doesn't matter…it was long ago." He turned away and she had to close her eyes, because the sight of his back hurt her so terribly. He put the shirt on the back of a chair and moved it closer to the stove.

Eleanor tried to calm herself but it was impossible. She didn't move away from the door. "Why were you flogged?"

He was at the sink, taking a cup of water from the pail. It was a moment before he answered. "It was a test."

"A *test?*"

He slowly faced her. *"It doesn't matter."*

"It matters to me!" she exclaimed.

His gaze was searching, and he sighed. "Elle, it was sport for the guards…the new inmate…the traitor that would soon hang."

She hugged herself. "There are so many scars," she whispered.

He didn't answer.

She bit her lip. "They picked on you, didn't they? It wasn't one time—they flogged you many times."

His chest heaved. "You don't need to know."

She wiped the tears trickling down her face. "I do need to know, Sean."

"What difference does it make? They're scars.... I've healed."

"Have you? Because I don't think anything has healed except for your skin," she said fiercely.

He turned away, leaning on the sink.

Eleanor hesitated, then allowed her heart to lead her. She walked up to him and before he could react, she slid her hand over the mass of puckered scar tissue. His back became rigid; he stiffened.

"Why did they put you in solitary confinement, Sean?" she asked softly, her hand still on his scarred back.

He didn't move now. His breathing was labored. "I killed an inmate."

She was shocked.

He turned abruptly and she was faced with an expanse of his strong throat. His movement caused her hand to brush his arm, and she stepped back. "You killed an inmate?" she said in disbelief.

He wet his lips. "Don't...look at me...like that."

"I don't understand."

"I had to protect someone…a boy, really!" His eyes flashed. "No one else would!"

She covered her mouth with her hand, cutting off her own gasp. How much had he suffered and how much more was there to tell? How much anguish could any one man bear? "You were protecting a boy?"

His gaze glittered. "He'd been accosted…I had to stop it."

She inhaled. She thought she understood Sean's meaning and it was too terrible to contemplate.

"He died anyway…the boy, Brian. He died from the next assault. I didn't understand that world…if not one bastard, there's another."

Eleanor turned away. She couldn't stop crying now. She wept for some boy named Brian and she wept for Sean.

"Elle, don't cry," he whispered in a harsh plea.

She didn't want to cry, so she nodded and wiped her eyes.

He caught her wrists, surprising her. "It's over now.… That hell…it doesn't matter."

She didn't refute him, because it would always matter to her. She became aware of their proximity, his strong grasp and his wet, earthy scent. Moisture clung to the well-defined planes of his chest, and excitement surged in her body. Slowly, she lifted her gaze to his.

Would she always feel such a powerful attraction? And how was she going to manage it? "Sean, why were you put in solitary confinement for two years?"

He dropped her wrists and moved a step away from her. "The warden was dismissed shortly after my confinement. The new warden was a drunk. I didn't know then.... I didn't know anything until I escaped." He met her gaze, anguish and revulsion mingling on his face. "I thought I would be in that black hole for the rest...of my life."

She swallowed hard. "You mean, the second warden never knew you were there?"

He nodded. "But it was fortunate...otherwise I'd have hanged."

She could not imagine being locked away in such a manner and not having any idea of what was happening or how long such torture would last. "Surely someone came to see you in those two years? I mean, you were fed, weren't you—"

He cut her off. "There was a slit in the door. They fed me like a dog...the guards thought it very entertaining. The warden didn't know I was there...the guards knew and didn't care.... I saw no one, Elle...no one until the day I escaped!" His shoulders heaving, struggling with his fury, he slammed his fist into the side of the tin sink.

Eleanor flinched. "Those *bastards*. How did you escape?"

He glanced at her over his shoulder. The question seemed to surprise him, but oddly, his stiff body seemed to relax. "I took the warden hostage."

"So the warden—the second one—realized your existence?"

He shook his head. "Another warden...Lord Harold.... Very sorry for the inconvenience! Came to apologize." And Sean laughed, the sound bitter and shocking. "I was *desperate*."

He was staring at the bottom of the sink. Eleanor laid her hand on his back. The skin there rippled as he shuddered. "You must have been planning what you would do the moment someone, anyone, actually came to see you."

He turned abruptly to face her. "Yes."

His eyes were so hard and cold that she cringed. He had been through so much and in that moment, he frightened her. But she must never be frightened of him, because she had her own mission. "Thank God it is over."

His brows arched. "Is it?" And he walked away from her.

She now leaned against the sink, watching him.

"What about the trial? Obviously you weren't there, yet you were convicted."

"It's done all the time.... Surely you know that? It's a military measure." He pulled out the other chair and sat down. He cradled his head on his arms, as if exhausted.

She tried to think, no easy task when she wanted to take him in her arms just to hold and comfort him. "Are you certain your conviction is legal? Maybe it can be overturned."

"Maybe." He looked up, his eyes flat. "Probably not."

"Sean, you're never going to suffer like that again!"

"Don't feel sorry for me."

Their eyes held. How could she not feel sorry for him? She knew that if she dared to speak further, she might push him away, but she had to go on. "Is that what you dream about? Those years spent alone in the darkness and solitude of that cell?"

His face tightened.

"Sean?" She dared. "Is it Peg? Is that who you dream about?"

He leaped to his feet. "Why do you have to pry? Why?"

"I am going to help you, Sean," she managed to say firmly. "I am going to help you forget all the horror of the past few years."

He was incredulous. "Like hell!"

"Don't you want your life back?" she cried. "Or is it Peg that you prefer?" And the minute the words slipped out, she regretted them.

He was furious. "You never stop…do you?"

"Don't go. I'm sorry! I won't pry anymore. Sean!"

But it was too late—he was already out the door.

SEAN PAUSED in the courtyard behind the cobbler's shop, leaning against the building, closing his eyes and trying to breathe. Why did she have to pry? Did she know that her prying was like taking a sharp knife and stabbing it in his gut, then twisting it in the wound?

Peg was dead. He wasn't going to talk about her, not ever and certainly not to Elle.

He covered his face with his hands. He had the oddest urge to go upstairs and let her put her arms around him. A part of him seemed to think that if he did that, she could chase away the demons. But he would never give in to such an urge, especially not now, not after the other night. He knew how his treacherous body would respond to the innocent act of her comforting him. He had never burned with so much heat; he had never felt so desperate and explosive. She had become such a beautiful woman, and the fact that she was so tempting confused him. But he was certain of one thing: he was going to regret the few moments of passion they had shared for the rest of his life.

And as he stood there, his rigid arousal was proof. He had come to the courtyard because he had been frightened by her question and he'd needed to escape—not just Elle, but Peg, his guilt, the past. But somehow the grief and guilt had turned into need and desire. It was jumbled up now, together, like an unwanted obsession.

That morning he had gone to the banks of the river and had used his spyglass to take a good look at the HMS *Gallatine*. She was sixth rate, carrying twenty-eight nine-pounders, but she looked as if she was fast. He had also called on O'Connor, who had agreed with him; McBane might be just the escort to take Elle back to Adare. He was a gentleman, so he would behave honorably toward her and probably give his life to protect her. O'Connor had said he would attempt to make contact with McBane. If he could not, he said he could escort Elle back himself.

"Sean?"

He tensed at the sound of the soft feminine voice. He turned.

Kate stood beneath the roof's overhang, smiling at him. "It's raining," she murmured. "Why are you standing outside?" The rain had lightened into a soft but steady drizzle.

He knew exactly what she wanted. He had always known when a woman wanted him, even as a boy, when the women had been girls. He had never really understood why the female of his species looked at him once, looked again and then took up the chase, but he had never lacked for female companionship because of it. He had had his first lover when he was thirteen years old and he had been taking lovers ever since. Like all the O'Neill men, his virility was extreme.

Except for the past two years, when an unnatural celibacy had been forced upon him. And then there was the other night, when he'd briefly lost his mind, taking Elle, not even in a bed.

Kate approached, her gown damp and clinging to her curves. Moisture had gathered on her face, and the skin of her chest above the lace-edged bodice of her dress. "Are you all right?" she asked.

He knew what she wanted and he wanted it, too. He was hard and desperate. And she wouldn't play games; she wouldn't demand his love in return for sex. He could simply walk with her to the livery, just across the courtyard, and they could bed down in a clean stall. "I'm fine," he said, not moving.

Her dark gaze searched his face as she paused before him. "I am glad," she murmured, cupping his cheek.

There was no reason not to take her hand and put it where he needed it to be—except one. And she was upstairs in that atrocious flat, waiting for him. She would know what he had done the moment he walked in that door. She would take one look at him and know—and she would be hurt, impossibly so, again.

He hated himself for already hurting her. How could he hurt her another time?

Kate slid her hand down his neck and over the bare, warm skin of his chest.

It was hard to breathe, hard to think. But he managed to realize that Kate might not assuage his lust, because she wasn't the one who had inspired it.

Kate smiled and moved her hand low, dipping her fingers into the waistband of his breeches.

Sean inhaled and grasped her hand firmly to remove it. Her eyes lifted and her cheeks flushed. He began to apologize, the words on the tip of his tongue, when he knew they were not alone.

Elle stood beneath the building's overhang, eyes wide.

He pushed Kate away, forgetting her in that moment. He knew he should shout at Elle, remind her that ladies do not spy, but no words came. He just stared—and she stared back.

Elle whirled and ran back through the arched overhang and into the building.

Sean realized Kate was standing beside him, her eyes wide with surprise and comprehension. "I'm sorry," he said.

"She isn't your sister," Kate gasped.

He didn't hear her—he was already racing after Elle.

ELEANOR REACHED THE FLAT and slammed the door closed behind her. She was shaking wildly, uncontrollably. She could not stop seeing Sean standing there with Kate, the moment thick with lust. She didn't hesitate—she threw one of the bolts.

Then she backed up, breathing hard. Hadn't she known he was bedding Kate, or preparing to take her to bed? She'd spied on him a dozen times with his lovers and she knew all the signs. Why should she care? He wasn't even the same man anymore, and she didn't love the man he had become. Her decision was to heal the man he had become, so she could have her best friend back. If she was ever fortunate enough to succeed, there would be other women, because

Sean was virile and passionate. She was going to have to accept it sooner or later, so why not now?

He pounded on the door. "Elle. Open up."

She stared at the locked door. Being childish, she said, "No." She hated his chasing other women and being chased by them!

The banging stopped. "Elle. Open the door and let me in. I'm wet…and cold."

"I doubt that," she said. "I think you are very hot." And desire stabbed through her, painful and full.

He wanted a woman, and she had this raging need, too. She turned away from the door, shaken and confused. Why did her body have to be so aroused? Why did she have to feel so feverish whenever she looked at Sean?

"Open the door…so we can speak, damn it."

She had the inkling that she should not open the door. She went to it, slammed the bolt free and backed up.

He walked in, gave her a dark look and closed the door, locking it. "I would have thought…you'd outgrow your need…to spy on me."

"I wasn't spying," she lied. She had seen Kate from the window and her every instinct had urged her to go down to the courtyard. "We needed water and you forgot to take a bucket. I was bringing one to you."

"You were spying." He folded his arms against his chest. Eleanor stared, because unfortunately, it remained bare. His forearms thickened, both pectoral muscles bulged. Eleanor was aware of staring but could not look away. *Couldn't she help him through his torment and share his bed at the same time? If she did not, there would be someone else, and it wasn't as if she were a virgin anymore.*

"Listen," he said, his tone thick. "I don't want Kate."

She met his gaze. "Yes, you do."

His cheeks were flushed. "No...not Kate."

She went still. The air pulsed around them, and her own body pulsed, as well. "What do you mean?" she said breathlessly.

He made a helpless gesture, and then his gaze slammed to her chest and lower, to her hips. Abruptly he closed his eyes, as if that might stop him from looking at her in such a bold and male manner, and he turned his back to her.

Eleanor swallowed. Was he telling her that he wanted her? Because she wanted him desperately, as much as she ever had, if not more.

He was fighting for control, but whether it was to manage his anger or his lust, Eleanor did not know. "Elle...I didn't sleep with Kate...I haven't and I won't."

She did not understand. She stared at the horrific web of scars on his back. "Why not? You never were very discriminating in the past."

He just stood there, his head almost hanging, his back rigid, his shoulders stiff, and he did not speak.

Eleanor managed to inhale, although she continued to shake. She laid her hand on a vein of scars. "I don't understand. You could be through with Kate by now."

"Don't," he breathed.

She stroked her hand down the vein of scars. "Sean," she murmured. A tremor passed through him. She laid her other hand on a different set of scars; leaning closer, she pressed her mouth to the apex of puckered-up tissue.

"Not...good," he gasped.

She sensed that his surrender was imminent. Barely able to breathe, she shifted forward until her soft breasts, the tips aching and erect, pressed into his back. She moved her mouth against his skin, against the ribbed scars, kissing him slowly, repeatedly. He shuddered and whispered hoarsely, "Do you want me...to hurt you?"

She clasped his shoulders and when she spoke, her mouth moved against his hot, rough skin. "No. I've been hurt enough. Sean, you won't hurt me."

And she kissed the side of his neck, which in contrast to the scars, was soft and smooth.

He moved, breaking free of her, facing her, eyes wild and hot. "Why? Why do this...seduce me... again?" There was desire in his tone but there was so much panic, too.

Her body was so feverish she felt insane. "Because I need to be with you, too! Because you are a passionate man—and I am a passionate woman." *And because I love you,* she thought.

"Don't," he said harshly, "make this any harder... than it is."

Her mind raced, but blankly, and her blood hummed. "Sean, you've changed," she whispered, "but I still want you, even more than before."

He was still, his gaze wide—a battle there. And very slowly, he said, "I can't hurt you...again. Please!"

"You won't." Even as she spoke, she knew she was lying—she knew she was going to become hurt, hugely so. Her heart told her that. But everything had vanished, all logic, all of her plans, her resolve, were gone. There was only a dully lit, sparsely furnished and cheap room; there was only her and Sean.

"You need to go back to Adare." His eyes were intense, brilliant, on hers. "You need to marry Sinclair."

"And you need to go to America. I know that. But

what does that have to do with today, tonight?" she asked softly.

He just stood there, breathing hard.

She was breathless, too. "Sean?"

He was begging her now with his eyes. "I can't give you...love."

"I'm not asking for you to give me anything more than pleasure," she whispered, and in that moment, she meant her words. He blanched. "I am asking you for pleasure, Sean. I need you to give me pleasure, now."

And his face turned crimson, his gaze silver and bright. He moved, groaning.

Eleanor cried out and then she was in his arms and their mouths were open and fusing. His body was pressing against hers. "Elle," he gasped against her mouth, already unbuttoning her shirt. *"Elle."*

Eleanor gasped as his hands covered her breasts, beneath shirt and chemise. Briefly he tore his mouth from hers to look into her eyes. He smiled.

She was stunned, but there was no time to think. He arched her backward over his arm, kissing her hard and furiously. And then he half lifted and half dragged her to the bed, climbing over her and finding her nipple with his mouth.

Exquisite sensation, part pleasure, part pain, shot though her. Eleanor felt faint and she began to seek the wild pleasure that was cresting over her. She wanted Sean to *hurry*.

And he was fumbling with her trousers. She felt him pulling them off, her drawers vanished. His mouth moved back to her face, her lips, her throat, her breasts. His hands were shaking, covering her skin in the wake of his mouth. Eleanor could not stand the sheer pleasure his mouth and hands were inflicting; her body had become so turgid, she thought it might break.

Suddenly his hands settled on her hips, anchoring her to the bed. He started exploring the flat expanse of flesh around her belly button with his mouth and tongue. Eleanor tensed; his mouth was causing the flesh of her sex to expand impossibly, to throb with a terrible urgency. She wriggled helplessly beneath his laving tongue as it delved lower and lower still. She gasped when he began to stroke the cleft of her sex. She went still, while her heart threatened to explode in her breast, her body surging.

Eleanor began to break apart and as she shattered, his tongue became bold and insistent, reckless and adept. She shattered again and again and he fed her cries relentlessly, until she had nothing left to give.

He lifted himself up and moved over her. She

looked at him and he met her gaze, his eyes impossibly hot. "I need you," he said roughly.

She knew and she smiled, cupping his cheek.

He slid one strong arm beneath her, bent and kissed her again, the kiss filled with urgency but controlled, restrained. Then he reached down to free himself. And his heavy loins pressed swiftly against hers. Eleanor gasped, new stirrings building rapidly again.

And Sean hesitated. Eleanor met his searching gaze. "Are you certain?" he asked.

She touched his face, the curved scar there. "Yes." She had never been more certain of anything, she realized.

Sean nodded, eyes drifting closed. Sheer need written all over his face, he moved against her, pressing into her warmth. *"Elle."*

Eleanor took his face in her hands—his beloved face. "You won't hurt me," she whispered. "Hurry, Sean, I love you!"

He cried out. Sweat—or tears—trickled. He kissed her, and then began to move, eyes tightly closed. The love swelling in her chest was replaced with something urgent and intense. Eleanor held on to his shoulders, the tension spiraling quickly, impossibly, and then it broke apart.

Sean gasped, moving harder and faster, as she spun wildly through the room, the ceiling, the universe. His cries became harsh, mingling with hers, and he reached completion, too.

Eleanor slowly floated back to the bed and the earth. She held his damp body as he moved to his side and she began to think. She was afraid that she loved Sean as he was, as much as she loved the man he had once been. In fact, no matter how he had changed, she had never loved him more. She kissed his moist cheek, afraid of what might come next.

His body had been utterly limp and relaxed. Now he stiffened. His head lifted and their gazes met. His stare turned blank. "Are…you all right?"

Eleanor was alarmed. How could she love the man he had turned into? How could she not? And where did that leave her? Even though he had so much passion, that wasn't necessarily love and she had promised herself that she didn't need his love—she only needed him whole and healed again.

"Elle…Eleanor?"

And she hated it when he corrected himself. "I'm still Elle, just grown-up."

His stare was odd and unhappy.

Eleanor reached for her shirt, drawing it closed over her breasts. She slid her bare legs under the sheet, pulling it up to her waist. "Yes." She swallowed, smiled. "I am fine. That was…lovely."

His eyes held hers.

She somehow kept smiling.

He didn't smile back. But he hesitated, as if he was uncertain, too.

She forced lightness into her tone. "I am fine. Making love—I mean, sharing your bed—was wonderful. And that is all it was, of course. That is all I want, I mean."

He stared at her as if she were the Loch Ness monster.

Her smile vanished. She fought the rising hurt. "Because that is all you want. Passion, a bedmate, a lover."

He sat up, turning aside so she couldn't see him straighten his breeches. Then he glanced at her. She was now hugging the sheets to her neck. "I want you safe…that is what I want." He stepped from the bed. "I'll go for water so you can bathe."

She didn't want to bathe. She knew she must not push. "You want me safe—at Adare."

He started for the door. "Yes."

She knew she must not add, *with Sinclair.* But one conclusion was inescapable. He was very attracted to her, but if he had any deeper feelings for her, he would not be able to send her home to her fiancé. If he had any deeper feelings for her, he would want to take her to America with him.

At the door he suddenly turned. "You are impossibly beautiful…Eleanor."

She tensed. She did not like his expression or his tone, and she knew a "but" was coming.

"You deserve more than a night…in my bed."

She didn't hesitate. "Yes, I do." And she almost wished she hadn't verbalized what remained in her heart.

He was so clearly unhappy and resigned. "I'm sorry," he said.

Eleanor pulled the covers higher and watched him walk out once again.

CHAPTER THIRTEEN

THE FLAT WAS SUDDENLY achingly empty. Eleanor inhaled, trembling. A few moments ago, when they had been making love, she had felt closer to him than she ever had. Yet now, clearly, he was regretting what they had just done and what they had just shared. She knew he had been through more suffering than any one man should ever bear, but she just couldn't understand why he couldn't accept their need for one another—why he couldn't allow love to grow between them.

She began to dress, refusing to feel hurt, trying to understand, yet failing. Maybe, when she knew more about the past four years, his behavior would be comprehensible. But how much time did she have before he left for America and she was forced to return home?

Eleanor suddenly winced. She realized she had stepped on a sharp object with her bare foot. She glanced down, surprised to see a very tiny carved figurine on the floor. Instantly she knew it had fallen out of the pocket of Sean's breeches earlier and she retrieved it. It was a ship with a single mast, the details exquisite. Because of its size, she felt certain it had been carved for a child.

Unease filled her. Why had Sean kept this tiny boat in his pocket? How many secrets was he keeping? First there was Peg, and now there was some child in his past, as well?

He entered the room. Their gazes collided and he looked away, going to the wood bathing tub in the room's corner. "I'll fill it so you can bathe," he said, not looking at her. He tossed the pail of water in, but before he could leave Eleanor went to him.

"Sean. Wait."

He stiffened, glancing at her. "Don't."

"I don't understand you!" she cried. She knew she should leave this subject alone now, but she couldn't.

"I know. You can't...not anymore." His gaze held hers now, searching and agonized. "I've changed. We have agreed on that.... I was honest. I said I couldn't give you anything but an hour in bed...you said you understood me. But you weren't being honest, were you?" He was accusing.

She hesitated. "I thought I could settle for passion, but I was wrong."

He paled. "I need to get more water."

She seized his arm. "That was far more than passion, Sean!"

He turned, incredulous. "You don't…know anything. You were innocent…until the other night. I don't want to discuss this." He jerked away and left the room.

Eleanor sat down hard on a chair at the table, and then realized she still held the carved ship. She put it down. He had come very close to saying that she was wrong—that their lovemaking had meant nothing to him. Had he been so blunt, it would have been too hurtful to bear.

She hugged herself. One thing was clear. She needed time to be with Sean, to help him through his misery and to change his mind about what he intended. But the British were on their trail and in a matter of days, he could be bound for America and she could be on her way home. Her heart lurched with panic at the thought.

He returned, not looking at her, his cheeks flushed. He added another bucket of water to the tub. "I'll wait in the courtyard," he said tersely.

She leaped to her feet. "Did you book a passage to America?"

It was a moment before he spoke. "Not yet."

She was so relieved that she exhaled loudly.

He faced her grimly. "Elle. I mean, Eleanor." He wet his lips. "It was a bad idea. This is my fault, again. I take full blame.... Please don't cry," he added, a sharp plea.

"I'm not crying."

"But you're hurt.... I can see it in your eyes and on your face," he exclaimed. "I have hurt you."

"I don't understand how you could touch me and kiss me the way that you did, and then try to claim that it was bedsport! You loved me when I was a child— don't you dare deny it!" she cried, when he seemed about to protest. "And when I became older, we were best friends—we did almost everything together! Now I'm a woman and we also share passion—we have done everything together, haven't we?"

"Don't do this," he warned.

But she could not stop. "I know you were locked away by yourself for two years. I know they flogged you brutally. I know that soldiers died that night in the village— I know you blame yourself! But Sean, that is over now. It's the past. Why don't you want to take me with you?" she cried, genuinely bewildered. "Why? Are you trying to punish yourself for something? Do you think to deny yourself any happiness, ever again? I made you happy a few minutes ago—I could make you happy again! We could share a bed every night, and a life! We're already best friends! I could have your children, Sean!"

He was rigid now and stark white. "You need pride. You can't beg a man...for love."

She felt like slapping him silly. "I'm not begging you for love. I am pointing out the obvious. I think you do love me—or at least care, deeply. Can you deny it?" she challenged. And then she was afraid to breathe.

He was silent, clearly refusing to speak. His temples throbbed.

"I didn't think you could," she said firmly, but she was trembling.

"I do not...want...to hurt you...again," he ground out.

"You will hurt me very much if you disappear from my life forever," she said fiercely. "And who will take care of you in America? Who will heal those scars?"

He jerked. "I already said...they're healed."

"And we both know that is a lie," she retorted.

Their eyes clashed. "And if...we're captured?"

Her heart leaped with hope. She dared to go to him and touch his arm. "What if we're *not* captured?"

He stepped back, shaking his head. "You don't understand...the British soldiers...what they can do."

"But not to me!" she cried. "I'm a woman, a lady, the daughter of an earl. Sean, if we let Cliff help us, we won't be caught. He's as dangerous as any Barbary pirate."

"I don't want him hanging beside me!" Sean shouted at her. "And I don't want you hurt because of me!"

She jerked. He was so distressed that she despised herself for pushing him. She hesitated, then whispered, "There's more, isn't there? There's something terrible that you haven't told me. Something that is making you so afraid for me, for Cliff, for all of us. Oh God, Sean—what really happened to you in that prison?"

His face appeared so stiff it might crack. He shook his head as if he could not speak, and a terrible silence ensued.

Eleanor was afraid to even begin to imagine what demon really haunted him. "You know you can trust me," she finally said. "Whatever you are hiding, you know your secret is safe with me."

He inhaled harshly. Another long moment passed before he spoke, and then his tone was low and rough with strain. "I *can't* give you what you want.... *I can't, Elle.*"

And suddenly she could feel his pain pouring from

him in huge, aching waves. Had he begun to cry, she would not have been surprised.

So she walked over to him and put her arms around him. He didn't move. "I won't push you anymore, Sean," she whispered, reaching up to stroke the hair at his nape. "But let me comfort you. Surely you can allow that."

For one more moment, he was still and she felt him fighting himself, his breathing harsh, uneven and ragged. Then, when he had gained control, he stepped back from her. "You are a fine woman," he said, his eyes becoming soft. The corners of his mouth lifted in the barest imitation of a smile.

She touched one corner. "You used to have a dimple. I want to see it again. I saw it before. You smiled at me, just before you took me into that bed."

He shook his head in some kind of denial, but whether he refused to acknowledge that he had actually smiled, perhaps for the first time in years, or that he wished to ever smile again, she did not know. Then his glance fell to the table and he started. "Where did you get that?" he cried.

Surprised, Eleanor watched him rush to the table as if it were a matter of life and death. Instantly the toy boat was gone, shoved into his pocket. He turned, his gaze incredulous and accusing.

And Eleanor was terrified of what that toy boat meant to him. "I found it on the floor," she explained slowly, her mouth dry. "Sean, why are you carrying that figure around? Is it a keepsake?"

His expression was tight. "Yes." He turned away, reaching for the bucket.

She went to the door and barred his way. "I don't understand. What does it mean? Who gave it to you? Is it a child's?"

He ground his jaw. "Excuse me."

"Is that a child's toy?" she cried again.

For one instant, as if disbelieving, he was silent. And then he exploded. "Yes, it's a child's. It belonged to Michael...Michael, my son. Michael...who is dead."

He pushed past her and slammed down the cramped staircase but she did not move, paralyzed with shock and fear.

Sean had a son? A son who had died?

She was so stunned that it was hard to think. Her heart drummed with painful force. He'd slept with so many women, it would not be strange if he had a bastard. Most men did.

Eleanor sank into a chair. But his son was *dead?*

She hugged herself, beyond worry now. Was this the cause of his grief, his bitterness, the shadows in his eyes, his sorrow? Was this the real cause of his pain?

Sean returned, dumping the last bucket of water in the tub. His movements were angry.

"I didn't know you had a son," she whispered. "Sean, I'm so sorry." As the final comprehension settled over her—he'd had a child and his son was dead—tears filled her eyes.

He suddenly faced her. "It was my duty to protect him."

She quickly went to him. She took his hand. "How did he die?"

He met her gaze. "The troops set fire to my home. They couldn't find me...so they killed him." He pulled away, shaking. "I don't want to talk.... Why won't you let me be?" He went to the stove and knelt there, clearly intending to replenish the fire.

Eleanor followed and knelt behind him. "I understand how painful this is," she soothed. She caressed his back. He continued to tremble, fighting his emotions for some kind of self-control. She had never loved him more and she had never wanted to protect him as she did now, from this kind of grief and loss. "It's not your fault," she said, and without even knowing it, she had slid her arms around him.

He didn't move. "It is my fault."

She had been right; he was blaming himself for a terrible tragedy. She wished now she had been wrong. "No. The officers who allowed those men to burn your home, they are the ones responsible for Michael's death. You are a fine and honorable man. Had you been there that day, you would have died in his place and we both know it. You cannot blame yourself." She reached for him to turn him to face her. "Sean, look at me."

He allowed himself to shift and he obeyed, his gray eyes lifting to meet hers.

She clasped his face. "You have to stop blaming yourself. Blaming yourself won't bring Michael back. But you know that."

His eyes flickered with anguish. "How many times…did I save you?" he asked in a whisper.

She didn't answer, trying not to succumb to the same grief he was feeling.

"But I failed Michael," he said slowly. "Why?"

A tear had finally spilled. Eleanor caught it with her thumb. His gaze locked with hers. She became still, her hands on his face, as the anguish shimmered, becoming desperation. She wanted to tell him that he could not run from Michael's murder forever. Instead, she slid her thumbs over his skin. He flinched, his eyes turning hot.

Nothing mattered, Eleanor thought, except that he was so wounded, in so much pain, and he needed her now. Even if only temporarily, she could soothe him. She stood, taking his hand as she did so and bringing him to his feet, too. "I love you so much," she murmured unsteadily.

He stared at her and his eyes filled with tears. And then he shook his head.

She did not know if it was a denial of her declaration or a protest of what she intended, but she knew exactly how to comfort him now. She closed her eyes and floated her lips over his.

He stood utterly still, allowing her to kiss him, and she tasted not just his firm lips, but the salt of his tears.

And then his arms were around her and he was kissing her in return, deep and desperate.

THIS TIME, WHEN HE MOVED onto his back, Eleanor moved against his side, laying her cheek on his chest. She felt his body tense in response and she prayed. Then, slowly, his hand slid over her arm, closing around her. Eleanor squeezed her eyes shut against sudden tears. *He wasn't pushing her away.* This was a beginning, and she was acutely aware of it.

He didn't speak.

She waited until she had recovered some of her own composure, now thinking about his son, Michael. She had so many questions but she did not have to debate with herself to know that now was not the time to raise such a painful subject again. Besides, if possible she wanted to remain just where she was, in his arms, in his bed, being gently held, for as long as possible. This time she wasn't deluded—their passion did not signify any change of intention of his part. She intended to cherish the moment. Eleanor laid her hand on his chest, caressing him, but in a manner meant to comfort, not arouse. She wanted to press her lips to his skin, with all the love she was feeling, but she restrained herself. Then her stomach growled loudly.

She looked up as he looked down. His eyes were soft and searching. And, very faintly, he smiled. "I will get us supper."

Her heart leaped in wild elation at the sight she had just witnessed. She smiled back, her chin now on his chest. "It's dark. Maybe this is not a good time to be roaming the city streets."

His somber expression had returned, but his eyes didn't change. He kept staring at her face, as if he were seeing each and every one of her features for the first time and as if he wished to memorize them. "I'm hungry, too," he said. He added, "Dark is better. I can slip through town without anyone…seeing me. And it's not far…to the inn."

For one moment, she laid her hand on his taut belly, relishing the smoothness of his skin and the fact that he was allowing her such liberties. Then she recalled the thick and coarse web of scars on his back and she sobered. She sat up. She never wanted him to suffer that way again. "I'll get supper. I'll go to the inn."

He was staring at her breasts. "No."

Eleanor realized he was admiring her and she felt a heady sense of allure. Her instinct was to raise the sheets, but she did no such thing. "Sean, I am not a child anymore. I do not need to be protected at every twist and turn. The inn is around the corner...."

"No." He handed her an edge of the sheet, placing it over her breasts. "Ladies are modest," he chastised.

She had to smile. "But we agreed long ago that I am not a lady."

And he smiled in return as he slipped from the bed. "How could I forget?"

She ogled him while he was reaching for his clothes. He suddenly glanced at her while stepping into his breeches and he blushed. "Ladies are not so bold."

She shrugged. "You are beautiful.... Why can't I stare? Men stare at women all the time."

He sighed and reached for his shirt, which was now dry. "You can't…it's improper…you know that."

"I hate being proper," she declared, meaning it.

He went still, a faraway look coming to his eyes.

Eleanor had a vague recollection of a different time and place, when he was young and she was younger still. "Sean?"

He slowly turned, his gaze drifting over her and from the look in his eyes, she knew he was seeing her as a child in braids, not as the woman he had just taken to bed. Then his gaze sharpened. "You are a lady…just an unconventional one. Do not ever forget it."

"I pretend to be a lady when I have to—which is most of the time," she rebutted. "You know I despise wearing dresses and having tea and going to balls. I haven't even learned to dance properly."

He glanced at her, amused. "Only you…would dare to be so honest."

"Sean, I see that dimple," she said, and it was the truth.

He straightened in surprise, his soft smile vanishing.

She wondered if he was determined to grieve. She slid from the bed. "Sean…seeing you smile is wonderful."

His eyes widened. "You should get dressed." As he spoke, his cheeks turned red.

She was so comfortable with him that she hadn't even realized she was nude. She jerked the sheet from the bed and wrapped it around her. "I think you must know every inch of my body intimately by now."

His color increased.

"But I don't mind," she exclaimed.

He seemed displeased now. "Elle, I hope you only act so bold…with me. No one else could understand…or accept it."

She folded her arms. "Oh—you mean, like Sinclair?" And her heart raced with anxiety.

He lifted his chin. "Him, too."

Had someone tied a rope between them, the tension could not have suddenly been greater. But Sean turned away. Eleanor seized his arm. The words slipped out. "You don't really expect me to return to him? Not after all we have shared this day?"

He pulled away, buttoning his shirt and clearly refusing to answer her.

He still thought to send her back to Sinclair. "You spent the afternoon making love to me!" she cried in genuine shock.

He was angry. "We already discussed this."

"There was no discussion and that was yesterday. There was an order, a directive—it was your decision, not mine."

"Why do we have to debate again?" he demanded.

"Because it was one thing to have made a foolish mistake once—a meaningless and foolish one—but it's another to willfully deceive a good and honest man when we both deliberately chose to be lovers!" She was furious.

He glanced sidelong at her. "Nothing has changed…. Sinclair is *protection* for you." He started for the door.

She was so stunned with disbelief she just stood there, staring. Then she said, "I don't need protection from the British—but you will never believe that, will you?"

He faced her. "I was an animal…in a cage. It was madness…it was hell. This time, I will hang. And you? Do you want to spend your life in the Tower? Or do you prefer a privileged existence as Lady Sinclair?"

She wasn't furious now; she was determined to understand him. "You are not being rational. No one is going to lock me in the Tower. Is this irrational fear somehow connected to what happened to Michael?"

He refused to answer her.

"I can't leave your bed and then take vows with Peter," she said honestly. "You must see that it would be despicable."

He cursed. "I knew it was a mistake. I have already arranged for you to return home tomorrow. And we agreed you would pretend innocence with Sinclair—you promised."

"I promised no such thing," she gasped. "And our one-sided debate was before you spent an entire afternoon enjoying my favors," she added.

He held up his hand. "Don't," he warned.

"Don't what? Don't insist that you do the honorable thing? I already made that mistake, didn't I? And you already refused to marry me," she said with some bitterness. And no matter what she knew and understood, his failure to want to take her as a wife genuinely hurt. "I'm not a fool. I would hardly play that card again."

"Then what game are you playing?" His eyes flashed angrily.

She swallowed hard. "I can't leave you like this, Sean. I meant what I said before. If you go to America alone, there will be no one to take care of you. You said no one can help, but that's not true. I can help. I will help. I am your other half." And somehow, she smiled through her tears.

He was ashen. "I would die," he said, so low his words were almost inaudible, "before placing you in that kind of danger."

They were at a terrible impasse; he refused to listen to her and she could not understand his fears. "And I would die before leaving you now—this way."

"No!" He was incredulous. "When will you understand? It's not safe. I should not have returned for you...you would be married now. Safe and married to Sinclair! Damn it, Elle!"

She was ill that he could be so adamant after what they had shared. "You might want to send me home—but into the arms of another man? I don't believe it! You want to be with me! You *need* me, Sean!" she cried.

"I need no one!" he shouted. "I need air, water, food...you need *me,* not the other way, and you always have!"

She recoiled.

"So cease insisting otherwise, damn it! I never asked for this...love! Never, not once, ever!" He was on a furious tirade. "If things were different, maybe we could be together.... If things were different, I could be honorable and make you my wife. But you are engaged...as it should be! Forget me! Forget this!" He gestured wildly at the bed. "You need to marry Sinclair, not me—not a traitor who is bound for the gallows.... And damn it...if you are having my child...he will raise my son as a bloody Englishman! He will never suffer indignation...outrage...injustice...anything!" he cried out, smashing the wine bottle, now empty, from the counter.

Eleanor flinched. How the truth hurt. "You're right. I have always needed you and loved you. And you…what? You hated my affection, my trust, my loyalty? Just like you hated my lovemaking a moment ago?"

He was panting hard. "Not fair."

"No, this isn't fair. It isn't fair that you left me four years ago, missing you terribly, without a word—perhaps while you were enjoying a liaison with someone else. It is not fair that you came home now, and swept me back off my feet on my wedding day! It is not fair that you took me to bed, but refuse to be a gentleman and do what is right. No, it's not fair, Sean."

He stared.

She wet her lips. She could not stop now. "You have hurt me so much since you left and now again, since you came home. Sean, do you realize that you never hurt me, not genuinely, in all those years when we were growing up together? You were my hero."

"Stop," he whispered.

She shook her head. "Maybe you didn't need an annoying brat spying on you all the time—or a young woman who gladly rubbed her hands raw to help you rebuild your home. In fact, I am sure you would have had a pleasant boyhood growing up without me, just as I am sure you could have rebuilt Askeaton without me."

"I'm sorry," he offered.

"No! You had your say and now I have mine. You

need me. You are suffering from the pain of Michael's death, and the two years spent in prison, and maybe even more than that—I don't know. You need me as you have never needed anyone or anything before. You need me *more* than air, food and water!"

He reached out to grasp the back of a chair.

"Do you know what else I realized this afternoon?"

He didn't move, his gaze unwavering.

"I love you with all of my heart—not just the way you were, but the way you are now."

He closed his eyes tightly. "Then you are mad," he said.

"Yes, you are probably right. But today I have seen the truth. You are running from Michael's murder. So be it. But you can't run from me. I want to be your wife. And if I have to, I will wait—for as long as it takes."

He inhaled, turning white. "No."

And she began to tremble. "I am not going home to marry Sinclair, Sean."

"I said *no!*" he roared. "When will you understand? *I married Peg.* I am not marrying you!"

CHAPTER FOURTEEN

ELEANOR KNEW she had misheard. It was simply impossible that he had married another woman. But her certainty wavered as she stared at his flushed face and angry eyes. Her heart began to pound so swiftly she felt faint and dizzy. She had misheard, hadn't she? Or was she in the throes of a nightmare?

She gripped the back of a chair. The room tilted wildly. "You're not married," she choked.

He seized her arm, steadying her. His gaze was searching and their eyes met. "Peg is dead."

The room was a blur. He was a blur. How could this be happening? Her entire life, she had followed him, chased him, laughed at him, with him; there had been thousands of moments that they had shared. They had swum together, raced their horses, dived off cliffs. There had been card games, hide-and-seek, tug-of-war. And every time she had been in trouble, he had appeared, miraculously, to rescue and save her. The day she had fallen off her pony while following the hunting party, she had been lost and scared. When she had gotten caught in some weeds in the lake, she had been terrified. It hadn't mattered—Sean had always been there.

She had loved him from the first moment she had set eyes on him and she had never stopped loving him, not even after he had so callously taken her innocence.

He had married someone else.

"Here." Sean suddenly handed her a mug of water. "Take a sip. You'll feel better."

She ignored the mug. *How could he have married someone else?* "Why?" She managed to breathe, her heart suddenly numb, her lips as frozen. She became frightfully cold, in her bones.

"She's dead, Elle. Because of me…they're both dead," he said harshly. "You should sit down."

Somehow she was seated. Her face was wet and she realized that she was crying. She tried to focus on him but he was a haze now, his handsome features blurred. "How could you marry someone else?" she heard someone ask—then realized it was her.

He gripped her hand. "It wasn't like that," he begged tersely. "I didn't love her."

Was he lying now? She simply could not understand his relationship with this other woman—a woman he had decided to marry. She just looked at him, in acute grief and disbelief.

"Why are you staring?" he cried. "It's been *four* years! So much has happened in the interim! You were marrying Sinclair...I married Peg, and now it's *over.*"

She couldn't comprehend him at all now. All she could understand was that he had been married to another woman. He had left her to marry someone else. It was the single greatest betrayal of her life. If he had felt the way that she did, that they belonged together no matter the circumstance, he would have never been able to bring himself to marry someone else. Marriage was *forever.* He had chosen to be with another woman for the rest of his life.

And it did not matter that she was deceased. His choice, his decision and his betrayal was what mattered now.

"How long?" she choked out, wiping at her tears. "How long were you married?"

He shook his head. "Not long. Please don't cry."

She somehow met his pale silver eyes. "But you were supposed to marry me," she heard herself whisper.

He stiffened. "I'll go get supper," he said decisively. He strode from the room, and then turned. "Bolt the door."

Eleanor did not move. The refrain haunted her

now. *He had married a woman named Peg.* Her mind turned cruel, intent on torture. She saw an unbearably beautiful woman, Irish, of course, perhaps another earl's daughter. She would be blond and short, because Sean didn't like tall women, and almost too beautiful to even look upon. She had probably been like Lady Blanche Harrington, the woman Tyrell had almost married. Blond, beautiful, perfect—impossibly elegant and gracious to a fault. She saw Sean with the woman, his wife, laughing, adoring, smitten.

She tried to remind herself that he had said that he hadn't loved her. She started to weep. She knew Sean well enough, especially the way he had been before his incarceration, to know that he had cared for this woman. He had cared, perhaps deeply—perhaps the way he currently cared about her, Eleanor.

There was more than passion, Sean!

You don't know anything…you were innocent until the other night!

Eleanor wept harder. She was a fool. He had used her, obviously, the way he used women like Kate. She had been naive enough to think his lovemaking was just that. Had he made love to Peg with the same explosive desire? Surely he had—after all, he had chosen to marry her! The truth was that she was no different from Kate or any other housemaid or farmer's daughter—because she wasn't Peg, because he hadn't waited for her, because he hadn't cared enough to take her hand in marriage, because he had chosen to spend his life with someone else.

She hated the other woman, God she did. It was wrong—that woman was dead. And then she realized that it was Sean she hated.

Eleanor could not breathe. She began to choke for lack of air. But it didn't matter—she didn't care if she lived or died. She only knew one thing. She had to get away from Sean. He was a traitor, in every sense of the word. He had been a traitor to her, to them.

She was never going to forgive him.

She stumbled down the narrow stairs, too late realizing she remained barefoot. Weeping, she did not care. Outside a hundred stars were twinkling in the night sky and the far end of the street was lit with a single cast-iron gas lamp. Eleanor ran.

It didn't matter where she went. It only mattered that she run as hard and as fast as she could go—it only mattered that she escape her own heart and all the pain consuming her.

And then she turned a corner and saw three British soldiers swaggering up the street. They seemed boisterous and drunk. Eleanor ducked into a doorway, where she hid.

Sometime later, the soldiers long since gone, it began to rain.

Eleanor did not notice. She was too cold to notice the ice in her heart and soul.

HE WAS ILL. He walked slowly up the stairs to the room over the cobbler's, unable to stop recalling Eleanor's shock and grief. But she had overreacted to the fact that he had been married, considering that Peg was dead. She had acted as if he had betrayed her. But he had been in shock over the massacre in Kilvore when he had taken his wedding vows. There had been no time to really think it through. The burden of grief had been overwhelming. And he had never, not once in their relationship, indicated that he might love her the way she loved him.

Promise me you will return for me?

I promise.

He stiffened. He had known when he had left her standing at Askeaton's front gates that she had taken his promise in a literal manner, when it had not been made that way. Was this entirely his fault?

The first thing he had done upon returning to Adare was to spy on her, confront her, and then make love to her. And yesterday he had given in to his wildest desires, spending the afternoon with her. He shouldn't have touched her even once. Of course she would have expectations, because she did not understand, really, the danger she was in. Any woman gently born and bred would be expecting marriage from him—but Elle also expected his love, when he had nothing in him to give to anyone, not even her.

"DO YOU, SEAN O'NEILL, take this woman to be your lawful wedded wife? To cherish and to hold, in sickness and in health, until death do you part?"

Sean had been ill then, too. He had stood beside Peg in the small village chapel wearing the smith's dark Sunday suit; Peg was clad in a simple white dress and a borrowed wedding veil. He had looked uneasily at Peg, aware of performing a monstrous duty, suddenly feeling crushed. She had been crying with joy over the impending union, but her tears were also those of grief, for the deaths of her father and friends. For an interminable moment, he had not been able to speak his vows. Peg's image had wavered, her blue eyes turning dark and amber, and Elle had stared expectantly at him. He had been stricken, for the first time in months, thinking of Elle and home, becoming vaguely aware that everything was wrong. But Peg had whispered, "Sean?" And in panic, he had faced her again, then glanced at

Michael, who was waiting eagerly for him to marry his mother. Some in the congregation were weeping, still grieving for the loss of brothers and cousins, fathers and sons in the massacre earlier in the week. He had to protect Michael and Peg. Grimly, he faced the priest. "I do."

SEAN JERKED, realizing he stood in the dark, dank stairwell, lost in the past. He hadn't thought about his wedding day even once since then; he'd actually forgotten it—or buried it with his memories of that entire week. Peg and Michael were gone; Elle was not. And now he had to admit to himself that he hadn't told her about his marriage because he had known it would upset her; he could add that to the long list of his crimes against her, his sins.

He started up the stairs. He had not been able to protect his wife and son, but he would not fail Elle. Until she was safe at Adare, with Sinclair, he had no other cause. And he would not think about the other man taking her to wife and to bed.

He hesitated halfway up the dark, narrow stairs. Leaning on the wall, he began to shake. What was happening to him? How had he returned home only to become so caught up in Elle's life—to become so caught up with her? His life had turned cold and black the night Peg and Michael died. It was too late, but now, standing in the dark, aching and alone, he thought of Elle and the stairwell became warm and bright with light. But then, Elle had been the sunshine in his life. When she smiled, he was warmed impossibly, and not just in his body, but in his heart, his soul.

And if he dared to remember being with her in bed, if he dared to remember being in her arms, he might have to admit that she was far more than sunlight and peace—she was his siren call. But it was so terribly dangerous to do so. If he thought about sharing a bed with her, he might explode—and he might decide not to return her to her waiting groom.

But now, he did not know how to best apologize to her and he did not dare attempt to console her. Sean continued up the stairs. Before he reached the top step, he saw the light spilling into the hall and he froze. The front door was wide open.

He dropped the bag and ran to the room. He took one look inside, already knowing she was gone. The flat was empty. He cried out, smashing his fist against the wall. *Where did she think to go?* Panic began, mingling with raw fear. Peg's faded black-and-white image floated before him in the room, then it was followed by the coldest and most frightening blue-eyed stare he had ever seen. He started to sweat.

He reminded himself that if Reed still had a command in Ireland, he could be anywhere in the country or to the north, near Drogheda. The man was cavalry, his regiment stationed as needed or upon request. He reminded himself that, while Reed had become the monster in his dreams, the man had undoubtedly forgotten Sean's very existence years ago. Reed was never going to touch or hurt Elle.

He turned to go, then whirled back again. Instantly he saw the lace-up boots he'd gotten her.

She was in the city, but she was barefoot. He was distressed as he charged down the stairs, but he reminded himself that was fortunate, for she would not get very far that way.

A few moments later, Sean was mounted and trotting down the street. He could cover much more territory astride than on foot. But Eleanor could be anywhere.

Did she think to walk home?

Knowing her, she might.

He had calmed some of his panic, but a very genuine fear for her safety remained. A beautiful woman, alone on the public roads, dressed as a man, was sure to attract attention from every unsavory sort, even if she eluded the soldiers. Sean spurred Saphyr on.

DAWN WAS SPREADING a pale gray blush across the harbor just southeast of the city. Sean sat the stud on the low rise of a hill, too frightened for Elle to be exhausted. He had quickly realized that if she chose to remain in the city and hide, he would never find her. He had decided to ride north toward Limerick, but she had been nowhere to be seen on the main roadway. He had given up when he realized that she could not have gone that far on foot.

Of course, he did not know if she remained on foot. If she had somehow gained transportation, then she might be on her way home. He should be relieved, but there would be no relief until he knew she had arrived safely at Adare.

He needed his wits now, but they were failing him. Where was she? Was she all right? What if she had been accosted, assaulted, worse? Had she been apprehended by troops? He was on the verge of panic, making it hard to think.

Then one thought filled his mind. Cliff and his brother intended to help him, regardless of his wishes. There was a harbor just below him, where the ferries ran between Cobh and Cork. Sean stared down at the gulf of water that lay between the harbor and the island, and the shoreline of Cobh's jumbled buildings. He had purchased a spyglass the previous night and now, he began to study the panorama below.

A dozen dinghies and sloops were at berth in the harbor, a few fishing boats already putting out to sea. The only large ship in their midst was the HMS *Gallatine,* an incongruous sight, as the naval base was on the island's other side in Cobh. He lifted his spyglass, for a wider-ranging look—and smiled.

A frigate, far larger, more heavily gunned and quite ominous, her hull painted red and black, rode her anchor some meters away, all sails reefed, the standing rigging vast.

Only Cliff had a frigate painted in such bold colors. If he was not mistaken, that was *The Fair Lady,* oh yes.

Sean spurred his mount down the hill, leaving Cork well behind. If he had realized Cliff might be nearby, had Elle, as well? He was afraid to hope, but he would give anything to find her safely aboard that ship. He was worried enough now that he would beg Cliff for his help in finding Eleanor.

He left the stallion at the closest dock, where he seized a small fishing boat. He was no sailor, but he quickly untied her moorings and began furiously rowing toward *The Fair Lady.* Halfway there, he heard the watch call out. By the time he reached the ship's hull, several sailors stood there, throwing down hooks and a rope ladder. At first glance, Sean mistook the trio for Moors and pirates. But the man at the railing was no Moor. Although bronzed from the sun, his tawny hair covered with a red scarf, a gold earring hugging one ear, and a short, Turkish-style velvet vest over his linen shirt, it was Cliff standing above him.

The small boat secured, Sean quickly scrambled up to the deck of his stepbrother's ship. Cliff threw his arm around him, steering him across the deck, past numerous cannon, and to the captain's cabin. Sean took an inventory of the stepbrother he barely recognized. He was heavily armed, a huge sword with a bejeweled hilt sheathed in its scabbard on his hip and a dagger winked out from his belt. A pistol was in a shoulder holster. Cliff clearly meant business and Sean was reassured.

"Are you mad?" Cliff said, low. Then, in a voice of command, "No one is to approach this ship and no one is to leave her."

Cries of "Aye, cap," sounded.

"I am pleased to see you…too," Sean muttered. "What? No gold rings?"

Cliff laughed then, and gestured Sean inside. Sean stepped into a large cabin painted a dark, surprising red. A red Chinese rug, laced with green, blue and gold flowers, covered most of the wood floor. A vast canopied bed was centered in the room, also furnished in red and gold, not far from a dining table with four burgundy velvet chairs. A Portuguese desk with spiral legs faced the door covered with maps and charts. Sean's gaze swept the room and his heart sank.

Cliff booted the door closed and embraced him, hard. "Sean, damn it!"

Sean's attention turned to his stepbrother, whom he had not seen in well over four years, as Cliff had been sailing the West Indies before his departure. Cliff was actually two years younger than he was, but because of his bold nature, in many ways he had seemed a peer while growing up. They had been especially close, perhaps because they were as different as night and day. Sean was cautious, conservative and responsible, Cliff a hellion from the day he was born. He met his brother's blue gaze and found it curious, intent and deeply searching. "It has been a long time."

"It most certainly has." Cliff folded his arms across his chest. "We arrived last night, close to midnight. As soon as the British realize I am here, you can be certain I shall be watched." His gaze slid over him again, from head to toe. His smile faded.

"You barely resemble the brother I grew up with. Are you all right, Sean?"

Sean was well aware that he resembled a villain far more than he did a gentleman, but he certainly had no time to explain. "You hardly appear...the nobleman's son."

"I have no use for fashion and airs at sea. What has happened?"

"Have you seen Elle?" Sean asked grimly.

Cliff started. "No, I have not. But she is with you, isn't she?"

Sean sat down. "No. She is not with me." He tried to breathe, the panic rising all over again. "I need your help...I am afraid."

Cliff clasped his shoulder. "Tell me what has happened," he said very calmly. "And we will make our plans."

Sean looked at him. "She left.... I went to get supper and when I returned...she was gone."

Cliff was wary. "Why would Eleanor leave you, Sean? My understanding is that she is deeply, if foolishly, in love with you. After all, she did leave Sinclair at the altar."

Sean met his stepbrother's penetrating, but not disapproving, eyes. "I am a fool, Cliff. I told her the truth...that I had married another woman."

Cliff's eyes flared with surprise. It was a moment before he spoke. "I begin to understand. I had no idea. Who is this paragon? And where is she?"

"No, you don't," Sean said grimly. "Peg is dead, as is her son."

Cliff stared. When he spoke, his tone was harsh. "I am sorry for your loss, Sean. But you surely did not expect Eleanor to withstand your news? She has been in love with you for as long as anyone can recall. She waited for you to return, to her, Sean. We watched her pine for you for years."

"I never promised her..." He stopped.

"So you did promise her something?" Cliff was clearly angry.

Sean shook his head. "I said I would come back and I meant it. I did not anticipate rotting in prison...for two years!"

"What possessed you to take up arms against the British?"

"I tried to stop the villagers...from assaulting the Darby estate," Sean replied.

"Are there any witnesses? Because Colonel Reed swears he saw you leading the villagers, not attempting to stop them."

Sean froze. "Reed?"

Cliff reached out to steady him. "Colonel Reed

called on Tyrell, and I have been apprised of the conversation. Apparently he is leading the manhunt for you."

Sean cried out. He felt the ship tilt and spin. "Cliff! Reed is a murderer—he murdered Peg and Michael!"

Cliff's eyes widened. "You think he murdered your wife and her son? Are you certain?"

"Oh, I am certain—and I fear he might harm Elle! You must help me find her!" He was consumed with fear and panic.

Cliff grasped his arm. "Are you in love with my sister? And if so, why in hell did you marry someone else?"

He jerked away. *Was he in love with Elle?* "We married two days after the massacre. I married Peg because she was with my child…and because I thought to protect her and Michael from the British troops. They needed me, Cliff, and Michael needed a father. But I failed them— Reed got to them when he could not get to me. Where is Reed now?"

"The last I heard, in Limerick. Sean, we will find Eleanor. Rex, Devlin and Rory McBane are at the Stag's Leap Inn in Cork—they will help. I can see you are very frightened for her, but she is not the one in danger. Reed may be a murderer but he would never harm Adare's daughter. That would be political suicide! You must relax on that count. I am far more concerned about you. I wish to set sail immediately and take you to foreign shores. There is no point in your staying here. I haven't given my men leave so we can be gone within hours—the tides will be favorable until midmorning."

"I am not going anywhere!" Sean exclaimed furiously. "You don't understand. Reed is dangerous. He has no morals. His men raped my wife, Cliff, and beat her…she died from their assault. She paid for what I did…it was punishment for my sins. Elle is barefoot, dressed as a man, penniless. She is alone, somewhere in Cork or on the roadway to Adare! It's bad enough that any scurvy might accost her! If the soldiers find her, she is finished!" He had to sit down. He could barely draw a deep breath.

"Reed asked about her and your relationship with her."

Sean began to shake.

"But Eleanor is clever and determined, not to mention very strong, and a better shot than most men. Is she armed?"

"No."

Cliff was grim. "That is unfortunate. How upset was she when you told her about your marriage?"

"I may as well have stabbed her in the heart."

"Yes, you may as well have. Well, I know my sister. She might be heartbroken, but she will rebound enough to protect herself. She will probably return to the flat you were hiding in. But I will send word to Rex and Devlin. They will look for her on the road to Adare, and we will sail from here immediately."

"I am not going anywhere! I will leave when Elle is safe," Sean erupted. "Not a moment before then."

Cliff stared. "You never answered me. Are you in love with her?"

Sean's heart leaped strangely. He didn't dare contemplate the question. He walked to the porthole, which was open, and inhaled deeply. The seas were so calm. "I have to rescue her. I have always rescued her. It is my responsibility to see her home...and safely wed to Sinclair." He suddenly turned. Cliff was regarding him with quiet skepticism. "Cliff. Promise me you will make certain...she marries Sinclair."

"I do not understand," Cliff said slowly. "If you have feelings for my sister now, and she loves you, as well, why send her back? Why not take her with you? That is clearly what she wants—and I begin to think you want it, too."

Sean was furious then. "And what if we are captured by Reed? Elle needs to marry Sinclair!"

"I am very sorry about your wife, Sean. I think, however, that I am beginning to comprehend all aspects of this crisis," he said slowly.

Sean turned away, feeling ragged now. "We need to find Elle. I need weapons."

Cliff hesitated. "Sean." He moved to stand in front of him. His gaze was direct. "Will Sinclair take her back?"

Sean understood Cliff's meaning. Cliff wanted to know how far his relationship with his sister had gone. Somehow, he met his gaze. Somehow, he did not flinch or look away. It was hard to speak, and not because of any physical limitations. "Elle need only tell him…that she ran off with her brother…that she is the most loyal of stepsisters," he said.

Cliff stared, his eyes darkening. "That wasn't what I asked. You would never take advantage of her." It was not a question.

And he could not stop himself from tensing. Worse, he felt his cheeks heat.

Cliff's eyes went wide. Sean had no time to react; the blow took him in the face, knocking him off of his feet. On the floor, he looked up. Cliff towered over him, furious, a dagger in his hand. "You bastard! You rotten bastard! If we hadn't been raised as brothers, I would cut off your balls, one by one and hang them out to dry!"

Sean pushed to his feet. "Go ahead," he said. "Land another blow. You are right…I was wrong. I am a bastard. Do as you will."

Cliff clearly fought the need to do just that. Then he shook his head. "Bloody hell," he said fiercely. "No wonder Elle left you. Why would you ever tell her about your dead wife, anyway?"

"I don't know," Sean shouted. "I don't understand myself anymore!"

Cliff stiffened, as if taken aback.

A huge silence fell.

Sean sat down. "I am begging you for your help." He looked up. "She must go home. She must marry Sinclair, before anyone even thinks of charging her…with any crime, any conspiracy…before Reed ever finds her himself."

"You should marry her, not Sinclair," Cliff responded sharply.

"And then we can hang together! That would be a sight for the countess…don't you think?"

"You hardly let me finish. If the circumstances were different, I would stand you at the altar myself, no matter what you wanted." His brilliant blue eyes flashed. "All right. I am agreed. I shall contact Rex and Devlin immediately and we will concentrate our efforts on finding Eleanor. And then what? What if finding her takes days? What if you are captured in the interim?"

"My escape is not the priority," Sean said.

Cliff's gaze narrowed. "You do know, Sean, that you behave very much like a man in love."

"How the hell would you know?" Sean said, instantly uncomfortable. "Or have you changed so much that you have taken that particular fall?"

Cliff smiled, briefly amused. "I am not certain I shall ever fall, as you have put it, but I have watched your brother turn into a besotted fool over Virginia and my own brother almost give up the entire earldom for Lizzie. I think I can recognize the affliction in another man."

Angry now with everyone, especially Cliff, Sean snapped, "I don't care what you think."

"You might think to pander to me, just a bit, as we have devised a plan. I am to be the decoy and while the authorities pursue me, Devlin will sail you away from here."

"I don't want you involved…. I don't want Devlin involved. I will find my own passage. Thank you," Sean said grimly. He started for the door.

Instantly, Cliff barred his way. "I refuse to be denied. You cannot do this by yourself."

Sean seized his arm. "Let me go by, Cliff," he

warned. "I allowed you to beat me a moment ago.... I warn you, I am not the same quiet boy you once knew."

Cliff hesitated, clearly debating. Then he stepped politely aside. "Very well. I am not afraid of you, Sean, but I can see you remain selflessly noble. How will I contact you when we find Eleanor?" He walked to the desk and unlocked it. He then handed Sean a double-barreled pistol, a pouch containing ramrod, carbine and flint, and one of the daggers he had been wearing.

"You said that McBane is with Rex and Devlin?"

Cliff nodded. "You do not know him, but he is married into the family."

Sean almost laughed. "Actually I do know him, and he knows me—but as John Collins. Tell McBane. He will know how to reach me."

"I grow more curious with every passing moment," Cliff said dryly.

"I am sure that you do." Sean hesitated. "Cliff, just keep her safe. Give me your word."

Cliff studied him. "You forget, she is my little sister. Of course I will keep her safe. I would die in order to do so."

"Thank you." Relief overcame him then.

Cliff threw his arm around him. "Have a care, damn it," he said gruffly.

Sean nodded and pulled away.

CHAPTER FIFTEEN

CAPTAIN BRAWLEY was uneasy. He had been in command of the small garrison at Kilraven Hill in County Limerick for almost two years, by default—his superior officer had died in a carriage accident and he had never been replaced. And ever since the earl of Adare had stepped down from the position of magistrate, Brawley had been performing those civil duties as well. But the headquarters of the fort were no longer familiar. Two new aides were in the anteroom, having usurped his aides' stations and his personal office had been taken over by Colonel Reed. In fact, Colonel Reed had taken over his command.

Reed sat at Brawley's desk, flipping through some files with impatience and a brilliance that Brawley had become far too familiar with. Brawley knew he was reviewing paperwork relating to his regimental command, but a likeness of Sean O'Neill was front and center on the desk, and another one had been taped to the wall behind him. Brawley wanted the earl's stepson apprehended as much as anyone, especially as he was almost certain that O'Neill was endangering Lady Eleanor. He knew that she would never run away with a felon. He was utterly convinced that O'Neill had somehow misled her into abandoning her groom and leaving Adare with him.

But Reed stared at O'Neill's poster in his every spare moment. Brawley knew he carried a folded-up page in his interior breast pocket. He had seen the captain, in the midst of a drill or reveille, suddenly take the poster from his jacket, unfold it and simply stare. Reed had the coldest, brightest eyes Brawley had ever remarked, especially when he looked at O'Neill's likeness.

Brawley did not like his command being hijacked, but more importantly, the captain's intensity made him uneasy. He had reviewed the O'Neill file extensively. Reed's regiment had been stationed at the county garrison during that fateful night when the villagers had rebelled. His troops had quelled the rebellion but not before the Darby estate was destroyed and almost every man in the village had been killed. Reed had been the one to file the initial report. And he had been the one to apprehend O'Neill and escort him to prison a week later.

And now he was in Limerick, hundreds of miles from his current command, intent on apprehending O'Neill once again. Brawley felt certain that this manhunt had become highly personal for the captain.

In response, Brawley had penned a letter to Major Wilkes, who was in command of the southern half of the country. The letter merely requested clarification of his role in the current manhunt—while mentioning Reed's intervention in a district not assigned to him. But Brawley had yet to send the letter. A soldier to the core of his being, his every instinct was to accept authority, to obey orders. He wished to avoid sending the Major such a letter if he could help it. He wished to give his superior, Reed, the benefit of the doubt.

Reed now looked up, his blue eyes pale and brilliant. "Brawley. What is it?"

"The troops have returned from Limerick city, sir. If O'Neill is there, he cannot be found. We have searched every single house, every home, every shop and stable." Brawley spoke literally. The manhunt had been intensive. As far as he was concerned, O'Neill could not be present there.

Reed leaned back in his chair, smiling without mirth. "He isn't there. De Warenne sailed out the day after O'Neill escaped from Adare. *The Fair Lady* has been a few miles from Cork since midnight last night. I believe O'Neill is in Cork."

Brawley felt a flicker of excitement. "Sir! May I request permission to take a dozen soldiers and proceed directly there?"

"You may not," Reed said, standing.

Brawley was stunned and disappointed. "Sir, Lady Eleanor may be in danger. You know I believe he has taken her hostage."

Reed waved at him. "I doubt it. Even you said she willingly left with O'Neill."

"That is how it appeared," Brawley said uneasily. "But I do know her somewhat. She is a great lady, sir, if original. He may have persuaded her to come with him, simply to use her as a hostage. She must be rescued before any harm befalls her."

"And she will be, when O'Neill is apprehended." Reed went to Brawley and clapped his shoulder. "I have spies in Cork, Captain, watching the de Warenne ship. Sean O'Neill will walk right into the trap I have set for him, you may count on that."

Brawley met his blazing gaze and shivered.

A knock sounded. Both men turned. A young man stood there, red-faced from exertion, sweating heavily. He was not in uniform, but Brawley thought him vaguely familiar. Reed gestured. "Sergeant Lewes, come in. What have you learned?"

Lewes rushed forward. "O'Neill boarded *The Fair Lady* at dawn, Colonel. He met with de Warenne for about a half an hour."

Reed's brows arched, and he smiled. "Well done! Where is O'Neill now?"

Lewes hesitated. "I don't know, sir."

Reed's smile vanished. "What the hell does that mean?"

"Colonel, sir! I left my post to report to you the moment he left the ship. Those were my orders, sir."

"You fucking fool," Reed cried.

Lewes paled.

"Your orders were to discover his whereabouts," Reed added, flushed with anger now, "and to relay those whereabouts to me. Who is on the watch?" Reed demanded. "Or did *The Fair Lady* sail away, as well?"

"John Barret, sir, is spying on the ship."

"You are dismissed," Reed said harshly.

Brawley was stunned by the developments he had just witnessed. He hadn't known that Reed had men stationed in Cork, spying on Cliff de Warenne. Obviously Reed wished for him to be in the dark, and while it wasn't his place to question what his superior did or how he did it, he was uneasy yet again. "Sir, I am very familiar with Cork, its outlying neighborhoods, the mayor, the aldermen and some of its citizens. I also know Cobh."

"I am aware of that, Captain. I have read your file, not once but several times."

Brawley was silent, uncertain as to what that comment signified. He could have easily supervised the mission, and they would now know where O'Neill was. But his captain was intent on capturing O'Neill without his help, or so it seemed. But why? Was this a matter of glory, or something else?

Reed was cold. "I have more men in town," he said. "I have heard it whispered about that a Blueboy helped O'Neill in the first place. Yesterday I broke one of them, Captain. Now there is a traitor in their midst. When O'Neill contacts his treacherous friends again, we shall hear of it."

"Sir." Brawley was sweating.

Reed lifted a brow and waited.

"And if he thinks it too dangerous to contact a Blueboy this time?"

"Then he will need help from his brother. That is why, in light of this new information, you are to proceed to Cork with a detachment. You may camp outside of the city. Take one or two men and supervise the watch on *The Fair Lady*. I will send word to our new spy. Either way, we will locate O'Neill."

"Yes, sir," Brawley said, relieved to be seeing

action. Now, he could only continue to hope that Eleanor de Warenne was well, and that her stepbrother did not think to use her in order to flee the authorities.

"Your orders remain. Apprehend O'Neill, dead or alive—it doesn't matter, as this time, he will hang."

"Yes, sir."

"And should the opportunity present itself, you are to apprehend the woman."

Brawley started. "I beg your pardon?"

"If you discover Lady de Warenne's whereabouts independently of O'Neill's, she may have useful information. You will apprehend her and bring her directly to me."

His distress escalated. "Yes, sir."

And Reed knew, for he seemed amused. "Calm yourself, Captain. If you are right, the lady has far more to fear from her outlaw stepbrother than she does from me. Besides, I doubt you will discover her alone." His eyes glittered.

Brawley knew there was an innuendo in the colonel's words, but he simply failed to understand it.

AT LEAST HE WAS ARMED, Sean thought as he entered the doorway at the base of the stairs that led to his flat.

He remained sick with worry and knew he would stay that way until Eleanor had been found. She was hurt and angry, and she was also stubborn. She had no intention of coming back to him. If she did, she would have returned hours ago.

And now, his stepbrothers and Devlin would begin a massive search for her. Surely they would find her, and soon. He started up the stairs in the dark. He would continue looking for Elle, as well, but he needed an hour of rest.

Suddenly he faltered, his gaze penetrating the shadows on the landing, only to discover a pile of rags which had not been present earlier. Then Sean realized that the rags were far more than clothing; he cried out.

"Elle!"

Elle lay curled up there against the wall, shivering, her eyes meeting his. He knelt, reaching for her, quickly realizing that she was soaking wet. She flinched, pressing him away.

"It's me," he said quickly, ignoring the protest and pulling her into his arms. Her skin was wet, icy and cold, frighteningly so.

She pushed him away. "The door is locked," she said hoarsely.

Still kneeling, his gaze found hers. His heart twisted at the raw grief he saw in her eyes. She remained devastated by what he had done, but she had come back to him, anyway.

"I know. I didn't want to leave it open in case the British found the flat. You need to get warm," he said quickly, standing. His hands were shaking now as he tried to fit the key in the lock. Had she spent the night in the rain? Why hadn't she found shelter!

"I only came back for Saphyr. I am going home," she said, her tone so low it was barely audible.

He turned. She remained seated on the floor, holding her knees to her chest. Her feet were filthy and he realized that one foot was bleeding. She stared, her eyes accusing.

He realized he needed to somehow explain his marriage to her—but how could he, when it hurt too much to even think about it, much less speak of it? And even if he did explain, then what? He saw from her eyes that she hadn't forgiven him for his betrayal and that she never would. "You need to dry off. I have an escort for you—you can't think to ride about the country alone."

She shrugged.

He hesitated and then held out his hand.

She looked away, the tip of her nose already pink, turning red.

"Elle...Eleanor. Let me help you up."

She didn't answer, standing by herself, wincing as she did so.

His heart raced with more alarm as he pushed open the door, going directly to the stove. He quickly started a fire, straining to hear what she was about. She entered the room but then paused and he did not hear her close the door. He didn't hear her move, either.

The fire crackling, he closed the door to the stove and stood. Slowly he glanced at her, his stomach clenching.

She looked as if she had almost drowned. He ignored the sight of her wet blouse and chemise, mostly transparent, clinging to her breasts. He glanced down to look at her bleeding foot, and instead, his gaze lingered on her long legs, encased in wet doeskin. Shaken, he tore his gaze lower. "What happened?"

She shrugged and started limping across the room.

He realized she meant to drop directly into the bed. He reached her side and grabbed her arm. "You need to change from those wet clothes."

Her golden eyes lifted. "I don't think so. Not if you remain in the room."

He deserved her suspicion, her lack of trust. But he just stared, stricken, because this was the first time in his life that she mistrusted him.

She stared back, her gaze filled with hostility, hurt and suspicion. "Maybe you should visit Kate. That way you can leave me be."

Her words stabbed through him like a knife. He wanted to tell her it hadn't been like that. "I'll wait in the hall," he said instead, slowly leaving the room. At the door he glanced back, but she hadn't moved. He realized she was crying.

He had finally broken her heart. Too late, he had the terrible feeling he would never have it back.

Sean stepped outside, closing the door, trying to fight sudden panic. This was as it should be, he told himself fiercely, because she would recover from this and then she could give her heart to Sinclair. He turned and kicked the wall so hard that pain shot right up his leg to his knee, but he could not find calm or relief. It was finally over.

When a sufficient amount of time had passed, he knocked but there was no response. Sean carefully peered into the room. The spare suit remained hanging on the wall and Eleanor was in bed, wrapped up in the blanket. He saw her shirt on the floor, stained with watered-down blood and knew that at least she had cleaned her cuts.

He went inside, bolting the door behind him. "You need to be in front of the fire," he tried, but as she had to be nude beneath the blankets, it wasn't the best of ideas.

She didn't respond.

And because he was concerned, he went over to her. She was either asleep or pretending to be asleep, but shivering periodically, the shudders violent. He hesitated, uncertain of what to do. She needed far more warmth than that single blanket could provide and he wanted to inspect her wounded foot. But she hated him now. He had no doubt of that. "Elle?"

There was no answer and he realized she was deeply asleep after all.

He sat down at her hip, wondering if she had been up all night, wandering the streets of the city, heart-broken and alone. He could no longer live with himself. He had hurt the one person he cared most about in the world.

Do you love my sister?

The question felt like a trap. He wasn't going to take the bait. What he really felt didn't matter. He saw that he had taken her hand and was gripping it. It was icy cold.

Sean gave up. He tore off his boots and he climbed under the covers with her, taking her into his arms. She remained as soft as a rag doll and as cold as ice.

He had done this. "Elle, I'm sorry." He kissed her

cheek and he started to cry. "I should have told you about Peg the moment I came home.... I was afraid. I knew you would hate me for marrying her... I never loved her."

He was holding her so close that she was wrapped in his arms and legs, her face against his shoulder. He lifted his head so he could stare down at her face. Her lashes had fluttered. And gazing at her, his heart surged powerfully. She was so beautiful and so strong, so brave. He lowered his head, tucking hers beneath his chin. "How could I have ever loved Peg? I love you." And too late, he realized the words he had just spoken were the truth.

He closed his eyes, holding her even more tightly, allowing himself to finally realize and identify his feelings. He was stunned by their enormity, their intensity, their power.

He knew what would happen if he dared to love her. She would suffer, as Peg had suffered. And he was a doomed man. Nothing had changed, except that his heart wanted something he could never have—and had no right to have.

"S-S-Sean? I'm c-c-cold."

He stiffened as their gazes met. Hers was not coherent or focused.

He tried to smile at her. "I know. You'll be warm soon. Warm...and safe. I promise."

Her mouth curved and the trust he thought he'd never see again filled her eyes. "I am safe," she murmured, kissing his jaw.

This time an entirely different part of his body went rigid. He reminded himself that she was more asleep than awake, and possibly ill, if not delusional. She hated him, and the trust he'd seen in her eyes was a cruel reminder of what he would never again genuinely have and had never really deserved. The present was proof of that.

Suddenly her cold hands were inside his shirt and against his chest. She sighed and began to rub the skin there and then his nipples.

Sean seized her wrist, restraining her. His mind told him to get out of her bed, now, before he succumbed to temptation. Because he was now acutely aware of just how naked she was, how soft in some places, how lean in others, and the way they were intimately entwined. And then he felt her body soften.

Stunned, he realized she had fallen asleep, this time deeply, the shivering having ceased. He sighed, shaken but relieved, and then he pulled her closer. He kissed the top of her head, thinking about the feelings he had just discovered, allowing the wonder of his discovery to wash over him. He did not know when he had first fallen in love with her, but she had been his life from the moment they had met. The swollen feeling in his heart might have been joy and hope combined, had he been a different man in a different life. He decided not to analyze it further. He felt awed, as if in the midst of a miracle, and he knew he must cherish this brief moment and cling to it for as long as he could.

Reality must wait.

And when dawn broke another time, he crept from her bed and made the necessary arrangements for the future they would not share.

WHEN ELEANOR AWOKE, it took her a moment to recall where she was.

Sunlight was pouring into a small, sparsely furnished flat. A fire was crackling in a cast-iron stove near a tin sink. She lay in a simple bed, with a single pillow, a sheet, a thin and coarse blanket.

And then Eleanor saw Sean.

He was entering the room, carrying an armful of wood for the stove.

In that moment, she recalled that he had come

back and she had jilted Peter Sinclair at the altar. They were in Cork, hiding from the authorities—and Sean had married another woman named Peg.

Overcome with the same sense that this could not be happening, she sat up slowly, holding the covers up to her neck. She had never ached with so much sorrow. *Sean no longer belonged to her and he never had.*

"What happened to me? Where are my clothes?" she asked, her tone sounding high and hoarse to her own ears.

He put the wood in the wicker basket by the stove, avoiding her. "You ran away from me." He glanced at her, his expression tight and hard. "You returned freezing cold and soaked."

And suddenly she recalled spending the night in a doorway, shivering and wet, crying her heart out, the sense of loss beyond anything she'd ever before experienced.

He stood and glanced briefly at her. "I bought you some proper clothing." He gestured at the wall pegs, where a muslin dress, underclothes, pelisse and bonnet were hanging. There were also shoes and stockings.

She wondered if he had any money left, then refused to worry for him. He was a traitor, not to the authorities, but to her—to them. She never intended to forget it.

"I suppose you expect me to be grateful for the clothes?" She was aware of sounding as bitter as she felt.

"You don't owe me...anything," he said sharply, and their gazes collided. He turned away again, finally flushing.

"I certainly do not," Eleanor retorted, now hugging the blankets to her breasts. He owed her everything, and she was never going to collect, because he had chosen a different woman over her. She wondered if her heart was ever going to heal and feel whole again. She didn't think so.

"Where are my trousers?" she asked grimly. She actually coveted the clean dress and underclothes, but would never say so.

He went to the clothes pegs and removed the feminine items. "I burned them," he said quietly, attempting to hand her the ensemble.

"How dare you!" she cried, and in that instant, she was enraged. "I want my trousers back!"

He started, and as if realizing she was slightly out of her mind, a wary look entered his eyes. "They're gone. You can't parade around...dressed as a man. When you are home, I am certain...you will talk Tyrell out of his clothes."

When she was home, tossed aside like leftovers.

That was what she was, used goods fit for the garbage. But he hadn't used Peg that way.

"I'll wait outside," he said suddenly.

"Oh, yes, with Kate! Is that where you got the clothes, from Kate?" She was furious.

"Actually, I bought them in a shop," he said carefully.

"But Kate's clothes would have been so perfect for me! Because I'm no different from her, now am I? I'm no different from a housemaid or a dairymaid or a farmer's daughter. I am no different from a *whore*."

He turned white. "For God's sake, don't do this," he said rigidly.

"Don't do what? Point out the fact that you have treated me the way you have treated all those trollops you took to the stables when we were growing up?" Tears of bitter rage filled her eyes. "How dare you burn my pants!"

He inhaled harshly. "I am sorry. I am sorry for everything. You are not a farmer's daughter and you are not a whore. I know you love me…I am a cad. I used you and there is no excuse." He turned to leave.

She slid from the bed, the blanket and sheet wrapped around her. "I don't love you!"

He stumbled, stiffened, turned.

"You were a rake when I was a child and I know

it firsthand. You remain a rake—and a cad! You are a *cheat,* Sean, a *liar* and a *cheat* and a *miserable cad!*"

He did not move. He did not speak. He was so still he could have been carved from stone, a beautiful male statue.

"Defend yourself!" she shouted, shaking in her rage.

He shook his head.

Eleanor didn't hesitate. She slapped him with all of her might across his starkly pale but handsome face.

He flinched, but otherwise, stood ramrod straight.

"Just so there is no misunderstanding, I hate you now."

He nodded and walked out.

ELEANOR PULLED her wide-brimmed bonnet low as she followed Sean to the dock, keeping her head and face hidden. He had disguised himself with a powdered wig, the kind some of the older, unfashionable men wore, as if their previous king still lived. Her heart had never felt heavier, but this was what she wanted now—to go home. Sean had said that Cliff would sail her to Limerick. The trip overland was much shorter, but she had wanted to avoid any and all conversation with Sean. He seemed to want that, too, and they had not exchanged more than a few sentences about their plans since their previous argument. Sean appeared to be in a hurry. She couldn't help wondering what that might mean. Were the authorities on his trail?

The piers were in sight, with many bobbing ships of all sizes and shapes. Instantly she saw *The Fair Lady,* at anchor some distance away. She also saw the British naval ship and at the sight of its flag, she shuddered. A few red-coated marines were on its decks, but otherwise the ship was silent and appeared deserted.

She folded her arms, filled with a new tension, brought on by the sight of the marines. "Why would Cliff take me home now when he could sail you away? The two of you have clearly conspired already." She refused to meet his gaze.

"Cliff is going to take you home. He and I are agreed." He was firm.

It was so difficult having a conversation with the man she had once loved so completely. All she wanted to do was escape him and never see him again, but he did not deserve to hang. "Do not mistake me," she said curtly, her gaze on the harbor scene. "I want to go home immediately. I want nothing more. However, I have decided that I prefer to go by land. Cliff can sail you away." And she finally met his eyes.

"As soon as you board, I will book passage…on another ship." He spoke very softly now but his voice had never been more intense. Was it pleading?

She felt herself flush. "I do not care what you do," she said, meaning it, "once you are out of the country. There are soldiers right over there. I will travel by coach."

His gaze was searching, so she kept her eyes downcast. "We don't have time to argue.… The plans are made. And Cliff will keep you safe."

The words slipped out before she could stop them. "And who will keep you safe, Sean?" Her tone was hostile.

"But you hate me," he said slowly.

A long, tense pause ensued. "I hate you…but I do not wish you dead," she finally said.

Then, suddenly, he spoke. "You will never forgive me, will you?"

She had to meet his anguished eyes. Trembling, she steeled herself against him. "No."

"I didn't think so," he said.

ELEANOR SAT IN THE BACK of the gig by herself, wrapped up in a soft wool cloak that belonged to Connelly's wife. There had been too many soldiers on the docks for her to board Cliff's ship, and she was travelling home by coach after all. The carriage was an open one, pulled by a single horse, and even though the sun was shining, it was a cold, bitter day. She shivered, but the coldness of her skin was nothing like the iciness in her heart. Connelly had offered to take her to Adare and she was finally on her way home. She was trying not to think or feel but it was so hard. She was never going to see Sean O'Neill again.

How had her life come to this single point in time?

Memories she and Sean had made together over an entire lifetime were her only companion now. But the remembrances were so painful now, even the pleasant, happy ones, because all hope was gone.

Their lives had diverged long ago when he had chosen a path that had led him north, away from Askeaton and into another woman's life. How odd it was that a single twist of Fate had briefly brought them together. Now, with every breath she drew, their steps diverged again, but this time, more widely. There would be no more miraculous twists of Fate. Their paths were never going to cross again. It shouldn't hurt, not after all he had done. But, dear God, it did.

Eleanor shuddered, filled with grief. The adage was that time healed all wounds, but she knew hers would never heal. Hatred was a refuge, but she could never genuinely hate Sean. She would cling to her anger for as long as she could, but her heart knew it was a sham.

There was so much regret.

Connelly suddenly glanced back over his shoulder, his face stiff with tension.

Eleanor felt a frisson of dread. She, too, turned.

A dusty cloud filled the air, signaling numerous riders behind them, rapidly approaching.

Connelly saw it, too. "We have company, my lady. Probably a hired coach, but you never know. Could be cutthroats an' thieves—or worse."

Worse, of course, would mean soldiers. For the first time since running away with Sean, Eleanor started to realize the situation she was in. In a way, she had been an accomplice to Sean's escape. She remained certain, however, that no officer would ever condemn her for what she had done. After all, she was Adare's daughter.

Eleanor clung to the carriage door. Connelly slowed the gig. The cloud of dust was replaced by a half a dozen riders, all except one wearing the blue uniforms of a regiment of Light Dragoons. And the officer in red was none other than Captain Thomas Brawley.

Instantly she was afraid for Sean—and fiercely

relieved she did not know his exact plans. Trembling, she realized she must convince the troops that Sean had left the country days ago, that he was already far out to sea. And in that moment, there was no hatred, only a fierce and loyal desire to protect the man she had known and loved her entire life. Lowering her voice, she said, "We have done *nothing* wrong."

Connelly was white. "They'll hang me if I am found out," he said.

Eleanor's mind sped with excuses and explanations. She hadn't seen Sean in days—he had left the country immediately, and she had been ill and stranded in Cork. "Let me do the speaking," she said tersely to Connelly.

Brawley rode up to her. "Lady de Warenne!" he cried with evident relief.

She somehow smiled. "Captain."

He instantly dismounted. His gaze moved swiftly over her, the inspection clinical, not bold. "Are you all right?"

Eleanor marked his concern but was now worried about the treachery she suspected had led the troops to her. She glanced at Connelly, but he was pale with fear and she was certain he was not the traitor—if, indeed, there was one in their midst. She must use all of her wits now, she thought fiercely, and if Brawley was concerned for her, she would play him, too.

She extended her hand to him. Unfortunately she was trembling. "I have been through an ordeal," she said softly, allowing tears to fill her eyes. "Thank God you are here."

"What has happened to you?" Helping her from the carriage, he took her arm and led her a short distance away, so they might speak somewhat privately. "Where is O'Neill?"

"He is gone," she gasped. More tears came. "He abandoned me in the city days ago, sir, and I was lost and alone. After wandering the city in the rain, I became terribly ill, with fever. I woke up on a farm and this kind farmer not only cared for me, but once I recovered, he offered to take me home."

Brawley's gaze moved over her face. "You still do not look well, Lady Eleanor. I am sorry you have suffered such a terrible ordeal, but I must ask another question—do you know where Sean O'Neill has gone?"

"I only know that he took a ship, but I do not know where he was bound." She regarded the captain closely, breathlessly awaiting his reaction to her story.

"Did he tell you the name of the ship?"

She shook her head, relieved, as Brawley seemed to believe her. And to continue her pretense, she said,

"How is my fiancé?" She let more tears fall. "He will never forgive me for what I have done."

Brawley produced an immaculate, white handkerchief and he handed it to her. "He was vastly concerned when I last saw him, Lady Eleanor. I am certain, once you explain, he will forgive you. O'Neill forced you to leave with him, did he not?"

Eleanor accepted the linen, dabbing at her eyes. How could Brawley think that, when half of the county had seen her chasing Sean in her wedding gown? "I was worried about him, as you know. I wanted to detain him, and when he would not stay, I was determined to go with him so I could learn the truth. Once we had fled Adare, there was no going back. He told me from the very first hour that he would leave me the moment we got to Cork."

"He is unconscionable," Brawley said grimly.

She tried to think. Brawley was going to insist that he escort her home. There did not seem to be any way around it. "I must get home and I have promised a considerable sum to O'Brien for so kindly taking me back." She did not want to reveal Connelly's real identity. "If you could allow us on our way? I am very eager to reassure my family that I am well, and I miss Peter terribly."

"Lady Eleanor, of course you are eager to return

to Adare. I would be delighted to escort you," Brawley stated firmly.

"That is hardly necessary. I do not want to deter you from your military duties and as you can see, I do have a driver and a carriage." She smiled at him.

He seemed stiff and uncomfortable now. He tugged briefly at his high, tight collar. "I am afraid I have orders to the contrary," he said.

She tensed. "Orders? What orders?"

Brawley wet his lips. "I do beg your pardon, Lady Eleanor. But my orders are to escort you to Kilraven Hill."

Eleanor was stunned. *You must go home, to Adare and Sinclair. He can protect you, Elle. I will not have you risk your liberty, your life!*

And recalling Sean's strange words, words she had not been able to genuinely comprehend at the time, she became afraid. "Why would you have orders to take me to the fort?" she asked slowly.

"My commander wishes to speak with you." He tried to smile reassuringly and failed. "I have no choice. I am sorry but we must proceed to the garrison there."

Sean had insisted she could be charged with various crimes because of him. She had not believed it. She was becoming frightened now. Surely her father would never allow anything to happen to her. "Am I a prisoner, sir?"

He flushed. "Of course not! Colonel Reed merely wishes to speak with you. I shall be delighted to escort you home, as soon as the interview is concluded."

Eleanor said uncertainly, "But I have told you everything that I know, sir."

"Lady Eleanor, you may unwittingly possess some more clues as to O'Neill's destination. You may be able to identify the traitors he has been associated with. Colonel Reed merely wishes to ask you a few questions. I know you are tired and distressed and that this is highly inconvenient. On his behalf, I do apologize, but I must bring you to Kilraven."

Clearly she could not manage Brawley now, not to her satisfaction. Still, he might be more pliable at some future time. Eleanor nodded, summoning up all of the grace and dignity she could manage. "I understand that you are merely doing your duty, sir. I will not resist."

"I hope you do understand, Lady Eleanor," Brawley said fervently. "It is my greatest regret that I am inconveniencing you in your time of need."

Eleanor somehow smiled.

CHAPTER SIXTEEN

DEVLIN O'NEILL ENTERED the great hall of Askeaton with long, purposeful strides, tossing his greatcoat at his valet. "Where is my wife, Hughes?" he began.

But he did not have to continue. The two solid oak doors that yielded to a large yet intimate salon opened and Virginia appeared, crying out. She instantly rushed across the flagstone floors and into his arms. "Devlin!"

He embraced her once, hard, then quickly led her back to the salon. "Hughes." He spoke as if still commanding a warship. "We are not to be disturbed."

"Yes, Sir Captain." Hughes closed both doors behind them.

Devlin met his wife's frightened eyes and his heart turned over. Once, his life had been a black hole of obsession; Virginia had been unfortunate enough to be his worst enemy's niece and he had cruelly and ruthlessly used her as an instrument of revenge. He wasn't certain when he had fallen in love with her, but he thought he had loved her at first sight, when she had stood on the deck of an American merchantman in high seas, trying to take a sniper shot at him. He had been intent on mayhem and piracy, but even while boarding the enemy ship, he had admired her audacity and daring, not to mention her unusual beauty.

She had become his mistress and then his wife. She was everything now—his dearest friend, his untiring lover, the mother of his two children, his guiding light. She was his heart. "Darling, you need not worry so."

"I need not worry!" she repeated in disbelief, as white as a sheet. She shook her head. "I wasn't sure I'd ever see you again! I thought you were in Cobh!"

He took her small hand in his. Even after so many years together, he was amazed by how tiny and delicate she was. "Before leaving the county, I learned of a schooner here in Limerick, newly arrived. I have purchased the *Gazelle.* She is small but swift and smart and she will suit our purposes nicely."

Virginia faced him, both of her small hands on his broad chest. "I must come with you, Devlin. I am terrified that we will never see one another again."

He was dismayed. "I have every intention of returning to you. And what of the children?"

A tear began to crawl down her cheek. "You know I can't leave them. But they could come with us. No matter what happens, we would be together as a family."

"Absolutely not."

"How small is the *Gazelle?* How many guns does she carry—how many marines?"

Unfortunately, his wife had learned a great deal about ships and naval warfare. He hesitated.

"Devlin!" she cried.

"Darling, she only carries nine guns." He saw the panic fill her eyes. "Virginia, I am not going to engage the British. She is exceedingly swift. The British will be following Cliff," he reminded her. And to lighten her mood, he smiled. "Cliff intends to lead them on quite a merry chase! His arrogance knows no bounds. He is enjoying his mission and I feel certain he thinks to lead them across the entire Atlantic Ocean before they ever realize they have been duped. Knowing my brother, he will serve the officers a fine crow supper in his island home."

Virginia wiped at her tears. "If your plan works, how will you return home?"

"I do not want you to know any details, as my absence will eventually be remarked. I have laid a paper trail to France—you may insist I am attending to business in Paris. But when I return, I will not be on the *Gazelle*. Have no fear, Virginia. I am coming home."

He had never seen her this afraid, not since that terrible day in her native land when she had thought him killed in action during the war between their countries. "Darling, I must help Sean."

"I know. You remain the bravest man I have ever met—and the most steadfast," she whispered.

"It will only be a few months," he returned, finally allowing his real emotion to creep into his tone. His life had changed. Once, he had avoided land like the plague, never spending more than a few days in any port. Now, he avoided travel in the same way. He had not seen his wife and children in three days, and it felt like three years. He hated leaving them now, but he must save his brother from the gallows.

"We will be waiting for you, Devlin," Virginia said, forcing a smile. "I am sorry I am acting so spineless. I am so glad you could come home, if only for a few hours."

She knew him so well. "I must set sail before dawn and speed the *Gazelle* to Cobh, Virginia." He met her violet eyes. "I do not want to waste any time."

Virginia raised her face to his. "Neither do I."

Devlin crushed her in his arms, claiming her mouth

with the same hunger he'd felt upon first seeing her on the deck of that ship, six fateful years ago.

KILRAVEN HILL WAS an old garrison, established centuries ago during the latter part of Queen Elizabeth's reign. Some of the original stone walls were still standing. About five hours from Limerick and Adare, the fort had certainly been close enough for Eleanor to be familiar with it, but she had never once visited the command. Now, as her carriage passed through the curtain of wood stockade walls, Connelly seated beside her in manacles, she shivered. Brawley had claimed that she was no prisoner, but in that moment, she felt very much like one.

Connelly was no longer pale. He had spent the past few hours in silence, and occasionally she had heard him pray. Eleanor had tried to reassure him but had then given up. He was a commoner, an Irishman and a Catholic, and he had aided and abetted a traitor's escape. If he was fortunate, he would be deported, not hanged.

"My lady," he suddenly said, facing her. "I have prayed for you, too."

Eleanor's heart danced with renewed anxiety. "Mr. Connelly, you have placed yourself at great risk to usher me safely home. The moment I arrive there, I will do my best to see to it that you are freed."

He shook his head. "I have a wife and two children. I'm afraid for them, too."

Eleanor touched his arm. "I will take care of them," she said, "and it is a promise."

Relief softened his eyes.

The carriage halted before a large stone building, and Brawley was already opening her door. "Lady Eleanor?" He smiled reassuringly at her. "We are at the garrison's headquarters. Please?"

"What will happen to O'Brien?" she asked, stepping down from the carriage with Brawley's help.

"He will be imprisoned until his trial."

"So he has already been charged?" she cried.

Brawley flushed. "Not to my knowledge."

"Is there any justice in this world?" she demanded grimly. "Has it not occurred to you that he may be innocent of the crimes you wish to accuse him of?"

Brawley lowered his eyes. "Lady Eleanor, we have had spies in Cork for days and Connelly was identified as a Blueboy almost immediately by our men. We have a witness who will testify that he aided Sean O'Neill from the moment O'Neill arrived in the city. But you are right. This may be a misunderstanding and I have been too quick to judge."

"Thank you," Eleanor managed stiffly. She was aghast that Brawley knew Connelly's real identity. The fact that she had been covering for him made her look like an accomplice.

But Brawley did not remark on it. He ushered her inside, his expression grim. Clerks and staff sergeants were seated at desks in a large room, attending to their duties. Across the room, Eleanor glimpsed an open door and another office, dominated by a large desk. Brawley indicated that she precede him to it.

Her heart raced madly. She had had several hours to brood in the carriage and she knew what she must do. In a terrible and ironic way, Fate had intervened again, placing her in the position of being able to help Sean elude the authorities. She might never see him again, but she could lead the authorities astray in their search for him by feeding them false information.

Eleanor stepped into the office. The moment she did so, she saw Sean's likeness taped on the white wall behind the desk and she blanched. The poster was too far away for her to read, but she knew it was a poster offering a reward for Sean's capture. Her stomach lurched sickeningly.

Brawley smiled reassuringly at her. "I will have tea and biscuits brought in. The colonel has been summoned. He will be present shortly."

She stared at the poster, barely hearing Brawley. She fought for her composure, when what she wanted to do was seize the poster, read it and then rip it to shreds. Instead, she breathed deeply. Then she lifted her gaze to the young captain and smiled at him. "You have been terribly kind. Thank you for making this ordeal somewhat bearable, Captain."

"I would there was no ordeal at all, Lady Eleanor."

She smiled again. "Can you send word to my father that I am here?"

He started. "The earl is in London, bent upon attaining a pardon for your stepbrother."

Hope leaped in Eleanor's breast, but she did not change her expression. Brawley bowed and left, closing the door firmly behind him. So much excitement began. Her father was a great man of power as well as wealth, and when he was determined to succeed, he never failed. Surely he would attain Sean's pardon and this nightmare would finally end!

She didn't dare think about what the end of his fugitive status would mean for her. There was no time for more hope and certainly not for procrastination. She went to the desk and passed behind it. She stared at the poster, her conviction hardening. The page declared that Sean was armed and dangerous, an escaped felon and a traitor. He was to be apprehended by any means necessary, dead or alive. A reward of 10 pounds was being offered.

She reached for the poster, enraged, about to rip it from the wall. An English voice stopped her.

"You may have it as a souvenir, if that is what you wish."

She dropped her hand and stiffened. Then she rearranged her expression into a distraught one, summoning moisture to her eyes, and she turned.

A pair of remarkably intense and terribly cold blue eyes met hers. While the colonel wore a soft smile on his pale, oval face, the expression did not reach his gaze. Eleanor tensed.

And the colonel bowed. "Lady Eleanor de Warenne, I presume?"

Her heart was racing wildly. She reminded herself that she had no reason to fear this man. He was an officer and a gentleman. "Yes. Colonel Reed?"

He was studying her with such a brilliant regard that her alarm increased. And then his gaze swept her from head to toe, slowly and carefully, so as not to miss a single detail. She stiffened. The examination was somehow crude and base. He was judging her as a farmer did during the purchase of a prospective horse. She pulled the brown cloak she wore together, holding it tightly closed over her breasts.

"Would you like the poster of your stepbrother?" His pale brows rose. His tone remained far too neutral.

"I hardly wish a souvenir of the terrible ordeal I have suffered."

"I am sure your ordeal has been a trying one," he drawled. No light flickered in his eyes. "Come, please, sit down. Clearly you are exhausted. You must tell me all about it."

Eleanor hesitated. The desk was a large physical barrier between them and she was oddly reluctant to come out from behind it. Having no choice, she walked around the desk. As if he understood that she did not wish to come too close, he firmly took her arm. She flinched. This man was making her unbearably nervous, and she was angry with herself for reacting so hysterically to his rank and uniform. She had a plan to execute, one that would free Sean. She managed to allow him to guide her to a chair.

Reed went behind his desk, where he sat facing her. "You will tell me all about it, won't you, Lady de Warenne?"

She remained unbearably rigid. "Of course," she breathed. Then she dabbed at false tears. "I am such a foolish woman, sir. When I glimpsed my brother after so many years of separation, I was overcome! I had recently learned he was a fugitive, but I knew he could not be guilty of any crimes! I went with him because I had to learn the truth. I did not realize that once we left Adare, we would be pursued and that I could not simply turn around and go back." She now dared to look at him, to see if he believed her story as Captain Brawley had.

He was smiling. He was actually *amused*. And in that instant Eleanor knew she could not manipulate this officer as she had young Brawley.

"Shall we cut to the chase, Lady Eleanor?"

She was rigid. Brawley had the right to call her in such a familiar manner, as he had been a guest in her home, invited there by her father. This man was a stranger. He had no such rights. "I beg your pardon?"

"I must locate your stepbrother, and I am an impatient man. So shall we cease with your nonsense?"

Her heart beat hard. "It is Lady de Warenne, Colonel." He dared speak to her so boldly *and* so rudely? She was stunned.

He laughed, the sound mirthless. "If it pleases you, Lady de Warenne. Where is O'Neill?"

"He is on his way to Sicily, sir."

"Sicily? I thought you were not privy to his plans."

So he had taken a moment to speak with Brawley. "I dissembled, Colonel. Sean begged me to keep his plans to myself, but I am cold and tired and I want

to go home, so I have decided to tell you everything."
She managed a placating smile. "I will tell you the
truth, so you will let me go home sooner rather than
later. Do we not still have naval forces in the Medi-
terranean? I am sure you will locate Sean there if you
make the effort."

Reed leaned back in his chair and he simply stared
at her, until she felt her cheeks grow hot. Then he
spoke. "And suddenly you wish to see your *stepbrother* caught?"

He had inflected mockingly on the word
"brother." Eleanor trembled and hoped he did not
notice. But she must play the fool now. "My stepbrother is a gentleman, sir, not a rogue or an outlaw.
I know this is a terrible mistake and that once he faces
the authorities, the entire affair will be resolved. I
have never been more certain of anything and I do
wish for him to come home! I tried to reason with
him but he would not listen to a word I had to say."
She sighed. "But that is Sean. He is so unreasonable
at times."

Reed's vague smile never slipped. "And which
ship did he set sail on? And when did he disembark?"

"I don't know which ship he sailed on. But he left
me in Cork the morning we arrived, four days ago—
the day after I was to be wed." She tried to appear

angry and upset now. "He simply left me there, alone and lost! For that I shall never forgive him, sir!"

"How outrageous," Reed said with obviously false sympathy. "So you spent three days alone in Cork and only today, the fourth day, did you decide, suddenly, to attempt a return home?"

"I was very ill!" Eleanor exclaimed. She relished a chance to tell a part of the truth now. "I wandered the night in the rain. I became unconscious. I cannot begin to tell you how ill I was—I slept in a doorway, sir! It was several days before I regained enough strength to beg for help, like any common vagrant, and then that sweet farmer was kind enough to offer me a drive home. Of course, I will reimburse him for his efforts on my behalf."

He made a soft disbelieving sound. "Of course. That sweet farmer is a Blueboy and you know it. He is a traitor to the Crown, intent on revolution and anarchy. And that is before he came to the aid of your outlaw *stepbrother*."

Eleanor blinked, as he had spoken with heat and anger. His regard slid down the bodice of her inexpensive white dress. When he spoke, his tone was impassive once again. "So you spent the entire time in Cork vagrant and homeless in a doorway?"

She knew her story was a doubtful one. "I was delirious for two days, Colonel. And then I wandered to a farm, which is where I woke up. Do you doubt my word?" she cried with indignation, quickly recapturing her cloak and covering her body with it.

Still smiling politely, he stood.

Eleanor became so tense it was hard to breathe.

"I think you are an utter liar."

She cried out.

And he stared, his smile gone, his eyes brilliant with fervor, the room becoming terribly, unbearably still.

She finally stood. "How dare you," she managed, beyond shock. No man—or woman—had ever spoken to her in such a disrespectful way.

"Sit down." It was an order.

She ignored it. "I think not! In fact, I am going home. You, sir, are no gentleman and you will be hearing from my father, the earl." She was livid now.

And Colonel Reed began to laugh at her.

Eleanor was disbelieving. Genuine dread began.

For Reed now walked around his desk toward her. "Your father, my dear, is not in this country."

"Sir, this is not appropriate behavior," she protested.

He smiled. "Utter lies are not to my liking… Eleanor."

And in that instant, when he dared to utter her

name in such a disrespectful manner, she knew she was in danger. Suddenly, she recalled Sean's fear for her safety. Suddenly, she began to understand why he had been afraid for her. She backed away from the colonel until she hit the wall. "It is Lady de Warenne."

He did not pause.

She stiffened impossibly as he approached her, incredulous now, for he only halted when an inch separated them.

"Do you really think me a fool? An utter idiot?" he asked softly.

"Move away," she commanded desperately, as his breath feathered her face.

"I am the one who gives the orders here," he reminded her. "You may cooperate, and you will be sent home, relatively unscathed. Or you may lie—and pay the consequences. They will be dire."

She tried to breathe. "How dare you treat me as if I am some commoner, sir! I am a lady, and—"

"I believe we both know you are no lady."

She gasped.

He leaned close. His mouth moved over her cheek when he spoke. "I know a whore when I see one."

She responded on instinct, striking at him; he seized her wrist with so much force that in another moment she knew it would snap in half.

Eleanor inhaled sharply in pain, the room turning hazy. Hot waves knifed through her wrist and the gray room turned black. Miraculously the pressure was eased and salts were placed under her nose, when all she wanted to do was to faint and escape him. "No," she begged, turning away from the offending odor.

"You will give me what I want," he said harshly. "And you certainly will not be allowed to faint."

"No," she gasped. But he kept the salts there against her nostrils and the world stopped turning. The terrific pain became a terrible throbbing, but one she could endure. She opened her eyes and met the most ruthless gaze she had ever seen. She did not think her wrist was broken but she somehow knew he would have enjoyed inflicting even greater pain if he could have done so.

Never had she been so afraid.

"O'Neill is your lover and you are nothing but a traitor, no less than he is," Reed said savagely. He put his arm around her.

Eleanor struggled uselessly until she realized he was only forcing her to the chair. She sank into it and dared to clutch her wrist. She tried to breathe and to think, but she was too afraid to plan or scheme now.

"How unfortunate that you had a fall on the stairs,"

he said. "The next fall will even be worse. I imagine a broken limb might result."

She went still.

"Yes, Eleanor, I will break you into a dozen pieces to get what I want. I want your lover. He should have hanged for the death of my men two years ago. This time, he will pay for his crimes."

"You are mad," she gasped, and she finally understood Sean's fears. She was in grave, mortal danger. "My father, my brothers—"

"They will never know what happened to you! If you force me to abuse you, I will make certain you disappear without a trace." He suddenly seized her face, lifting her chin. "So do not make me hurt you, *Lady* de Warenne. If you value your life, you will tell me where O'Neill is. And I will even spare you the infamy of any punishment for your involvement with a traitor."

Eleanor was still. This man was insane. He had just threatened her life and she believed him capable of doing as he said. Worse, he was so arrogant that he was not afraid of her family. This man might even be right—if she simply disappeared, who would ever suspect an officer of her murder?

In that moment, she realized she was powerless.

Eleanor was briefly incapable of thought, of

reason. Her entire life she had been the Earl of Adare's treasured daughter. She had always been revered and treated with deference and respect. During her lifetime, Sean had been there to defend and protect her, should the need arise, and with him her three brothers and her stepbrother, Devlin. It was almost impossible to comprehend that she was in the hands of a madman who was not afraid of her family and that her rank, her breeding and her station meant nothing to him.

But how could she betray Sean?

"We both know O'Neill is in Cork. I have spies there—how else did I know to apprehend you on the road?" Reed cut into her horrified thoughts.

Eleanor did not speak. She was shaking like a leaf with fear.

He made a harsh sound. "Tell me where he is."

Eleanor had to marshal her thoughts. She was in grave danger, but she would never betray Sean. She had no death wish, though, either. That meant she needed to escape Reed's clutches. "I don't know."

He seemed surprised. Eleanor waited for some inevitable horror—she thought he might whirl and break her wrist.

But when he turned, he was holding a thin,

delicate sterling letter opener with a beautifully carved horn head.

Her heart sank and then raced wildly. The blade was as fine as that of a stiletto.

He smiled and lifted a tress of her hair. "Do you treasure yourself at all, Eleanor?"

She was relieved—he intended to cut off her hair. She began to breathe, as she could not care less if he turned her bald—it would grow back. And then he shocked her, slicing through the ties of her cloak so it fell to the floor.

She started to leap to her feet but he took his hand and pressed his palm against her bare décolletage, forcing her back into the chair. He met her shocked gaze and smiled. "This can be long and rude, or short and swift. Where is O'Neill?"

"I don't know," she answered, agonizingly aware of his hand on her body.

He took the letter opener and lifted the edge of the bodice of her dress with it. He met her gaze and waited for her to understand what he intended. She failed to even swallow now as she realized he was going to cut her dress off her, as he had the cloak. "Do not," she gasped.

"Modesty from an Irish whore? How odd."

She was so afraid that moisture trickled between her legs.

"Where is your lover?"

Eleanor closed her eyes. She was too afraid to pray.

And when she refused to speak, she felt and heard the fabric of her bodice tear. She gasped, eyes flying open, as he calmly sliced through the first layer of white cotton, taking the blade down between her breasts, down her torso and to her waist. There, he flicked at the fabric so it fell apart, exposing her body in her transparent chemise.

Instantly Eleanor closed her eyes and tried to think. She was defenseless, powerless and now, being sexually molested in a way she had never dreamed. But she could not give up Sean. What did he intend? Would he disrobe her? She could survive such cruelty and humiliation. Would he rape her? She would rather die than suffer his touch and invasion.

"Look at me," he ordered.

She opened her eyes and met his cold, brilliant gaze. "What will you do?" With great dignity, she gathered up her torn dress and held it together.

He smiled, amused. "I will proceed until you tell me what I must hear. Do not make me do this, Eleanor."

"I am not making you do anything," she somehow

managed to reply. "You do not have to go to such foul ends for what? To avenge your men? Sean did not lead the rising!"

"God, the lot of you, cutthroats and savages, as thick as thieves, and it never changes." He laid the letter opener down and cupped her chin. "Did you know my mother was an Irish whore? And in the end, she murdered my father. You remind me of her, really, not in appearance, but in spirit."

"Do not blame me for what your mother did to your father!"

He paced slowly around her chair. "I have dedicated my life to bringing justice to this heathen land, but it is an impossible and thankless task." He stared down at her. "Perhaps you do not know where he now is. Tell me where the two of you were hiding in Cork."

"Surely your spies have discovered that."

He struck her hard across the face and walked away from her.

Eleanor cried silently, until the throbbing of the right side of her face dulled and eased. How much more of this abuse could she stand? She was going to be tortured and raped, because Reed had a personal vendetta against everyone and everything Irish, and he feared no one. She had to postpone this interview; she had to gain time, because if she had time, she would find a way to escape.

Reed now sat on the edge of his desk, regarding her skeptically. "Are you in love with him?" He laughed with disbelief. "Such loyalty, and for what? Rape, torture, an inglorious death at the bottom of the sea? And does he love you in return? I doubt that," he added.

Eleanor did not hesitate and the painful reality of Sean's marriage to another woman fell away. "I love him," she said, "and I will never give him up."

He eyed her and spoke with relish. "I wonder if he ever gave you a thought while he was in bed with his pretty redheaded wife, night after night."

Eleanor choked on mortification, stabbed with hurt. Reed was right—Sean hadn't been thinking about her when he had been married to Peg, she felt quite certain.

"Ah, so he has already hurt you. He married Peg Boyle—not the Lady Eleanor! I, would have chosen you—your attributes are far more pleasing, and far more vast." He smiled, directing his gaze at her breasts.

He was beyond disgusting. Eleanor refused to speak.

"Oh, come. Let us talk about Sean's married life. Shall I tell you about Peg Boyle?"

Eleanor had to look at him. She remained ill, but she would hear him out now, because she was desperate to know something about the other woman, even though she was aware that he was manipulating her.

"She was very pretty, all flaming red hair and flawless skin. She was petite—perfectly so, really. You do know that a man enjoys a small, tight woman? She was very feminine, very seductive."

Eleanor bit her lip to keep herself from making a sound.

"But I never had a chance to sample her wares. My men were the ones who did that."

Eleanor was stunned. "I pray you are lying!"

"I am telling you the truth. I could not directly capture him and I made certain she paid for his crimes. Are you prepared to give your life for him, as well?"

Eleanor managed to look at him. "I am prepared to die."

He stared, his smile vanishing. His voice dropped to a silken whisper. "She did not want to die—she fought to the end. If death doesn't frighten you, I will have to find a far crueler fate. Of course, you need only confide in me, and you will be spared any further insults."

She tensed as he approached. "Even if I told you where Sean is now, you couldn't let me go. I would tell my brothers what you have done and you would pay a terrible price."

He leaned close. "You cannot triumph over me. You do not want to see any of your brothers assaulting a British officer, do you?"

She realized she was trapped. Even if she escaped, Reed was never going to pay for what he was doing to her, because he was right—she did not want her brothers seeking retribution against a British officer.

"O'Neill is a dead man, with your help or without it. Now I suggest you think about what it will be like to service an entire prison of convicted felons, thugs, cutthroats, murderers and thieves, because that is what I will do—I will lock you away where you will never be found and throw you to the scum of this earth. Think on it." He suddenly walked out.

Eleanor collapsed in the chair, shaking wildly. She believed him. She suddenly doubted her ability to withstand his threats. The man's madness knew no bounds. She wiped her eyes and stood, staggering from a sudden surge of dizziness, and she made her way to the window.

Twilight was settling but the fort remained distinct. Brawley might help her. If he knew how she had been treated, she had not a doubt he would protest vigorously. No gentleman would ever allow such cruelty to be inflicted on a woman. But the two soldiers standing outside the building were not familiar and a black despair claimed her.

Reed terrified her.

And she knew now that he was going to break her.

CHAPTER SEVENTEEN

BRAWLEY PACED just outside of the office where Reed was interviewing Lady Eleanor. It was simply incredible, but Reed had barred him from the interview, just as he had refused to allow Brawley to offer her refreshments. Eleanor de Warenne was clearly exhausted and her face was pinched and pale. She had suffered a trying ordeal and he remained deeply moved by her distress. He wished to alleviate her circumstance, but Reed would not let him.

He no longer trusted his superior. The interview had gone on for too long, and it *was* an interview—not an interrogation. Just as he had that unwelcome thought, a cry rang out—a cry of distress.

He turned to the staff sergeant. "Did you hear that?" he asked, for the office behind that closed door was now ominously silent.

Sergeant Mackenzie met his gaze. "Yes, sir, I did."

Brawley hoped he had imagined that cry. He wanted to barge into the room. What in God's name was happening in there? He reminded himself that Eleanor de Warenne was very distressed and it would be natural if she shed tears over her stepbrother. But surely Reed would politely remove himself from the office, so she might have a moment to compose herself. When he did, Brawley intended to insist that he be able to bring her a glass of water. But Reed did not come out.

Brawley knew that Reed was no gentleman. He was a career officer—his father had been the son of a butcher who had risen through the ranks, making captain. The man was a commoner with enough wit to rise through the ranks, just as his father before him had done.

Another ten minutes passed. In that interim, Brawley strained to hear, but only silence came from behind those closed doors. And then Colonel Reed stepped out.

Brawley stiffened. Reed never paused. He beckoned for Brawley to follow him as he crossed the anteroom and stepped outside into the night.

Reed spoke swiftly. "You may now bring Lady de Warenne her tea. You are to sympathize with her fully. You are then to aid her in an escape."

Brawley was stunned. He did not understand. "I beg your pardon?"

"Do not be a fool now," Reed said with his characteristic impatience. "I expect you to help her escape tonight. You realize, of course, that she will lead us back to O'Neill—if he is still in the country."

Brawley did not think so. "Sir, I believe she will return to Adare, as that is her destination."

Reed looked at him as if he were a gaping, drooling idiot. "I do not care what you think or believe, Brawley. I expect you to follow orders. You plan an escape with her, one that is credible—and we will follow her like a fox to its lair."

He was sweating. "Sir, is Lady Eleanor a prisoner?" Otherwise, why would she have to escape?

"She has lied about O'Neill. She is not free to go. I know you are smitten with her, but she is a traitor, just like O'Neill."

Had he not been in uniform, he would have drawn his sword and demanded a duel. Instead, Brawley stood there, thinking about the letter he had written to Major Wilkes. Before leaving Kilraven Hill to intercept Lady Eleanor, he had sent the missive by courier. He had been ambivalent about doing so; now, he was fiercely relieved.

Reed made a sound of disgust, shaking his head.

"Take her the tea, plan the escape and report back to me," he ordered. He stalked off into the night, reaching into his interior breast pocket as he did so.

Brawley watched him unfold the poster advising the public of O'Neill's escape and the reward for his capture. He was repulsed.

And now, apparently, Eleanor de Warenne was a prisoner, or so she thought. But he was to aid her in an escape. Nothing would make him happier, especially as he was certain she intended to go home, where she would be safe.

Brawley took one moment to produce a handkerchief and mop his brow, then he went into the building. He ordered an aide de camp to retrieve the sterling tray with its teapot, cup and saucer, and biscuits, and follow him into the room. Before entering, he knocked.

There was no response.

Brawley pushed open the door. The room was in shadow, as not an oil lamp had been lit, but he saw Eleanor instantly. She stood as still as a statue by the window, staring at the door where he had just entered. In the shadows, in her white gown, her long hair entirely loose now, she was without any doubt the most beautiful woman he had ever beheld.

"Captain," she said hoarsely.

He smiled and turned to the aide. "Light the lamps, please." He went to the fireplace and knelt, quickly striking a flint and starting a fire as he was certain Lady Eleanor must be chilled. As he did so, both lamps were lit behind him. Brawley stoked the fire to make certain it was well on its way as the aide quietly retreated, closing the door behind him. Then he rose and faced Lady Eleanor.

She remained at the window, her eyes huge and dark in her face, which was shockingly pale, except for two bright spots of pink on her cheeks. It was then that he realized she was standing strangely—and he saw that she clutched the front of her gown.

In shock, he realized it had been ripped. "My God! What happened?" He tried to tell himself that she had caught her dress on the corner of some sharp object.

"It doesn't matter."

"Of course it matters!" Brawley felt his cheeks flame and he jerked his eyes up—her knuckles were white. He dragged his gaze to her face. And now, for the very first time, he saw a mark on her cheek—a vivid red welt.

He was no longer aghast. He was ill.

He rushed forward. "Please, allow me to help you now," he choked out. Reed had done this? Reed had struck a woman? Torn her gown? What else had he done?

Tears filled her eyes but did not fall. She kept her head high. "Thank you…thank you, Captain."

He touched her elbow, indicating she must sit down in the closer of the room's two guest chairs. She did so, collapsing into the seat.

"I will summon the garrison physician," he said.

She shook her head. "Help me…please… Thomas."

He went still and their eyes held. She had never called him by his given name before, and he hadn't even been aware that she knew it. He was overwhelmed—by her anguish, by the ordeal she had just been through, and by the lady she was. "Of course I will help you," he said. "But first, I fear you need medical attention."

"My face will swell. I don't care. I would like it very much, though, if you would wrap my wrist. It is rather useless now, and I do plan to use it."

She was the most courageous and dignified woman he had ever met. He remarked her bruised wrist. He was too much of a gentleman to ever ask what else Reed had done, but he feared the worst. Reed was clearly insane. "I will be right back," he managed.

"No!" She leaped to her feet, seizing his hands,

the torn gown falling apart uselessly. "Do not leave me alone! He might come back! Send someone else for linens, please, I beg you!"

He turned his back to her and began unbuttoning his jacket, aware that his hands were shaking. How could this have happened? Would he ever forget the sight of her, in her state of dishevelment and fear? He handed his jacket to her without looking at her and he waited until he heard her putting it on. When he did glance at her, she wore his jacket and he knew his face remained red. However, he went to the door, demanded that his aide bring linens, and then closed it.

"Thank you," she breathed in relief.

"I am taking you out of here tonight," he announced.

Hope flared in her eyes. "Is there a way? Is there a way that we can escape this fort—and that madman?"

"There is a way and I will find it," he said firmly.

She closed her eyes, breathing hard. When she looked at him again, she smiled.

ELEANOR DID NOT KNOW what time it was, but they were traveling down a carriageway under a full moon. She thought it was close to midnight. They had slipped out of the fort just minutes ago, on foot, Brawley having arranged for two horses to be tied up in the woods, waiting for them. She wore someone's shirt and the cloak—she suspected the shirt was Brawley's. They seemed to be alone, without pursuit. It had been too easy and Eleanor was wary.

The road ahead diverged. One route led south, to Cork, the other northeast, to Adare and Limerick.

She halted her mount, facing him. She was terrified of Colonel Reed. A part of her wished to go home to Adare, where she would be as safe as a princess in a fortified tower, but her desire to warn Sean that a madman was now on his trail was far stronger than her cowardice. "We should be in the woods," she said, breathing harshly. "He is going to discover that I am gone and he will set chase."

"It doesn't matter," Brawley replied. His gaze was direct, meeting hers. "He is following us even as you speak."

She cried out and started to spur her mount to whirl and flee, but he seized her reins. "Lady Eleanor! I am staunchly loyal to you now! You must pause to hear me out."

Eleanor was so frightened she could barely understand him. But she owed her life to Thomas Brawley and somehow, she had come to trust him. "What is it?"

"He asked me to aid you in an escape. He believes—erroneously, of course—that you are returning to Cork and your stepbrother. He hopes that you will lead him to O'Neill. But you are going to Adare, and I will see you safely there."

Eleanor stared. He was helping her escape Reed; he was betraying his commanding officer for her. Brawley was an honorable man, one every officer should emulate. However, Sean's life was at stake. Eleanor rode her mount closer to him, so their horses rocked together. She did not care for what she must do, but she reached for him.

"Lady Eleanor?" he asked.

She leaned close. "I owe you more than I can ever repay," she whispered—and she touched the spring clip on his shoulder belt, releasing his carbine. She quickly reversed it, sliding the safety catch to remove the bolt lock, although she did not quite aim the barrel at him.

He gaped at her.

"Thomas!" she cried. "I am so sorry, but I am going to Cork, not Adare! Reed is a madman and I must make certain Sean has fled the country. If Reed has treated me with such disdain, what will he do to Sean?"

Brawley was starkly pale. "He insisted you would go to him, but I refused to heed him. I believed you would go home, where you will be safe! My dear lady Eleanor, please reconsider. You are right—Reed is mad. However, I have already sent a letter to Major

Wilkes. Reed will not be allowed to continue on in this vein."

"I hope you are right. But I must warn Sean."

"Then let me escort you to Cork, Lady Eleanor. Please. I am a gentleman. I cannot allow you to ride this road at night, by yourself."

Eleanor did not want to implicate him in her plot. "If you escort me to Cork, we can say that I escaped you here and you pursued me to the city limits," she said slowly.

"Yes, we can." He understood that she would not lead anyone, not even him, to Sean's hiding place. He nodded and held out his hand. "Please?"

She returned his carbine to him. A cloud overhead passed and the moon illuminated the roadway. Spurring their mounts, they charged off into the night.

He HAD BOOKED passage not to America, but to France. From Normandy, he would then find a fare to the United States. His ship, a small French schooner, was setting sail the next day. Sean felt as if he were in the midst of a surreal nightmare.

He was chopping wood for Farmer O'Riley, as he felt he must do something to contribute to the man's selfless actions in hiding him. But his actions were mechanical, because there was no thought, no feeling. He was dazed and numb. He was vaguely sorrowful; there were nameless, unidentifiable regrets.

But Elle was safe at Adare by now. She would have arrived late yesterday. He could not rejoice, but he was relieved.

He swung the ax and split the heavy cord of wood. Although the gray skies were ominous, threatening rain, he did not feel any chill on his skin and he had removed his shirt. The only chill he felt was in his soul. The future loomed, and somehow it had become as black as the hellhole where he had been confined for the past two years.

Sean wished he could unravel time. He no longer knew who or what he was. Before he had wandered so recklessly from Askeaton, he had been whole. And briefly, in these past few days, he had started to feel like that man, with a heart and soul, with a past and a future. That odd awareness had vanished. Elle had taken it with her.

Sean heard a rider approaching and he stiffened. He was in the yard behind the house, not far from the small wood barn where O'Riley kept his prized sow. He quickly moved to the house, pressing to the wall, ax in hand. And he peered around the corner.

His heart stopped.

Eleanor was leaping from a cavalry mount, clad

in the white dress he had bought her, a man's shirt and the brown cloak. She started to run for the front door, but Sean knew that no one was home. He stepped into sight. "Elle."

She halted and whirled. "You didn't leave!" she cried.

His heart had come to life. It sped wildly, madly, insanely, beating hard with pleasure and joy. He had needed to see her one more time. It was drizzling now, but the yard was drenched in sunshine. He realized he was smiling.

And smiling in return, she rushed toward him.

When he reached for her, he saw the bruise on her face, which was mottling now, gray, blue and green.

She went into his arms. "It's nothing, really. Kate told me where to find you. Sean, there is news!"

A vast sense of dread and alarm had overcome him. He managed to tear his gaze from her bruise to her eyes. A terrible fear was reflected there. "What happened?" he asked quietly, reaching for her hands and removing them from his shoulders.

She winced. "There is a spy amongst the Blueboys, Sean. You are not safe here. Connelly and I were waylaid on the roadway by troops."

He stared at her tightly wrapped wrist. Blood drummed in his head, in his ears, deafening him.

Suddenly Peg's blurred image came to mind. He tore his gaze from her wrist to her eyes.

"I fell from my horse," she said with urgency.

He had never heard a more outrageous lie.

"He tripped," she tried to explain.

"How badly are you hurt?" he asked, a dark, dangerous need settling over him.

"I'm not hurt." Her smile was brief and strained. "Sean, I must warn you— Colonel Reed is at Kilraven Hill and he has confessed to murdering your wife!"

Shock immobilized him. For one instant, even his mind was paralyzed.

"He is a madman," she whispered, and tears came to her eyes. "He is coming after you, Sean. I had to come back to warn you!"

Reed had done this to her and he knew it. He knew it the way he knew that it was drizzling and about to pour. "You are to tell me everything…Eleanor," he said, his tone so hard even he didn't recognize it.

She jerked away from him. "Sean! There is nothing more to tell except that he purposefully set his troops on your poor wife. I am very afraid of him and you should be, too."

His heart beat now, hard but slow. A calm had descended. "So a spy informed on us. You were apprehended by troops and taken to Reed…at Kilraven Hill."

She was staring at him, wide-eyed. Her face was utterly pale, causing the dark bruise to stand out garishly. "Nothing happened," she said.

He felt a convulsion ripple through him. "How did you get here?"

She swallowed. "Captain Brawley helped me escape."

He tilted up her chin.

Tears filled her eyes.

"Don't lie to me," he warned.

"But I'm fine."

"He struck you, didn't he? Did he touch you, too?" And in his mind, Reed turned red, bursting into flames.

She started to shake her head no and then the emotion changed, becoming an affirmation. She started to cry, two large tears slowly tracking down her face.

He was going to kill Colonel Robert Reed.

"It's all right," he soothed, taking her by her arms. "Elle, I'm here now, and I will never let him touch you again."

She nodded, her gaze glued to his. "I was so afraid."

"What did he do?" he asked, amazed at how calm his tone was, when he was beyond rage.

She had trouble speaking.

He leaned down and brushed her lips softly with his. "Tell me, Elle."

She nodded. "He was so rude. Sean, he is not afraid of anyone, not father. Not Ty, not anyone! No one has ever addressed me as he did, much less—" She stopped, more tears falling.

He pulled her close and held her. She buried her face against his chest, gasping in anguish. He held her more tightly. He had to know. "Did he rape you?"

"No."

He stared and she stared back. "Then why are you wearing a man's shirt...over your gown?"

Her mouth crumbled.

Sean unfastened her cloak and tossed it into the dirt and mud. He reached for her shirt and saw his hands shaking, betraying his own fury and anguish. He began to unbutton it. Elle reached for his hands to stop him but he ignored her, and as each button was released, the tear in her bodice became increasingly visible. He pulled the shirt open. Two pins kept the front of her gown closed.

He was suddenly sick enough to retch. "Don't lie to me."

"He didn't...do what you asked. He used a

blade—a letter opener—on my dress." She looked away, closing her eyes, starkly white.

She had been cherished, respected and protected her entire life. His worst fears had come true. Reed had reappeared in his life and he had gotten his hands on her. He saw no difference between cruelty and molestation and rape.

He pulled her close again. She held on to him tightly. He stroked her back, her hair. "Where is Reed now?"

"I don't know," she murmured against his chest. "Brawley was allowed to help me escape—Reed intended to follow us, correctly thinking I would return to you. Sean, the things he said to me!"

He met her anguished eyes and stroked her hair again. "Once you are safely back at Adare, you will begin to forget…that anyone could dare to treat you so dishonorably. Where is Brawley?"

"I left him hours ago. We agreed he would not be privy to your whereabouts. I think we eluded the troops, but obviously Reed must be lurking about Cork."

He nodded. It would not be hard to lure Reed out of whatever rat hole he was in. And he began to relish the prospect of facing him and taking his bare hands to his throat, so he could slowly choke the life out of him.

She understood him completely, because she said,

"You can't assault another officer. You cannot—I will not allow it."

He touched her left cheek, which was not bruised. "I am sorry, Elle, but Reed is going to pay…for his murdering ways."

"He will kill you."

Sean thought that likely. Lying smoothly, he denied it. "I will strike when he least expects it…in the dark…like a coward. He will never know what hit him and this will be over, Elle. You will be able to sleep at night."

She shook her head fiercely. "I am not the one with nightmares! I am not the one who cannot sleep peacefully because of what Reed did to Peg and Michael! Do not seek vengeance for me. I am fine, Sean." She inhaled. "Please, do not go after Reed. Father is seeking a pardon for you in London, even as we speak. There will be no pardon, not now, not ever, if you assault Reed!"

"I could never live with myself if I let him walk away…from what he has done to you!" he cried.

"I am *fine!*" she cried, weeping. "But I have never seen such a look in your eyes. Nothing I say will change your mind, will it? You are going to seek vengeance now and we both know that will be your death."

"Don't cry for me," he said, wishing he could

have somehow spared her this. "Come here." He pulled her against his chest again.

She didn't press her cheek there; she strained upward, seeking his mouth, her lips urgent, frantic. And it crossed his mind that this was the end for them. He was going to walk away from Elle in order to avenge her, and then he would hang—if Reed's troops didn't slaughter him on the spot. In that moment, his body stiffened with a huge, desperate, consuming hunger.

She felt the change in him. Elle pulled her mouth from his and met his gaze, hers wide, surprised.

He took her hand. "Come." He pulled her behind the house, into his arms and to the ground. She cried out, her response filled with the same desperate need.

Their mouths mated and quickly, so did their bodies. Thrusting his tongue deep, he moved her skirts aside, reaching for her. She gasped with pleasure, reaching for the buttons on his breeches. Sean hesitated, overcome as her hands skidded over his length, his thickness. And his last thoughts of revenge vanished.

He lay back, gasping for air, and she pulled the breeches apart. Her long hair fell over him, entwining there. He could not stand it and he was prepared to beg, but he did not have to. She slid her tongue

over him and he found her face, holding it, whispering her name. "Elle."

And then he moved, reversing their positions, their gazes briefly meeting. Instantly he pushed his body between her legs and he slid deeply into her.

She threw her arms around him, clinging, as he rode her. "Don't let me go," he said. "Ever."

FOR ONE MOMENT, Eleanor lay in Sean's arms, realizing that she remained as deeply in love with him as ever. She was so afraid now, not just of Reed, but of what Sean planned. Still breathless, she sat up, arranging her skirts. "We have to go. Sean, is Cliff's ship nearby? Even if it is being watched, *The Fair Lady* is our best chance to escape."

"I want you aboard that ship," he said decisively. "You're right. We have to go." He stood, turning his back and quickly fastening his breeches.

She leaped to her feet, realizing what he intended. "Damn it! You think to drop me with Cliff while you commit suicide?" She began to bargain desperately. "Don't do this, Sean. If you insist that I go home— to Sinclair—I will. You can go to America and I will go home."

He faced her, sadness in his eyes. "It's too late for negotiations. Let's go. We'll ride double."

Eleanor balked. "No. I am not leaving you so that you can destroy yourself and your life."

He stared at her, his expression stone cold. "Don't make me force you onto that horse."

Eleanor had never seen anyone so determined, but she could not give up. "If you love me at all, you will choose to live—and not go after Colonel Reed."

He stiffened. Anguish flickered in his eyes. "That is not fair."

"Nothing is fair!" She thought she sounded hysterical.

He shook his head, anger darkening his expression, and started for the other side of the house where she had left the cavalry mount grazing. And Eleanor heard the riders.

So did Sean. He whirled, eyes wide. "Get in the house," he said tersely. "There's a trap door by the bedstead. Use it."

She had only an instant to decide. "I'm not leaving you. You don't even have a weapon!"

"I have my hands," he said, giving her a furious look. He started around the house.

Eleanor ran after him, expecting to see Reed and his men riding into the yard. Already envisioning Sean's attack on the officer and the consequences, she could almost see his slain body on the ground.

But Sean halted and she collided into his back. Then she saw Devlin, Tyrell and Rex.

They had halted their horses on the other side of the front yard. For one moment, the men stared at each other. A huge silence had fallen—and then Eleanor saw the three of them look at her.

She didn't care if their recent lovemaking was obvious. She ran past Sean. "You have to stop him!" She turned to Devlin, because he was Sean's older brother and Sean had always deferred to him. "He intends to murder Colonel Reed!"

Devlin leaped from his mount, as did Tyrell. Rex still rode astride, a superior horseman in spite of his handicap. Devlin reached her first. His gaze moved over her features and then he went to Sean. The brothers stared and Devlin cursed. "Bloody fool!" Then he embraced Sean as if he were a child, holding him for a long moment.

Eleanor had never been more relieved. She now faced Tyrell, as Rex limped toward them, leaning on his crutch. "You have to stop him, Ty."

"I intend to do my best. You are hurt."

"Barely!"

He tilted up her chin and stared into her eyes. "You have a choice to make, Eleanor. You must choose between Sean, who may never survive these events, and Sinclair, who remains at Adare, waiting for your return. And there is little time."

Eleanor turned to look at Sean.

Devlin had released him and Sean was staring at her, his gaze wide and intense.

"There is no choice to make," she whispered. Nothing had changed. Sean was her life.

Sean was grim as he moved toward them. "She chooses Sinclair," he said.

Eleanor cried out. And she saw tears forming in his silver eyes.

Tyrell said, the weight of authority and danger in his tone, "Do you care to explain yourself to her?"

Sean didn't even look at him. "Elle." He stopped as if he could not speak.

She was crying, and she shook her head, her silent way of begging him one last time to change his mind.

He had become pale. "I must do this. I could never bear the burden of what has happened…if I allowed Reed to get away with what he has done."

"I am fine," she whispered, the lie now solidly etched in her mind.

"You are not fine! And he will pay for his monstrous behavior! We both know…I will not survive this day."

She went to him. She was sobbing now and could not get a single word out.

But he smiled at her. "If things were different, if I could redo my entire life, I would have never left Askeaton four years ago. If I were not a fugitive…I would marry you. Elle, I love you."

Eleanor lost her ability to stand. It wasn't Sean who caught her, it was Tyrell.

"I am going to take you to Cliff," Tyrell said softly. "Rex and Devlin will stay with Sean."

She shook her head, wanting to tell him that she would stay until the very end. She was not leaving Sean's side now.

Hoofbeats thundered.

And Eleanor knew it was Reed and his troops. She staggered upright, turning, Tyrell keeping his arm around her as a dozen soldiers galloped into the front yard, blue coats and white shoulder belts gleaming. The troops halted, Reed at their forefront.

A terrible silence fell, punctuated only by the blowing horses and their jangling bits.

Sean was smiling.

Eleanor could not look away, sick with fear.

He glanced at Devlin. Devlin unsheathed his sword, the same long saber he had worn as a captain in the royal navy, and tossed it to him. Eleanor felt her heart lurch with dread as Sean caught it easily by the hilt. His gaze returned to Reed.

Reed smiled. "A viper's nest—or should I amend my choice of words?" His saber rang as it appeared in his hand.

Sean did not answer. He strode past Eleanor and Tyrell, past Rex, toward Reed.

Reed spurred his mount forward. "An entire nest of Irish traitors," Reed murmured, sounding pleased. "O'Neill, you are under arrest."

"Dismount." Sean spoke softly, so softly his words were almost inaudible; yet somehow, everyone in the yard knew exactly what he wanted.

"Arrest him," Reed said, dancing his horse aside and just out of Sean's reach.

"Coward." Sean's cold smile never wavered.

Reed's smile vanished. He promptly leaped from his horse and he was far too agile. Eleanor's dismay increased.

The two men faced one another like fencing masters, swords poised high to strike. Sean's eyes glittered—and so did Reed's.

"En garde," Reed murmured.

And Sean struck—but Reed parried the blow.

Eleanor knew that all of her brothers were superior swordsmen, but Sean had not held a sword in two years—if not more. He was at a terrible disadvantage. Her heart slammed as she watched the two men swiftly engage. Their swords rang and clashed, blow after blow, stalemated. Sean advanced; Reed retreated. Reed advanced, Sean retreated. The seconds turned into agonizing minutes; Sean's face was gleaming with sweat. Reed's face was as wet, but now both men were fiercely focused and determined. Someone was going to die that day. Their swords clashed and rang again.

Sean feinted and thrust—suddenly the tip of his blade was in Reed's blue jacket, in his shoulder. Sean pulled it back and the tip was bright red with blood.

Grunting, Reed thrust back and their swords braced and locked.

Eleanor began to have hope.

Sean thrust viciously again and in disbelief, Eleanor saw Reed's sword clatter to the ground. Reed froze, as did Sean. And then Sean laid the tip of his blade against Reed's heart. He smiled.

"No!" Eleanor screamed. "Sean, do not!"

Sean visibly stiffened.

"Apprehend him," Reed ordered.

A dozen swords rang. A dozen troops surrounded them and a dozen blades were instantly aimed at Sean's head and body, inches from his flesh.

Eleanor knew it was over. She could feel Sean now, with her, inside her, a part of her very being, and she could read his every thought, feel his every desire. He wanted to kill. He was about to kill. And the troops would slaughter him in return.

A shot rang out.

Sean's sword was blasted out of his hand.

Stunned, Eleanor saw Rex standing in a firing position, his entire weight balanced on his crutch and left leg, a pistol pointing directly at Sean and Reed.

The yard came to life. Even before Reed spoke, Sean was seized by several soldiers.

"Shackle him," Reed spat.

"No!" Eleanor cried.

Sean was dragged toward the milling horses and troops.

Eleanor started to pull away from Tyrell.

"Eleanor!" He gripped her hard, not allowing her to go after Sean.

And she hated him. "Let me go!" she shouted. "Let me say goodbye! Ty, let me go!"

He pulled her close. "No."

"Mount up and move out," Reed snapped, already on his charger. He rode his bay toward them. "I have no quarrel here, especially not with you, Sir Captain—" he looked at Devlin, and then at Rex "—or you, Sir Major." He wheeled the bay, lifting his arm and flagging his troops onward.

Sean was in their midst, astride, his hands manacled in front of him, as the mass of men moved out.

Eleanor fought Tyrell now. She kicked and scratched and he suddenly let her go. "Eleanor, don't."

But she lifted her skirts and ran up to the cavalcade. She ran past one huge horse and another and then darted between the chargers. "Sean! Sean!" She reached his mount's side and seized his leg.

He stared straight ahead as if he could not hear her. "Sean!"

His jaw was clenched, his temples throbbed. He refused to acknowledge her in any way.

She could no longer keep up with the trotting horses. Her steps slowed. On each side, the horses jogged past her. She stumbled, not caring if she fell and was trampled. The last troops had passed and she stared after them as they disappeared around a bend in the road.

Someone paused beside her; it was Tyrell. "Come, Eleanor, it is time to go home."

CHAPTER EIGHTEEN

IT WAS POURING HEAVILY when Eleanor arrived at Adare. She had traveled from Cork with Rex, his mount tied to the carriage behind them. She was sick with fear, so much so that she could not breathe properly. Images of Sean being captured by the British haunted her. She would never forget the stoic expression on his face as he had been led away, refusing to look at or even to acknowledge her. By now, he was at Kilraven Hill, imprisoned there.

He had finally admitted that he loved her. There should have been joy in her heart, not such sick despair. She had shredded the fine linen handkerchief one of her brothers had given her. Still clutching it, she looked at Rex, who had been silent for most of their journey, clearly as immersed in his own thoughts as she was. "Reed is a maniac," she suddenly said. "He might think to harm Sean just for amusement—or worse, hang him before there is any word from London."

Rex reached for her. "And that is why Tyrell rode directly to the garrison, to impress upon the colonel that he must await further orders or suffer serious consequences."

"Ty has no idea with whom he is dealing!" Eleanor cried. They had been traveling up the long gravel drive and the house had come into view, stately and gray, the stone walls gleaming silver in the rain. "Reed isn't afraid of him, or Father or anyone else in this family."

"Devlin is with Tyrell." Rex spoke with great calm. His mouth curved into a slight smile. "I cannot imagine any man facing them both without some fear. If Reed has somehow convinced you that he fears no one, I think it was a sham. He is a bully, Eleanor, that much is clear. Bullies are invariably cowards."

And briefly, Eleanor felt the slightest flicker of hope. "He did not seem cowardly to me."

His expression became rigid. "You are a defenseless young woman. He is a bully and a coward and he will inevitably pay for his behavior toward you."

Eleanor knew Rex intended some terrible fate for Reed, but she could not think about that now. Miserably, she stared at the house as their carriage halted. "Maybe we should go to London to find out what Father has managed," she said. "But on the other hand, I do not want to leave Sean. Rex, I have to see him."

Rex reached for her hand and grasped it firmly. "Eleanor, Peter remains at Adare."

He had her full attention now. In some disbelief, she faced him. "Peter is here? Waiting for me?" She was dismayed.

"I am afraid so. I think you must exercise some great control and dissemble now. It will not serve anyone to allow Peter to realize you are madly in love with Sean."

Eleanor was stunned that Peter was in residence, but then, it had not even been a week since their ill-fated wedding day. Her mind tried to grapple with the notion that she was about to face him now. "I can't manage this. Not now, not when I am sick with fear for Sean's very life."

"You have to manage," Rex said firmly. "But he will surely understand that you must go directly to your rooms." He gave her a nod of encouragement.

There would be some respite then, at least until the morrow. But Peter would want an explanation. "I must let him down," she whispered. "And I have no heart left to even attempt an apology or to find some pleasant way to do so."

"I must advise you against being honest with Sinclair. Eleanor, if Sean is not pardoned, you could still be in jeopardy yourself."

Eleanor understood that she was a conspirator to Sean's escape, and Reed and his troops had seen her with Sean when they had apprehended him. "I am a traitor, too. I cannot deny it now and I do not want to! Maybe it is for the best. If Sean hangs, I can hang with him." She meant her every word.

"Don't say that!" Rex cried, turning pale beneath his dark skin. "He is not Romeo and you are not Juliet! I am going to tell you what to do, and for once in your life, you will listen—and obey! You will not explain yourself to anyone, Eleanor, except for Sinclair, and you will tell him the story you told Reed. You missed your stepbrother, and believing in his innocence, you wanted to hear the truth from him. Somehow, in the excitement of the moment, you left Adare with Sean. You did not purposefully aid him in another escape, but once having left with Sean, there was no going back. He abandoned you upon arriving in Cork—and you returned to warn him about Reed after your capture. He is your beloved *stepbrother*, Eleanor," he said harshly. "*Nothing* more."

Eleanor hugged herself. "There are a dozen witnesses to the fact that I escaped the garrison and went right to Sean. What sister behaves in such a manner?"

"A sister attempting to warn her brother that a

madman is on his trail!" Rex snapped. "Before this is over, marriage to Sinclair might be for the best. It might be your only option."

Eleanor gasped. Then she shook with fury when she realized the stand Rex was taking. "Never! I can't marry him—I love Sean! And in case you did not hear, he loves me."

"I did hear. But it is too late. Sean might hang— but I will be damned if you will spend the rest of your life in the Tower."

She shook her head, tears spilling. "I love Sean. I am his *lover!* And I am not going to deny it."

Rex appeared furious. "If Sean survives, he is going to have to answer to me for *that!* So you intend to tell Peter everything? He loves you, Eleanor, and he has been nothing but honorable toward you. He is at Adare even now, sick with fear for you! And you will hurt him with the truth?"

She became still. Peter deserved so much more than she could ever give him. "Of course I will not tell Peter the truth. I have hurt him when he never deserved it and I do not want to add more injury now. But I can't marry him, Rex. I am in love with Sean."

"Even Sean wishes for you to marry Sinclair," Rex said, his dark eyes flashing.

Eleanor turned her back to him, staring out of the

carriage with more dismay and sudden fear. Sean had been insisting she marry Peter all along. And he had insisted that she do so in the same breath that he had finally declared his love for her. She glanced at Rex. "In one way, you are right. I will tell Peter what I told Reed, as it is a much kinder version of the events."

Rex sighed. "Eleanor, I am not trying to be harsh or cruel. I am only trying to protect you, in the event that this situation becomes even worse than it currently is."

"I understand that. But why don't we forget about my fate, as it is hardly in the balance now."

"We will discuss this again tomorrow," Rex said, his tone softer, "when Tyrell has returned."

Eleanor had a dreadful feeling then. "Surely you are not thinking of forcing me to the altar when Ty comes back?"

He smiled grimly at her as servants appeared, rushing from the house through the rain, but did not answer.

Horrified, Eleanor realized he was contemplating just such an act. But she had no chance to really press, for her door was opened. The countess stepped from the house to stand above her on the wide stone steps, and then Peter appeared there, as well.

Eleanor stumbled, her heart lurching, as she

stepped down from the coach, aided by a footman. Her glance went from her mother, who was pale but smiling wanly, to Peter Sinclair. He was as pale, but he wasn't smiling and his stare was searching. She was briefly overcome with nervous dread.

Peter was a gentleman. As Rex had pointed out, he had done nothing but love, honor and respect her. In that instant, every moment she had spent with Sean in the past few days flashed through her mind's eye, including every act of passion. She felt her cheeks heating as her heart accelerated. "Mother," she whispered, tearing her gaze from Peter's rigid face.

Rex took her arm firmly, and with his crutch, began limping to the stairs. There he let her go, and Eleanor preceded him up to the front doors. She stole another glance at Peter, who could not seem to take his riveted gaze from her. The countess cried out, beginning to fight tears, and Eleanor went into her arms. "I am all right," she said.

"And Sean?" the countess asked, holding her hands, her blue eyes wide and frightened.

Eleanor fought for self-control. "He has been captured, Mother." When the countess started to stagger, she cried, "But he is alive and he isn't hurt!"

Her disclaimer did not matter. The countess

swooned but Peter Sinclair caught her. Lifting her into his arms, he glanced at Eleanor. "Are you all right?"

She nodded, filled with guilt.

He quickly carried the countess inside, Eleanor and Rex following. When he laid her on an upholstered bench in the entry hall, her eyes fluttered open. Peter stepped back as Eleanor knelt by her mother's side, taking her cold hands in hers. "Mother?"

The countess met her gaze, her own moist with tears. "Are you truly unharmed?"

Eleanor nodded. "I am dirty and hungry, but otherwise, no worse for wear." And that was the only lie she had ever told her stepmother.

The countess studied her and hesitated. Eleanor knew she had grave doubts about the veracity of that statement. "I have been so frightened for you, and for Sean. Where did they take him?"

"Kilraven Hill," Eleanor told her. She knew her mother had a hundred questions that she wished to ask, but did not dare.

The countess sat up. "Darling, you need to rest. I will order a hot bath drawn and send supper to your rooms. Of course, I will attend to you myself."

Eleanor understood. The countess wished to whisk her away to a safe retreat, and would visit her there. "I do need to rest. I am exhausted," she said.

Then, her heart pounding, she slowly stood and turned to face Peter. She became aware that she was trembling, and she felt her face flame.

An interminable moment of silence passed, one filled with tension and strain. But Eleanor saw both relief and anguish in Peter's eyes. How much did he guess? she wondered.

"Sinclair," Rex said, breaking the silence. "I'd like a word with you."

Peter's gaze remained fixed on Eleanor. "May I have a word first with my fiancée?"

Eleanor's heart sank. How could he still think to marry her? Or was his choice of words merely formal, as there had been no official breach of contract?

"Eleanor has been through a terrible ordeal," Rex said firmly. "One that has included apprehension and interrogation by the British, when she is innocent of any and all wrongdoing. She must retire to her rooms."

Peter blanched. "Eleanor, are you hurt?" he asked. His regard strayed to the bruise on her cheek.

She shook her head, daring to approach. "I have had a terrible time," she somehow replied. "Peter, I am sorry for everything."

He took her hands, his gaze on the bruise on her face. "I thank God you have returned to me," he whispered.

Eleanor did not know what to do. She wanted to pull her hands from his, but did not dare.

"Are you certain you are unharmed?" he asked, sounding shaken now.

"Yes. I owe you an explanation," she began, but he interrupted.

"Your mother and brother are right. You must retire to your rooms. You need rest and I am calling your family's physician. As soon as you are feeling a bit better, we can speak."

Had she really forgotten how kind and considerate this man was? "Thank you," Eleanor said.

He just smiled slightly at her.

THE PRISON CELL had light and air. Sean saw that even as he was shoved inside by a soldier from behind. That fact could not quell his rising panic. Because the gray daylight creeping through the single window could not seem to ease the sudden darkness of the cell and he could not breathe. He heard the iron door slam shut behind him; he heard the lock turn and click. He began to choke on his fear and had he been laid in the raw earth, dirt piled on him, he could not have felt more terror.

Reed laughed softly. "Do we weep now, O'Neill? Like a child—a girl?"

He had heard the soblike sound, too, and it had come from his own chest. Sean leaned against the stone wall, facefirst. He wasn't entombed and he wasn't forgotten; this was not like the other time. This was not an eternity of hopelessness and hell. This was a prelude to a swift, certain death.

He thought of Eleanor, whom he loved. Surely, once he hanged, her part in his treason would be ignored. She would be spared Peg's fate... wouldn't she?

It had become impossible to breathe now. There were only bars in the window, no pane, but his lungs couldn't seem to comprehend that. His heart raced wildly, sweat streaming down his body, and he was shaking uncontrollably, his nails digging into the stone.

"Don't worry," Reed said softly. "Your stay here won't be long. You will hang in days, O'Neill, because I intend to see justice served."

The stone scraping his forehead hurt, but he didn't care. Sean clawed the wall and fought for air and sanity, but calm refused to come. "Eleanor?" he gasped.

"Your lover is undoubtedly in the bosom of her family," Reed said softly.

"She is innocent!" Sean cried. "She is my step-sister!"

Reed laughed. "She is your Irish whore and we

both know it. So lovely, so soft, I am sorry I never had the chance to finish what I began with her."

Sean cried out, turning. "I am going to kill you, you sonuvabitch," he choked out.

Reed laughed. "How? With words? You should have seen the terror in her eyes when I cut her dress, O'Neill. Oh, she is a very fine woman, indeed."

Sean lunged for Reed, but he stood on the other side of the bars and he backed out of reach. "You will pay for what you did."

"Perhaps she will pay for what you have done?" Reed asked softly.

Peg's broken, battered image came to mind, this time so vividly he saw her every feature and all the blood. Peg remained gray but the blood was red—darkly and vividly so. Sean was determined then to kill Reed before he hanged, even though he was behind bars. How to entice him into the cell, so he could wring his neck?

"But then, as she is as guilty as you are and the world will soon know it, she can pay for her own conspiracy. I think that would satisfy me far more than her rape or death. She will spend the rest of her life impoverished, imprisoned and alone, a woman forgotten, a woman of utter inconsequence."

Sean gripped the bars, controlling the impulse to

lunge for his captor again. He fought to breathe and he fought for his temper.

"There will be justice, on all counts," Reed said coolly.

"I am glad to see you intend justice, Colonel," Tyrell said flatly, startling Sean as he and Devlin strode into the corridor from the anteroom. "It should be much easier to obtain with all of us working for the same honorable end."

Sean finally drew in the air he so desperately needed. *Tyrell and Devlin were there. While his fate was undoubtedly inescapable, they would never allow harm to befall Eleanor.*

"Justice requires that O'Neill swing and you bloody well know it," Reed said.

"No. That would be another injustice, and I am reminding you right now that my stepbrother has suffered the gravest injustice already at the hands of the military—at your hands. He was incarcerated in a British prison for two years. He was falsely convicted. Adare is in London as we speak. There will be a full inquiry into the events of that night in Kilvore and Sean's apprehension, imprisonment and conviction."

Sean felt some small surprise, as he hadn't considered the possibility of an inquiry of any sort. There was so much authority in Tyrell's tone and manner that real comfort came from his words.

Reed's smile was thin. "Is there a point? Because if so, my lord, I fail to comprehend it."

"There was a witness to those events, Colonel, and my brother is bringing him to London. Sean never committed treason and once that has been proved, he will be pardoned. I am warning you now that you will keep him safe—and alive—until that day comes," Tyrell said coldly.

Reed replied but not as smugly as before. "There are no witnesses. Every man in that village rose up in arms, and every one was killed—except for O'Neill."

"You are wrong. There is a witness and his testimony will clear Sean," Tyrell said flatly. "But that will not be enough. Your actions are going to be scrutinized as if you were a rat being dissected under a laboratory microscope."

Reed stared, then laughed. "Such bluster. Who allowed you in?"

"Brawley. And if you think to deny me access to my stepbrother now, after two years of mistaken incarceration, you should think again."

Reed's eyes flashed. "There is no witness. I have done nothing wrong!"

Tyrell smiled dangerously. *"You touched my sister."*

Sean tensed. How much did Tyrell know?

It was a moment before Reed spoke. "I interviewed her—showing all the respect she was due. Apparently she tripped and fell when she was first brought to the fort. I would never touch a lady."

Tyrell leaned close. "Your career is at an end, Colonel."

Reed started. Then he snarled, "Do not threaten me." He stalked out.

Sean leaned against the wall. The hatred had receded, and so had the panic. He felt strangely calm. "Ty, don't. Don't bait him—he is too dangerous. He may go after Elle when he is through with me."

"I am not afraid of him, Sean. In fact, I intend to destroy him."

"Then you will have to get in line," Sean said.

Ty's brows lifted. "You have done enough, I think, so I suggest you leave Reed to me."

Devlin stepped past Tyrell, gripping the cell bars. "You are ill," he said bluntly.

Sean almost laughed. "I am past being ill." But he wiped the sweat streaming from his brow.

"How can I help you *now?*" Devlin asked grimly.

His brother somehow knew that being in a cell again was like being buried alive. Sean shook his head, forcing himself to take deep, steadying breaths.

He briefly closed his eyes and then opened them. "There is not enough air in here," he said with some difficulty. "But I know it is all in my head."

"Do you have a fever?" Devlin finally asked.

Sean shook his head. "No—but I am mad. I have finally lost my mind." He sat down on the floor, staring at it. Neither brother spoke. He finally said, "I don't care about myself. I am prepared to hang…it has been my fate all along and I can no longer avoid it. But Elle…" He looked up. "You must protect Eleanor. Find a way, Dev, to extricate her from any involvement with me. Reed has threatened her."

"Reed is going to find himself on a convict ship bound for Australia," Tyrell said grimly. "Damn it! Eleanor is involved and a dozen troops know it. Did you purposely appear on her wedding day to sabotage her future—her life?"

Sean recalled Eleanor, standing before her dressing mirror in her wedding finery, breathtaking in her beauty. His heart caught. He had meant to say goodbye, not steal the bride.

"He has been through enough and we are wasting time with recriminations," Devlin said coldly.

Sean spoke slowly. "There has to be a way, maybe a trade…her liberty for my life."

"No!" Devlin snapped.

"You don't understand." Sean looked at him. "I will gladly hang if she can live to a ripe old age with all of the creature comforts she deserves."

"I do understand. I understand that you are in love with Eleanor! There will be no such trade. First things first." He was commanding. "Runners have been looking for Flynn. Cliff is now on his way to Kilvore—if he isn't there already. They will find him, Sean. You will be cleared of all of these charges, one way or another."

"How can you be so certain?" Sean asked, because he recognized the hard gleam in his older brother's eyes. It was a ruthless light Sean had thought he would never see again.

Devlin smiled without mirth. "You might not recognize Flynn when you next meet him," he said.

An impostor would be brought forth if Flynn was not found. Hope flared—but it was too dangerous to entertain for long. "Soldiers died that night. In the end, I picked up arms, too."

"You tried to stop the rebels," Tyrell exclaimed. "And you are a nobleman, not a peasant. Amends need to be made. Then there is the case of your wife and son. They deserve justice, too."

The guilt that had lain dormant for the past few

days suddenly arose, clawing at Sean. "How? How do you know anything...about them?"

Sympathy filled Devlin's eyes. "Eleanor told us, Sean. I am sorry."

"Then you must know the entire story," Sean said harshly. "They paid...for my crimes. Reed made it so."

"Then an inquiry might lead to his imprisonment," Tyrell stated.

Sean slowly stood up. There was hope again—and with it, Eleanor's beautiful image, her eyes soft with trust and love. Then Peg's countenance appeared, dancing uncontrollably in his mind, so focused now that she could have been lying in his arms, dying. His heart lurched with dread and raced with fear. Peg had been brutally tortured and murdered because of him, and only God knew Michael's fate. How dare he hope for anything, much less a future with Eleanor?

He was powerless now, once again, and he must not forget it. There was no hope. His life was over and only a miracle could change that. He no longer cared. However, he cared about Eleanor's life, as he always had.

As much as he hated the idea of her wedding Sinclair, of her warming his bed, keeping his home and bearing his children, the other man loved her. He was powerful, wealthy, titled and British, and he would give her a good, long life.

He faced his brother and stepbrother. "You're both wrong," he said. "There is no justice in Ireland and there never has been. Reed is going to walk away freely from his sins and I am going to hang for mine. And even if I don't, I am going to America—alone. As for Eleanor…I do not love her in the way she wants." He saw Tyrell start. "She threw herself at me. She is a beautiful woman. And I am not the man you once knew. Do I have to be any clearer?"

Tyrell was ashen. "If this is a jest, it is in very poor taste."

"You know I was always a rake." Sean shrugged. "Two years alone in a hole, and then Eleanor offered me something I had no wish to refuse." He did not bother to continue.

Tyrell was so furious he was at a loss for words. He stared at Sean as if he faced an oddly misshapen monster he did not and could not know.

Sean waited; Tyrell cursed him and stormed out.

Devlin just looked at him. "That was utterly convincing. Why, Sean? I am going to make certain you are freed."

Sean shook his head. It was hard to speak. "I want

her safe. You make certain she marries Sinclair," he said harshly. "I want…your word."

Devlin stared, then responded. "I'm not giving it."

CHAPTER NINETEEN

ELEANOR PAUSED on the threshold of the gold salon, trembling. Peter was the only one present in the room and he was seated before the fireplace, staring into the flames. He was clearly brooding.

It was late the same afternoon. Eleanor hesitated. Her intention had been to remain in her rooms for as long as possible, ostensibly to rest, in truth to avoid Peter. But she could not rest, not when Sean was imprisoned just a few hours from Adare, his life hanging precariously in the balance. To make matters even worse, she was acutely aware of Peter's presence in her home and how unfairly she had treated him.

She owed him more than an explanation—she owed him an apology. She had begun a letter to that effect, and had quickly realized that was the coward's way out. She had to end their engagement, once and for all. "Peter?"

He leaped to his feet, stunned to see her.

She wanted to smile, but she simply could not. She meant to come into the room, but her feet would not obey her mind and her legs did not move.

Peter rushed to her side. "Eleanor! Why aren't you upstairs, resting? At least until the doctor arrives and has thoroughly examined you?"

She bit her lip. "I can't rest." She hesitated again, wishing he were not so kind and caring, then she walked past him into the room. "We need to speak, Peter."

He stood frozen at the door.

She slowly faced him, her hand lingering on the back of a tasseled chaise. "I cannot begin to tell you how sorry I am for what I did on our wedding day."

He was pale. He closed the door. "I understand, Eleanor," he said hoarsely.

She was surprised. "How can you even begin to understand? May I explain?"

He came forward, his cheeks having turned pink. "I understand that Sean is your stepbrother. I have heard that you doted on him as a child. I also heard he was incarcerated in prison for two years and no one in your family knew if he was dead or alive. How terrible that must have been for all of you!"

Eleanor could not believe that he would be so sympathetic. "My family came to the conclusion that he was dead, but I never really believed it," she whispered.

"I am so happy that he is not dead," Peter declared.

Eleanor had to sit down. She felt faint.

He sat down on an ottoman facing her. "I know the character of the woman you are," he said fiercely. "I know you would do anything to help those you love and hold dear."

Eleanor could only nod. When was he going to accuse her of infidelity, disloyalty, deception? Wasn't he going to demand an explanation for her behavior?

"Your family insists Sean is innocent. I am soon to be a part of this family, too, Eleanor, and I would ally myself with all of you."

She remained stunned by his gracious behavior. She studied him, trying to find an accusation in his eyes. There was none. Did he mean that he still intended to marry her? She would not tell him any more lies. "When Sean appeared, Peter, I was overcome. Until he told me the truth, I had no idea he'd been convicted of treason and sent to prison. When I realized the authorities were searching for him, intending to hang him, I had to go with him. Foolishly, perhaps, I was determined to help him escape the country in any way that I could."

"I understand," he said simply. "But the authorities must never know."

"How can you understand?" she cried, leaping to her feet. "Why don't you hate me? I left you standing at the altar! I *jilted* you, Peter, or so it appears. And that was not my intention!"

He took her hands. "I understand because I love you," he said.

Eleanor froze. When she could breathe, she said, "How can you love me now?"

"How can I not?" he returned quietly.

She pulled her hands from his and turned away. Peter's anger and accusations would have made her task much easier. She did not know what to do in the face of such loyalty and trust—both of which she did not deserve. She realized she was going to have to tell him the entire truth. "I love Sean," she began slowly.

He instantly stepped around to face her. "Eleanor! I know you love all of your brothers! I know you love Sean. And I have sent my father to London to aid your father in obtaining a complete pardon for him."

For one instant, her mind could not comprehend such generosity. "Lord Henredon is a cousin of the Prime Minister."

"Yes, he is." Peter took her hands again. "My father

will do everything in his power to secure Sean's pardon. He is well connected and I am optimistic."

Eleanor had to sit. She gazed up at Peter, trying to understand. "Why are you doing this?"

He didn't quite smile. "You are soon to be my wife. Your troubles are my own. If Sean is your brother, he is my brother, too. When will you realize that I would do anything—*anything*—for you?"

Tears came to her eyes. "You still wish to marry me after I jilted you at the altar?"

"You left me for a noble cause!" he cried, flushed. He knelt before her, taking her hands again. "You are a woman of honor, Eleanor, and of great loyalty, and I admire that as much as everything else. I trust you. How could I not? And I will do *anything* to take you to wife."

Eleanor felt her cheeks flame with guilt even as she wondered at his use of words and his fervor. "Peter," she began quietly, still determined to tell him everything, "you should not—"

He leaped to his feet, interrupting her. "When we receive news of Sean's pardon, we will marry immediately, but this time, without such a spectacular fuss."

Her heart slowed, but beat in a peculiar manner, hard and thick. She stared at Peter. She had no doubt now that he loved her, but she wondered if he knew the truth about her love for Sean. There was something so unnaturally fierce in his desire to trust her and believe in her.

"Sean will be pardoned, Eleanor. My father is never thwarted in these matters. I am sure we will hear of his pardon soon, and then we will celebrate our union."

She was still. The room had become still. Peter's message was suddenly resounding. He had sent his powerful father to London to help Edward in his quest for amnesty, and he expected their marriage to proceed after it was obtained. In that moment, she felt trapped and outmaneuvered. But was that his intention?

Was he offering her a trade? Was Peter purposefully bartering her hand in marriage for Sean's liberty and life?

If not, what would he do if she told him that she would not marry him? Would he recall Henredon from his mission?

"Eleanor, I thought you would be pleased with my news," Peter said stiffly.

She stood, managing to smile. She was trapped after all, but then, this was a small price to pay for Sean's freedom. "I am very pleased. Peter, thank you. Thank you for all that you have done on my stepbrother's behalf."

He did smile. "You need not thank me, Eleanor.

You need only promise me that, this time, you will not jilt me at the altar."

She thought he was making a jest, yet she also wondered if he meant his words, too. "Of course not," she said. "You need only set a new date, and your bride will be there."

He beamed, and she saw relief in his eyes. "Then let us share the good tidings with your family."

Eleanor nodded. He seemed satisfied and she knew that their unspoken bargain was sealed.

ELEANOR HAD TO KEEP reminding herself that this turn of fate was as fortunate as could be. Sean was going to attain his freedom, and all she had to do in return was marry a nobleman who loved her. They found the countess in the music room, sitting at the piano, her fingers on the keys, but making no effort to play. She looked up, her gaze wan, and managed a tired smile.

"There is hope," Eleanor said softly, leaving Peter's side. She went to her mother and sat down beside her on the upholstered piano bench. "Peter's father is in London, and he is also seeking a pardon for Sean. There is great hope."

The countess put her arm around her. "I am too afraid to hope."

Eleanor bit her lip. Then she glanced at the threshold of the room, where Peter stood. "Peter and I are marrying the moment we receive the pardon."

The countess started and her gaze went to Peter. He smiled at her and bowed. "With your permission, of course, my lady."

Mary turned a confused regard on Eleanor. "Darling?"

Eleanor simply smiled at her, the expression forced. "I wanted to share our news with you, first." She kissed her mother's cool cheek and stood. "I am going back to my rooms to rest."

Mary nodded, apparently speechless.

In the corridor, Eleanor was about to excuse herself from Peter when she heard a ruckus in the front hall. Tyrell's commanding voice sounded—and her heart leaped uncontrollably. Peter took her arm. "In light of the absence of your father, perhaps we should inform your brother as to what we now intend?"

Eleanor barely heard. Was Sean all right? Had Tyrell seen him and spoken with him? And what about Reed? She managed to nod as they hurried through the house and into the front hall.

Tyrell was disappearing into the library by himself as they entered. "Ty!" Eleanor ran after him.

He turned. He had shed his jacket, and his boots

and breeches were muddy and wet. Even his ruffled white shirt was spotted with mud and rain. His gaze went from Eleanor to her fiancé. "Why aren't you in your rooms, resting?"

Her spirits sank. He was so terribly grim. "I can't rest. I am too excited." She managed a wide smile. "Peter has forgiven me for my very lacking behavior and we will soon wed."

His expression did not change. His gaze held hers and Eleanor knew he suspected everything. "I am pleased," he said carefully. "Peter, I am more than glad to have a celebratory drink with you. Eleanor, why don't you excuse us?"

She dug in her heels. "Ty, there are some matters we must discuss." Her heart threatened the boundary imposed by her rib cage and chest.

His gaze became blank. "Of course. Peter? I'd like a brief moment with my sister."

Peter bowed. "Take as long as you like." He left the room.

Eleanor did not hesitate—she ran to the two oak doors and closed them. Panting, she faced Tyrell. "What happened? How is Sean? Did you see him?" she cried.

"Spoken like a true bride," he said darkly. He turned and poured a large Irish whiskey into a glass.

She ran to face him. "Don't you dare berate me now for the true love in my heart! I am sorry I do not love Peter, truly, I am! Is Sean all right?"

"He is as well as can be expected, I think," Tyrell returned flatly. "What the hell happened to him, Eleanor?"

She understood every aspect of the question. "He was locked up in a small, dark cell, Tyrell, and for two years he did not see, speak or hear anyone. That is, he was very much buried alive. Before that, they tortured him—they flogged him. And before that? I already told you that his wife was deliberately raped and murdered by Reed's men and that his stepson died in a fire set by those soldiers. All to pay for his supposed crimes. He is racked with guilt."

"He is almost unrecognizable," Tyrell said slowly, appearing pained.

Eleanor choked. "You should have seen him a week ago, when he could hardly speak a coherent sentence. You should see the scars on his back—you should have seen his eyes—dark, bleak and hopeless."

Tyrell stared at her. After a pause, he said, "You are doing the right thing by marrying Sinclair."

She fought tears. "I have no choice. I have made the Devil's bargain—to marry a man I do not love in order to free the man I do love."

Tyrell set his now empty glass down and clasped her shoulder. "He has changed, and not for the better. I will always love my stepbrother. But he is not the man for you, Eleanor. He can only bring a woman pain—and I do not think he is capable of the great love you wish for."

Eleanor was afraid Tyrell was right. But she shook her head and her heart spoke for her. "Just before he was captured, Sean began to find himself. He began to smile. He started to speak of the past—and to share his demons with me. I know that if I was given the chance to stay with him, I could help him find his way back to all of us. But I am not being given that chance. I am going to marry Peter and Peter's father is going to obtain that pardon. And Sean is going to be alone with his scars and wounds." She bit off a sob. Who would be there for him now?

"He won't be alone," Tyrell said gruffly. "Devlin and Virginia will succor him. We all will."

No, she thought, unbearably saddened, they would not all succor him—for she would be in Chatton, a loyal and loving wife to another man. She turned away so her brother would not see the depth of her misery.

Tyrell spoke from behind. "This is for the best, Eleanor. I would be afraid for you, if you stayed with the man he has become."

She whirled. "You are wrong! Sean loves me, and he would still give his life to protect me."

"A life with him would be so dark and so bleak that he would hurt you more than anything else. You must trust me now."

She did not tell him that she would give anything to share that dark, bleak life with Sean, even if he did hurt her. "Is he being treated fairly?"

Tyrell nodded. "But it would be best if he were not imprisoned for very long. I do not think he can mentally manage incarceration of any kind now."

She shivered with fear. "I need to see him."

"No."

"I am not asking for your permission. I am telling you that I will go to see him, even if I must do so alone and without escort in the midnight hours of the night!" She glared. "And as I have already suffered unspeakably at Colonel Reed's hands, it is your duty to make certain I safely visit Sean."

"You will jeopardize your future with Sinclair!" Tyrell exclaimed.

"No, I won't. I have lied enough, and I will tell Peter that I must visit Sean."

And Tyrell capitulated. "Fine. I will take you tomorrow after breakfast."

ELEANOR HAD ASKED Tyrell to wait outside for her. As an aide led her to Sean's cell, she was as eager to see him as she was afraid of what she might find. When she approached, she saw that he lay on a pallet on the floor, and for one moment, even though it was midmorning, she thought he was asleep. But it was bright and sunny outside, as if to compensate for the previous day's downpour, and daylight was pouring into the cell. Sean's eyes were open, she realized, and he was staring at the ceiling, his breathing shallow. Eleanor ran to his cell, crying out. "Sean!"

He suddenly looked at her and then lunged to his feet. "Elle," he gasped.

Instantly Eleanor saw cuts on his forehead and face. "Please let me inside," she said to the aide, trying to fight her fear.

"Sorry, no one goes inside," the solider replied.

"He's hurt!" she shouted, fury erupting. "He's ill!"

"He's mad," the soldier said. "Crazy like a loon." He walked away, cell keys jingling, and returned to the anteroom. The door slammed shut behind him.

"He's right," Sean said harshly. "You shouldn't be here."

Eleanor gripped the bars, facing Sean. She understood his panic and hoped to calm him. "Sean, everything is going to be all right. Tyrell is outside, and in a day or two, you are going to be released."

His eyes told her he did not believe her. "You shouldn't have come," he said. "Did you see Reed?"

"No, I didn't. Brawley let us in." She reached through the bars to touch his wet cheek with her fingertips. "I have good news."

His gaze remained on hers. "What news could you possibly have?"

She fought to smile. "Peter's father is related to the Prime Minister. He is also in London, seeking your pardon. We are all optimistic, Sean."

Sean stared, his face hard. In that moment, Eleanor knew he understood what she had done.

She tried not to cry. "I have no choice," she whispered. "This is a pact, unspoken but a pact nevertheless. His father is fighting for your pardon and when it comes, we will wed."

"Good," he said harshly. And his breathing became shallow again.

"Don't! Take a deep breath, Sean!" she cried. "I love you so much—I would do anything to see you go free."

He held up his hand. It was shaking. "This is *good*. This is what I *want*! You will never wind up…like Peg."

She couldn't stand him blaming himself for her

death, not for another moment. "You didn't murder her. You married her—and that is far different. *Reed* ordered his men to savage her. *Reed* murdered her."

He struck out blindly, hitting the iron bars. They rang. "It is my fault. When will you understand? If I hadn't married her…she wouldn't have been made to pay for what I did. I was supposed to protect her…I was supposed to love her. I did none of those things!"

"You would have protected her if you had been there that night—I know it, because I know you," Eleanor cried.

He backed away. "I can't even see her face anymore. I don't even remember what she looked like."

In that instant, she felt his burning pain and all of his raging guilt. "Oh, Sean. You have to let her go. If she really loved you, she would not be blaming you for what happened, and I am certain she loved you very much."

Sean just stared, and his tears finally fell. Eleanor didn't know what to do, because she had never seen a man cry like this. So, she waited.

When he spoke, his voice was thick. "She used to look at me with such confusion. She didn't have to ask, but I knew…. She couldn't understand why I didn't love her."

Eleanor didn't know what to say. "She was so fortunate to be your wife. I'm sure she felt that way."

He covered his face with his hands but failed to hide a sob. "Maybe I can forget what I did to Peg...but I can't ever forget Michael. God, Elle!"

Eleanor stiffened. Sean had only spoken about Michael once before. Suddenly, she realized he hadn't been able to talk about the little boy. Her senses told her that the child was as much the key to Sean's torment. "How old was he?"

He met her gaze. "Six."

"What color was his hair?"

"Red. Wildly red, like the sunset." More tears fell, but he smiled. "He was a rascal, Elle...always in trouble...but I knew he just wanted my attention."

She smiled, wiping her eyes. "He adored you, didn't he?"

Sean nodded, now incapable of speech.

Eleanor reached through the bars. "You can tell me, Sean. Tell me what really happened to him."

He looked blankly at her. Confusion and anguish covered his face. "That's just it...I don't know...no one knows. A sweet, innocent child...he probably died in that fire begging me to come, begging me to save him...waiting for me.... I didn't come."

Eleanor reached through the cell bars as he moved

closer to them and their palms entwined, clasping. And then he was leaning against her, the bars between them, weeping in grief, the terrible sounds coming not from his chest, but from his blackened soul. Eleanor managed to slip her arms through the bars and around him. "I'm sorry." There was nothing else to say.

Sean wept and she held him.

And when the tears were finally spent, he was still. He let her hold him awkwardly through the cell for another moment, before he inhaled raggedly and stepped back. Their gazes met. "He was a good boy. I wanted to be his father," Sean said.

"I know." Eleanor watched him carefully. She thought he had finally spent his grief and if so, then one good thing had come of this day.

He inhaled again. "I let them both down, Peg and Michael."

"You did not let anyone down. You tried to stop the uprising, you took your family and fled Kilvore, and you could not have known the soldiers would seek revenge on your family in the adjacent town."

He sighed. "I keep thinking 'if only.' If only I hadn't been at the inn that day, if only I hadn't married Peg, if only I had stopped the villagers from attacking the Darby estate. Elle...I am tired of thinking about what might have happened—I am so tired of thinking about the past four years."

She was relieved. "You should be tired of thinking about it. Sean, I know you hoped to punish yourself, and you succeeded. You can't go back in time to change anything that happened. You are such a good man. Why do you think that Peg loved you? That Michael wished to be your son? Because they both knew how noble you are."

Sean made a grudging sound. "I never thought to marry her, Elle. She told me she was with child a few days after the massacre. I was in such shock, she'd lost her father, and suddenly we were exchanging vows."

"I understand."

He studied her quietly. "Do you? Do you genuinely understand? Have you forgiven me, Elle?"

She smiled at him, recalling the anguish his betrayal had caused. "I do understand. I understand completely because I know you so well—and that is why I have forgiven you."

He smiled, relief in his eyes. "I thought about you that day. I was so uncomfortable. There were so many memories. You were such an impossible child. Just before I left Askeaton, I couldn't reconcile that child with the woman you had become. The night I left, do you remember it?"

She was thrilled. "I will never forget. I tried to kiss you and you were horrified." She actually blushed.

"I was afraid," he said, in a matter-of-fact manner.

"It doesn't matter." But now she truly began to understand what had happened to them, as she had grown from child to woman.

"Doesn't it?"

"We agreed, there is no going backward."

"But I let you down, didn't I? You trusted me yet I left you—I failed *you.*"

"You could never let me down," she whispered, meaning it with all of her heart. "You promised me you would come back, and you did. And I will always trust you, Sean."

His gaze held hers. It did not waver. "That promise meant something different to each of us."

She tensed, somehow knowing she would not like whatever he intended to say next.

"I'm glad you're marrying Sinclair."

Those were words she had never wanted to hear. *"Don't."*

"He will take care of you and he loves you. Once, that was my duty and my responsibility. Now, it will be his."

"You sound as if we are over! We will still be friends!" she cried fiercely. "That will never change!"

He gave her an odd look. "I don't think friendship is possible anymore."

She cried out, aghast. "I may become Sinclair's wife, but I will always love you exactly the way I do right now. You will always be my best friend—you will always be the one I turn to when in need!" She fought the urge to cry. "You are my heart, my soul!"

His mouth turned down, forming a hard line. A terribly intense moment fell. After the lifetime they had shared, after all of the pain and passion, Eleanor wanted to know if he also felt that their love would survive anything, even her marriage to Peter.

He finally said, "You have to go forward."

She shook her head. "And away from you? Never." Then, as he was not about to expound, she asked, "What will you do, when you are released, a free man?"

"If I am freed, I am going to America."

She was stunned. "You will go home. You have to go home to Askeaton—it is where you belong."

"With you and your husband a few miles away at Adare? No, I don't belong there now."

She felt the rush of more fear. "Of course you do! We never finished all the rooms! I can come over to help you, from time to time, when Peter and I visit Adare in the summer!"

"You cannot marry him and have me, too."

"You're my *best* friend! Of course I can!"

"Elle, stop! Everything is about to change. You are going to be another man's wife. You will have his children. And it won't matter where I am or what I am doing, because you will be happy—you will have forgotten this…us."

She was aghast. "How can you think such a thing? Forgotten us?" she echoed. "I will never forget this—us—you! Sean, promise me that, when you are freed—"

He cut her off. "No!" he cried. *"No!"*

She stared, stunned. "Don't ask me to let you go," she begged desperately.

"Don't cry!" He reached through the bars, "Please, this is for the best."

She fought for composure. "It is best that I uphold my bargain with Peter and marry him. I am committed. But it is also best that you live in your home, where you are loved, where you belong—and we will remain good friends."

He laughed bitterly and shook his head. "This debate is absurd, because I will probably hang. You should go."

It crossed her mind that this was the end, then, for them, because he saw no possibility of continuing their relationship. He was so resolved. She did not move, panic consuming her. She could not bear losing Sean this way. "I can't go—not now, like this!"

He slowly looked at her. "I am happy for you…Eleanor."

"No! It is Elle—it will always be Elle!"

He inhaled slowly, deeply. "You are going to have a good life. There will be children—maybe even an impudent girl, just like the child you once were. I am very happy for you."

She shook her head. "I'm not leaving, not yet. When will I see you again?"

He stared. "You know that is not a good idea. You know this is farewell."

She cried out, clinging to the bars.

And Sean turned away, calling for the guard.

CHAPTER TWENTY

"DARLING?"

Eleanor was in her mother's hothouse, wearing heavy leather gloves, a trowel in hand. Although it was frigidly cold out and terribly damp, inside it was warm. She wore a light wool shawl over her cotton gown as she repotted several plants, all exotic species of roses. Eleanor had never had any inclination to garden until the past month, but her mother's hothouse had become her refuge, where she could toil in the heated and humid atmosphere in isolation, her only companion her numb heart.

"Darling?" Peter dared yet again, his tone filled with hesitation.

Eleanor was still, not turning to face him, aware that he stood in the entrance to the hothouse. An entire thirty-two days and six hours had gone by since she had been to Kilraven Hill to see Sean. In that time, her fiancé had treated her with the utmost respect and even more caution, as if afraid that she might break should he say the wrong word or use the wrong tone. Eleanor spent most of her waking hours in the hothouse, but when the weather permitted, she would don Sean's shirt and her breeches and gallop across the hills on her stud, alone. She slept late and went to bed early. She slept with Sean's shirt in her arms. There was no word from either her father or Lord Henredon.

Eleanor took a breath, smiled firmly and with resolve, and laid the trowel down. She turned to face Peter. "Hullo," she said brightly. "Have I forgotten the time again?" She knew what time it was. She wore a small pocket watch pinned inside her bodice, and actually, it was thirty-two days, six hours and twenty minutes since she had left Sean's cell.

She knew she should not be tracking time. After all, it was over, he had made it clear that he would not budge. If she dared to recall their last conversation—which she did not—she would be rushing outside and demanding a horse, any horse, so she could gallop to the fort to see him another time and beg him for any other recourse to their lives.

Peter smiled and approached, closing the door to the hothouse behind him. Perspiration instantly appeared on his forehead and cheeks. "I am going to Limerick with Rex. Do you need anything?"

"Something to read would be wonderful," she lied. She had never had the patience to read before, just as she had never had the patience to garden, but locking herself in her rooms for hours at a time, she would insist she was engrossed in a new novel. There was a stack of such books by her bed, all untouched. Rex knew. He had come into her rooms unannounced one morning when she was supposed to be reading and had found her staring out of the window into the fog. He had instantly ascertained that of the half-dozen tomes on her bed table, not a single one had even been opened. He hadn't said a word. Instead, he had asked her advice on his domestic affairs—apparently he was in need of a housekeeper.

Eleanor knew he wished to distract her; he had definitely become her favorite brother.

Now Peter nodded, his gaze searching. "I thought you might be ready for another book," he said with an obvious effort at good cheer. "How is the planting coming?"

"Very well," Eleanor said, gesturing behind her. Reading was impossible, as it required mental concentration. Planting required a repetitive physical act and she was quite good at it. "Take your time, Peter, enjoy yourself in town," she added.

"We'll pause for a light dinner." He hesitated and

then took her gloved hand as if he wished to raise it to his lips. Eleanor tensed, then told herself to relax, as he could not kiss her hand—the glove was covered with soil.

Peter looked her in the eyes and leaned forward, brushing his mouth to her cheek. His own gaze had become dark. "Eleanor, I despise seeing you so morose!" he suddenly cried with fervor. "Maybe lingering here as we await some word regarding your brother's fate is not the best idea. Maybe we should sail for Chatton. I am certain Cliff would not mind transporting us to England."

Cliff had remained in the country, *The Fair Lady* now at port in Limerick. Eleanor was certain he would not leave until Sean had received a pardon, just as she was certain he intended to break Sean from jail and sail him away, should that pardon be denied. In fact, he had spent several nights at Askeaton with Devlin, Rex joining them, and she knew a conspiracy had been formed to answer the worst scenario. Devlin, of course, had left shortly after Sean's capture. He, too, was in London, drumming up support for Sean's pardon at the Admiralty.

"I can't leave," Eleanor said firmly. She did not attempt to smile now. "If your brother was in the jeopardy that Sean is in, you would hardly desert him now."

Peter was grim. "You are right, of course. But this is taking so terribly long. We have had one brief missive from your father, which merely said he was hoping for the best. I am beginning to worry, darling."

Eleanor withdrew her hand and hugged herself, mindless of the dirt. "Your father and my father combined could *never* be denied," she said fiercely. It was a refrain she believed with all of her heart, as there was no room for doubt. "And now Devlin is in town, too, and he remains a naval hero."

"I know you are trying to be brave," Peter returned seriously, "but it breaks my heart to see you so saddened, Eleanor."

He could not know the real cause of her sorrow. "We will hear something soon," she insisted. "Very soon, I am sure."

"You are so brave!" he exclaimed. "At least Cliff and the runners found Flynn. He is our witness to the events of that horrid night."

Eleanor pulled her gloved hand from his. Flynn had been brought to Adare two and a half weeks ago by a triumphant Cliff. Word had immediately been dispatched to the earl. "I am certain that Father will appear at any moment with good news," she said firmly.

Peter clasped her shoulder and she was forced to face him. His gaze held hers. "I want to cheer you," he said after a long pause. "How can I do that?"

"Bring me a new novel," she said with a smile. "You know that will cheer me considerably."

He turned away, but not before she glimpsed sadness in his eyes. And Eleanor became concerned. Did Peter suspect the truth? That she was frantic for Sean's fate and grieving over the loss of their friendship? She had been so careful to be social and charming, to choose the right words, the correct replies. Her smiles, while artificial, were well rehearsed. And should he make a jest, she was quick to laugh at it—she was always the first to do so.

"I will see you at supper, then," Peter said quietly.

Eleanor hesitated, and then she ran to him impulsively. "Peter!"

Surprised, he faced her.

"Thank you for your kindness and understanding," she said, meaning it. "I am sorry I am not more amusing."

He pulled her into his arms. Surprised, Eleanor stiffened, as they had not shared an intimate embrace since her return. "I do not want you to dissemble to make me happy," he said earnestly. "I only want to see your eyes sparkle with laughter and joy again."

She remained tense, but less so. "I will become my old self again, I will. I just need to know that Sean is going to walk away from all of this a free man."

His gaze searched hers, and Eleanor instantly recognized the need there. Her heart raced in some alarm. "I cannot imagine our fathers failing," he said quietly. "Eleanor?"

This was inevitable, she thought. After all, as soon as they received word of an amnesty, they would marry on the following weekend. It had been planned. And that night she would share Peter's bed. She intended to give him all of the passion she could muster—he deserved far more and that was the least she could give. She hoped, vaguely, that in time, she could give him more than friendship, loyalty and respect. It didn't matter. She would be the perfect wife; she had made up her mind. But then her mind betrayed her will and she thought, *Maybe one day, Sean would return to Askeaton and they would pick up the shattered pieces of their lives; maybe, when they were older, their temples gray, they would finally become best friends once more.*

Peter's lips brushed hers, jerking Eleanor into the present. Instantly she reminded herself that she must not wish for a future that, in all likelihood, would never be. She somehow smiled and returned Peter's gentle, uncertain kiss.

"I do not know whether I should be so forward now," he whispered.

"If you wish to be forward, it is your right. We are affianced," Eleanor said firmly. She closed her eyes and waited for another kiss. This time, she returned it with more fervor.

Peter finally stepped back, appearing dazed and smitten. He touched her cheek. "You are beautiful, even when you are up to your elbows in dirt. Until tonight, then."

Eleanor nodded, still smiling. Then he whirled and strode from the hothouse.

Eleanor began to tremble. She sat down quickly on a stone bench, her temples throbbing with a migraine, her knees uselessly weak. Once, long ago, Peter's amorous kisses had moved her. Now, she could barely will herself to suffer through them. Somehow, she thought grimly, she was going to have to change that.

And then she heard a soft jangle, not from the vicinity of the front door, but from a distance behind her. She turned, her eyes widening.

Cliff stood behind a huge palm, staring at her. She could not imagine how he had walked in without either her or Peter hearing him; he must have used the hothouse's back door.

He strode toward her. He was wearing a beautiful navy blue coat over a silver waistcoat with tan pants; he made a conscious effort to dress fashionably when at the house. It didn't matter. In spite of the attempt, he looked dangerous, more like a buccaneer pretending to be a gentleman than the genuine article. The sheathed dagger he wore beneath the jacket was visible and did not help the impression he made. Neither did his huge gold spurs.

Eleanor leaped to her feet. Every day someone from the family went to Kilraven Hill to visit Sean, the only exception being herself, as she could not go and would not be welcome if she did so. All of her brothers were kind enough to honestly tell her how Sean fared when she asked. Of course, she only did so in a privy moment. She wrung her hands. "How is he?"

"Are you all right?" he asked instead, his tawny brows lifting.

"Didn't you just visit Sean?"

"No. The countess went with Lizzie today and they have yet to return."

Disappointment claimed her. However, there was never anything new to report. Sean continued to have some anxiety and with it, occasional bouts of claustrophobia, but apparently he was becoming more skilled at controlling these moments. Her brothers insisted that he was in good spirits. Eleanor felt certain that they all lied and that he was resigned to his fate at the gallows.

Cliff laid a hand on her shoulder. "If you cannot kiss your fiancé, how will you bear his children?" His tone was kind.

She felt herself blush. "I believe it is done all the time."

"So you are a woman of the world now?"

"I think everyone already suspects that."

He actually blushed, as the extent of her relationship with Sean had been carefully ignored by one and all, but his eyes turned black. "He admitted the truth to me, Eleanor. I almost choked him for it."

She tensed in genuine alarm. "I do not need defending— Sean needs defending."

"Your honor needs defense and you know it as well as I do. This was not the subject I came to discuss but upon brief reflection, there may never be a better moment."

She was more alarmed now than before. She glanced toward the hothouse door, but it was closed. Peter was surely long gone; in any case, she lowered her voice. "I have no regrets. I gave Sean my heart a long time ago and I will never take it back. I know that you disapprove of everything that transpired in Cork, but I don't care. If I had the chance to go back in time, I wouldn't change anything."

Cliff folded his arms across his broad chest. "Are you with child?"

Her heart skipped. "I don't think so."

His brows lifted.

"This conversation is too intimate!" she snapped. Because the truth was that she hadn't had her month-lies yet. Eleanor hadn't dared to face the possibility that she might be carrying Sean's child. Worrying about Sean's fate was enough of a cross to bear.

Cliff stared at her.

Eleanor knew she flushed. She turned away, but he seized her arm. "Is there a chance that you could be with his child?" he asked very firmly.

Her color increased as she met his unwavering regard.

He realized her answer and his eyes widened. "Have you thought about this at all?" he demanded incredulously.

She pulled away. "I can't think about it now," she said unevenly. But she didn't have to consciously think about it. For she knew she would be thrilled if she could bear a child of Sean's into the world. And she also knew that if she did turn out to be carrying his child, she would have to tell Peter the truth. Eleanor had no idea what would happen next. She doubted Peter would be able to forgive her such a trespass. Surely he wouldn't want to raise another man's child as his own. On the other hand, he loved her and had the most generous spirit she had ever witnessed in anyone. As for Sean, he had made himself clear. If freed, he was leaving; if there was a child, he wanted that child raised by Peter.

"You had better start thinking about it," Cliff said sharply.

And suddenly Eleanor knew there was news. She seized his sleeve. "What is it? Why are you here? What have you come to say to me?" She was terrified.

He put his arm around her to support her. "I have news, Eleanor," Cliff said, and he smiled. Her eyes flared with hope. "Devlin's ship has been spotted off the coast and his signal flags have been raised. The earl is with him—and they have Sean's pardon."

SEAN NO LONGER feared sleep. Since being apprehended this final time, sleep had become an ally, for suddenly it was deep and, for the most part, dreamless. And when he drifted into dreams, he was swept far back in time to places that were warm and inviting—places he longed to go. There were lazy summer days chasing a young barefoot Elle across the lawns of Adare, days filled with laughter and hope; there were evenings spent at Askeaton, during those early days when the manor was charred and ruined, evenings in which he and Elle were too exhausted to do more than eat a quick supper and tumble into their separate beds. There were wild madcap rides and equally wild races, there were days spent swimming at the lake. There were supper parties when she was home from her first Season. In his dreams, he marveled at her beauty and could not understand how he had been so blind and oblivious for so long. There were also moments of lovemaking, during the days they had spent in Cork, moments that were wild, hot, intense....

"O'Neill!"

Sean heard his name but refused to heed it, because he was with Elle at Askeaton when she was on the verge of womanhood, before they'd ever made love. There was whitewash on her nose and love in her eyes and he could not understand why he'd been such a fool. Even at fifteen, she'd been so lovely and so wonderful. He could not heed the officer calling him, because her hands were blistered from all the labor she'd done to help him that day and he was going to bandage them before he left her again. For even in his sleep, even dreaming, he somehow knew that his life would soon be over. His family had been filled with hope this past month but he'd refused to allow himself such a luxury. He was afraid that if he woke up, he would not be allowed another moment to sleep and dream and relive what should have been.

"O'Neill."

Sean gave up. He sat up, leaving Elle and his home far behind, and he faced Captain Brawley, who had entered his cell, Devlin with him. He hadn't seen his brother in a month, as Devlin had gone to London to plead for his life. Grim, Sean stood, realizing that the sands of time had finally run out. He stared at his brother and Devlin smiled widely at him.

Oh, God, was it possible he was to be spared?

"You've been pardoned," Brawley said.

Sean was in sheer disbelief.

"It's official—you're a free man," the young officer added, and he shook his hand.

Dumbfounded, Sean looked at Devlin.

"It's true," Devlin said, and he embraced him hard. "Congratulations."

He was free. Devlin's wide smile and Brawley's pleased expression began to sink in. *He was free. He wasn't going to hang.* My God, he was going to *live.*

He had to tell Elle!

"Everyone is outside," Devlin added, clapping his shoulder. "We will celebrate tonight!"

Sean remained incredulous and amazed. Suddenly he was leaving his cell with his brother, who kept a hand on him, as if knowing he was too shocked to navigate his way outside on his own. The moment he stepped into the anteroom outside the prison block, he saw his mother and the earl, beaming and crying at once. Then he saw Tyrell and Lizzie, wreathed in smiles, and Virginia, Rex and Cliff. They were smiling, laughing, grinning. And in that next moment, he realized that Elle wasn't there.

Elle hadn't come.

Mary cried out, embracing him, tears of relief falling. He held her, stunned by the fact that Elle wasn't there, but his shock was passing now. In its place was a frigid reality. Of course she hadn't come. It was over. She was with Sinclair. Had she married him yet? He had been so careful this past month not to ask about her.

"Sean, I have prayed for this day," the countess said, clasping his face. "You are so thin! Will you come home to Adare? Please?"

His heart lurched and hurt. He reached for the earl's hand but his stepfather pulled him forward and embraced him instead. "Welcome home, son," he said, his gaze moist.

"Thank you, Father. Thank you for what you have done."

The earl now shook his hand, and did not release it. "You are my son. I would give my life for you, Sean. But I could not have succeeded without Henredon. My pleas initially fell on deaf ears." His gaze held Sean's.

Sean understood. Peter's father had been instrumental in achieving the pardon. But of course he had; now Eleanor would fulfill her end of the bargain. The earl seemed to comprehend the situation in all its intricate diplomacy, but was uncertain of what Sean intended toward his daughter. "Then I owe him—and Sinclair—my life."

"Yes, you do," the earl said, his gaze direct. "But you owe yourself a future of joy, as well."

Sean tensed. There would be no joy, not without Elle. But that was as it should be, wasn't it? He turned away, to face his oldest stepbrother.

Tyrell stepped forward. "We have had enough drama in this family to last a lifetime. And I agree that a vast celebration is in order." He smiled. "We can plan to celebrate well into the holidays."

Rex limped forward. "Welcome back." He hugged him with one arm.

Cliff slapped his shoulder. "You are forgiven," he murmured.

Startled, Sean met his gaze.

"But you need to meet with Eleanor," he added softly and firmly, his words clearly meant for Sean alone.

Sean was shaken, not sure what Cliff's last directive meant. Then Virginia came forward to greet him and he finally met Tyrell's wife.

Sean smiled at them all and glanced at Devlin. His brother smoothly said, "I think Sean might need a quiet night at Askeaton. And I will certainly hold a fête to celebrate his return in a few days. Mother? Why don't you come home with us? Edward? Perhaps you can spend a day or two there with us at my home?"

"I would love nothing more," Mary said, smiling. She slipped her hand in Edward's, who nodded in agreement.

Sean was oddly relieved. He should want to celebrate but he did not. Sean glanced past the family and through one of the chamber's open windows. Outside it was a pale, gray November day and a few soldiers were passing in the yard. But Elle did not stand in the courtyard waiting for him. Of course, he really hadn't been expecting her to be there. She remained with Sinclair—and that was what he wanted.

He wondered how long he could lie so baldly to himself.

THERE HAD BEEN a celebration, after all. Numerous bottles of fine burgundy wine had been consumed, followed by brandy, but it was well past midnight now and the earl and countess, Devlin and Virginia had all retired to bed. Sean sat alone in the salon before a roaring fire, staring into the flames.

He was finally beginning to believe that he was truly a free man and the horror of the past two years was over. But he could not find joy—and he could not find relief. There was only this deep, dark sorrow and an equally terrible regret. He needed to see Elle one final time—but if he did, he was afraid of what might happen.

She owed Sinclair marriage; *he* owed the man that marriage, too.

He rubbed his face. Sinclair and Henredon were responsible for his life. He could not go to Elle now and tell her how much he missed her and how greatly he loved her. He had heard that they would be married within days, on the weekend, and he knew he had to leave the county before that. So now there would not even be a goodbye.

No, they had already said goodbye, a month ago, in his cell.

I will never forget you!

You will always be my best friend.... You are my heart, my soul!

Elle's stricken image filled his mind. Sean desperately wanted to comfort her, and there was so much he wished to say now. He wanted one more chance to see her. This time, he would tell her far more than goodbye—he would tell her that she was his other half, his best half, that he loved her and he always had, and that his life was going to remain empty and bleak without her.

He stood, taking the bottle of brandy and slamming it against the wall. He couldn't go to her because he didn't trust himself not to steal the bride another time, and damn it, he was an honorable man and he was going to do the honorable thing.

He was going to leave Askeaton, and this time, leave Ireland, so she could be free. In time, Sinclair would make her happy; in time, she was going to forget him, no matter what she claimed.

"Sean?"

Sean turned stiffly at the sound of his brother's voice. Devlin's gray gaze was searching. "I can't sleep."

Devlin entered the room, as usual, not missing a thing, his regard going to the broken bottle and then back to Sean. "You're a free man now. It's obvious you're in love with Eleanor. Why are you doing this?"

Sean made a harsh sound. "She made a pact with

Sinclair. Their marriage for my life." And as he stared at Devlin, he thought, *he is right*. Why am I doing this? He could not stand the idea of Eleanor marrying the other man. He was Elle's hero—no one else could ever have that right.

"Break it," Devlin said softly.

Sean did not hear; he had started for the door. It was time he and Sinclair had a conversation. He owed the man, but he could not give up the love of his life. He had a future now, and he wanted Elle to be it.

"Take a carriage," Devlin called. "The roads are wet."

Sean did not answer—he was already gone.

CHAPTER TWENTY-ONE

SEAN HAD ALWAYS been able to come and go as he pleased at Adare. Having ridden like a madman through the night, he entered the house as if he still lived there. A quick exchange with the doorman told him where Sinclair was housed. Adrenaline flooded him as he strode through the halls of the sleeping house. The dialogue he wished to have with Sinclair could not wait until the morning. Sean hurried into the east wing and pounded on Sinclair's suite.

A brief moment passed and the bedroom door was flung open, Peter Sinclair standing there in his nightgown and cap, looking utterly dazed. They had never met and Sinclair instantly became fully awake. "I beg your pardon? Is there a fire?"

Sean knew he should not despise the other man and in truth, he did not. But he was jealous and he felt it in the marrow of his bones. "Sinclair, this cannot wait. We need to speak."

Sinclair's blue eyes hardened. He stared and it was another moment before he spoke. "O'Neill?"

Sean inclined his head. "Yes."

"Five minutes then," he said, stepping back into his rooms to dress.

Sean waited in the hall, pacing restlessly, fists clenched, acutely aware that his life with Elle was at stake. Sinclair's door opened and he appeared in a dressing gown and trousers. Their gazes clashed.

Sean reminded himself that this man and his father had saved his life. "I am vastly indebted to you and your father," he said without preliminaries. "And there is no way I can ever repay you both."

Eyeing him, Sinclair shoved his hands in the pockets of his wrapper. "I would do anything for my fiancée," he said firmly. "There is no need for any kind of payment." And his resolute gaze locked with Sean's.

"Really?" Sean remarked. "Why not?"

"We are soon to be brothers," Sinclair said. "That is how I have been thinking of it. And of course I would attempt to save my brother from hanging."

His words were utterly distasteful to Sean. "And being brothers through marriage, we will also be friends?"

Sinclair's gaze did not waver but he appeared distressed. "Of course. You need not have come tonight,

O'Neill. If you wished to thank me for my efforts on your behalf, it could have waited until the morrow."

And Sean knew that this man was no fool. Aware that they were true adversaries now, he chose his words with care. "I have come to thank you, but there is more." He saw Sinclair flinch. "Everyone thinks highly of you, Sinclair. I have been advised that you are a gentleman and a good match for Elle. I am aware that you love her. I am aware that you can give her all of the comforts she should have, not to mention a title. I have been supportive of the match. I think highly of you, too."

Sinclair was rigid. "You spoke in the past tense," he said slowly.

Sean knew he flushed. "I met Elle when she was tottering about, falling down more often than not, a precocious and spoiled two-year-old child." He smiled, recalling her demanding nature and the way she would ride piggyback on his shoulders. "Since that day, I have spent my entire life looking after her. It is my nature to protect her—it is my inclination to want what is best for her. That is why I approved of your match."

Sinclair flushed. "I have heard the family lore. I understand that you two were close. Why else would she be this devastated these past weeks, in regards to your situation with the authorities?"

Why else? Sean thought grimly. He was tired of dancing around Sinclair now. "I think you know the answer."

Sinclair started. "Eleanor is terribly loyal. She adores her family—especially you, her stepbrother and her hero."

How much did he suspect? How much did he know? And what would Sean have to do to get him to back down? "She is very loyal—on that point, you are right. Sinclair, it is more than that. But you already know that, don't you?"

Sinclair appeared terribly unhappy. "For God's sake, my father, at my request, has moved mountains to save your life, O'Neill."

"Is that what you really want? A marriage based on gratitude, the repayment of a debt?"

Seeming to breathe hard, Peter said, "I fail to comprehend you, O'Neill."

In a way, Sean felt sorry for Peter Sinclair. "I grew up regarding Elle as my stepsister. I no longer think of her that way."

Sinclair's eyes widened. "I beg your pardon?"

"I have always loved Elle. I love her now even more deeply than before, as the woman I wish to share my life with."

Sinclair shook his head. "Damn it! Don't do this

now, O'Neill! I adore her! I did everything possible to attain your freedom so she would not be crushed! You owe me!"

"I know you love her," Sean said grimly. "And I owe you my life, I do. But I cannot pay you with the woman I love. I've come for my bride."

Sinclair seemed devastated. He turned away, trembling, then turned back. "She is in love with you, too, isn't she?"

"Yes."

He made a harsh sound. "I have tried very hard to pretend your love does not exist. Of course I heard the whispers, the rumors! What are you really saying? Did you abduct my bride deliberately—to foil our wedding?"

"It wasn't planned," Sean said, feeling far too much sympathy for the other man. "And I didn't know the extent of my feelings for Elle until the authorities captured me in Cork."

"Are you asking me to give up my bride?"

"Yes."

The moment was interminable.

"Like hell!" Peter cried. "She cares for me, and you have nothing to offer her except a life of toil and hardship. You are penniless and in disgrace! I can care for her as if she is a queen! If you really love her, *you* will be the one to let her go. *You* will want her to have the life I can give her."

Sean was furious, because Sinclair was right. It was many moments before he spoke, and when he did, his tone was quiet. "You would marry her, knowing she is in love with someone else?"

Peter couldn't seem to speak, either. He was struggling, Sean realized, with the vast complexity of his emotions. But then, so was Sean.

And Sean realized the man was as deeply in love as he was. "Peter," he said slowly. "What would you do…if she is with my child?" His intention was not sabotage; he simply had to know.

Peter turned white, eyes bulging.

Sean prayed, knowing his prayers were not to be answered.

Peter shook his head, breathed hard and deep. "*Damn you. This* is how I have been repaid!" He inhaled. "I can no more stop loving Eleanor than I can will my heart to stop beating. If she is with child, so be it. I will raise that child as my own. I will honor and cherish it as my own. You need to go, O'Neill. And I suggest you go far away, as we are marrying in two more days."

Sean was reeling. Sinclair not only loved Elle, he would raise their child as his own. He could give Elle everything—he could give a child everything—and Sean owed him his life. There was only one possible recourse—to honor his commitment to the other man.

And Sean performed the greatest feat of his life— he bowed. Then he turned and walked out.

ELEANOR STARED AT her troubled and pale reflection in the mirror above the vanity chest, aware that her eyes revealed her turbulent emotions. Sean was now a free man—and he was only an hour's ride from the house. But in two more days she was marrying Peter Sinclair. She was at her wit's end. It was so hard to hold on to her pride and sanity; it was so hard to stay at Adare.

A knock sounded on her door.

Eleanor was confused—it was eight in the morning. She assumed one of her brothers was at the door, because no maid would disturb her before she left her room. She got up and answered the knock and was stunned to find Peter standing there. His eyes were red, as if he had been up all night—or as if he had been weeping.

She tensed. "Peter?"

"We need to speak," he said. In the most uncharacteristic manner, he walked past her, right into her sitting room, apparently oblivious to the fact that no man should be alone with her there.

Aware that he had something of tremendous importance to divulge or declare, Eleanor closed the door, absolutely indifferent to the impropriety, as well. "Peter, you seem distressed."

He faced her, waving his hands, unable to speak.

Eleanor felt certain he had been crying. Suddenly she was very alarmed. "Oh, God, please don't bring more bad news!"

He shook his head. "The news is good, I think."

"Then why do you appear as if someone has died?" she cried.

"No one has died." He took her hands in his. "I love you with all of my heart, Eleanor. I have from the moment we first met, and I always will."

Eleanor was more alarmed now than before. Acutely aware of Sean's freedom, she felt as if a coffin was being closed on her, burying her alive. She hesitated. "I am very fond of you. You know that, don't you?" she began.

"Shh," he said, a tear appearing on his cheek. He pulled her close and kissed her gently. "I have come to say goodbye."

She had to have misheard. "What?"

He pulled her closer. "I am a gentleman, Eleanor. If there is any one thing that defines me, it is that.

How can I force you into marriage when I see so clearly how much you love someone else?"

She cried out, and she felt her cheeks burn with guilt.

"Will you admit it? You love Sean O'Neill. You are fond of me, as you have just said, but that is all it is. You gave your heart to O'Neill many years ago—and I know you well enough now to know that you will never take it back or place it elsewhere, with me."

Eleanor staggered. "Peter, you have been so kind. I am prepared to marry you on Saturday, as we agreed. I am prepared to be a good wife—perfect, if I can somehow achieve that. You saved Sean's life! And I *am* very fond of you."

He wiped his eyes with the back of his hand. "You are *prepared* to wed, you want to *achieve* perfection as my wife."

"But I mean my every word," she declared, still stunned.

"Because you owe me for Sean's life?"

She did not know how to respond. "Yes," she whispered.

"I love you enough to let you go. He can't give you the life I can, but you are a woman of passion and I know, as much as I wish I did not, that you will not be happy with a fortune, not when the man you love is not at your side. I am breaking off with you, Eleanor, so you may go to Sean."

She was in shock. "Peter!" she cried, reaching for his face. "I won't abandon you, not if you tell me you still wish to wed. I do owe you. Sean and I, we both owe you! I will try to make you happy!"

He shook his head. "I thought I could marry you in this fashion, as repayment of a debt, but I can't. I thought I could ignore your love for another man, but I can't. I love you enough to want happiness for you, even if that means handing you over to O'Neill."

Eleanor began to cry. "I have never met anyone as generous and selfless as you."

"I have never met anyone as passionate and courageous as you," he replied unsteadily. "O'Neill was here earlier. By now, he must be home. You had better go to him, because he was very upset when he left."

Eleanor nodded, about to turn and go. Instead, she threw her arms around Peter Sinclair and she held him hard, for the last time. Then she ran.

As SHE GALLOPED the distance from Adare to Askeaton, she thought about Sean's resolve that she marry Sinclair. Then she thought about that night when he had left her four years ago, mindless of her pleas not to go. She was afraid of his rejection. Two years in prison and the loss of Peg and Michael had turned him into such a dark, wounded and complicated man. But she would never give up on their future.

Her stallion was heavily lathered and blowing hard when she flung herself from its back in front of Askeaton Hall. Eleanor ran toward the front doors when they opened. Sean appearing, coming down the steps. He was carrying a satchel—and it was déjà vu.

Eleanor halted, panting.

Her gaze fixated on the damned satchel. Somehow she tore her eyes from the bag to his tightly drawn face. "Where are you going?" she gasped.

He came forward. "I told you, I am leaving the country. What are you doing here?" he demanded, eyes wide.

How could this terrible night be happening all over again? "You can't go—you can't leave me!" Eleanor began to shake.

"I can't stay—I don't trust myself to stay," he said grimly.

"What does that mean?" she cried, reaching for his hand. To her surprise, he clasped it so hard the gesture hurt. It was as if he was determined to never let her hand go.

"I stole the bride a month ago—I don't think it

would be wise to test my resolve another time," he said tersely.

She shook her head. "I'm not marrying Peter."

"We both owe him," Sean said fiercely. "And I am leaving so I can be a man of honor."

Their eyes held. And Eleanor began to realize that Sean wanted to abduct her from the altar again. "Sean, he has broken it off."

Sean's expression mirrored confusion. "What? I just spoke to him—we had it out. As justice is on his side, I am the one who must leave you both to your future."

"No." Eleanor somehow smiled, realizing that Sean had gone to Peter to fight for her and their love. "Peter has broken off the engagement because he is noble and selfless and he knows I love you."

Sean stared, incredulous and disbelieving at once.

In the moment that ensued, Eleanor held her breath.

"He is walking away from you—because of me, of us?"

She managed to nod. He was starting to smile but he seemed dazed. "What did you say to him?" she asked.

"I told him I loved you. Not as a stepsister, but as the woman who is my entire life—and my entire future." His gray eyes softened. "Elle, I love you. In fact, I cannot live without you."

Eleanor started to cry. She reached for him and he put his arms around her. "When you declared your love in Cork when the troops had captured you, it felt like a dream—it felt too late. I have waited and waited to hear you say those words freely, meaning them!" she cried, laughing at the same time. "I have waited a lifetime to hear you declare your love for me, Sean!" She was giddy with joy, as all the darkness and torment dropped away.

He cradled her face in his hands. "And I have been a fool, not to see what has been right under my nose…for the past twenty years."

"How could you know that a tiny two-year-old child was your fate?" she teased.

He became terribly serious, his gaze searching. "Maybe I did know—maybe that is why I spent my life taking care of you. I still need to take care of you, Elle, no matter how resourceful you may be…I want to spend the rest of my life protecting you."

His tone had softened to a murmur and his face had lowered; Eleanor closed her eyes as their mouths drifted together. She sighed; inside, her nerves fired, her blood quickened. She could barely believe that this was really happening—that the future was theirs.

"May I do that?" he murmured, rubbing his lips across hers another time.

She clenched his shirt and answered, "Only if you make a very honest woman out of me."

Both brows lifted in mock confusion. "But you are a terribly honest woman."

She tugged warningly on his shirt. "I am serious! Are you going to marry me, Sean? Finally?"

He smiled, and the light of his smile filled his eyes. "Damn it, Elle! Will you not let me take the lead? Ladies do not propose marriage!"

"This one does!" she cried, her heart thundering as she awaited his answer.

He dropped to one knee. "Will you do me the vast honor, an honor I do not deserve, of becoming my wife? Will you allow me to cherish you, honor you, protect you and love you for the rest of my life? Will you bear my children, keep my home? Will you forgive me for not coming to my senses sooner?"

She nodded, speechless, as he stood upright. It finally sank in—Sean loved her. He was returning her love, and they were posed to embark upon the most wonderful journey of their lives, their future. "Sean, this feels like a dream. I have been waiting for you for so long."

He pulled her close. "I know. I just didn't know that it could be this way between us. It was so hard watching you become a woman. For the longest time,

I couldn't believe you were growing up. Elle, I need you. I need your smile and your laughter, I need your hope. I want to stay away from that place of darkness and guilt. I don't ever want to go back there. I've found light and peace with you."

"You are never going back to those shadows, Sean," she whispered. "I will make sure of it."

"Then come with me into the future—our future." He smiled tenderly at her.

"You couldn't stop me if you tried!" She smiled back, insanely happy, as he put his arms around her.

"Foolishly, I did try," he said with real regret. "Elle, could you be with child?"

"It seems more likely with every passing day." Eleanor searched his eyes. "I want your child, Sean, as much as I want our future."

He thought about Peg. Suddenly he could recall her vividly, in full color, and to his surprise, there was no guilt, no regret, just a vague sadness. And he thought about Michael.

Elle whispered, "If it's a boy, we can name him Michael."

He started. "I'd like that."

Eleanor reached for his face. "I will go wherever you wish to go," she said softly, kissing him. "And I know you won't believe it, but I will follow, not lead."

And Sean wanted to laugh, because he didn't believe it, not for a minute. But her warm, strong body was stirring up too many recent memories, and he paused before kissing her back. "I like it when you lead," he said, "as long as I am there to follow—and pick up any pieces that might come undone in your wake."

Impatient now, she kissed him, long and slow and very intimately. "I am definitely leading now."

It was a long, long time before he was capable of speech. "Good," he whispered. "Now let's announce our news."

And arm in arm, they went in search of the earl and countess of Adare to share their joy and good tidings.

EPILOGUE

Kilvore, Ireland, February 1819

THE DAY WAS GRAY AND RAW, the wind blustery. Eleanor sat beside Sean in the back of a handsome four-in-hand. Sean had fallen silent upon entering the quiet village, but because she held his hand, she knew he was not tense. She placed his hand on her swollen belly, because their child was kicking, and he smiled warmly at her.

"Are you all right?" she asked softly.

He had been gazing at the street lined with white-washed, thatch-roofed cottages. An occasional pedestrian hurried by, fighting the wind and the cold. "I am fine. I know I should be sad, but I'm not. I'm filled with anticipation, Elle."

She smiled, relieved. "You should be," she said. His demons were finally gone.

They had married the weekend she should have married Peter. The ceremony had been a very small one, with only immediate family in attendance. The earl had given her away, of course—when they had gone to him to announce their intentions, he had instantly approved of the match. Lord Henredon had been furious, apparently having it out with Edward. Peter Sinclair had not only left Ireland, he had left Britain, as well. Eleanor had heard he was in America and that he had gone West—as he did not need a fortune, he had become an adventurer.

She had broken his heart and he had not stayed for the wedding, but they'd shared a final goodbye. Eleanor had had the chance once more to thank him for his magnificent gesture and to tell him how much he meant to her. Peter had wished her a lifetime of happiness.

Their coach halted. Sean got out, a footman opening his door for him. Sean helped Eleanor down, a bouquet of flowers in her hand, and she gazed out at the village cemetery, a soft sorrow creeping over her. She no longer hated Peg and she wished she could have had a different fate. Sean took her hand and they entered the cemetery, neither one of them speaking.

It was a few moments before Sean found Peg's grave. The small stone had been placed there by the villagers of Kilraddick. It was engraved and read:

Margaret Boyle O'Neill
Beloved Daughter and Mother
1790–1816

Eleanor laid the bouquet of flowers down at the base of the small gray headstone and glanced at Sean. The same sadness she was feeling was reflected on his face and in his eyes, but it was a far cry from the grief and guilt that had once consumed him. Then he appeared puzzled. "Where is Michael's grave? Why isn't he buried here beside his mother?"

Even if they had never found his body, there should have been a grave beside Peg's. Before Eleanor could respond, she heard a shout and she turned. A small wiry man was at the gate by their coach and she recognized Jamie Flynn instantly.

There had been a huge inquiry into the events at both Kilvore and Kilraddick. Shockingly, other witnesses had been found and brought forward along with Flynn. Colonel Reed had been court-martialed and dishonorably discharged from his service, but before he could be tried in a criminal action for the murders of Peg Boyle and her son, he had vanished. Rumor held that he was on his way to the West Indies, a haven for military men turned pirates.

Flynn approached, beaming. "I was wondering if you'd ever get here, my lord."

"Flynn!" Sean grinned, hugging him warmly. "It is Mr. O'Neill, and you damn well know it. I am not titled."

"You're *his lordship* to me," Flynn said stubbornly. "You said you were coming in February, and you truly come back." He had left Limerick two months ago, after giving his testimony.

"Yes, I have come back—with my wife. And we are here to stay."

Flynn was thrilled. "I thought you meant you'd come to visit!"

"We have other plans," Sean said softly, and he smiled at Eleanor, pulling her close.

"You heard we got a new lord up at the house—but no one's seen him yet."

Sean exchanged a glance with Eleanor. She had to smile as he spoke. "I know. Times have changed, Flynn. It's a new day, and a new era. There'll be no more instances of tyranny here."

Flynn was confused. "My lord, I mean, sir. How do you know? Do you know his lordship? Can he be a good man?"

Sean continued to smile. "I am the new lord, Flynn," he said softly. "I bought Darby's estate."

In fact, the earl had bought the estate for them as their wedding gift. Flynn was stunned, gaping, tears filling his eyes. "My lord, this is a grand day, indeed! I got to tell everyone!" He wiped his eyes with the back of his hand. "And, my lord? This is a great day for you, too."

"What do you mean?" Sean asked, bemused.

"Look over there," Flynn murmured, but he was grinning from ear to ear.

Eleanor turned to glance in the direction Flynn had indicated. A young boy had paused just outside of the cemetery gates. The boy was bundled up in a heavy winter coat and a knit cap, but he turned to stare at them as Flynn waved him forward. The boy hesitated, and then started walking toward them.

"I got to go tell everyone the news," Flynn cried, rushing past the boy and from the cemetery.

"Oh, God," Sean suddenly gasped, his eyes widening.

Eleanor was alarmed. "What is it?"

But he didn't hear her. "Michael?" he cried, starting toward the boy. "Michael Boyle O'Neill—is that you?" He began to run, stumbling.

Eleanor cried out, incredulous.

The boy nodded, his eyes huge. "I'm Michael Boyle O'Neill," he whispered. "*Papa?* Have you really come back?"

Sean cried out, throwing his arms around the small boy. To his credit—as Michael was only eight years old and he hadn't seen Sean in two years—Michael accepted the embrace without protest. Suddenly realizing what the separation might have done, Sean released him. "Do you know who I am? Do you remember me?" he asked, dropping to one knee.

Michael nodded seriously. "You married me mum. Ye were me papa. Flynn told me, but I remember, too."

"I'm still your papa," Sean said, clasping his cheek. "I thought you died in the fire! What happened, Michael? Where have you been staying?"

"The O'Rourke family took me in after the fire and moved to Raharney, where there's more family," he said, starting to smile. "But they came back here in the fall. Flynn saw me when he came back from the courts. He said you would come back, and you did. Do ye mean it? Ye'll still be my papa? Missus O'Rourke says it's real hard to feed us all—she's got five of her own children."

Sean stood, tears slowly falling, and he nodded, wiping the tears with the back of his hand. Then he reached into his pocket, retrieving the small, carved boat. Michael's eyes went wide. Sean clasped his shoulder. "Do you remember this? It belongs to you."

Michael nodded, speechless.

"I have kept this in my pocket since the fire. Do you want it back?"

Michael nodded, taking the boat and holding it tightly to his chest.

Sean took Michael's small hand and he turned to face Eleanor. "Elle," he said thickly. "This is Michael. My son."

Eleanor's heart was thundering in her chest. Sometimes, she thought, still stunned, life could be fair. Sometimes, there was justice in this world. And she looked at the little boy and felt joy and love. She thanked God for such a miracle. "Hello." She came forward. "I'm Eleanor. I am so happy to meet you, Michael." She had never meant anything more.

As astute as children so often are, he looked from her to Sean and then back again. "Are you going to live with me and my papa, too?" His eyes held curiosity.

"I would love to—if you don't mind."

He blushed. "I don't mind." He looked at Sean. "She's *tall*," he said, making Sean laugh. "And pretty."

"She is very tall and she is very pretty," Sean agreed, taking Michael's hand. "And she is my wife, now, Michael. Do you mind?"

He bit his lip, flushing anew. "No," he said slowly, clearly thinking about it. "I don't mind."

He patted the boy's back. "Let's go see our new home." Sean turned to Eleanor. "Thank you."

She let him take her other hand. She said softly, "You have nothing to thank me for."

"I have everything to thank you for," he corrected as softly. "Shall we walk?"

Arm in arm, they started up the street, Michael now dancing ahead of them and pointing out every home and person they passed. That cottage belonged to the O'Briens, who were cobblers by trade, and that was the baker's, John O'Dare. Villagers came out of their shops and homes to greet them, smiling and doffing their hats, the women curtsying. Sean and Eleanor were greeted as "my lord" and "my lady," no matter how often Sean corrected the mistake. A gap-toothed vendor pressed hot chestnuts into their hands and the butcher offered them a leg of lamb, wrapped in paper. A woman came out to hand Eleanor a silk scarf. Eleanor thanked her profusely. More offerings followed—cups of hot tea, a jug of whiskey, cookies still warm from the oven—and their coach, traveling slowly behind them, was the repository of all the gifts.

And then they had left the last house behind. Ahead were two tall stone walls and wrought-iron gates; on the hill behind the fence was the big house.

It remained charred by the fires that had destroyed it but the dark stone and gaping windows were oddly welcoming. Eleanor glanced at Sean and their gazes locked. It would take many months to renovate the estate, and she could not wait to get down on her hands and knees with him to tear up the floors, not that he would let her do too much in her state. But when they were done, their home was going to be as magnificent as Askeaton, of that there was no doubt. She thought about her child tottering through the halls—she thought about Michael chasing after the toddler to catch him or her before he or she fell.

And for the first time, Eleanor knew she was having a girl.

"It's burned," Michael said in an awed voice. "An' they say it's got ghosts!"

"I doubt there are ghosts." Sean smiled. "We are going to rebuild, Michael, room by room, the three of us. Will you help Elle and I?"

Michael nodded eagerly.

And as they passed through the front gates, Eleanor glanced at the inscription on the brass plaque that she had ordered placed there. The estate has been renamed in Peter's honor. It was now Sinclair Hall.

DEAR READERS

I HOPE YOU HAVE enjoyed *The Stolen Bride!* For those of you who are familiar with my novels, you know it was a departure for me. I am well-known for strong, "Alpha" males, not wounded heroes who must take a long and difficult journey to recover their own power and in doing so, find true and eternal love. But Sean and Eleanor first appeared to me in *The Prize* and I knew instantly that theirs was a great love story which had to be told.

As you may or may not know, I first introduced the de Warennes in *The Conqueror* in 1989, a powerful and passionate love story set during the Norman Conquest. One medieval followed it a few years later, *Promise of the Rose.* I never intended to develop another family saga at that time and certainly never envisioned bringing this powerful dynasty to nineteenth-century Ireland and England. When I began *The Prize,* the hero was Devlin

O'Neill, whose ancestor, Liam O'Neill, was Queen Elizabeth's favorite pirate—*The Game*. But the de Warennes instantly insisted upon making another appearance in my life. And suddenly Devlin's stepfather became Edward de Warenne, the earl of Adare, and a whole new generation of powerful, passionate and privileged de Warenne men were born.

Sean and Eleanor's story is the third de Warenne novel set in the Regency period. *The Prize* and *The Masquerade* preceded it, telling the stories of first Devlin O'Neill and Virginia Hughes, and then Tyrell de Warenne and Lizzie Fitzgerald. Cliff's story is next in *A Lady at Last*.

He is the greatest gentleman privateer of his era; she is La Sauvage, a pirate's daughter. He is wealthy, powerful, privileged and accustomed to the greatest beauties in the world; she is used to running wild in the islands, she cannot read or write and has never worn a dress.

He had secretly admired her from afar, for no one has as free a spirit.

She has openly admired him for years, for no one is as handsome, as powerful or as great a sea captain.

Then Fate decides it's time to intervene and her father is hanged…and Cliff rescues her. With the snap of that noose, he becomes her protector, her champion, her guardian. And because it was her father's last dying wish that she go to England to meet the mother she has never known, he decides he will be the one to take her.

A Lady at Last is a huge, powerful and passionate love story. Cliff is one of my all-time great heroes, incredibly arrogant at times, and so obtuse when it comes to his feelings for Amanda, but he is so passionate and so powerful he can be forgiven his flaws. Amanda's journey is one of slow but certain discovery, as she navigates her way through society's scorn, her mother's rejection, love, desire and heartache.

Please check out my new Web site, *www.thedewarennedynasty.com!* There you can meet all the de Warenne and O'Neill men and the women who dare to love them. Visit The Lounge for sneak peeks of works in progress that no one has seen, as well as additional excerpts from yet-to-be published books, characters monologues, diaries and my own thoughts on my heroes, heroines, stories and the plots I am still planning. And don't forget to enter my contests, including the chance to win a trip to Adare, Ireland.

Finally, do not shy away from my first paranormal romance, *Dark Seduction.* If you have loved my historical heroes, you will love the *Masters of Time—*

powerful medieval Highland warriors sworn to protect innocence throughout the ages. You will meet Alpha heroes at their most arrogant, their most sexy, and their most infuriating; but these great Masters are men a woman will gladly die for.... Please check out *www.mastersoftimebooks.com* to meet the Masters.

Happy Reading, and see you at King's House in the summer of 1820!

Bda Joyce

Desire is the first weapon—*The Masters of Time*

Turn the page for an exciting preview
of the next novel of the de Warenne Dynasty
A LADY AT LAST
Available December 2006

DE WARENNE'S GAZE took in the pistol in her waistband and the saber she held. Then his gaze lifted.

I hate him, Amanda thought. *He would take a fancy lady to bed, but not her; she wasn't good enough for him.* She strolled forward. "Your son will be a good swordsman one day."

His eyes were guarded. "Yes, he will. What is that?"

She slowly raised the saber. "My sword." She smiled at him. She was very adept with a saber—she could beat Papa. Fencing wasn't about strength; it was about balance, agility and skill.

"Do you wish to fence?"

"I heard the blades, and I thought we were under attack." She took her pistol and laid it aside on the deck.

His eyes widened. "So you came up here to help my men defend the ship?"

"Of course," Amanda said. "I am no weak-kneed gentlewoman to swoon at the sight of battle. But I am rusty—I haven't had a chance to fence in a very long time. Do you care to engage?" she asked. Not giving him a chance to respond, she stepped forward and aggressively thrust her blade.

He reflexively blocked the blow. "Your sword is not blunted, Amanda," he said carefully.

She felt her lips widen. She thrust again—he parried. "I won't draw blood, de Warenne," she said, but she thought maybe she would, just so she could see the look in his eyes. A terrible excitement consumed her. With it was her rage. She thrust and he parried, but took a step back. Elated, Amada went on the offensive. His eyes widened but he merely blocked each blow, allowing her to drive him ruthlessly and rapidly back into the larboard railing.

She laughed, triumphant. "You can do better than that, de Warenne! Surely you are not afraid of my naked blade?"

"You remain very angry with me. I understand," he began.

She was furious. He knew nothing! She thrust and he parried; she feinted and then slipped through his defenses, instantly cutting a long line into his fine, fancy shirt. She withdrew, heady with the scent of victory. "You understand what?" she asked sweetly.

He glanced at the long tear, very surprised, and then he slowly looked up at her.

"I did not draw blood," she said, exhilarated now. She laughed at him.

"You were fortunate," he said, color flooding his cheeks.

"No, I was careful. I chose not to take your blood, de Warenne!" She thrust so swiftly that, before he could defend himself, she had taken the three top buttons off his shirt, causing it to gape open, revealing the two thick muscles of his chest.

Above them, someone laughed.

De Warenne was disbelieving.

"Fight, de Warenne," she said fiercely, panting. She was determined to savagely exchange blows— she would ruthlessly engage, there would be no quarter! "Or show your men that you can be outplayed and outfought by a *child*."

He suddenly thrust.

Amanda blocked the blow, but barely. He thrust again and again, driving her back across the ship before she even knew what was happening. In mere seconds, she had her back at the rail and sweat was pouring down her body, pooling between her breasts and legs. She was even more furious than before at his display of skill.

He smiled. "Come now, darling. I have no wish to fight with you, especially as your blade is not blunted. Besides, we both know you cannot best me."

But she would try. She would make him sit up and take real notice of her. She was not a fancy lady, but she could match him in every other way. Amanda growled and attacked. She thrust hard and he met her, taking a step back, a step aside, until they were moving rapidly in a vicious circle of hard blow after hard blow. Iron rang. Sweat burned in her eyes. Of course he was master here. She hadn't expected to win. But she wanted to somehow hurt him. There was nothing she wanted more—she wanted him to feel what she had felt, damn him!

Her arm was aching now. She was at her physical limit, but she would not give up. "Damn you!" she gasped, and she halted, pretending to be exhausted and ready to submit to his mercy.

He bought her game, a grin appearing on his handsome face. "Well done," he began.

Amanda feinted, thrust and sliced off the rest of his shirt buttons. He was so surprised he simply stared down at his shirt, now shredded in two. Then, slowly, he looked up at her. His blue eyes were brilliant, hot, but he slowly, boldly smiled.

He wasn't angry. She understood the heat, and a

huge, savage sense of triumph rose up in her. He might not want her with his fine intellectual mind, but just now, she had provoked him so thoroughly that he wanted her right then. She knew, beyond any doubt, that reason had been conquered by lust.

"What's wrong, de Warenne?" she murmured seductively. "Maybe it isn't a fancy lady that you really want."

Before she had even delivered this last call to arms, he attacked. He had the edge of both shirt and chemise hooked over his blade, and with one flick of his wrist, blunted tip or no, her clothes would be ripped in two.

She stilled, breathing hard, her body pulsing in frenzied excitement. "Go ahead," she managed. "Take my clothes."

His face hardened. He slowly lowered the big, blunted tip of his sword between her breasts. "I believe we are done," he said harshly.

She stared at the tip, then lifted her gaze. "I am *not* done."

His brows lifted. "I have my blade against your heart, darling. In actual battle, you would be dead."

"Most men would prefer me warm and alive in their beds," she challenged tauntingly.

His eyes blazed. He removed the sword, tossing

it aside, and it clattered across the deck. "You have won, Amanda," he said. "I concede defeat."

He was turning to walk away. Amanda thrust, catching the top buttons of his breeches, and cut them free. He froze.

"Maybe," she said softly, "my opponent would be as easily deceived as you have been and throw his sword aside too soon, falsely thinking himself in no further danger. Maybe, in real battle, skill will have little to do with the victory. Turn around," she ordered.

Incredulous, he faced her.

She could not keep her eyes on his face. His breeches gaped indecently and she had revealed an interesting portion of his anatomy. More interesting was the rigid line so visibly swelling there.

Her blood drummed in her veins and swelled in her own body. Aware of flushing, she pushed her blade against his heart, somehow tearing her gaze away from his manhood and lifting it to his face. "Yes, I win," she said flatly.